The Hour of Remembering

Grace laughed. "Ok, Gram, I'll peel and you talk."

"By now, you've heard every story I can tell. But I've always said it's a grandparent's job to tell the family stories. Still, I think you got a full load from your grandpa and shouldn't need to hear much more from me." As she talked, she was rolling out the crusts.

"Sometimes I feel like I'm still in school. It's the history, all the stories. They're just not written down. And every time someone tells more, I find another detail I hadn't heard before, or maybe had never caught. How do you remember so much of it, Gram?"

"Now I mean it, Gracie, you peel those apples. We're going to need them soon enough. As for all these tales, well I think they hang around in the corners of this old house and finally just fall onto the heads of everyone here. But you just listen to whoever is telling because you will have to tell others."

"I want you to tell my children all you've told me."

"It may not happen the way you want, Gracie." Her voice was soft, regretful.

THE HOUR OF REMEMBERING

The Hour of Remembering

A NOVEL

Paul A. Mascitti

Burlington, Vermont

Onion River Press
191 Bank Street
Burlington, VT 05401

ISBN: 978-1-949066-94-4

For Mary Ann, who believed.

Contents

"Only be careful, and watch yourselves closely so that you do not forget the things your eyes have seen or let them slip from your heart as long as you live. Teach them to your children and to their children after them."

Deuteronomy 4:9

In grateful remembrance to a generous community of
fellow writers.

Shamuel ?   Kelty

Died 1804________ I____   I
         Shamuel I Elishabet   ___ ___ ___ Archelaus ___ ___ Arthur ___ ___ ___ Jane   Orvis
                     1784-1850------------------------m. 1800------------------------------d. 1807

                          ------------------------------------ m. 1810---1790-1840

                                         Seth-?   Benjamin-?   I   Caleb-?   S.O. --------m. 1839-----Madeline Eikenhous

                                                                                                   1820-1877   I   d. 1873

                                                                   Lillian   Hatti   Ike----m.1861---------Lucy Jackson
                                                                   1844-1920   1842-1918   1840-1917   I   1848-1923

Charles-----   Eudora   Jackson----m. 1889------Emma Drinkwine
d., 1923 I   1866-1940   I   1877-19
Earle---------------------   ----------------m. 1923--------------------------------Grace   Archelaus   Stewart   Andrew   Phillip
1900-1971   I   1906-   1900-1943 1899-1918 1890-1918 1894-1918

              Alden   Phillip   Marjory   Stephen   Joseph------m.1961--------Rachel

              1933-   1932-1939   1931-1962   1929-   1926-   I   1940-

                                                       Kel   Michael   Sarah----------m.1983----------Steven

                                                       1963-   1967-   1964-   I   1963-

       KELTY FARM FAMILY TREE   Lucy   Mike
                                                                                1983-   1984-

1

NOVEMBER 1981: THE CONFLICT

"Kelty Farm, still pretty much the same piece of land my great-great-grandfather, Arthur, built this house on. He had a sawmill on the river and down in the valley he had sheep we don't have anymore. But he cleared fields that we plant again every year, and hillsides that now are orchards. Arthur had a family that remains. I am the last Kelty, though I gave up that name when I married over sixty years ago."

She squints to thread a needle, her white hair waving in the late afternoon breeze. She puts down her needle, puts away the thread in her basket. Drawing her sweater around her shoulders, she settles back in her chair.

"Almost all the Keltys born here are buried on the hill above. They lie in neat rows, each one accounted for, names on marble tablets. Sometimes I think they're waiting for me. I rock in my chair on this old porch where they each sat in their turn. The rocker sets the pace for my thinking, for all the stories they told, for the lives lived in this house.

"I'm Grace, the last Kelty to walk this land. I was born in this house and, please God, I'll die here. When I die, I want to know someone else is keeping what was mine and making it their own." She looks down the valley and up at the sky. She puts down the quilt-patch she is sewing on. She massages her fingers with each hand in turn.

"Too overcast today to see a sunset, but I love to see the patterns light makes in our valley. Makes me think about the pattern of the quilt I'm working on. Quilting is quiet work, lets you think. One thought wanders in, leads to another and another. I'm alone so often I forget to keep things to myself. Sometimes my thoughts just spill out of my mouth."

Grace sits back in the chair and looks across the valley. "That's Joseph's house over there, across the valley in the orchard. My Earle said, 'What does cutting down a few trees matter if your son wants to build a house and stay on the land?' He and my father planted that orchard. It never was the trees that mattered..." Her voice falls away and she continues to look at the house. Then she looks away and picks up her sewing again.

"This house has stood the storms, sheltering our family all these years. We built on as we needed, accommodating our numbers, our comfort. Then when the house was its largest and all but empty, Rachel wanted her own house." She stares intently at the quilt patch and stabs at it with the needle.

"Joseph is my oldest. I have other children, but they've gone off, living lives away from here. Joseph has stayed, keeping the Farm alive. We've been farmers six generations on this land, and Joseph's children will be the seventh. This used to be farm country, now there are only four left in the township. Because there are fewer of us doesn't make us less important, it makes us more important." She pauses, again looking toward the house on the opposite side of the valley. "Not everyone understands that. Even some that should understand don't.

"I've always wondered what Rachel wanted from him, my Joseph. He was a quiet man, already thirty-five when she came along. He was set in his ways, content. I just didn't ever know what she wanted." She rests her hands in her lap, then takes a hankie from her pocket and dabs at her nose. She pulls her sweater tighter over her shoulders.

"She came here, a girl with no family of her own, fresh out of college. Suddenly Joseph looked like the end of the rainbow to her. She married him and started changing him.

"Never one to be happy, not here, she had to have her own house. 'A house of my own, a house of my own.' It gave me shivers every time she said it." Grace examines the stitches on the quilt block then puts it down in her lap. "It put me in mind of the first Mrs. Kelty on this land, Elishabet, my great-great-grandmother. Arthur Kelty built this house for Elishabet.

"Elishabet was unhappy, never satisfied, never content. I heard tales from her grandson, my grampa Ike. When her husband Arthur was lying in his grave, well, that's when she first realized he'd loved her, had made this farm for her, worked himself to death providing for their family, never hearing a kind word from his wife." She rocks a moment and shakes her head.

"I hate to think this, but Rachel is discontent in the same way. Building her a new house was only the start. Next, her things had to be better, that having a baby wasn't going to stop her from having a job— no, not a job—a career! It wasn't enough to be a farmer's wife and the mother to his child. And then the second and third child came along, and Rachel built onto the house and hired help to run it." Grace rocks harder, her hands gripping the arms of the chair.

"Imagine, a stranger picking up after your kids, making your supper, washing your dishes…" She slows the rocker to a stop.

"Well, it was clear from the first that Rachel and I were not cut from the same cloth...

"Most of my grandchildren live away and I don't see them often. We write and call. I feel in touch with them in those ways. Then there are Joseph's three, his son Kelty, his daughter Sarah, and the youngest, Michael."

She begins to rock gently. "I have to smile when I speak of Kelty. He was named for the old family, for my parents. He works with his father on the land. He may go to agricultural school. He's a good boy. There's a lot of my father in him. Kelty is his father's son.

"Then there's Sarah. She used to like to make cookies with me and bring some home. She used to watch me quilting, always talking about the colors and patterns I was working with. Once, she asked if I could tell the future by looking at the pattern of the quilt. I told her that the person who slept under this quilt would be covered with my love and would sleep safe and warm." Grace chuckles softly.

"Her eyes got so big, as if I was really telling the future. I loved her so much at that moment. I could see she trusted that every word I said was the truth and set in stone.

"Sarah doesn't come often anymore, and she doesn't stay long when she does come. She's returning to college tomorrow, promised to spend this night with me. She'll come, but her heart's not in it. Seems she's more her mother's daughter than her father's.

"And Michael, well, he's his mother's too, no question.

"I go to their house for supper on occasions… birthdays and such… I like to see them happy, see my quilts on their beds… But we're not as close as I wanted us to be… as family should be. I know whose door to lay that at." She rocks a moment then stops, putting her sewing aside, looking out over the valley.

"Elishabet started a tradition, one most people don't know about. On the way up the hill, round back of this house, when they were carrying her husband to the grave his sons had dug for him, she insisted they stop and open the coffin. She covered Arthur with a quilt she had made. It was the first sign of her wanting to care for him.

"That's been the way each of the Keltys on the hill was laid in their graves, wrapped in a quilt. I saw my gramma put one on my grandfather, my mother put one on my gramma. I put quilts on my mother and my father, another on my son, Phillip, one on Marjory. I wrapped my dear husband, Earle, in one, too. This is a loving custom women in our family have.

"But I can't depend that Joseph's wife will do that for me. I brought it up once with Rachel. She thought it was funny. She said home burial was out of style, that she wasn't going to have any part of it." Grace sighs.

"I have the quilt picked out. It's one my mother and my gramma worked on together. It has patches from my father's work shirts and… Well, I guess it would be hard to explain why it's important to me. It is, that's all." She begins to rock gently, folding her quilt block.

"I know I could talk to Joseph about this. I just think it's a woman's place, part of caring for her family. It makes me cold, and very lonely, to think of lying in my grave without my quilt." The chair slows, stops, and Grace rises slowly. She grips the railing, looking once more toward the other house, then goes into the house and shuts the door.

* * *

The light is on in a bay windowed room in the house across the valley. Rachel is seated at a desk. She works at a calculator then checks figures in an account book. She closes the book, takes off her glasses and sits back in the chair. She runs her fingers through her hair.

"That's all of this desk I can take for one day." She stands, walks to the window. "Feels good to stretch. Everyone says Rachel loves her home office, and I do. But even I get tired.

"I didn't start out liking these apple trees outside this window. I didn't start out liking anything here, except Joseph. Joseph…" She hugs herself, lost in thought,

"I met Joseph when he drove up to school with my roommate's brother. Here was this big man standing behind the girl's brother, hardly looking up, not meeting my eyes, never seeing my face, saying little when he did speak, and blushing red faced when I spoke to him. I can tell you, I'd never had that effect on anyone before. I was intrigued and went out with them when they asked." She smiles, chuckles a little.

"It was fun. I experimented as to what would bring Joseph out. I found that if I talked to others, he would look at me. So, I talked to everyone else, knowing he was looking right at my face. If I talked quietly to my girlfriend, he would talk to her brother. I listened and began to know him.

"When we said good-bye, I told him I'd had a good time and asked if he'd call me." She laughs. "He almost choked! When he left I laughed a lot about him. I didn't know what to make of him.

"The next year I saw Joseph often. When he wasn't there, I thought about him. The summer before my last year of school I got a job in a town near here and boarded with my girlfriend's family. I hardly saw Joseph at all. Then her brother brought us to Kelty Farm one afternoon." Rachel smiles to herself.

"This is my favorite memory. Joseph was in a field, haying. He didn't have a shirt on... was all sweaty, his fair skin red from the sun, hayseed stuck to him. He was embarrassed but I never saw a more beautiful man. His father wanted him to go with us but Joseph said it might rain later and they had to get the hay in. He told us to come back the next day to swim and picnic, and he would show us the Farm.

"That was the first time I really looked at Joseph as a man. He was older than other men I dated, and he had gotten where he was going. He was so at home on Kelty Farm, so in charge of everything he showed us. He didn't mumble. He spoke directly.

"And something changed for him that day. He looked into my eyes when he talked. And... he began to smile. He told me long afterwards it was that day during the picnic he first knew... he loved me." She draws in her shoulders for a moment, letting out a sigh.

"That picnic changed my life. I began to really see Joseph. Past the shyness, I saw a quiet man, competent... confident. Behind the confidence I found a man with deep values, bonded to the place he lived. I knew then I wanted to possess something as completely, as passionately, as Joseph possessed that land. I wanted to live with a passion for something so utterly my own. I wanted what Joseph had... and I wanted Joseph." Rachel plays with the scarf at her neck.

"I loved him. I wanted to be with him. I don't think he ever asked me to marry him, it was an understanding we came to. I met his family, his sister Marjory, the brothers and their wives—they were more my age—and his parents. Everyone was so kind. They seemed to open up and take me in. I didn't see any rough spots—not then, anyway." Her fingers play down the rows of buttons on her blouse.

"I didn't notice, and Joseph never said anything, but I think his mother held back from the first. When we announced we were going to marry, a lot of things went undecided… like where we would live. I wanted a house in town. Joseph wanted to live on Kelty Farm. I thought we could build a house there. He said everyone always lived in the homestead. I suggested we remodel a wing. He said his folks liked it the way it was. I wanted to have some new furniture. Joseph said what they had was just fine.

"I began to see how stuck he was here. It was too late. I loved him. And I was young; I thought I could change the world.

"It pains me now to realize how inexperienced I was.

"We lived two years in the old house, in those small dark rooms filled with furniture. His mother did all the cooking, all the cleaning. I felt like a guest in a rundown hotel." She returns to her desk chair, straightening up her desk. "It's not as if anyone was unpleasant… It was the disapproval. I found an interesting job in town. Going to work and coming home, I sensed it from her. Some days she told me what Joseph had for lunch, as if I had missed an important event. Other days she told me Joseph hadn't come in for lunch, as if my being there would have made some difference.

"I was beginning to get discouraged. Then Joseph started talking about babies. I looked at him. I said it one time: 'I want my own house.'"

Rachel folds her hands on her desk. "That's all. Every time I heard about babies, I looked at him and he knew what was standing in the way." She laughs.

"I laugh now because it didn't really work like that. I never denied Joseph anything and suddenly I was pregnant. Then he began to talk about a house."

She sits back in her chair, relaxing. "One evening we sat on the porch, looking across at the orchard. The setting sun was pouring light through the trees straight to our feet. We turned to each other and at the same time, we both said, 'That's the spot!' The next day we walked through the orchard to the very place we had picnicked years before. We measured and drove in stakes. With every strike of the mallet, I felt his ancestors' hold on Joseph loosen. We were making a change from the old ways. I began to breathe easier.

"When we told the folks, his father was happy, but his mother held back. When we tore up the trees on the space we needed, his father was cheerful but his mother… As the building rose, we drank a toast… except his mother." Rachel rolls her shoulders, moving her head from side to side. She sits back in the chair.

"I shouldn't think about all this. I should stick to things I can control, things I'm more at home with, like business. I started in a small insurance and realty company and now I'm a partner. My work is an extension of me, of who I am. It's what I do. I needed to have a business life—let me say the 'C' word, a career. I was educated for it at great effort on my part, at great expense to my parents. I'd be unfaithful to all that if I wasn't working.

"I've maintained my family and reached for goal after goal on the job. I've stuck with it with little support from anyone at home. As opportunities opened up my income grew. We have the kind of security a family needs, and the kind we never would have if we depended on the Farm.

"I know how rare it is when one family stays on the same land nearly two hundred years. But this wouldn't be a farm, at least not our farm, without the day in, day out sacrifice my husband makes year after year. And he couldn't devote himself that way if I wasn't holding up my end." She leans forward again, folding her hands on the blotter.

"I don't make quilts. I don't make jams and breads. I don't have ancestors buried on the hill, each one with a story that makes them more alive than when they walked.

"This farm goes on because of me. Joseph's mother couldn't run this place. Joseph never complains but we wouldn't be caught in this backwater life except for her. Because I can be content with my home and the children growing up here, he's been able to stay.

"It's time and more than time we were free to make a change. I bide my time. My day will come. I need to be patient." She stands, walks to the window looking out into the night.

"It's going to be a cold night. It's early for this cold. This is take-it-or-leave-it weather. And there's not much chance we'll get to leave it, not any time soon at least. I hope it doesn't snow as early as last year. Joseph worked in the woods till almost Christmas to get all the firewood orders filled. Winter slows him down, though he says he loves the snow.

"Well, I don't love the snow, no, nor winter tires, heavy coats, boots, gloves or hats. The driving hasn't gotten easier over the years, the winding icy road out of the valley, ten miles into the office and ten miles home again every night.

"It's no coincidence this land has been in the family so long—who else wants it? Kelty Farm! There isn't even a Kelty working it anymore. But my husband wouldn't have any peace anywhere if his mother had to see Kelty Farm go out of the family. After she passes on, when she's finally gone, I don't know how long we'll stay.

"So, I wait, tending my children, bending them like twigs toward lives in a world larger than the Farm, urging them into educations that will make them dissatisfied with this small place, with small lives, knowing they'll move on when it's time, knowing it will be easier for Joseph to let go of the Farm then." She pauses.

"I never liked these trees outside the window. I wanted to cut them all down and have a yard. Joseph said no, that his father and grandfather had planted them.

"I wanted the house bigger. Joseph said no, we would have the homestead when his parents passed.

"I wanted to name the baby Joseph. I wanted to name the baby after my father, or his father, or some other name altogether. Joseph said no, we would name the baby Kelty.

"I've heard the old family stories. I know the traditions about naming the baby with family names. I gave in. I let it happen. It was a mistake. And in all my years here, it's the only thing I regret.

"I let the baby be named after Joseph's mother's family. I thought it would be the last payment on the land, the land they still call Kelty Farm. And I was careful to interest my son in other things, to send him off to various camps, to places he would taste and want more of.

"But I was busy. There were other babies. And my career... Now it looks like he wants to follow his father on the Farm. But I'm insisting if he's going to farm, he gets the education to go with it. That could change things.

"I've made a lot of compromises to achieve the stability I didn't have when I was growing up. I gave in as often as I had to to get my way, to have what I wanted. And it hasn't all been selfish. I did it for my family's future, for their lives to be better than mine. I'm close to realizing the fruit of my long vigilance." She walks to the door, looking one more time around the room, then puts her hand on the light switch.

"I don't owe a son to this land, to this life. In a few short years, a very few short years, all my children will be in college, off the land, and I will retire. Joseph may have had enough by then. There's a chance we can break free. If his mother is gone, maybe we can leave. Maybe..."

2

1840: ELISHABET, MORNING AND AFTERNOON

They seem somehow embarrassed, these giant men, these sons, four strangers who came from my body.

They stand in front of me, feet shuffling, hands raking through hair or hands in pockets, shoulders slumped.

They don't look at me. Their eyes are cast down at their muddy boots or at each other's faces.

They don't speak. They cough and clear their throats. They seem to want something from me.

"Your father's dead?" I tremble at the sound of my voice echoing their announcement. These words have import, but I cannot discover in their faces how they apply to me.

"Yeah. He's gone. Must have dropped soon's he got in the barn. Just nobody noticed him right off. Can't have been dead an hour yet."

I know this one is Caleb. The taller one is Seth, but he hasn't spoken, he just keeps looking at Caleb. "So where is he now, your father—your father's body?" I ask, not sure why.

Caleb looks at his brothers, waiting to see if one of them will answer. He glances at me then quickly away.

Fear? Is he afraid of what he sees?

"Downstairs. We carried him in. He's at the bottom of the stairs... Where do you want him?"

His voice falls away. He and the others, all of us in this house, have a natural reluctance to words with each other. I know they are not like this in the woods, the fields, the barns. I hear them talk and laugh, but never in the house, never with me.

"Want him?" I ask.

"Yeah. Where do you want him?" Caleb asks again.

Want him? I ask myself.

"Want him..." I want to plead with them to go away, or at least to tell me what they require of me. Their faces are for each other and not for me. I wet my lips with my tongue. I feel I should say something, but I can't think what. I glance back into the room at my chair.

"Do you want him in the kitchen, on the table?"

I look up quickly, trying to guess who has spoken. Benjamin—or the other? None meet my eyes.

"Want him...on the table? In the kitchen?" If he's dead, why would they want him on the table?

"Mother," Caleb speaks—he is neither the youngest nor the oldest, but the smallest of the sons— "we'll send for some of the neighbors. The women will help you prepare Father—Father's body—to bury him. Do you want to bury him in town, in the church yard?"

He is reluctant to say it, but there is more. I see it in his face, in all their faces.

"If not the church yard..." another says. Seth.

"If not in the church yard... Tell me."

"We could dig a grave on the hill, above the house, around on the other side. Father liked it there..."

The silent one. This from the silent one. I don't remember him speaking before, I don't recognize his voice. Of all these strangers, he is the one I know the least.

"I liked it there, too. It's where I wanted my house, but he built it here because there is water here." I don't know why I tell them. It was thirty years ago.

I look back at my chair, then at them. They seem worried. They glance at each other; they clear their throats.

I can't stand up anymore. I walk past the bed to my chair by the low window. From here, I see that these men are yet children, wanting someone to direct them, wanting someone to tell them what to do, that they will be all right.

"Yes. Yes. That's all right. Yes. Send to the neighbors. Tell them we'll have the burial at noon, no, two o'clock tomorrow. They'll have to be home for milking. Tell them two o'clock. Make a coffin or send into town for one. Don't tell the women to come. I don't want any of them church do-gooders here. I don't want them."

They look at me now, done looking at each other.

The squeak of the rocker on the floorboard is comforting.

"Tell your wives to cook. We'll feed everybody tonight, and likely tomorrow people will bring food."

"Where do you want us to put him—Father's body, I mean." Caleb. Yes, this time I know it is Caleb.

"I suppose you'd better bring him up here. On the bed."

They seem relieved. They shuffle from the room, nearly falling on one another in haste. They clamber down the stairs, four pairs of feet in heavy shoes making more noise than is seemly.

It is quiet. The squeak of the floorboards comes to me.

I spend so much time here, in this room that I think of as mine, though I share it with him. This is my fortress. It is here I feel most safe, here that I feel strong if ever I do.

If I open this window or that, by some trick of air it is possible to hear voices at the carriage barn or in the yard. I keep the windows closed most of the time. I don't want to think of anyone being here, in the yard or at the barn. I don't want to think of anyone at all.

The room is much as it was when he first brought me here to see the cabin. If I'd known I'd be sitting here this many years later, still looking at the clay he chinked the logs with, I'd have insisted he do a better job.

But he was young, and I thought there'd be time to do better, for him to do it better, for him to do it so's I would be satisfied.

When I first came into the cabin, I was surprised how big it was, though it was all one room and this was just the sleeping loft above the main room. There was a cold cellar under the floor, and there was some work started on a barn across the yard, but the cabin was built first as I asked, as I needed before I'd say yes and marry Art.

And even more important to me right then was not to spend another winter, another day, another hour, under the same roof as Arc's family... Maybe I wasn't as choosy, as demanding as I'd a right to be just then. Maybe I didn't notice the crude clay drying between rude log walls, the uneven windowsills, the rough flooring.

Maybe I was seeing the silence I seek, even now, here in this place he built for me.

"A house of my own," I told him. His mother wouldn't have me live amidst her unmarried sons, though I'd married her oldest and lived in the west till he'd died. Her Christian heart made her take me in but didn't make her treat me well.

I tried to think of a place to be other than there, under her roof, with all those Kelty men. And her.

There was nowhere.

Nowhere.

She used me bad. She thought to drive me out with hard work, but I stayed. She thought to drive me off by threat of marriage, but Art, her youngest, he told me he'd have me.

I wanted to laugh. I would have laughed, but I didn't laugh anymore even then.

He said he'd always loved me, even when Arc and I had married nine years earlier. Course, he was a kid then. Puppy eyes for his big brother's bride, like enough.

I'd told him I'd marry whoever would build me a house of my own.

"He was a man that did what he needed—no talk—he just did it. He was like that, Art. When he wanted something, he reached with both hands."

Now I hear them on the stairs. They scuffle. They're in the hallway outside the door. I'll open it for them. They are quiet. They know I'll open the door. The latch clicks loudly, the hinges complain.

They stand before me, bearing their father between the pairs of them. They are trees, but children, these sons of the father from my body.

I have no friend among them.

They shift with their burden. I glance at Arthur's body, and they start forward into the room.

"He's too dirty to put on the bed. Take his clothes off in the hallway, then bring him in."

They back out again, closing the door.

Am I shut in or shut out from them?

I hear a wordless bustle. I go back to my chair. I rock.

The door opens. Caleb and Seth come in each holding a knee of the under-suit-clad body. Benjamin and the other each hold an arm and a shoulder.

They come forward, out of step with each other, jostling their way into the room.

They stop beside the bed. They look at one another for a signal. They deposit the body onto the bed.

Caleb leans over his father, taking him under the arms, straightening and centering him on the bed. Ropes complain through the mattress beneath Caleb's knee.

The other shifts his father's legs. His hands seem reluctant to let go the stockinged foot he holds an extra moment.

"You might as well take that off him too."

They study each other's faces. I can see they think it is not their place.

Caleb leans over his father, hesitates, then slowly unbuttons the length of the front of the under suit.

I grip my chair to see his hands so gentle on his father.

He rolls the body to one side, freeing one arm and shoulder, then the other. He pulls the suit by a wrist cuff on either side under the body, then, lifting each foot, he slides the garment free. He scans the unclothed figure on the bed.

The quiet one reaches for the edge of the quilt that hangs to the floor and brings it up over the body, then goes to the other side and does the same, leaving only the head exposed.

My fingers and knuckles are hurting me, and I relax my grip on the chair. I watch their faces.

Only Caleb looks toward me, his silence asking if I require anything more of them. I say nothing. They back out of the room, shutting the door.

Again, I wonder if I am shut in or shut out.

My room is quiet. I fold my hands and rock.

"You men. Why do they bring you back to us women when you are dead? Maybe it's to return you to your source. All the days you live, the only time a man comes to a woman is when he's born, when he's sick, when he wants to make his children, and then when he's dead. Why is it women's lot to birth him, care for him, and tend his needs even unto death?"

I am surprised at my anger. I stand and walk to the bed

You look so small, Art, so quiet. You are a do-er, you're never quiet.

You are the form and likeness of the man who lay beside me on that very bed just last night. You look like you need some sleep and then you'd be ready to go again.

You look as I see you in dreams, waiting for me, waiting for me, wanting to talk to me...

"What would you say, Art, if you could speak now? What would you have to say to me? How many nights we lay side by side in that bed, separated by inches and by silence."

I put my hands on the footboard to steady myself. I watch his chest for the familiar rise and fall I expect to see even this moment or surely the next.

"You look like a baby, wrapped in that quilt, dependent, needy…and insignificant. You never seemed insignificant to me, Art, never, not since I said yes to you, and we came here as man and wife. You were hardly twenty, Art. I was sixteen when I married your brother, ten years before."

I gaze at his face and for a moment I see him as he once looked. The thin grey tufts over his ears are bushy black unmanageable curls. The closed eyes are open and sparkle green, a warm green that never leaves me, following me around in any room. The body always in motion.

"Where did you go?"

I need to sit. I go back to the rocker.

Someone knocks at my door. I cross the room silently and stand behind the door.

They knock again.

"Mother?"

It is Seth. They would send him.

"Mother, may I come in?"

His voice is louder, insistent, yet filled with dread. He is a man who does as he has to rather than as he wants. The burden of being the oldest weighs on him.

"No. Don't come in."

I don't know what I want but it is not his presence.

"Mother…"

"I'll have him ready soon. See about a coffin and bring some saw-horses in by the fireplace. I'll call you to come up when he's ready."

"Mother, I've done all that."

He seems to be apologizing, as if maybe he should have waited to be told.

"Mother? Did you hear me?"

I do not answer.

"Mother? May I come in?"

"No. I'll call you when he's ready."

My voice sounds tired but I'm not tired. It just is all so inevitable, as if I've waited thirty years for this day, for this man to leave me too.

I hear Seth's slow tread down the stairs. After a silence, I open the door, needing to assure myself he is gone.

Cooking smells fill the hallway from the kitchen off the lower level connected by the stairs.

Closing the door, I lean against it, feeling its solidness, barrier to the world, guardian of my peace in this room.

Art's face is calm, patient.

"You built this house."

Did I say that, and to him?

"You built this house, these two rooms just for me."

I sit down in my chair and look at him on the bed, the afternoon light shining on his pale face.

"When the babies started coming, you made a kitchen with a sleeping area above, then the 'ell' with the dining room and two more bedrooms over that. The kitchen and dining area made this cabin a house, you said.

"You laid floors, dug cellar holes, raised roofs, all so easily, with so little talk, built on, built over, making the pieces into a whole. You built the dam and the mill, you logged the land, sold the lumber, bought the sheep."

I rock. My feet don't leave the floor. My knees bend in the going and the coming. My back fits the chair. My hair, coiled into a white bun held with a net, cushions against the headrest.

Outside I hear a handsaw biting its way through a board. I hear the sound stop and then, after a time, start again as if the sawyer saws another board or had rested in the middle of a wide board.

"Certainly, one of the boys."

I rock.

"They're all builders, these sons of yours. But you built this house for me."

I rock.

"Did you know I thanked you? I always wondered if I should just say thank you. I thought you'd know. I married you, I cooked and kept house. I worked beside you in the woods, in the fields. That was to thank you. I lay beside you at night, I bore your children. You can tell me nothing now, but I hope you know I thanked you."

The sun has moved off Art's face.

The sound of the sawyer in the yard below is more insistent.

The day is moving on. The task is before me.

I bring the basin and the pitcher close to the bed. I throw back the quilt.

I take his hand and his arm follows. The hand is not warm and flexible as ever before when I felt its touch. It is cold. It is the first time I ever reached for it myself and it is cold.

The cloth glides along your smooth skin, the skin of a younger man than I know you to be. Your arms are brown, your upper body less so, and your lower body not at all. Your elbows are very dark, and leathery like your knees. You are a lean man today as you were so long ago when we married. I rinse the cloth, wet it again and continue what must be a ritual. He is already as clean as anyone needs to be.

I've asked "why" about washing a body before burial. No "why" I have ever asked has been answered my whole life and I have stopped asking.

I find your nakedness so touching.

I pause.

I remember our wedding night in this very room. Before I had the lantern blown out, you had your clothes off and started to get into bed naked.

I stopped you.

"You don't expect that of a decent woman!"

You were chastened. You put on your under suit and apologized.

I can hear your voice as you returned to bed.

"Don't mind me none, there, Elishabet. I got carried away with myself. I'll learn. It won't happen again."

And it never did.

And suddenly, now, I regret that.

I was a dutiful wife, fixing the fire, setting out a breakfast of a morning, baking beans and bread at noon, and a hot supper at evening.

Each night we lay together in this room, on this bed covered by my hand done quilts.

I never reached for you, nor spoke when you made your intention, your wants clear. I let you take what you would have, but I gave nothing.

"I regret that."

I roll him onto his side and wash his back. Again, it is brown and dark to his waist, then fish belly white.

The skin is so smooth I am reminded that he is six years younger than I.

"You never knew this, Art. There was another time when I saw you naked, you and the boys. I was walking in the woods near the water in the valley. I heard shouting and splashing. I stayed in the cover of the trees, but I moved closer. It was at the pool in the river near where all the Elms are, there by the big rocks. You had all been in the fields and were washing before supper, I think. This was ten years ago. You swam and rough housed together in the tree-shaded pool. You dived from the flat rocks.

"At first, I was shocked to see all of you naked in the daylight, and I turned to go. But the lightheartedness of the moment held me, made me long to be part of it, to share... something... something that did not include me. There was no way to join but I stayed, unseen, and followed the fun with my eyes, my heart lifting with every moment.

"Your bodies were sun-browned from the fields, your arms bulging from good health and endless day-to-day work. You were unconscious of the animal grace, the pagan grandeur of your bodies. I caught my breath again and again as I gazed on such forbidden beauty.

"That night when you held me in the embrace of your body, I know I responded in a different way. I know I did. But you didn't remark, and it was not our way to speak."

I drop the cloth into the basin, pouring water over my hands from long habit, not because they have been soiled by my task.

It is finished. I have washed you. Now, I suppose I must dress you.

In the yard I hear the chewing sound I associate with the hand drill I have seen used so many times. Art and I used it on the maple trees in the spring, and when he made furniture. I smell the rise of sap as I think of it, and I see in my mind the curl of the waste wood as the hole is made. I hear the thump of the pegs being driven. I know what has been made in this yard in front of the house while the dead wait inside.

"Mother."

I listen.

"Mother."

"Yes?"

"Do you need some help? I know you said you'd call when you were ready, but everything is waiting downstairs, and I wondered if you need some help."

I don't answer. I don't know what help there is. Art is dead. Art has left here and only his body remains.

"Mother? Do you hear me?"

"Yes."

"May I come in?"

I go to my chair and seat myself. Soon this burden will pass.

"Yes."

Seth again, and the other, the silent one. They glance at Art, at each other, at me, and back to each other, then away. It seems to be painful for them to see their father lying there unclothed. They wait a long minute, perhaps waiting each other out.

Seth gives in first. He always does.

"You've washed him?"

"Yes."

"Should we dress him now?"

"Surely before you take him downstairs."

They wince. Perhaps there was another answer but perhaps there could have been a better question. They are yet children, these men.

"There are clothes in the press by the door. Take the newer suit, the black one—and the shirt in the drawer under that. The shirt on the left is newest, I made it for Christmas. Use that. There are boots behind his chair over there, a new pair, hardly worn."

The quiet one opens the press and I watch him find the suit. There are only two there. He picks the shirt out of the drawer, his eyes on the whiteness of it.

"Find a ribbon to make a tie. There should be some behind the shirts. Look underneath the other shirts if you don't see it. Yes, that one will do."

"Mother, you want to use the new shirt, the new suit, the new boots? Are you sure?"

"I said to, didn't I? This is the head of the family, the Master of Kelty Farm. This is an important man in the community. How can we expect people to know this if we don't act like we know? People will come and they must see that we honor him, respect him. This is not anyone else, this is your father who gave us all his best. Can we give him less, his last night in this house he built for us?"

I glare at Seth. He absorbs my glare, a question still on his face.

"The new boots?"

"The Master of Kelty Farm will be buried with new boots. Do you have any other questions?"

I wait. My rocker is still. I feel coiled, ready to spring.

"What about under things?"

I glare at the quiet one too.

"He won't need those."

They look at each other but do not question me further.

"Dress him there and carry him down to put in the coffin. I'll come down and see everything's right before anyone comes. I don't want to be on display for the neighbors or anyone from town. I have no friends among them."

I begin rocking again. I hear the complaint of the floorboards and I know where I am, where I belong.

The quiet one looks at his brother and then begins to dress his father. Seth stands uneasily, waiting for the moment to say something, to ask me for more of what I have none of.

"What is it…"

"Some folks are here already…"

"Well, they've come early. Ask them to wait outside."

"One is Doctor Fitch, and another is Doctor Cord."

"Two doctors when none is needed. Isn't that the way."

"Doctor Fitch is the minister at the church Father sometimes attended. He came to ask if he could see you. Doctor Cord is the medical doctor. He came thinking you might want him yourself."

"Tell Doctor Cord Mr. Kelty is already dead and there's no business for him here today. And tell Doctor Fitch my mind is made up. There'll be no church yard service, everything will be done here in Mr. Kelty's home, and burial will be on his land. If he wants to officiate, there'll be a small stipend after the funeral tomorrow, and nothing but food till then."

"Mother, I can't talk to those gentlemen that way."

"Then they'll never know the truth, for I will not see either one of them tonight."

"I'll tell them."

I glance up. The quiet one. Yes, maybe he is the one to tell them.

"And we'll bring the coffin up here. You can see Father arranged as suits you and then we'll carry him down. We'll tell you when everyone is gone and you can have some private time with the family, or alone if you want that."

He does not look at me as he speaks, this quiet one, but keeps on with his task. Today is the most I have heard of his voice. I feel a distance between us I always suspected, but a like-mindedness that is a strange comfort.

"Who is tending to the grave? Shall I go up and show you where to dig?"

I address them both, but the quiet one goes back to the dressing of his father, and Seth looks at me with pain on his face.

"The grave is already dug. We dug in the center of the pines at the top of the hill. As you follow past the house, along in front of the hill, and then up the other side, you come right to it. It's very sandy and dry up there."

I know it's dry. That's why the house is here and not up there. But I told them that earlier. I remember my surprise that it was still on my mind after all these years.

"That won't do. The hill faces west like the house. On the farthest side going that way, the side closest to the house, walk to the edge, to where it drops away, then back up about ten or twelve feet. Put the head there, facing the sunset, his back to the east. That's where I wanted the house, where I wanted to live. That's where he'll lie." I rock.

Seth clears his throat.

"What is it?" Is it as painful for him to speak to me as it is for me to answer?

"Christians are buried facing east and the sunrise, waiting the call to rise on the last day."

"On Kelty Farm, sunrise only means more work. Sunset sometimes offered rest. I want him to face west." I rock. Seth pauses, then turns away.

I watch the silent son dressing the father, how much care he shows, how gentle he is with a cold, unfeeling dead man. Where did these men learn that gentleness, that care?

"There are pines there. It's a big area, but the pines have grown up…" Seth again.

"Your father cleared that land. He was going to build the cabin up there, that was his first plan."

"Mother, that was thirty years ago. The pines have grown up. They are all over up there. It's very thick."

"We'll cut them down." The quiet one again.

Seth turns to his brother.

"Between now and tomorrow afternoon? What are you thinking? And what help will you be with your wife ready to give birth any hour? Don't promise things you can't deliver, Brother."

Seth's anger is not for his brother, but for me.

"Brother," he answers without looking up from his task, "some of the men who come tonight will stay or come back early tomorrow to help. It's no more than we've done for others many a time. We'll find a spot between the trees where Mother says to dig. We'll only cut the trees along the edge and any that are in our way. We'll drag them out of sight. Later we can clear the hilltop."

"But the place will be full of roots and stumps then, and we've already dug one grave."

"The grave's just a hole that's not needed. Fill it back in. We can pull the stumps. Pine roots will just dry up in sandy soil. They won't bother. Go tell Benjamin and Caleb to bring the coffin up here, I'm almost finished."

Seth digests this, looks to me. I can tell him nothing more. He leaves us. There is silence as the door closes. I rock.

"Thank you for letting me dress Father."

"Thank you…," it's hard to say this, "for knowing what I want."

The silence again.

"Your wife is the good cook."

"Yes, Madeline."

He seems surprised I would know. I don't know them all, but I know which one she is.

"She's going to have our baby tonight."

"Your first?"

"Yes." He has more to say.

"What?" He is reluctant, or naturally keeps his own thoughts. I wait. I stop rocking.

"I was thinking…"

"Yes?"

"…they say it's a boy. Maybe I would name him Arthur…"

I wait. I sit still.

"Are you asking me or telling me?"

"Asking," he says, looking directly at me.

"I think those would be big shoes to fill for any little baby, a big shadow to grow into. And the Keltys were not such lucky people that any one of them could share their luck. No, I don't think it's a good idea."

"I think Father was a very lucky man."

I rock.

"I'm surprised you would say that when here, he died so young. He was not yet fifty. My father lived to be seventy."

"What was your father's name?"

He is finished now. He stands beside the bed unable to move away from his father.

"Shamuel. And so was my brother's. Neither were lucky, nor do I wish to hear the name again. But do what you will. You don't have to please me."

"I'd be glad if I did. I'd want to."

"Why?" I am startled, but curious beyond my control.

"We all do."

"Why?" Again.

He looks at me. He is so calm, his father's son.

"You're our mother. We respect you. Father would expect that."

"Respect? I can't believe you know me well enough to respect me. And your father is dead now, you are not subject to him." I look away from him. I rock.

"I've been taught to respect my mother. And my father is still my father though he's dead. I'll give up nothing he taught me. Nothing."

His eyes blaze on his last word. If I wasn't seated, I would want to sit now.

"Father told us some of the circumstances of your life. You have done nothing to earn disrespect and I'd better never hear anything for you from anybody but respect." He puts his hand flat on his father's chest as he speaks to me, looking directly into my eyes. I long to have that touch he squanders on his dead father's body. I wipe away a tear.

"Not many feel as you do."

"All who live in this house will...and do."

I rock. I look away. I cannot look at him. I cannot see his reluctance to let go of his father. I cannot understand his respect. I'm not sure I can pay the price for it.

Something bumps the door, then it opens. Seth.

"Should we leave it out here?"

"Bring it in," his brother orders with quiet assurance.

Little Caleb has the front, and tall Benjamin has the back, the weight being on Caleb. They set it down beside the bed. I have second thoughts about a coffin beside my bed. I know someday mine will sit exactly there.

The four of them look at me, waiting for me to say something. I say nothing. My rocker is still.

They signal to each other, these men who are used to working in team. They carefully place the body in the coffin. They arrange and fuss over details.

I see they have made the box from thick pine. Each panel is solid, cut to size from wide boards, drilled and pegged. I notice the pegs along the bottom and on the ends. There are holes in the top edges waiting for more pegs. It is skillfully done as Arthur would have taught them.

But I forget myself and they are waiting for approval. I leave my chair, my safety, and stand among them looking down on the man inside the box.

He is so small; they are so large. Nothing is a right size.

"He looks uncomfortable."

"He looks fine, Mother." Seth again.

I look at the quiet one.

"Put a pillow under his head."

He reaches for the near pillow on the bed.

"No, not that one. Take the one from my side, it's smaller, it will fit better." He does. Benjamin lifts Arthur's head and shoulders and the pillow is slipped under.

"Yes. Better. There's nothing under him. We'll put a quilt under him."

"He's fine, Mother. It's all right as it is." Seth.

"Which quilt, Mother? How do you want it?" The quiet one again.

"There should be something under him. We'll fold a quilt and cover the bottom of the coffin."

"The coffin isn't deep enough for much thickness. It isn't right to lift him in and out like he was a stone. He's fine as he is. People are downstairs waiting." Seth.

"Brothers, lift him onto the bed. Mother, what will you have us use?"

"There's a lap robe on top of the press. It will only need folding once and is long enough, I'm sure."

"Seth, get the lap robe. Benjamin, you take the boots. Caleb, you take the shoulder on this side of the bed, and I'll hand him across the coffin." The silent one.

The Father is so easily handled. He is a corn doll in the hands of these giant children.

"Take the pillow, Caleb. Give the robe to me. Is this what you want, Mother?" He looks to me. I nod. He knows. "Caleb, the pillow, please. There, now let's put him back."

The doll is in the hands of the children.

"Yes, that's what I want." I straighten his coat and lapels, his tie, the shirt. The silent one pulls the trousers over the boot tops. Caleb smoothes his father's hair. I take a brush from my dressing table and brush the hair back from the forehead, back from the ears. I touch the still face. It is cold.

How could this vessel have held life?

"We'll take him down now, Mother, if you will." He looks at me. I say nothing. "Benjamin and Seth take the foot. It's lighter but you go down first. Caleb, take that side, I'll take this."

They maneuver out of the door, shuffle in the hallway then go down the stairs slowly.

I suddenly see they are dressed in clean clothes and are ready. I shut the door, look at the empty, rumpled bed, and go to sit in my chair. I need some peace. I rock.

I hear many voices but no words. Some of the sound comes from downstairs, some from the yard, and other sounds I know not their source. I rock.

Someone is at the door.

"Mother Kelty? I have a tray of food from the kitchen."

I rock.

"Mother Kelty? I'll leave the tray here. I'll come back later."

I rock. I rest my head and shoulders against the chair, my hands loose in my lap. I close my eyes. The squeak of the rocker on the worn floorboards is my anchor.

I grip the arms of my chair and dare to part the dark curtain of the years, perhaps to see what I have never recalled about Arc's death.

3

1807: ELISHABET

Archelaus is dead. It doesn't change anything for me.

He is on the bed as he has been for days, and I, too big with child to carry myself, do all the doing, the work of every day that will not wait while he has to die, and while I can hardly walk.

The horse stamps and snorts, calling me to her, to give her grain and water, to assure her all is well. The chickens jump onto the window-sill, pecking at the smoky glass to tell me to fill their pan and give them to eat.

I settle back on my low chair, swatting the flies, hearing the commotion of the animals outside. I try to think why all this depends on me. I fold and unfold my hands over the weakly kicking stranger inside of me. Who now will come to help me?

There has been no rain this summer. For days there have been clouds, even lightning and thunder, but no rain.

I ask myself who has brought me to this impossible juncture? Who but I myself, in my pride?

I, Elishabet, have chosen wrong at every turn, wrong to leave my father, wrong to choose this sad and weak man, wrong to follow after him through trouble and trial, through ill wind and bad land. When I finally could go no further, I pick a poor site for a cabin, in this bleak and narrow valley whose streams disappeared as summer came on, with no game to be had, and the earth itself inhospitable to my crops.

Withal, this man now lies dead upon my bed where I myself should be, burdened with this oncoming trial of birth. Yet, here am I, alone, uncared for, and at the end, unloved.

I look at the heart-shaped window in the rough wall of this cabin. A foolish gesture, this window, a wedding gift from the foolish and impractical man who came all this way only to die.

I reach toward the table, grasping its rough leg, pulling myself over the side of the chair, wanting to fall to the floor but forcing myself to stand.

* * *

I wash Arc's body. It is great effort to have water. I ask myself why I am doing this. I have no strength, and I spend what little I have tugging on his body, turning him, pulling arms into sleeves, legs into trousers. I button the shirt already knowing I will wrap him in a quilt for a shroud and no one will ever see the buttoned shirt, the clean clothes, the washed body. Washing a body to put it into the ground. Why?

I ask again. Why?

This is my favorite quilt. I have carried it when I left much behind, again and again culling my belongings, leaving much behind, leaving much behind.

This quilt is larger than the others. I fold the quilt over his body. I roll him one way and then the other, each time folding the quilt away from his face. I am reluctant to cover his face. I want to see his face until there is nothing to be done but to cover it.

Now comes the time. I see this face for the last time. I will never again feel the beardy stubble of chin against my soft breasts, my throat, my cheeks. I never will see the eyes as they looked through me, as if I was not there, and then suddenly see me, and tell me he wants me again. Again. Again, even when I am with child. Even when he is sick. Even before he died.

The cruel mouth, the cruel words, the biting teeth on my shoulder, the hurting words, the hurting words.

Cover his eyes, his mouth, his beardy chin and cheeks. Cover over his head. Wrap the quilt tight. Tie it with rope. Tie the quilt onto his body with rope. Roll to the edge of the bed. When it lands hard on the rough floor, it will land with a harsh thud. A hard landing. How many times did I fall hard on the floor, or against the wall? How many times?

This life made me angry too, Arc. I've been disappointed. I feel the rage. But I don't hit you. I don't push you, until…until…today.

I lean into a pull, budging the body only inches. I feel a weak kick from my swollen belly. Blackness.

* * *

I claw the soft earth of a flower bed, the only sod-free entrance to the dry earth.

Handfuls of tender roots are pulled from the ground and tossed to the side, finally buried beneath other handfuls of soil, dug away by bleeding fingers. At last, I have the hole knee-deep, and I know I am not able to do more. Even removing myself from this hole is a problem in my advanced condition.

I return to the useless struggle to remove Arc's quilt-wrapped body from the cabin, but I can do no more this day. I sink onto the bed and pray I too will die.

* * *

At some hour of the morning, I awake knowing the horse must be first on my mind. She is my best help at hand. I weave past poor furnishings and unlatch the door, wincing at the distance to the well. At last, I grasp the handle, needing seven hearty pumps to produce a single drop from the nozzle to the trough. Doubting my strength but not my will, wondering if will will have its way, with a "WOOSH…" the water splashes into my bucket. The horse draws near.

Gratefully I see the halter on her huge head. I thread my rope through the brass ring at her throat.

In the cabin once more, I tie the rope around the neck of the quilt-wrapped thing. I stretch the rope taut to the neck of the draft animal. The reluctant horse moves forward. By inches the body slices through the doorway. I guide the horse and its dragging burden nearer the edge of the waiting grave.

The horse lurches, pulling the burden past the opening. I yell in frustration. I try to drag the body back but cannot move it. I pound it with my fists. I lay on it and cry. There is no help from this shrouded man. I feel the burn of the rope on my muddy and bleeding hands. I am too young to be this desperate and alone.

Rain is falling now. I stare at the open grave, missed by so few feet. I try to move the horse back, but it will go no closer to the burden. There is nothing but to urge it forward. I lead it wide of the cabin corners so the dragging thing behind will not be caught. Slowly we pass each angle of the house and approach the waiting grave again. I cannot last. My strength is failing. Another burden imposes itself on me. I feel the first pangs of this coming birth.

With patience I do not own, I lead the horse step by step, stopping her as the shrouded thing is at the opening. I remove the rope from her great neck, and she walks away. I do not care.

I move to the side of the grave. This flower bed had been the bright place in my grey life. Now I put my hands on the quilted flowers and feel the man inside. This man could never put down roots and stay long enough to know a place. This man could not wait for babies to be born before moving on. This man twice buried my babies and now is dead himself. With rage, with pain, I push the dead thing. It rolls over the edge and lands with a thud that sickens my stomach, my heart, my soul.

The rain falls gently. Blackness takes me.

* * *

My dream is of a young girl with raven hair. Her flashing eyes count the males who would court her. She chooses a laughing man ten years her senior, a man who boasts, who is rash. She dances and dines at their wedding feast, New Year's Day, 1800. He toasts her, toasts the crowd and makes idle boast that he will soon leave for the west, "Where a man can come into his own…" She pouts pretty lips and stamps a dainty slippered foot, vowing not to leave her father's house this night or ever unless he takes back his word.

But her father, a proud and stiff-necked man of the Book, forbids her naysay, pronouncing a curse on a wife who will not follow a husband's wishes.

"Wives, be in subjugation to thy husbands," he quotes.

The idea of leaving takes root in the bridegroom's ale clouded head, and soon they are on the path through seven years that lead her to waking up in the rain beside the rude grave, another child insisting on being born.

* * *

In the bed, sometime in the night, the baby comes. I find it silent. It is dead as two before it, as its father is dead. I wrap it in a quilt. These quilts were wedding presents. Now they are shrouds.

I sleep.

In the daylight, the next or the following day, I put it in the grave with Arc and pull the muddy earth onto them.

They are together. I am alone.

4

1840: ELISHABET, EVENING, MORNING AGAIN

"Mother, may I come in?"

I rock. The floor squeaks. I look around to be sure of where I am.

The door opens. It is him, the quiet son. I am safe if I can be safe.

"Mother, people are leaving."

His voice is as gentle on me as his hands on his father. Where did he get such gentleness?

"Do you want to come down, or wait?"

"I'll wait. How is your wife? Who is with her?"

"Her sister has come to be with her."

"Has her sister attended births before?"

"Yes, and she has children of her own."

"Give your child a name from your wife's family. Maybe it will have some luck we can't give it."

"I'll come back for you. Do you want anything?"

"No."

He leaves. I rock. I could put on a black dress. But I would be doing it for the others, not for Art, not for myself.

I will do it for the others, but not tonight. I am wearing brown, a dress heavy for the season, plain. It will do. I rock.

Tomorrow I will wear my black dress. I rock. The squeak from the floor is a constant. I depend on it. It never leaves me.

"Mother."

"Yes."

"Everyone is gone now."

I go to the door. He is there. The quiet one. He is alone. He offers his arm. I'm not sure anyone has ever done that for me. We walk into the hallway toward the stairs.

"Will you want someone to stay with you tonight, one of the women?"

"None of the women…"

"Would you want one of the children to sleep with you?"

"Sleep with me? No. I will stay by the coffin tonight." I hadn't thought of this, but it seems right.

"I planned to stay with him tonight, too."

"Won't you be with your wife?"

"She has her sister. I am of no help to them. I want to be here."

We walk into the parlor. He covers my hand on his arm with his hand as we are confronted by the family of this large house. We walk toward the coffin, the bare boards of the coffin sitting on the sawhorses.

There is no time to think.

I did not want to see anyone. I did not want anyone to see me see him, here, as he is, as he never will be again after tonight.

We stand together. This silent son of his father has hold of my hand. I do not think I could withdraw it. I am not sure I want to.

Arthur looks still smaller than he looked upstairs.

"Where's the furniture?" The room is so large.

"We moved most of it into the dining room."

"Where did all the chairs come from?" So many chairs.

"It will be a wonder if we find all the places to put them back." He is strong, he holds my arm, my hand.

"Why are so many people here?" I didn't want to see anyone tonight.

"This is your family. We want to be with you."

He looks at me.

"You do? They do?" I feel surprise. I am surprised to feel surprise. I didn't think I could feel anything.

"Yes, Mother. We want to be with you."

"I expected to be alone," I whisper to him. "It's all right if you stay, but so many? I expected to be alone…with him."

"Let everyone stay a while…with you, Mother, then they will leave, and you can be alone." His voice holds me.

"Yes."

Art's tie does not look right. I want to retie it. But there are so many people here.

"I think I chose the wrong shirt. He didn't like that shirt."

I made it for him. He tried it on. It was just like so many others I made for him. But somehow it didn't fit the same. He didn't say so, but I knew he didn't like it. It stayed in the drawer. He chose the others over and over, but he never put that one on again. He didn't say anything, but he just didn't wear it.

"It looks fine on him. He'd be proud you chose it for him." His voice holds me. Why is he so gentle with me?

"You think so?" I look away from Art to this son.

"Yes. And we can't change it now. We wouldn't be able to change anything now. Everything is fine as it is."

"You think so…"

"Yes."

"How long are the others going to stay?"

"A short time. Then you can be alone."

"I need to sit down."

"I had someone bring down your rocker."

"From my room?"

"Yes."

I am surprised again. Surprise is the last feeling left to me anymore, surprise when anyone does something to please me, or interest me.

It surprises me when anyone even notices me, let alone tries to meet my need.

"Good. I'll sit down."

"Maybe you'd say something to the family."

"What would I say?"

"They want to know that you are all right, that you are not suffering. They want you to reassure them that our lives will go on as before, that the Farm will go on."

"They want me to reassure them?" To reassure them?

"Yes."

"What will I say?"

"Mother, tell them that we have all had a loss, but Father would want us to go on as before. Tell them that Father would want us to love one another."

"Love one another?" Love one another?

"That we must love one another in memory of Father."

I turn away from Art. This silent son is not the tallest of the sons, but he is taller than I am by a head. His arm is across the back of my shoulders. He is strong, so gentle in his strength.

There are many faces here. I don't see them well in the poor light. How long have I separated myself from the inhabitants of this house? How long since I thought of any of these as my children, my husband, my family?

When I sit at table with them, I enjoy the surprise of trying to recognize any of them. I never remember the wives, the silent young women in this silent house. I don't know the children, though there are not many.

They look at me now. I cannot say anything to them. I don't know them.

"I've got to sit down," I whisper. He holds me. He holds me.

"Mother would like to say that this is a sad time for our family, but that we must, in the absence of our father, we must love one another in his memory. Mother wishes you all a good night, and she plans to sit here a while."

His eyes hold me. The others look at me. Their empty faces all so much alike.

He leads me to my chair. I sit. I rock.

Faces come before me. Their feet drag on the carpet. They touch my hand, my shoulder. I rock.

I am alone. I rock. I rock. I rock.

From my chair I see his face in the coffin. Not any of his hair, but his forehead, his brow, his nose, lips, chin. He is so clean shaven, so young. I rock.

His sons have his looks. His sons. I rock.

"Out of my body, but your sons." All his sons. I rock.

Seth. His son. I rock.

Benjamin. His son. I rock.

Caleb. His son. I rock.

The quiet one. His son.

Until today, the quiet one. I sit.

His son… I rock.

…his son… I rock.

…his son…until today.

* * *

"Mother."

"Mother, we've come to sit with you.

The giants. The strangers. His sons. And the quiet one…

"I wanted to be alone." Alone again. Alone again.

"We'll sit with you a while and then we'll go." Seth.

"The flowers are nice." Benjamin. His son.

"Flowers?

"The flowers around here are goneby. Frost got em. These came from some of the gardens in town." Seth.

"Town? Came from town?" No friends there.

"The ladies from the church sent them from their gardens. They haven't had hard frost. Still have leaves on the trees, too. Good color still. Some maples. Oaks. Tamaracks." Seth again.

"I don't want their flowers." I stand. "Take them out of here. Take them out of here now!"

"What's the matter with a few flowers? They sent them out of the goodness of their hearts." Seth again.

"Let them keep the goodness of their hearts and may it do them precious little good as it ever did me."

"Mother, tell us what you want us to do." His voice holds me. His hand reaches for mine.

"I have no friends there. I don't want their flowers."

"Father had many friends there. And some of these flowers came from our wives' families. Some don't belong to the same church. Mother, we can't hurt their feelings. It's the only thing they can do for us now." His voice holds me. His hand holds my hand.

"Mother, we'll take the flowers out of here so they won't be in your sight tonight. We'll bring them back for the service tomorrow, and no one will notice in the meantime. Why don't you sit."

His voice holds me. He lets go of my hand as I sit.

"Brothers, bring the flowers into the kitchen." Even his orders are gentle. The brothers take the flowers away.

I rock.

They return and sit around me. I am their center.

"Father told us that you married his brother, Archelaus. That if Archelaus had lived, he would have been our father."

"Arc's children didn't live." They died, died, died...

"How many were there?" His voice holds me, holds me.

"Three. They died." They died. They died. They died.

"What were their names?" The gentleness in his voice.

"They died. They had no names." Died.

"Are they buried together?" The gentleness holds me.

"Maybe we shouldn't ask Mother about this." Seth.

"Maybe now is not the time." Benjamin.

"Mother. Mother..." The gentleness, the kindness...

"They are each buried different places. The last was buried with his father. Arc was a foolish man. He would not have had fine sons like Arthur, fine sons like you are."

"Did you love Archelaus?" Gentleness, gentleness…

"Love? No. I was a child. I didn't know what it meant to love a man. Any man. I didn't know how much it could cost a woman not to know love. I wanted to marry Arc. I thought he would start a farm. His family had land, land they didn't use. I thought he would start a farm, that we would live near town, that I would have my mother, my father and brother, my friends. I didn't know he was such a foolish man, to not care about what I wanted, about what he could have, that he would want to leave and take me with him. How could a man be as foolish as that, and how could I love him?" How? How? How?

"Mother. Mother. Stop, Mother." His voice holds me.

"Mother, we don't have any right to ask these things." Seth?

"Mother, we don't need to know." Seth? Caleb?

"Mother, you don't need to tell us." Benjamin.

"Mother, I need to know… I want to know…"

I will tell you anything, strange, silent one…

"What would you know? What would you ask me?" Ask me, silent one, quiet one.

"Mother, did you love Father?" Holds me, holds me…

"Love. Not every woman has the luxury of love."

"Then you didn't love…"

"We shouldn't know this. We shouldn't ask this." Seth.

"Your father built me this house. I married him. He worked very hard. I worked with him. He planted crops. I cooked his food. He chopped the wood. I kept the fire. He was good to me. I was good to him. He wanted me often, in his bed. I…"

"We shouldn't know this. We didn't ask this." Seth.

"He was kind. He was good. He didn't hit me. He didn't hurt me, nor blame me for things that went wrong. His children didn't die, didn't leave me. He didn't leave me, until today… Your father told you a lot, I can see. But he couldn't tell you what he didn't know." I can.

"What didn't he know?" Kindness. Gentleness.

"I was angry when we married. I was afraid." Afraid…

"What were you afraid of?" So gentle.

"Afraid it would be like before. I decided I would kill him before I would let it be like before…"

"Kill who?"

"I put a knife under my side of the mattress, a sharp knife…"

"Kill who, Mother? Not Father?" His voice holds me.

"Art."

"Arthur, our father, or Arc, his brother?" So kind.

"Art, before he was your father."

"We shouldn't know this…" Seth, the oldest.

"But he was kind and good. He was gentle. He didn't hurt me. He was patient. He was kind.

"Be kind to your wives. They want you to be gentle. A woman's body is different, not hard like a man's. Be gentle, be kind…"

"Mother. Mother." Gentleness.

"Are you gentle with your wife? Your wife who is birthing your baby tonight?"

"Mother…"

"Are you? Are you?"

"Yes. I'm gentle with her. We are all gentle with our wives. Father told us, every one of us…"

"Be gentle. Be kind. A woman's body is soft, not…"

"Father said that. He talked to us. He told us. We know, Mother. We know. Father said a woman should leave a man who is not gentle with her. Father said that to every one of us. He said he'd not have a son who was not kind to his wife, his children, his animals. He said the only one a man had a right to be hard on was himself."

"That's what he said." Benjamin.

"He told us again and again." Seth.

"He must have learned it because of you, Mother. He said he wasn't like the rest of his family."

"He said they didn't treat you well."

"He said he was the youngest and didn't know how to help you when you came back from the west."

"He said all you owned was the window and a few towels."

"He told you about the window and the towels? He told you about his family?" The hurt? The humiliation?

I rock.

"He said you brought back the window, the heart-shaped window that Archelaus had given you as a wedding present."

"He said all you had were a few towels you had woven for your bridal chest."

"He told us your parents were dead, your brother wouldn't take you, and the Keltys didn't want you."

I rock.

"Father said they worked you hard, and your health wasn't good."

"He said he worked harder so there were less things for them to ask you to do."

I rock.

"He did the worst jobs so you wouldn't have to do them."

"He never told me. I didn't know that." I didn't know.

"He told us to be kind to you. That you deserved better than you got."

I rock, I rock.

"We'll leave you, Mother. We know you wish to be alone. We needed to be with you a while. We all wanted some time to be with you and Father."

"You don't need to leave..."

"We had planned to sit up with Father this last night. We didn't know you needed this time."

"You can stay..."

"We'll come back at times during the night."

"I don't think anyone in the house will sleep much..."

"Brothers, I know I won't."

Laughter. He laughs too, but I see the worry on his face.

"I'm going to sit with my wife for a time, then I'll come back to Mother. Get what sleep you can, Brothers. We have much on our shoulders tomorrow."

They smile weakly at each other, tiredly. They nod to me, kindness on their faces. They touch each other's hands, arms, shoulders. They stand at their father's coffin, then, one by one, they slowly walk away.

I am alone. I rock. I rock.

* * *

"Young men are in a hurry. There's no need to be in a hurry. You'll have it as you want it, but no woman is in a hurry about these things. I know. You must listen to me. I'm your wife, Arthur. I'm older than you. There are things you haven't learned yet."

"I'll learn, Elishabet. You just tell me once. I'll learn."

I cannot see him in the dark but I can feel the heat from his body. He is so close to me; I feel some fear of him. I will not have it be like it was with his brother. I will not have it be like that. I think of the blade on the ropes beneath the mattress.

"A man can tell a woman what he wants and be gentle about it. A man does not have to hurt a woman to have what he wants."

"I won't never hurt you, Elishabet. I won't never hurt you. You only tell me if I do wrong and I won't never do it again."

His voice is eager as I know he is, as he would be, being so young. I was eager at first.

"Have you ever done this before?"

"I ain't never been with a woman. But I know what's to be done. I know that. I just ain't never done it myself."

So, this is a first time. He will be quick. He will want more.

"We will never have to talk about this again if you listen to me now."

"You tell me, Elishabet. I want you to tell me what I should know."

"You always be clean when you come into bed with me."

"I will."

"When you want congress with me, you put your hand on my leg, above my knee. If I don't push your hand away, then you slowly gather my gown and bring it up some. You touch me with your hand, and you wait till I'm calm and comfortable. Don't be in a hurry about this part. Do you understand?"

"Yes."

His voice is strained. He would be done by now if I had let him. I lay back, deeper into my pillow. He must learn to be patient. I may never have the chance to tell him again, and I will not, will not have it be as with Arc.

"After a time of gently touching me, you move over onto me, but you brace your weight on your elbows and your knees. You understand?"

"Yes, yes. I understand. What else?"

"Never ask me unless it's dark, and always keep the bedcovers over us."

He does not speak. I imagine he is nodding assent.

"You be slow and gentle. If I say you are hurting me, you must stop. I will not be hurt. You understand?" I think again of the blade on the ropes below me.

"You tell me and I'll stop. I don't want to hurt you."

Somehow, I believe him. But any man would say the same at this point. I don't know if a man can stop.

"You'll never hurt me. You understand?"

"I never want to hurt you, Elishabet."

I want to believe him.

"Gently, gently, you'll find how things fit, and you'll go slowly. Everything will happen as it should. You just go slowly."

"Slowly…"

"Slowly."

"Can I start now?"

"In a minute, Art."

"In a minute. All right, Elishabet. I can wait."

"Now there are sometimes of the month when this would be painful for a woman. There are sometimes of the month when a woman has The Blood. You can't ask during those times. Just like when a woman has a baby, there's a long time before and a long time after when you can't ask. So, if you put your hand on my leg and I push it off, don't ask. Don't make me shame you by telling you no."

"I won't, Elishabet. You tell me what you want and that's what I'll do. It will always be that way, Elishabet. I ain't never going to hurt you, nor shame myself. Never, Elishabet. Never."

I want to believe this man. I want him to be good to me. I will be good to him if he is only good to me.

"Can I start now, Elishabet?" He puts his hand on my leg above the knee.

"Yes, Art. You can start."

And so, the timeless ritual between man and woman began again for another man.

* * *

I stand and walk to the coffin. The candles at either end have burned low. There are shadows on his face.

"You were a handsome young man, Art."

I liked you as a little boy though I was too stuck on myself to notice you much. I was in love with the idea of being in love with your brother. He danced. He sang. He took my breath away and I felt powerful and wonderful because he wanted me.

But he was the child, Art. Not me. Not you.

You grew into a fine, loving, caring man. I watched you with our children. You had such patience, such interest. You talked to them, you looked into their little faces.

I...

This is hard, Art. Even though I'm alone here and only in my thoughts, this is hard.

I didn't let myself love you.

I didn't want to hurt you. I was afraid to love you. I didn't ever know that I knew what love was. I was afraid. Even after I removed the knife from under the mattress where it had cut the ropes. I was afraid. I was afraid to love.

I thought it would be easier if I didn't love you.

It wasn't. It was difficult not to love you.

I did like a lot about you. I liked how you laughed. I liked that a lot. You were cheerful. I needed that. I liked that. Watching you… I liked watching you. When you wanted something for your family, you reached with both hands. I could tell when you wanted something you didn't have yet. I watched you figure out how you were going to get it. I watched you turn it around in your mind, figure it out from every angle.

You would lie awake at night, looking into the darkness over the bed, never seeing the dark but the obstacles that were in the way of your having what you were set on having. You lined up those bumps in your road, those pitfalls that lay between you and your objectives.

You'd turn those problems, have a look at them every which way, seeing what you could, and knowing whatever there was to know so that in the morning you could come at it again, and, knowing where your strength was, and reasoning out where your best chance might lie, well, that tomorrow might be the day of your having what you were set about.

Some tomorrows hadn't come yet, but every day was another chance to try—and it was put into you to try—all the day long, try till the night comes. Every night until that long last night we all come to.

Beaten, thwarted, every night you said, "It's just for this night. It's only the night standing between this day's defeats and tomorrow's fresh start."

How I admired that.

So, you'd lay down, draining off your hurts, your pain, and soaked up the quiet, the peace of the darkness. You examined where to start anew on the morrow, by what path you'd travel and achieve your goal. At last, sleep would fill you and give your wants sinew for the morning light.

What a wonderful man you were, Art. I always knew it.

"Nearly from the first."

I wish I had told you. I wish I had told you.

"I wish I had only told you." I sit. I rock.

"How will it be now, Art? How will the Farm go? How will the family get on?" I rock.

"How will it be for me…" I rock, "…without you?"

"The Farm will go on all right, Mother. He taught us well. He worked with each of us. He taught us everything needed. He found what each liked, what we were good at, and helped to make us better. He worked us together and separately. The Farm will be fine. The family will be fine."

The quiet one. Quiet until today.

His face is so like to his father's young face. He is not as tall as Seth or Benjamin, yet taller than Caleb. His body is lean but broad, strong. A strong man, so gentle.

"As for you, no one can take Father's place, but you must lean upon your sons. We are you sons, Mother, as we are Father's sons. Now that Father is gone, you must come into the family more. We would welcome you. You sit at the head of the family. You help us with decisions to keep our Farm, our family strong. Your advice is needed, is wanted."

His words, his voice, his kindness and gentleness reach across the space between us, embracing me, holding me in safety.

The candle closest to us begins to sputter, then goes out. Some of the lamps in the room have gone dry. The candle at the head of the coffin remains. I look at Art. For a moment, it seems he is smiling as he often smiled in his sleep.

"I will go to my room now. I will rest, and I will come back when the neighbors arrive tomorrow. Though I don't know many of them, I know your father was a friend to all."

"You are our mother. We will stand beside you, our families with us. You are Mrs. Kelty of Kelty Farm. They'll know you."

"How will that be. I can't even imagine. I will need you to help me."

"I'll be there, and so will we all. Take my arm, I'll walk up the stairs with you and then I'll bring your chair."

"I want to take a lock of your father's hair. I meant to do it before, but now will be my last opportunity. I have scissors in my pocket. Take them and find a place behind his ear where no one will notice."

He leans over the reposing figure, gently, so gently searching. I hear the scissors come together. He has a thick lock of grey hair and he puts it into my hand, laying the scissors beside. He puts out his arm. We walk slowly from the room to the stairway and accomplish the stairs one slow step at a time. He does not hurry me. At my room, he opens the door and steps away.

"Leave the door open and I will bring the chair up."

Inside, I see the rumpled quilt in the low light of the lamp. I turn up the flame. The quilt on the bed will need washing. I fold it and put it on Art's chair. Art never sat in the chair except to put on stockings or footwear.

In the bottom drawer of the clothes press there is a new quilt and I unfold it over the bed. I have never used this one. I somehow wanted to save it for a special occasion or maybe a gift. My eyes tire easily these days, and I cannot make a quilt as fast nor as well as I have in the past.

The colors and patterns in the quilt are gentle, reminding me of willows and brooks. They seem cool and refreshing—promising. I never made another just like this one.

He brings my chair and puts it just in the right place over the squeaking floorboard. He bends toward me, kisses my forehead at the hairline.

"Good night mother. I will be with Father for this night if you have need of me. In the morning, we will do what we must on the hill, and it will be as you want it to be. Trust us."

"I do."

"Rest as well as you can. Much is expected of us tomorrow." He walks to the door, pulling it closed behind him.

"Good night to you…my…my son," I say before the click of the latch.

I look at the bed but I know I can not lie upon it this night. My pillow is gone. My husband is gone.

I reach into the back of the press and remove the box with the paper wrapping. I put it on the bed and slowly undo the covering which has kept the dust out for this long time. I remove the cover. Inside is more tissue. It is tucked into the sides, so carefully, so deliberately.

This is my wedding dress. Ten years ago, I tried it on. After twenty years, all the children, the work, it fit me well enough. I do think on my wedding day it was bigger than I needed.

It is black. It has tassels for the fastening. It has a black-upon-black design, subtle, not easy to see. There is a black shining trim at the neck and cuffs. It is the nicest dress I owned since leaving my father's house forty years ago.

Arthur had a woman make it for me from my sketch. He was not surprised at my choice of color because I was a widow at the time of my marriage to him. No one knew my mind enough to realize the terrible mourning I felt at having to marry into this Kelty family a second time. I had no choice.

How often in these later years Art urged me to order new dresses, new things. My mother taught me to be handy with a needle and I have been. I ordered as I needed, making my own things, often of the cheapest materials. Until my sons married, I made most of the clothing my family had worn.

Tonight, I will examine this garment to be sure it is a widow's dress and not a wedding dress. There is no one left who attended my wedding supper at the old Kelty house. I alone will know that this was my wedding dress.

I have never been interested in fashions of the times and this gown was not made to the fashion of its day nor is it likely to be today's style. It is high at the neck, gathered at the bodice, snug at sleeve and full in the skirt.

There will be a quiet time when everyone will be sleeping. I will go down to the kitchen and heat the irons to press out the years of storage wrinkles in the material.

This night I will weave the lock from Art's head together with a lock of my own white hair. I will entwine my white around his grey again and again, write a note to wrap the weaving in, then I will place it in a small opening between the wall and the heart-shaped window.

The window is at the far end of this room in the peak of the roof over this sleeping loft. Art put it there when he built the cabin. I had forgotten the window entirely and was not especially pleased to see it installed in prominence at my new home.

I understood immediately that it was something he was moved to do to please me, but I never mentioned it to him. I would as soon have forgotten it forever instead of being reminded of my past every night and morning these thirty years.

Still. I know he never meant anything but good.

"I know that especially today."

How many things I have learned about this man I lay beside each night since I came to this house. As much time and thought as I have given to him, I am amazed at all that has been revealed to me today.

"I wish…"

Well, I may get used to living with regrets.

I wish we could have done something about flowers of our own. The fields and woods and trees of our land are usually full of blossoms of one kind or another. It is late and frosts come early here. But that is as it is and is not worth regretting. There are many other things that are not so easy. I will have years beyond this night to frown and worry over them.

After this evening with my sons… My sons! After this evening with my sons, perhaps these years ahead will not be so bleak.

"Another gift from your hands, Art."

If there is time, I will sit in my chair. Perhaps I will sleep.

* * *

He has come to get me and offers his arm. I have learned to take it and walk at my pace. He will match it. There is no rushing on his arm.

"How is your wife?"

"It will be soon, but the baby isn't here yet."

"Is she strong?"

"Yes. Be thankful."

At the foot of the stairs waits the crowd of the most people I ever hope to see in my house. People press away from our path as if they would not brush against the twice widowed, twice Mrs. Kelty. I have avoided these people for years, not wanting to see the smug faces that secretly laugh up their sleeves at my marrying a younger brother after losing the older one under circumstance unknown and unexplained.

I know they sneer that I was a charity for my own in-laws who were none too gracious about doing their duty by me. I know they laugh at my childbearing by the younger brother as I never had with the older.

I feel the strength of this son's presence. I must lean on that...

We turn the corner into the room that never has been more filled nor less welcome so. Still, a path has been left for us and a chair has been reserved for me in the midst of my family. The minister stands to one side of the coffin. He too is dressed in black. He holds his Bible. May it do him more good than ever it has done me.

I sink into the chair. The Reverend mouths a prayer and begins his well-practiced words. This is not his loss; this is his job. I feel a hand patting my arm. I need not look to know which son this is. How is it that I only now come to know him or any of the others?

The greenery behind and around the coffin catches my eye. Someone has filled all the space with pine boughs, freshly cut and aromatic. There are strings of bittersweet swaged at odd lengths and angles, very much as one would find it in our woods. Here and there at a distance from the coffin are the floral offerings I had seen last night. They seem lost and late come to the natural greens that smell so good.

I glance at my sons to the right and left. They each smile and nod as they catch my eye. They seem pleased.

> "Know what happens when Christians
> die so that when it happens you
> will not be full of sorrow..."

Christians. Christians. Have I not been in the hands of Christians and have I been spared any sorrow?

> "...and the believers who are dead

will be the first to to meet the Lord…"

Art Kelty, when you rise, you will find your feet on your own land, on soil that you walked to your heart's content. May you rise and find it still Kelty Farm, and in the hands of your blood. You leave strong sons who are rich in wisdom you gave them. May they be blessed in their own children, their children's children, and their children.

"…we who are still alive

and remain on the earth will be

caught up with them in the clouds…"

After the example of your hard work, those who mix with our blood will cling to this land. They will husband it, hold it dear. How could they not? And they will love those who understand that this land where we are, is who we are, is what we are.

"…and remain with him forever

--so comfort and encourage each other.

1 Thessalonians"

Arc, I forgive you the deaths of our babies, I forgive your hard use of me, I forgive you all the sorrows of my aching heart. I will try, but I cannot now forgive you for teaching me not to love. For that sin I missed loving your brother in his lifetime. Maybe I can love his family —our family—before I lie forever beside the man who truly loved me, though he never heard a word of thanks for it.

"I hope Art knows. I hope he knows."

5

1847: ELISHABET, POSTSCRIPT ONE

"At last they sleep, the two, my watch dogs."

She fills soft felt slippers with her feet, though she feels nothing as she does so.

"My feet are as far away from me as dead children and husbands I dream of: I feel nothing from them either, and yet they are with me." Her voice is a soft whisper even to herself.

The windows tell nothing of the night, though her eyes have seen no light in years. Sometimes, by a window, she can hear a bird call, or a tree rustle as it brushes the house. She feels at the window for a draft, a stray gust of wind that might find a loose pane. In silence, this is her way to know the night.

Across the sill of her bedroom doorway, she begins the litany.

"I know how to turn the latch to make no sound. I know as I pause by the doors in the hallway, who sleeps calmly, who is overtired, who has a cold. I carefully avoid the last door before the stair. There, more often than not, I hear the rocking chair in the middle of the resting hours when all others sleep. That is the silent one, the one of all these brought forth from my body, of all this house full of strangers, he is the one most like to me."

54

Now at the top step, she continues.

"I know his eyes are empty now…"

She steps down one.

"…of the fear of me so many others have."

Another step.

"His eyes hold no longing to please me some still have." She pauses.

Down a step.

"They are void of the distaste, the distrust, the disgust some hold for me."

Down a step.

"In these years of darkness, in my quiet room, guarded by the two…"

A step.

"…I hear, I feel the whole household tiptoe by my door, ever shut."

She steps down a step.

"Sometimes of an evening they sing, they laugh, and I wonder…"

Steps down a step.

"…what they find to laugh at here where I have never laughed."

Down a step.

"And when I forget that I don't know them, when I forget that they are laughing and singing without me…"

She steps down a step.

"…sometimes I rock in my chair."

The last step.

"But then they stop."

She opens the door of the hallway into the kitchen, her slippers scuffing on the wooden floor.

"Of all those who quietly pass my doorway, among the many who wish to be unobtrusive, it is he, the silent one, whose boots walk steadily up the stairs and down the hallway, whose door rudely slams shut, who does not sleep in the night as everyone else does, and whose eyes I remember though it is my only blessing in my sightless years that I no longer see them burning."

She steps into the kitchen, surely to the stove, motioning flat circles inches above the cooking surface to know the state of the fire within. She scowls and steps through the darkness toward the woodbin.

"His are the eyes that hold no pity for me, no desperate wish to understand. No dread, no fear."

She probes layers of emptiness for the fuel she needs.

"In his eyes I remember something more terrible than in the others. I saw myself."

She swings her flattened palms from side to side, from front to back, lower, lower.

"Those lazy boys didn't bring wood in last night. Would serve them well to have a cold breakfast to start their day." She leans farther into the box, her middle resting on the top edge. There were always some pieces no one used. They would do today.

"And wouldn't their cold breakfast come back on me when they're all sick by tomorrow. Well, I'll make do with the little I've got here, I will."

Back at the stove, the iron side door complains as it swings open. She passes her hand slowly over the bottom of the chamber, a witch casting her spell. In the darkness her lips curl into a smile.

"Humph! Almost out! I'll be lucky now to catch it," she complains knowing she alone will hear.

Back to the woodbin, in a far corner she grasps the few straws, the chips, shavings, hoarded allies in a secret wish never to waste a match. To these ingredients she adds twigs, dry switches of elm, reeds form a broken basket. With all in gnarled and bent fingers, she returns to the waiting fire chamber. She scratches through the layers of ash, finding the hidden life within.

On this faint pulse of heat, she lays the straw, the twigs. Across these she layers the broken basket reeds, the switches. Lastly, and with great care, she crisscrosses the limb wood, some back to front, shorter pieces side to side.

She shuts the door making an unaccustomed clang in her haste.

"Dolt! Do you want the whole house down on your neck?" she hisses. She adjusts the flue, slides open the damper, turns toward the pantry before her hand leaves the spring handle.

Her waving hand meets the uneven surface of the agate coffee pot on the back shelf.

"Two inches off from where it was yesterday," she mutters, her brow furrowing. The ladle hangs off the back of the water bucket, another second to find. Twelve dippers full, counted off as the level in the bucket drops and the pot fills.

Third shelf to the right, round tin. Coffee beans, measuring spoon on top. Four grinding turns of the coffee mill, a transfer to the metal sieve basket, fit the lid, shuffle to stove—feeling warmer—slide the full pot to the back stove lid.

On the left of the sink, in front of the drafty window, the large mixing bowl. Below the shelf, the handle pulls open the tin-lined flour bin. Five dips of the one cup scoop-sifter. The sack on the floor inside the next door, four and a half cups of the cornmeal. (Fresh. Smells corn. A remembered golden-grainy color.) Lift the lid on the sugar jar. One cup, and a little. Baking powder on the first shelf, right of the salt cellars. Pry off the lid, spoon out dragging the spoon by the round opening of the can, mounding up the teaspoons-full, name the apostles, leave out the Judas. A teaspoon of salt for the Judas.

Mix. "One for the Father, two for the Holy Ghost. Three for the good Lord, four for His mother who bore the most."

Milk jar on the sill overnight. Pour off the cream, dump in the remains. Stir. Bottle of oil, three gulps of air into the bottle pours out a cup and some. Bowl of eggs on the sill, cool to the touch. Break five. And another. Stir the whole.

Large baking sheet leans against the end of shelf. Lard pail near the corn meal. Soft cloth in the pail, scoop the lard, rub the cloth on the baking sheet, along the bottom, four sides. Return the cloth, cover the pail, slide it back against the wall. Pour the mix onto the tin sheet, spooning its moistness against the low metal sides, swiping the spoon in the bowl, gathering the thickest mix, paddling the mix to the four corners out of the middle.

Carefully open the oven door, wave of heat hits face, slide sheet on middle rack. Lift stove lid. Poke at fire, add two sticks. Pull coffee pot to front.

She pauses, holds a breath, head inclined toward the door.

"I know that was a cow calling, but was it the first one?" She scowls. "Slow foot. On the morrow I must wake sooner."

She hurries the stairs, aching knees ignored.

She pauses to clear her throat at the first door. The rocking stops. On to her own door, lift latch silently.

Blind Grandmother. Cannot earn the bread, but can make the family's morning warmer.

6

1855: TEAMWORK

"Ike, you're fifteen, this is going to be your farm, and you'll have to know things that used to depend on a lot of different people knowing. Some of those people have died, some have left, some don't work much anymore. This Farm takes a lot of working at to keep it going." He sat back into the rocker, the porch boards complaining at the going back and the coming forward.

Ike perched on the top step by his father's boot, watching the toe dance to the chair's beat. He thought about fishing, wondering if there was time to drop a line near the big elm before the hands might come for a swim this afternoon.

"It wasn't so bad when Dad was alive. We were mostly family here then, all working together. We never thought of anything else, we just did what needed doing next, or what Dad told us to do." He cleared his throat.

"That was the thing about Arthur Kelty, and anyone would tell you this, he always knew what needed doing as if he'd been awake all night working everything out, seen the goal and then worked backwards from there so he knew, he really knew exactly what needed doing and when. You never found Dad unsure of himself."

A grey cat came onto the porch and Ike beckoned to it. It stood motionless but for a twitching tail, then took cautious steps toward Ike.

Just as Ike reached for the cat, it sprang into his father's lap and nestled, purring, into the older man's large hands.

"On any morning as we started our day, he paired us up, usually two to a team, sometimes with a brother, sometimes with an older and more skilled worker. We were seldom paired with the same man more than a day at a time. He set us off to do this or that, mending fences, pruning trees, marking trees to fell as was needed. We would split shingles, dig post holes, plow a garden space or field. It all depended how Dad saw our developing abilities, our growing skills or interests."

The cat winked several times at Ike, but Ike was guessing where to dig for worms to bait his hook if he did get the chance to fish the river today.

"When Dad sent us off to do a task, we knew, by God, we were the best men to do it. Anytime we would begin to lose our way, if the job wasn't going well or we were flagging, he would appear. It seemed he'd be there, and just at the moment when you'd begin to think, 'If Dad was here, he'd know what to do,' or, 'I wish Dad were here now...,' he'd be there."

Ike watched his father's knowing hands play behind the cat's ear, under its chin, along its belly. His father had a way with things, Ike thought, be it a stubborn mule, a wild–eyed horse, a stump to be drawn from a field or the cat nearest to hand. He played them all as easily as he played the instrument, his ancient violin that only screeched in Ike's hands.

"Of all the places he could have been just then, of the miles between one end of the Farm to another, or side to side, up hill and down, he'd be there when you began to know you most wanted him." He laughed and set the cat down on the floor of the porch. It rolled belly up to the sun.

"One time I learned that it wasn't only one's predisposition to a task that made Dad choose who was set to it or who you were paired with." He smiled broadly at Ike, though when he spoke of those days, his smile was often directed elsewhere. "My older brother, Seth, and I, God rest him, once got into a snit over something—and now I couldn't tell you what it was. But we'd had words and hard feelings without it coming to Dad's attention, or so we thought.

"So, came a morning after chores and breakfast, and Dad assigned me to work with Seth. The one person on the place I hadn't passed a civil word with in days. And I saw by my brother's face that he was no more pleased than I, but he knew, too, there was no use in saying anything to Dad. At the very least it would have brought the hard feelings between us out before our father, and neither of us wanted that to happen." The rocker stopped, and he leaned forward to Ike.

"As I look at it now, I know if either my brother or I had felt truly wronged we would have been most anxious to have our father's attention to the matter." He sat back in the chair and looked off across the valley. He smiled.

"So, there was nothing to be done but to start. We were to take the two-man saw and cut several logs into eight-foot lengths for the mill. Each log had to be peeved into place with a man on each end, moving in unison in an agreed upon pace. Next the saw was placed on the marked lengths and by forward and back pulls, in step with the other man, the saw would bite its way through the log.

"We had said only the words necessary to pace ourselves to the work and hadn't looked into one another's faces at all. Before we were two hours into the day my brother broke out into a laugh I can hear right now as if he were here and still laughing."

Ike watched his father's face split into a broad smile bordering on a laugh. Ike smiled himself sharing the moment. The cat still purred and stretched a clawed foot toward Ike's hand.

"Nothing could have surprised me more nor broken through the dark cloud in my brain quicker than to hear his hearty laugh. I stopped in my tracks, prepared to take fresh offense. I looked into his face and before I could ask the question, he burst into telling:

"'You know he knew, don't you, and knew too, that we'd never work a two-man saw and stay mad unless we were to kill one another! And Brother, I'd never kill a man who works as hard as you do!'

"We laughed and worked all the harder till it was noon and time to break for lunch. We returned to the house arms around shoulders, laughing and watching for that sly look on Dad's face he always got whenever he knew he'd made a good bargain."

The cat walked away, tail twitching as it passed behind the moving rocker. Ike wondered if he could leave now, if the worms would be hard to dig near the shady backside of the horse stalls, and if there was a hungry trout willing to be caught before supper.

7

───

1861: LILLIAN

The October wind blew aside her skirt and wrestled with her petticoats. She knew no one would be about at this late hour after the long day's work set by the sun. She let her skirt lift as it would and kept both hands on the tray. At the barn door, she was unnerved by the thump and click of the latch string lifting the wooden bar, and again when the door seemed to swing open on its own. She stepped through into a darkness unknowable, her movements sure. The door crashed shut as she set the tray on a shelf. Her hand reached, feeling along the cross bar, sliding it into place. She felt for the latch string and paused a moment before drawing it through.

No one else would enter the great barn tonight.

The stirring of the animals in the stalls were familiar sounds to her, and, from below, she could hear a constant shuffle of the cows, restless because of the wind. She stood with her back against the door, her body rocking as great screaming gusts hit the old planks so solidly bound together. She smiled into the blackness, sensing the warmth of the living creatures inside and the cold promise of snow outside.

The barn was her special refuge, and never more than tonight.

Retrieving the tray from the shelf, she chose her way as though it were light. Counting off the stalls on her right, she listened for the breath of the horses within.

63

"Jason, Stalwart, Susie," she counted, then the empty stall where Morgan the mule had been, Morgan, born sixteen years ago when she was born, Morgan who had bitten her father once too often and had been sold for his habit. "Micah, Trump," and the last empty stall. And then the wall of hay. Seven steps left to the door of the small room that was never cold.

And Luther who lay waiting for her.

The food on the tray was for later.

* * *

"You don't understand, Father. You never will."

"My precious daughter, it is you who doesn't understand. You're young, too young, perhaps, to comprehend the world you are so eager to rush out into."

"I know our life here well enough to not want any more of it."

"Our ways are hard but sheltering. We do not see need here, not real need. When we have a use for anything we acquire it. And while we do not squander, we have the means to have whatever is our wont." The man shuffled papers on his desk infuriating the girl.

"It hasn't been my experience that I could have whatever I wanted…"

"I think you purposely mistake my words. No one, dear Lillian, ever has whatever they want, though to be sure some have whatever they want for the moment. No satisfaction is had in life by the easy gain of whims and passing desire. Mature people expect to work for what they need and sometimes have a little more by the effort of their own hands."

"My hands will be worn down to the elbows before I have all that I want!"

"My father was Arthur Kelty…"

"You start every conversation that way, Father. You find any justification you need in those stories. They are part of all you carry around every day. Do you set them aside when you go to bed?"

"Lillian, you will not speak to me that way. I am your father, and you will respect me if not all who came before me. You will hear me out, young miss."

"If it's to be another story, don't start way at the beginning, about how the land was all stumps when your father got it, that somehow it belonged to the Keltys, but they were losing it till he took it on."

"Lillian, you think to hurt me by how familiar you are with these stories, but your easy recall of such details gladdens my heart, makes me know that you have listened long and carefully to the tales of your heritage."

"Whenever was there a choice but to listen? Yes, I have listened to you, to your aunts, to your brothers and their wives, to anyone and everyone that walks and talks of nothing but Arthur, Elishabet, and Kelty Farm, Kelty Farm, Kelty Farm. But when will I be listened to? When?"

"Daughter, I have taken thought of you, have watched your growth, your growing needs..."

"But you have no intention of listening to me. Even now, you choose the occasion to speak to me, not with me, nor to hear anything I might have to say."

"What would you tell me if I were to listen?"

"Oh, Father, dear Father. You could not sit in your chair to hear me. And you could never be silent long enough, nor could I stand against the disapproval in your silence to tell you my true heart."

"We both have other duties..."

"I have a duty to myself."

"Then say your say, unburden yourself, my girl."

"Where to start. The counting, the cooking, smoking of hams, canning, putting by—I get so sick of it all. Is there no season of rest? And the sewing, sewing, sewing—always another shirt, a skirt or blouse, a dress, small clothes, a slip... You can buy all that at any store, even right down at the village."

"Lillian, your hands have been so willing to sew..."

"I'd rather spin and weave and sew than anything else and yet I get to hate it. It makes me feel so useless, to be used up making what could be had for the sale of a cow or sheep—and we have many.

"Am I so little, to be used up in place of spending a small portion of what we have? Am I less than the worth of one cow that I am set to sew all winter on what could be bought by selling one, even one?"

"You miss the point, Daughter. Your sewing is a handiness that serves the family. As your mother cooks and cleans, and Hattie did washing and other chores, your talent was sewing, and whenever possible, you were left to that. Your skill is in clothing the family, and how we are seen by others reflects your skill in large measure."

"Father, Father, you miss the point. I am not Mother nor am I my sister Hattie, though she is at the end of her servitude to Kelty Farm…"

"Hattie married and now has all the chores that here were shared by you, your mother, and whatever hired girls we had. I never considered any work here servitude, and there are many here whose work is harder than your own. When you are older you will marry…"

"Older? I was born the last of your children and I have always been older, older than Hattie, and older than Ike, though my brother is near twenty-one. And marry? Who will l marry but a farm hand? Where do I go to be seen by anyone else but another me?"

"Hattie met young Norman at church…"

"When I'm seen at church, I'm in one of two dresses, each nearly worn out or reworked not to show the wear—oh, and I know all the tricks—attaching side panels, detaching the waist band and turning the front and back to the sides, putting on pockets over patched tear, shortening, lengthening, putting here a frill, there a flounce, an appliqué, a cloth flower…

"I'm tired of it all. I'm not going to have here what I want to have. I want to be free of the worry of it, of the not having of what would make me free of the worry of it. I'm tired…tired."

"Dear Lillian…"

"I'm tired of Mother working harder to keep me busy than the work needed to be done would take to do."

"Lillian…"

"I'm tired of your silence, Father, of your glances that tell me you disapprove."

"Lillian…"

"I want to unbraid my hair as I please, to stand in a wind. I want someone to see me, someone dangerous who would be excited by me. I want to go places and see things I'd never see here. I want to know things I can't imagine now, no, nor ever would here."

"My mother's first husband…"

"Yes, Archelaus, yes, he went out west…

"And he died out there."

"But he went! He wanted to go, and he went… Of all the stories, I've always thought I was most like almost-grampa Arc."

"You don't seem to know that his name is considered unlucky in our family, that we never name children after him, that he was not spoken well of in our family. That he isn't buried with the others on the hill."

"And I never want to be buried up on the hill. That's the reward for staying here till you die, for never going anywhere in life."

"Daughter, there are many who would wish for such an embrace as our family enjoys here."

"Father, I hate to shake your clear and certain view of life, but I am not among that number. I am not Ike who dotes on your every word. Ike would go off to a war to save the Union but will stay home to please you. He rides the countryside on beautiful horses, courting, visiting his many friends. Nor am I Hattie, farm wife Hattie, who will be her mother's daughter every way she can think to be. I am Lillian, and Kelty Farm will never be enough for me."

"What you are saying is that we could fill your closet with store-bought goods, and your dresser with gee-gaws. We could send you to every event from church weddings, to socials of the local young people and whatever else, and nothing would be enough. This discontent is inside of you and is not brought on by our ways. You express needs beyond your years, but you have yet to learn the patience that makes the having so sweet.

"There is yet another story of Arthur Kelty…"

"No! I don't want to hear another story."

"I have heard you, and now you will hear me. Sit still for this, it will go down easier."

"You will be waiting for your supper this night."

"Yours are not the only hands that work in this house. Now just you listen.

"Dad said for years he watched the river flow past, leaving him behind. In time he developed a longing to follow the river, into a lake, out of that and on to whatever ocean it must come to at the last. He said he never could do it because it would take him away from his life here, from his wife, his children, his duties. He said he wanted to be home at day's end, have supper at the table with his family.

"Later, Dad said it came to him that he'd rather follow up the river, see where it'd come from, to the streams and smaller streams, the brooks, the springs, that it would be easier to see where the river'd come from than where it ran to. Closer to home, you know. But he never went. Didn't ever have the time when he thought of it, he said.

"At the last, it come to him that what he was meant to see of the river was what came to him, right here where he was. And that time will come for you, Lillian."

"I know you mean well, Father. I just don't think you have heard anything I have told you. I don't want to follow the river in either direction. That would never be enough. I want to see the whole world."

"Don't you have any caution, Lillian? Are you so young you have no fear?"

"When have I needed caution? Fear? You, Father, have enough for both of us."

"I see disappointment ahead for you, young miss. You won't be satisfied to stay, and there isn't world enough but would break your heart if you were to have the whole of it."

"But I can't be satisfied to stay." Lillian turned her back to her father.

"And if you go now, no matter if I supported your ill-advised adventure, I see loneliness for you, danger, and no return though you'd always be welcomed. I can only counsel you to wait, to find the opportunity, a plan which will provide for your well-being."

"I'm watching for the day, Father. And it will be soon."

* * *

Luther hated waiting and especially waiting in the dark. He hadn't come early because he knew she'd be late, but now he was here in the dark barn, he wished he hadn't come at all.

Still, he felt that stirring again when he thought of her, that stirring that had no beginning, that wasn't there one minute then suddenly was the center of his thoughts. She did that to him. Was it because she was so damned ready for him every time? Hell, women weren't supposed to be ready. They were supposed to be reluctant, barely able to be talked into anything.

But not Lill.

The first time had happened by the big elm, on that hot August day when he was late from the fields and had gone down to the river to swim off some heat and hayseed. She had been on him before he really had time to think who she was.

Luther smiled into the darkness, remembering how ready he'd been himself. But a man doesn't get chances like that every day, especially with the boss's sweet young daughter.

For a while after that time, he watched for her, avoided the side of the table she served, avoided being alone in the great barn or any-where she might approach him. Every day he expected her father or her brother Ike to confront him, to end his job here, or to beat him soundly before sending him down the road.

After September all the work had been in the barns, and she seemed to know where he'd be. He smiled again, his hands anxious to be on her skin, around her soft neck, on her warm breasts, on her belly and legs.

He sighed, closing his eyes. "Lill is really something," he said to him-self. His shirt seemed to scratch at his chest. He unbuttoned it part way.

The smell of the leather harness hung on pegs on three walls filled his nose. He walked four steps left, his hand ready to touch leather.

He kicked a half-circle with his boot, finding the wooden chair. He sat, wondering if maybe this time she couldn't get away. What if her father found out? He'd come in with a horse whip!

"Calm down," he muttered to himself. "She's too clever for them, too clever for her own good, maybe." Inside a voice asked, "Too clever for you, Luther?"

"Lill's nothing special—just because her father runs this farm." Luther knew he'd never be more than a hired man here, never more than that.

"A hired man on a place like this is a lot," he told himself, "but not if you're married to the boss's daughter." He had seen that the family men worked twice as hard as any of the hired help.

So, what was he doing here? Sure, she was a hell of a roll, as fine as he'd known. But would it be worth the beating if the Keltys found out? The tack room door opened, announced by the smell of hay and the dull glow of the lantern. Her bare feet seemed to glow as she entered. Small fingers turned down the wick and the lantern scraped as she set it down on the hard floor. He put a hand out, saying, "Lill..." and his fingers wound into her hair.

* * *

His breathing was even. His eyes were closed. She didn't believe he was sleeping. She knew he would rouse himself again.

"Luther..."

"Lill, honey, I got to rest a while."

"Luther, let's talk while you rest." She moved a leg over his, her breasts against his side, her head nestled into his shoulder. He lay on his back, the buffalo robe between his naked body and the floor. His arm stretched beneath her head, reaching down to caress her back. Her right hand wandered across his hairy chest and down his middle. She felt him shudder and sigh. He seized her hand, holding it to his chest.

"What do we have to talk about, Lill?"

She heard the note of suspicion in his voice. She smiled to herself.

"Have you ever lived other places, Luther?"

"Where do you mean? Other farms?"

"Other places, like cities, other states. Places."

"I been to New York, but not to live. I didn't like it much. Maybe I was too young to like it. It was big."

"What do you mean, big?"

"Well, you know, big. Lots of houses, people, horses, too much of everything, and everything seemed dirty." He frowned into the dark at the memories. "Some of those people don't even speak English, at least not like we do. There was lots going on and I didn't understand what I was seeing. I didn't like it there."

"Did you ever go anyplace else, besides New York?"

"My family lived in Boston for a time, long ago. But that wasn't anything to brag on neither. And I didn't like it there. It was too big."

"Tell me what those places are like, Luther." His hand had let go of hers. Her fingers began to play in his chest hair.

"I told you already. Too much of everything. That's what big places are like." He reached for the end of the robe and pulled it up around her. "Are you cold? Do you have to go back to the house soon?"

"Do you ever think of marrying me, Luther?"

His body went stiff beneath her. There was a long empty moment.

"Gawdamighty, Lill. Can you see your father's face if I was to ask for your hand?" His voice was calm but tense.

She smiled.

"Someone's going to sometime, why shouldn't it be you?"

"Can you see us ever having any time alone, just you and me?"

"You mean like this, Luther? Like we are right now?" She began to make circles on his chest, larger and larger circles, dragging her fingers slowly across his stomach, feeling the taut flesh, the tight muscles that recoiled slightly at her touch. She began to rub her leg up and down his. He moaned agreement.

"You could build me a house, Luther, a house just for us, a place only for you and me. Mother said she and Father were going to do that when they first married, but no one would tell grandma Elishabet about the plan, so they ended up in the old house with the rest. But you could build us one. Father would give us the land, the lumber."

"Lill, your father would give me the end of his boot before he'd give me land to build a house."

He shifted his body, but not away from her. She trailed her fingers lower on his belly once more, lingering at the downy patch, the lair of the man thing. She felt for it, grasping gently, firmly, feeling the throb of life she expected. He moaned, seemed to hold his breath, then sighed deeply.

"You like what we do together, Luther?"

He rolled over onto her, guiding himself in to her again, he sighed, and began to withdraw, to thrust forward, to withdraw again.

"Luther, do you like what we do together?"

"Yes, Lill," he answered, his voice husky. His breathing became labored but controlled. He began to give a little grunt with each forward thrust.

"Luther, near Christmas I'm going to ask my father for money to buy me some things. I've got a small sum of my own as well. When I have it all together, I want you to leave with me. I want you to take me away from here."

He grunted. His back was beginning to arch and his breathing came harder.

"You hear me, Luther?"

"Yes, Lill, I hear you honey." He thrust deeper, faster.

"And you'll take me away when I'm ready?"

"Yes, Lill, yes, my little darling girl, yes, yes..."

"When I say I'm ready you'll take me, Luther?"

"Yes! Yes! Oh, my God! Yes! Yes!"

She wrapped her legs around his narrow back, crossing her ankles, pressing a heel into his buttock.

"Yes! He shouted again, and again, "Yes!" and held his breath in a quivering shudder.

She felt his hot seed spill into her, and she shuddered herself.

She smiled.

Men were so easy to love.

8

1875: KNOWING

"I see the Tinker's wagon has been here all afternoon, Lucy. What have you got him fixing that I can't fix?" Ike slid into the rabbit-eared chair across the table from his wife. He waited, noticing her hands folded tightly in front of her on the checkered tablecloth, her staring eyes locked onto her hands.

"What's the matter, Lu?" He reached across the table, closing her hands in his own. "Tell me. Is it Dad?"

"No, Ike, your father is fine. He's sitting out back in the sun. I didn't think he'd be warm enough and I wrapped him in a quilt. He said, 'Fool woman,' but he kept the quilt. He'll be all right for a while yet, and I've got some soup made for his supper." She sighed and looked away. Ike followed her gaze across the room to the wood cook stove.

"Is it the soup that smells so good?"

"It's more likely the roast chicken. That big red rooster took another run at me this morning and now he's in my roaster. I hope he'll be tender. He wasn't a chick anymore. None of us are, I guess." She sighed.

Ike felt her small hands slide out from beneath his, watched her stand and walk to the stove. She hadn't looked at him. He began to worry.

"So, where's the Tinker? What have you got him working at?" He sat back in his chair, beginning to have an uneasy feeling and not liking it.

She brought a mug of broth to him, setting it hard on the table, spilling some. She wiped her hand with her apron then went to the sink, returning with a cloth to wipe the spill, but it had spread, darkening the table covering. Her face clouded, the corners of her lips turned down, she closed her eyes.

Ike stood and moved to her side, gathering her into his arms. He was always amazed how small she was, this wife of twelve years, this mother of his son. She was so strong, ever moving forward even when in doubt. He admired her. He loved her.

"What's the matter, Lu?"

"Have you been out with the horses?" She nestled against his chest. "You smell like my father."

"Are you missing your father, Lu? Is that what's the matter?" He gave her a squeeze.

"Yes, and my mother, and Madeline, your mother. There's nothing I can do about it. And your father's moving slowly, even for the season. I worry about him, but all he says when I ask how he's feeling is, 'Fool woman.' People are slipping away from me, and time, and I can't do anything about it."

She tucked her face into his shoulder, and he knew she was crying but he didn't know what to do for her. He held her. He kissed her head. He inclined his head, putting his face into her hair. Strawberries. Her hair smelled like strawberries.

"You'll always have me, Lu, and Jackson. He's only ten. You'll have him underfoot forever, and then he'll marry and have a family for you to see after. Kelty Farm will be the home of a big family again, you'll see. You just wait and see."

She shook loose of his embrace, turned and walked to the stove again. She lifted a hot metal cover, dropped it back onto the pot with a clang, then took a cloth holder and lifted the cover again. Steam rose around her, and the aroma of the broth wafted to him as he stood rooted to the spot looking after her.

"Tell me what the matter is, Lu. Tell me."

She turned to face him, the stove behind her, the cover in one hand, a long handle wooden spoon in the other.

"It doesn't matter what I do, time passes, people change, grow older, die. And nothing I do will fix that. And Jackson is the only child I can ever give you. You tell me, Ike, how do I live with that?"

"Lucy, my dear wife." He dropped his hands to his sides, returned to his seat at the table, and picked up the mug of broth. "You're talking about things we get no choice about. Ask me how we're going to get through the winter, how we'll feed the animals till the pastures turn green again, how the crops will be next summer. I can tell you we'll do our best; we'll hope for better. That's how we'll get through life. Whatever comes, that's how we'll get through.

"There are no big answers, Lu, only little ones, only quiet voices that tell you it's all going to work out."

She turned back to the stove, putting more limb wood into the fire.

"Just that some days, the little answers don't answer the big questions, and the hole you're left with you could drive a wagon through."

"And this is one of those days, is it?" He took a sip of the broth. He began to relax, feeling now he knew the reason for his wife's mood. This was familiar ground. Lucy worried about this sort of thing all the time and in the end, she came to some answer that gave her peace. He sipped more of the broth. He just had to wait. He hated to see her suffering, but he had gotten used to the idea that there are things he couldn't help with.

"So, where's the Tinker. What have you got him doing?"

"He's resting in the back bedroom."

"Resting?" Ike said a little too loudly. "How much is he charging us for that?" He regretted his tone as Lucy turned to confront him.

"I know you think he only does half the job for twice the price; I know you'd rather he didn't come around at all, but Ike, we only give him worn out things to fix when we should have bought new, and you should remember that your mother set great store by that man. He was a good friend to her and has been to me." Then the fire in her eyes died down and the sadness returned. "He looked tired, and I told him to lie down and rest a while." She looked directly at her husband, her shoulders back, stiffening. "And if the day has come when I can't make decisions about who is welcome in my home then it's a sad day indeed."

Ike felt stung.

"My father said the Tinker was the only man he was ever jealous of. He didn't like him, and you can't blame me for not liking him either. Any friendship he had with my mother was because she always paid him for what she bought of him and then she gave him a meal at the family table too. Sitting out with the farm hands wasn't his style. No, he had to sit at the table engaging my mother in chatter while my father glared at him the whole meal through."

"Well, I've heard your mother's side. She said that the Tinker was the best company she ever had at the supper table and that your father was never more attentive and gentler with her than after the Tinker's visits." Lucy put her knuckles against her waist, her arms akimbo, and stared across the kitchen at her husband.

Suddenly the back door slammed shut with a bang. Both Lucy and Ike turned to face old Mr. Kelty making his way toward them in his slow, foot dragging gait. The colorful quilt hung over his shoulders and slid to the floor as he passed Lucy. She bent to retrieve it and heard him say beneath his breath, "Fool woman."

"Your soup is ready, Mr. Kelty," she said gently.

"And it's really good, Dad. Our Lucy makes a good soup," Ike called after his father, who disappeared into the hallway to the back bedrooms.

"Does Dad know the Tinker's here?" Ike asked quietly.

"He went to sit out back when the Tinker's wagon came into sight," Lucy said softly, her eyes on the hallway, expecting Mr. Kelty's return. As in answer, he shuffled back into the room to stand at his son's side.

"Son, do you know the Tinker is lying on the bed next room from mine?" His voice cracked but his eyes were clear. Ike was compelled to answer.

"Yes Dad. Lucy just told me."

"And how much are we paying him to use our bed?"

Lucy made a loud noise with the pots on the stove.

"Dad, Lucy thought he looked tired and needed some rest. He'll go along in a while."

"But not before he's eaten another meal off our table, I'll wager." He turned, disgust on his face, and began the long shuffle to the hallway again.

"Mr. Kelty, sit down with Ike and have some soup, now. You've been outdoors and the soup will cut the chill."

"Lucy's made you a good soup, Dad."

The old man turned, his face a scowl.

"You mean the last good rooster we had has made a good soup, don't you? There's no secret to making a heavy broth out of a fine rooster, is there? The trick will be to get a crop of chicks out of those lazy hens in spring without the rooster." He seemed to stand straighter, taller in his building rage.

Lucy was drawn in. "There'll be roosters enough in the young chicks from last spring. And maybe they'll be nicer to me when word gets around as to how much guff I'll take from old roosters."

"And maybe you'll learn that Ike is rooster enough for you that you don't need to keep an old Tinker man around."

"Dad!"

"Mr. Kelty! That was uncalled for, and you right well know it. Everyone loved Mrs. Madeline, especially you. I don't know what would make you say such a thing. You're probably cold and hungry. Why don't you sit down and have some soup? You'll feel better right away." Lucy pulled out the chair opposite Ike, waiting for the old man, but he made his way back toward the hallway.

"Fool woman," he muttered.

Ike and Lucy looked at each other. Lucy sat in the chair, folded her hands, and studied them.

Ike thought there must be a right thing to say to make her happy, to bring back the contentment he always felt from her. Nothing presented itself to him and the moment grew longer, more weighted.

"Let's we have our supper, Lucy. Jackson is eating down with the men; we shouldn't wait for him."

"Jackson is a lonely child."

"Don't think about that now. It would be a good thing for us to have our supper together, a good thing for both of us. And I've got to get back to the barn soon."

"The cows have to be milked; the farmer has to be fed." She got up from her chair wearily, walked slowly to the sink, reached into the cupboards, went to the stove, stopping at the table each time she passed to unload dishes, silverware, tumblers, water pitcher and food.

"I think it's wonderful the way you do that," he said.

"Do what?" she asked indifferently.

"Set the table. Put a meal out. Just all to once food comes up out of drawers, down from cupboards, out of pots and pans. As if it was all waiting for your touch to assemble here on the table, all ready to eat."

"Ike, I've done this so many times I feel like I'm on a track going round and round, doing the same things every day. Sometimes I think I know how that train feels when we hear its whistle from so far away."

There wasn't any blame in her voice, but he felt accused. Again, he wished he knew what to say to this usually contented and satisfied woman.

"Everything you do here is important, Lucy, important to me and Jackson, and all of us on the Farm. I don't know what we'd do without you. You mustn't take anything Dad says to heart." His eyes followed her around the kitchen, on her trips to the table, then away again. Finally, she sat opposite him in the chair she had offered his father. Her hand reached for the bread and Ike caught it, holding it mid-air over the table. Their eyes met.

"I want you to tell me that you know I love you, Lu."

"Oh, Ike, my darling man, I know you love me, and that's one big answer I'm not searching for. Rest assured."

He released her hand. She picked up the breadbasket and handed it to him, smiling. He felt relief, and sensed the tension run out of his shoulders. Knowing her, he knew she would never tell a lie.

* * *

"Mr. Della Vecchia, you don't seem any better. You must have some broth, and you must stay the night. If you aren't stronger in the morning, I'm going to send for the doctor."

"No, no. No doctorere. I should go. I will get to my wagon, and I go!" Saying the words, his old voice told of his weakness, his lack of strength to match his will. "Lucia, Lucia, you must aid me. It is my will to leave and be no trouble to you."

She tried to see in his thin and wrinkled face, his wispy hair, any possibility she could believe that he was able to leave on his own power. But no, she decided, he must stay.

"Rest, old friend. Accept the hospitality of my house. Perhaps in the morning you will have your way and leave on your wagon, but not tonight. I've had your wagon put into the barn and your horse has been fed as you slept the afternoon away." She plumped his pillows and felt his forehead, relieved there was less fever than earlier today.

"Ah, Lucia. You are the angel, the angel. Who would care for an old man, uh? Yet I know that this may cause strife in your house. I do not want that for you, Cara." The old man lay back on the pillow, his hair a light fog around his head, his heavy mustache and eyebrows made to match. His spare body barely showed its shape beneath her quilt.

"If there is strife, it will be mine to handle. You have nothing to worry about. You were a good friend to Mrs. Madeline, and now you are my friend."

"The old Signora, Signora Madelina. Yes. She, too, was an angel. And now you are the Signora, the young Signora Kelty. Yes. Yes." He looked pleased with himself.

"I guess that's true, but it does not feel true. I can hardly believe she's gone, though it's been over a year. It will always be her house, her family. I don't feel I've taken her place in any way, and nothing seems right to me since she left us." Lucy sat in the small rocker near the bedside. She felt drawn to the comfort of talking to this man she knew had loved Madeline too.

"Ah," he said gently, "but you have taken her place. I could feel it more today than ever before."

"Feel it? What do you mean, Mr. Della Vecchia? I could never take Ike's mother's place. Only Jackson is mine, and he grows more like his father and grandfather every day." She shook her head, surprised at the confidence she so easily shared. "I don't know why I'm telling you all this."

"But surely you do, Lucia. You know it is safe to talk to me. You know that." His quiet voice called for a response.

"Yes, I guess I do know."

"But of course, Lucia. From deep inside is this knowledge, is the knowing we have, one for the other, you and me. Yes, I am the man who comes to fix the pots, sharpens the scissors, the knives. I fix the broken chairs, put new caning in the bottoms. I, for many years have come, since Ike, your husband was a boy younger than your Jacksone' is now. And there is another knowing between us. I saw it right away, but you have been slow to see."

She looked at him. His eyes seemed to glow as a dying spark will sometimes catch a draft and come again to life. She was confused, but he was an old man, sick, feverish, and she was talking to him overlong.

"You need your rest, Mr. Della Vecchia. Drink the broth and sleep. Everything you need is on the dresser, towel, basin and water. I'll look in on you before I sleep, and again during the night."

"One thing, Lucia. You gave the old Senora the peace she needed when it was her time. You have taken her place, and she was glad of that. Do you not see?"

Lucy stopped at the door but did not turn to see his face, his eyes. She held the latch a moment then opened the door and slipped through, leaving it ajar behind her.

At the end of the hall Mr. Kelty stood looking at her. It was a moment before she made out his shape in the shadows of the gathering darkness.

"Is there anything I can get for you, Mr. Kelty? If you're cold there are more quilts in the blanket chest behind you." For a moment she wondered if he had heard but then he turned his back, stepped into his room and closed the door.

* * *

"Grampa says you want the Tinker man to move in with us right here in our house." Young Jackson sat at the table, cheeks ruddy from the outdoors.

"No, Jackson, Mr. Della Vecchia will leave as soon as he's feeling better. Everybody should have a warm place to be and people to care for them when they're sick." She hid her resentment that Mr. Kelty had talked about this to her son.

"Grampa says you take better care of the Tinker man than you take of him. He says..."

"Jackson, that's not so and I don't think that's what your grandfather meant..."

"Well, that's what Grampa says, he says..."

"Well, it's not true anyway. You always see me making the things Grampa likes to eat and hanging his sheets to dry outside when I wash so they smell fresh the way he likes them. I take very good care of your grandfather and I don't know why he'd say any different."

Lucy watched her son think this over. She smoothed his hair, touching the ever-present cowlick to no avail. No doubt when he had more to say he'd say it.

"I made some fresh molasses cookies for you."

His face lit up, melting her heart.

"Did you put raisins in 'em?" He held his breath waiting for the right answer.

"No, I did not, and I put sugar on the tops the way you like."

"Oh boy! Can I have some now?"

"Yes, and there's milk cold in the ice box."

She watched her son fly from the table to the broad shelf then to the cupboard for a tumbler. The trip to the ice box took him briefly from her sight but she heard the milk being poured, the door being shut, and then he reappeared from the pantry. His round face was alive with anticipation as he put three cookies and the glass of milk on the table near her, threw himself onto his chair and bit into a dark cookie.

He closed his eyes in the ecstasy of a nine-years-old. She silently wished his needs would always be so easy to meet. His moments with her were precious all the more since he had discovered his great love for following his father around on the bigger world of the Farm.

She heard a cough from the hallway.

"Where's your grandfather, Jackson?"

"He's down at the great barn. He wanted to go to the road across the valley, but Dad said for him to stay closer to home. I said I'd stay with Grampa but then he got grouchy, and I came up here." All this with more than half a mouthful of cookie, Lucy noted.

Another cough from the direction of the hallway.

"Is that the Tinker man coughing? Can I go see does he want anything?" his eyes searched his mother's.

"No, you finish your cookies. Take another if you want. If you're going back down to your grandfather, take him two cookies, take the ones without the sugar." She saw the question on the boy's face. "That's the way he likes his molasses cookies. He says it's the way his mother, old Elishabet, made them." She lifted a lid and put more wood in the stove, moved a kettle to the front.

"Grampa tells me a lot of stories about Gramma Elishabet. They all make me laugh."

"Madeline was your gramma, Elishabet was your great-gramma. And I've heard a lot of those stories too but never heard one that made me laugh. Anyway, it's good that he tells them to somebody. That helps him remember. You better listen carefully because he's the only one left that knows all those stories. He was here when most of them happened." She took a large mason jar from the cupboard. She set it on the broad shelf, moved the wire closure aside and removed the glass top. She heard another cough from down the hallway.

"Dad tells me a lot of them too, but Grampa always adds more story to Dad's telling. He knows all the stories better than Dad does."

"It's a grandparent's job to tell the family stories. Parents are usually too busy working and taking care of things to tell stories. Just you listen. You're a lucky boy to have a grandfather. All his brothers are gone, and some were younger than he, and their wives, even some of their children, though there weren't many of the Kelty children who lived to be old, and none of them live around here." She wrapped the unsugared cookies in a cloth napkin and put them on the table beside the boy. She touched the side of the kettle to see if the water was hot yet.

"All the Keltys are gone, right Ma? They're all in the burying ground and there's only us left. There's a lot of them up there and only four down here."

"That's right, Jackson," she said absently. She heard another series of coughs, the last ones muffled. She took a large linen towel from a bottom drawer.

"And when Grampa dies, there'll be just three Keltys." Lucy suddenly realized where the conversation was taking them.

"But that's nothing for you to worry about, son. And your grandfather will be fine as soon as spring comes." She stood behind Jackson's chair and put her hands over his shoulders and down onto his chest. She put her face into his hair, breathing in the hay scent of him, feeling the hardness of bone beneath the clean brown hair, feeling him squirm against her hands and face.

"I hate it when you hold me in a chair like this." He wriggled free of her hands, stood almost her height, looked directly into her eyes. He stared a moment, then flung his arms around her, hugging fiercely. "I love you, Ma," he whispered to her neck.

"And I love you, my sweet boy."

"I know you do, Ma."

The kettle began to whistle, and she loosened her hold of him as he released her, grabbed up the cookies, and ran out the door. She looked through the window after his retreating figure until he was lost to her sight on the path to the great barn in the valley. She filled the Mason jar with hot water, sealed the jar with a canning rubber, and rolled the hot jar up in the linen towel.

Another cough called her to the first bedroom down the hall. She opened the door finding the white-haired man under the covers but wide awake. He smiled weakly. She felt a flood of appreciation from his eyes.

"The angels sent me to one of their own to be sick."

"You have some sort of influenza but you're not going to the angels if I can help it. Save your strength, don't talk now." She pulled up the covers from the bottom of the bed and took out the cooling linen-wrapped jar, replacing it with the hot one. Putting it against the bottoms of his feet, she thought again of how white and beautiful his feet were. They seemed more like baby's feet for all their size.

"Santa Lucia. Who else would take an old man into their home for a week as you have done? And when will I be well. I should never have come. I should have died on the road."

"Please, no more talk of death. Jackson was talking about death just ten minutes ago." She picked up the covered chamber jar, finding it empty. She straightened his covers then sat in the low rocker.

"Jacksone'. Ah, the son. You will live long, Lucia, and Jackson will live longer. His young life is wrapped in gold."

"What a peculiar thing to say. Why would you say that? 'Wrapped in gold?'" She composed herself, thinking ahead to supper, to the men coming back to the house, to their needs. She sat to watch over the old man a while.

"Wrapped in gold...," he repeated and closed his eyes. "It is an expression to say that his life will be safeguarded, watched over. This is to say that he will prosper, be well."

She leaned toward him. "Still, how can you know?"

"Wrapped in gold..." he said softly.

"Don't talk now, just sleep. But I'm going to ask you about this again. Don't you forget."

* * *

"He's improving, Ike, the doctor says so."

"Lucy, you could raise the dead with two weeks of your kindness and care, but this old man isn't going too far on his own steam. We may get him to go down the road, maybe even back to where he came from, but you must know, Lucy, you must know he hasn't long to live."

Ike glanced into his wife's face, hoping he wasn't hurting her, hoping to see the resignation she had to come to. He had resignation. It was a part of how he made his living. Every day he made decisions that affected every living thing on Kelty Farm, and without the resignation, the knowing, how could he face the consequences of those decisions.

"I'm not looking that far ahead. The work for my hands right now is to get him well. Any worry about after that will wait. I just thought you might like to know that the doctor had been here and said Mr. Della Vecchia is improving." She pulled her chair out from the table, getting up, leaving Ike to think over his mulled cider.

Ike had grown up on this land, this farm, in this house, in this kitchen. He remembered days of aunts and uncles, cousins, neighbors, friends, farm hands, tradesman, all bustling in and out of the house, all underfoot in this big kitchen. Even before Lucy came here there were fewer people, but this house was the quietest now it had ever been. It wasn't like the Kelty Farm of his youth.

He didn't mind the extra person in the house, Lord knows, there were plenty of unused rooms in the old homestead. Extra people here didn't bother him at all, it was that his father didn't like the person Lucy had so easily invited into their midst. When Tinker was gone, maybe Dad would settle down. Lucy had stepped on the old man's toes on this one, and the old man wouldn't forgive her easily.

Time would tell. And Lucy could win over the devil himself if she had to. Ike looked around the kitchen, finding himself alone.

"If I know anything," Ike laughed to himself, "I know that. I'll just let the two of them work it over between them." He put down the empty mug.

"Well, back at it, Ike old boy," he said to no one.

* * *

It might be my imagination, Lucy thought to herself, but I'd swear his back straightened when I opened the door. She pulled her shawl closer, gathered her long woolen skirt and stepped down off the back porch onto the path to the end of the house. She walked toward the old man, careful not to step on the icy spots of the path. She unfolded a woolen throw as she approached, reaching out to put it over his shoulders.

"Mr. Kelty, if you insist on sitting out in this weather, you should do what you can to keep the cold off of your shoulders. You know they pain you afterwards." She dropped the warm covering over his shoulders and came around him to tuck the two ends into his lap. He shrugged. She stood in silence a moment and considered going back to the house.

"It's not too bad of a day for it being winter. Maybe we're going to get that January thaw they talk about every year." She tried to sound cheery, looking past him down into the valley to see what had his attention. The silence came again. Then he sighed.

"When I was a little boy, finally big enough to leave the house and walk around with my father, for the longest time all I ever saw of him was the back of his coat, his trousers, his heels. With my small legs I ran to keep up with him, watching my step so's not to fall. It went on like that for a long time. Whatever he did that I was allowed to go with him, he was there, and half done before I really caught up. My older brothers laughed at me, called me slow foot."

His voice was the voice of an old man talking to himself, reflective, introspective. His pause found Lucy holding her breath, unwilling to disturb the magic of the moment he was sharing with her.

"Then one day I ran out of the house up this very path. Pulling on my coat, watching my step so not to fall, I caught up with him. He had waited for me, here, just at the end of the house, just where the path changes direction. He had waited. And he held out his hand for mine. We stood here, right here, and we looked down into this valley for a long time. He pointed to the spot where the great barn is and he said,

'I'm going to build a barn right there. You want to help me, son?' I searched his face and I said, 'Yes Pa.'

"All that summer, at some point in the day he'd come get me. We'd walk down into that valley, and he'd tell me what we were going to do and then we'd do it. And I can tell you there were no days like them days, no days like them days."

His eyes were fixed, seeing a place only he could see. He paused, sighed deeply, and Lucy thought that might be the end, but she waited.

"I don't know who whittled the pegs, drilled the holes nor put the beams into place. But my father held a peg to a hole, and he'd have me pound the peg with the wooden mallet..."

Suddenly his arms took positions in the air, mimed the holding of the peg, the swing of the mallet. Lucy stepped back then reached for the woolen throw that threatened to fall earthward.

"...until I could get the peg to go no further, then he'd take the mallet and slam the peg home. And then we'd do it again. My arms would hurt, I could hardly hold the mallet because my hands would go to sleep all prickly, but he'd hold the pegs and I swung the mallet with all I had, one after another." He paused again, smiled, remembering.

"You couldn't but give him your best. You knew you'd give him your heart if he asked, so anything else seemed a small thing if it pleased him. And he'd shout! To hear him, you'd think that this peg was the making of the whole barn. To hear him, you would think this was the last one, and then this was the last one, and then this was the last. The same for kegs of square-headed nails on the siding, the roof. Every day, from the time he set the sills till we nailed the copper weathervane in place, it was like that.

"And no one can know..." He seemed to come to himself. He wiped his eyes for tears he felt but had not shed and he gazed at Lucy. He looked away, and a long moment passed.

Lucy put her hand on his shoulder.

"And no one can know..."

She waited. He straightened his shoulders.

"And no one can know how much I loved him. My father! He was the builder! By the time I was fifteen, he had built every building on this land that we still have today. And he built this house. It was a cabin, you know." He looked at Lucy again as if waiting for an argument. "It was just a cabin. He built it to get my mother to marry him. But he built on, he improved it every way he could think of, right up to the time Madeline and I got married, then he built another three rooms for us."

He shifted around on his seat, a dove-tailed box never meant to sit out in the weather, never meant to hold a man's weight. Lucy made a mental note to put a chair out here for just such a day that might come again, and maybe two chairs.

"My father set great store by Madeline. She came to us to cook. My mother was sickly for a time and didn't take part in the household. There was some trouble between the women, my father's two maiden sisters he had taken to live with us, and my brother's wives. It came to pass that we weren't getting anything to eat. One meal there'd be ham, and I mean only ham, and then a meal of bread, and only bread. My father put his foot down and got us a cook."

He laughed. He smiled, sadly, it appeared to Lucy, as someone does when they look inward and see a thing so clearly, a thing no longer with them. She thought he has been out of doors long enough today but was reluctant to say so and break this rare mood.

"Madeline was a little thing, hardly weighed more than a feather pillow. It wasn't long that the whole house was on its ear. All those women, and yes, every man, was falling over themselves to be of any help to Madeline. With her to direct them, the house was never in better order, and we ate food the like of which we hadn't seen."

Mr. Kelty smiled broadly, looking skyward, he shook his head in disbelief.

"And my father came to me, and he said, 'There's a woman would make some man a good wife.' He looked at me, the only one unmarried of his four sons. And he looked at me a while longer. And he said he thought he had taught me everything he could to make me a good husband and that now I should go ask Madeline to marry me."

He glanced at Lucy, then quickly away, and tears spilled. His mouth quivered, but he smiled. She put her arm over his shoulder, leaning onto him a little, her hand on his hand.

"And I asked her, and she said yes, and we were married right here, right here, where my father had waited for me that day, she married me. Oh, it was summer, and there were roses and every blooming flower burst out for Madeline, and everyone came. And the house was so hot we brought all the chairs out here in the shade of the house, and the preacher, Madeline and me, we stood right here."

He stopped. She saw the tension in his neck, the effort it took to control himself to go on.

"And then what?" she gently prodded

"And a year later, just a little more than a year later, my father, was dead, and Ike was born." He put his head down, closed his eyes. She became very conscious of her arm over his shoulder. She wanted him to know she is there, but she didn't want to intrude on memories.

"It was long ago, Mr. Kelty. A lot has happened."

"I wanted my son to have a home here, as my father had made for me. I wanted him to have a son, and he another. I want Kelty Farm to be the home of Keltys forever, just as my father planned. I look down into this valley and I have to look twice. Sometimes I see it with all the trees still standing that we cut down to mill for the barn. I see hillsides with sheep grazing and then I see orchards where the sheep used to be. I see standing timber waiting for the day we need more lumber for more building, or to sell against the day we have some other need."

He stood and his voice rose, his old body rigid, his arm raised with a fist. Lucy retreated a step.

"This is a place a family can stand through the times that come and go. This place is where my father is buried, and my mother. This is where rests my wife, where I will lie. And in death we will be held as we have been held in our lifetimes, by this land, this land that my father chose, that my father chose..."

His arm came back to his side. His fingers unclenched. He sat again and looked away to the point inside his own vision. Lucy paused, but reached for the fallen throw, replacing it upon his slumping shoulders.

"He must have known. He must have known that it would be like this. That this land would support us, that, yes! we would work hard, but the land would support our lives here. He must have known, but he was just nineteen when he came here. How could he have known?"

He turned, passing his question onto Lucy, asking, needing her to answer.

"Mr. Kelty, I don't know for certain how a person comes to knowing things, but it's something I think on often." She was surprised that he so plainly needed an answer from her. She thought what would give him comfort, what would be a good answer, a truthful answer. His eyes urged her on.

"Maybe knowing comes from what you've been told..., added to what you see..., to what can be..., to what you want? If you want a thing to be so, you look inside yourself and find if you have the strength it will take to make that thing so. You think on the time it will take to happen and you ask yourself if you've got that time." He watched her intently. She wet her lips. "Knowing a thing can come from all that, from asking yourself hard questions and giving yourself truthful answers. And trusting, trusting a thing has a chance to be. Then can be had the knowing."

"So, my father, Arthur Kelty, could have known so long ago that this would be a good home for us, that we'd still be here now, looking into the future?"

"Your father knew Madeline would be a good wife. He knew you would be a good husband. And whatever he told you I think you have told your son, because Ike is a good son to you, a caring husband to me, and a fine father to his own son." She returned her arm to his shoulder; her hand pressed his arm.

He smiled at her, taking her hand in his own. She was amazed at how soft his hands had become after all the years of callous. They were softer than her own, she thought, and maybe he was like his hands.

"You're a fine woman, Lucy, good for my son, good for Kelty Farm. It makes me happy to see you make this house your own, to see you content with our life here."

"Mr. Kelty, how could I not…"

"I'd like it if you would call me Dad, like Ike does."

"Oh, Mr. Kelty…Dad… How could I not be happy and content here? This is my home, and never more so than today. This is where all the people I love live. This is where my life is."

"And do you love us all?" He smiled, knowing what he asked.

"Yes, Mr. Kelty… I mean Dad, I love all the people on Kelty Farm." She returned his smile.

"It's a test of true love to love someone even when they aren't easy to love. I guess you've passed that test, Lucy."

* * *

"And how could I not be well again, Lucia, Cara, with all the love and attention you have lavished upon me? Certainly it would be ungrateful of me not to be well." The smile on his face was lit by his dancing eyes.

"Still, I want you to stay this night and then you can be on your way tomorrow. Let me put one more good supper into you and I'll rest easier. And it does my heart good to see someone appreciate my food."

"And there is a thing we must talk of, you and I, uh?"

"What's that, Mr. Della Vecchia?" She was aware of a feeling of warning, a sharp feeling between panic and relief.

"You, a happy person, have been happier in these last few days. Something good has come about and I am glad for you. But I see a sadness, an aloneness… This may not be the right word, Cara, but if you know the word, perhaps you would speak of it. Oh, I am but an old man, and you must tell me if you have a trouble. Listening is a thing an old man can do."

To Lucy, his voice was as inviting as his words.

"Old Mr. Kelty and I have reached a smooth place in our path. That, perhaps, is my happiness."

"Ah, a hard man, Mr. Kelty. And yet you love him, and Madelina loved him. Much riches for one man only." He sat back in his chair beside Lucy's chair near the bed, the small room was confining, intimate for two people.

"You knew Madeline well?" She felt herself on unfamiliar ground.

He glanced at her, taking a moment to adjust the blanket around his knees. "Yes. I knew her for most of the years I came here. Your question, I think, was did I love her? Again, yes. But to love Madelina could only mean to be her friend. And being her friend, could I ask for more? She was a virtuous wife, and the more did I love her for it."

Lucy saw humbleness in his answer, but no apology.

"Would you have wanted her to yourself?"

"How could I say no to that? And yet, would I have taken her from her life, here? No! Never! That would be to break her heart. She had only hard work, here, but for her, abbondanza! Everything! Her husband, her son and daughters, you, your son, her love of this Kelty Farm. How could I have offered her less and love her? No! No! To love her and to be her friend, that was my abbondanza. To come here, to see her, to fix a pan or two, she brightened my life. Her friendship, that was what she gave me, and I was a rich man for it."

His hands were loose in his lap. He did not rock his chair. His words were spoken softly.

"Did she know you loved her?"

"Did we speak of love? No. Did she know? Does a woman know when a man loves her beyond his own life?"

They sat in silence for a time.

"Why did you come back after she died?" She had to know.

He turned to her, searching, finally turning away again.

"He is still here, her husband," he began, "and you are here, and Ike, and your Jacksone', and this Kelty Farm. All that she loved. All still here. Should I not come to where she was happiest, where she was in life, where was our friendship? And soon I can never come again, so I have come as often as I could and not burden anyone."

"You are no burden, and I was glad to nurse you back to health this time. I've been glad to have you here."

"Unfortunately, Lucia, I came one too many times and you were burdened with this long time of caring while I was too weak to care for myself. For this I am sorry."

"The caring was mine to give, and I do not begrudge it to you. I'd be glad to have you return anytime."

His eyes searched hers a moment, then closed as he rested his head against the back of the chair.

"I am too greedy, to want more of what is not mine. I am at the end, and I have had already more than most get. I will not be here again. Tomorrow we will say good-bye, Cara, and we will not see one another again."

"How can you say that? How can you know?" she asked, a dread of his answer growing in her heart.

"In my life I have been sure of things that I could not know, and yet I knew. There is a knowing. It comes to some, will they have it or not." He again glanced into her face then lowered his eyes to his hands. "I think you have this knowing, and that you often wonder how you could know what you cannot know...but you do know."

He rocked gently. She took her gaze from his face. A silence came between them. Lucy wasn't sure if she had a question but hoped he would say more.

"If I were younger, I might wish to go to her grave. But there is snow, and it is a long walk for someone who is used to wagon wheels to do the carrying. Yet, I know she is not there, for if she could be anywhere, she is here, so I will not go. For now, I will go to that most fortunate of men except now possibly your Ike and ask the old master of Kelty Farm if he would have my wagon ready in the morning, and to offer payment for the care of myself and my horse."

Lucy began to interrupt but the old man waved a hand.

"No, no. This is a thing between men. I would offer and he will generously refuse. I will be in his debt. And... And I will say good-bye to him. We two, he and I, will soon be with our dear Madelina, though this time, I think, I will be first." He clasped his hands into a single fist and seems to be in fervent prayer. She could say nothing.

"And, mia Lucia, you must tell me to give me peace, that you understand about the knowing."

Lucy looked deeply into his eyes.

"The knowing? I can't say what I know. I have so many questions, I ask 'why' to so many things. What can I say to give you peace when I have so little peace about this myself?"

He nodded his head several times, his eyes down, his lips drawn tight.

"Lucia, you may have all the answers to your questions someday or you may come to where you don't ask. Inside, Cara, find the quiet place, the soft voice that speaks with the assurance of knowing. You have only to listen. I am right about this."

"Yes, I think I understand. And I trust I will understand more as time passes."

"Ah. Trust. Only trust, Lucia."

9

1900: EMMA HAS HER SAY

"Jackson, I've heard the same story about your name and your father's being after the mother's family. Three sons we've named without honoring my family and this time I'll have my way." Her petite hand nipped and worried at the baby's clothes, straightening a fold of the embroidered cloth.

Emma was a small woman but determined. He hadn't heard this tone from his wife often, but he knew it well.

"Now Emma, my dear..."

"Emma-my-dear and all, this son will be named for my father, though we'll use his given name, Archelaus. No one should be named Drinkwine."

"But Emma..."

"I don't care if the name was already used by the old Keltys."

"Archelaus is an ill-fated name in our family," Jackson said seriously.

Her hazel eyes sparked; her cheeks reddened. Her hair done in short curls around her round face framed her most determined look.

"Ill-fated?" she asked incredulously. "Are you going to tell me that ancient story about 'Almost-Grampa-Arc' again? How long does a curse last?"

"Might as well name him Jonah and be done with it."

"Fate wouldn't reach across three sons to get to the fourth. Superstition and such in this day and age!"

She stared at him, and he knew he had shown no sign yet but that he was backing off.

"If only it had been the daughter we have waited for," he said, hoping to deflect her anger, and move her from her stance.

"Jackson, it would have been a grace from God if this child had been a daughter after three sons already, but since we have a fourth son, I'll have him named for my father."

10

1913: AMAZING GRACE

"Gracie, I've got a surprise for you."

"A surprise? What surprise, Archie? Are you going to give it to me right now? It's not my birthday." Grace held her breath.

"It's something I built for you, and you have to use it now cause it won't be there later. Come down to the great barn."

"The great barn? Can we go now? What is it, Archie?"

"It wouldn't be a surprise if I told you now. You've got to see it; you've got to get on it. Just come with me."

Arc headed for the kitchen door, little sister on his heels. He smiled, hearing her catch the screen door behind him, knowing she would question him all the way to the barn. It was a lot of fun, doing things for Gracie. He was the closest to her in age of her four brothers, and even he, at thirteen, was six years older than she.

"Is it inside or outside the barn? Is it big or small?"

"Wait till you get there and you'll see what it is."

"Tell me, Archie. I can't wait. I want to know now."

"Gracie, good things are worth waiting for!"

"Ah, tell me, Archie."

The footpath wound down from the kitchen gardens, over the side of the hill and down the gentle slope to the floor of the valley. Most people from the house walked the path, avoiding the dusty road.

Grace skipped along almost at her brother's pace, but frequently falling behind.

"Wait up, Archie. Tell me about my surprise."

"You could walk faster than you're skipping."

"I'm too excited to walk! Are you going to take me for a ride somewhere? Is that what it is?" Grace was nearly out of breath.

"Well, you're getting close… It is a kind of a ride, but…"

"So, where are we going, Archie, where are we going?"

"You're getting the wrong idea. I'd better not say anymore." He smiled but slowed his pace to keep just ahead of her.

"Just tell me where we're going to go."

"No."

"Come on, Archie. Tell me where we're going."

Arc hurried on, refusing to wait, refusing to look at his sister.

"Archie, where are we going?"

Arc stopped, turning on his heel, fists at his waist.

"You're guessing all wrong. The surprise isn't that we're going anywhere. You're spoiling it! Now you're not going to be satisfied with what I've got for you."

The change in his voice and the hurt look in his eyes stopped Gracie in her tracks.

"No, I will be satisfied. I love any surprise, Archie. I'm just in such a hurry to love this one that I want to know what it is right off." She put her small hands against his chest and looked up into his eyes. "Don't be mad."

"I'm not mad at you, Gracie. I planned this for such a long time and now it's ready. Let's just go along, we're almost there." He took her hand and they walked side by side.

At the riverbank Arc looked across, thinking of the minutes they could save if they could cross on the stepping stones instead of walking to the bridge. The water was low enough and the day was dry. The stepping stones would not be slippery for his shoes but were not close enough together for Gracie to cross safely.

"We'd better walk to the bridge. It'll only take another minute."

"I can cross here, Archie. I do it every time Mama sends me to get Dad from the barn. Last week I crossed here carrying a jug of juice for him and I didn't have any trouble. Watch me!" She stepped toward the riverbank, her tongue at the side of her mouth, eyes intent on the first flat stone.

"No, Gracie!" Arc lunged for her hand, holding it tightly in his own. She stared at him.

"What's the matter? Phillip showed me how steady the stones are, that they don't move. I've crossed with Stewie and Andy. One time I sat on Phillip's shoulders as he ran across." She laughed. "He said I almost pulled his ears off."

"I remember. I was on the other side waiting for you and I saw Dad's face while Phillip was carrying you. Dad turned pale, even with his tan. That was the first time I ever saw him get scared, worrying over any of us."

"Well, I'm ever bigger now and I cross here whenever I want to." She pulled her hand free of her brother's and jumped off the embankment down the four feet to the top of the first stone.

Arc held his breath, his feet rooted to the ground.

She leaned forward, hands behind, leaped to the next stone, then the next and the next, only stopping half the way across the gently flowing water. Grace looked back at him, her face split by an enormous smile of achievement. She turned away and sprang again, flat footed, across the tops of each of the last four stones. She scrambled up the opposite bank, her skirts pulled daintily aside with one hand. Again, she turned back to him, laughing, her eyes alight, her red-gold braids tossing.

"Come on, slow foot!"

"Gracie! Gracie, don't you ever do that again!" he sputtered, more amazed than angry. He leaped across the stepping stones to her side.

"You could have fallen! You could have gotten hurt! You're too little to cross here by yourself, and you'd better not do it again. If I tell Dad or Mama, they won't let you out of the yard. They'll keep you right up there at the homestead all the time."

"Then don't you tell!" She laughed again. "Now, let's get over to the great barn and see my surprise." She ran into the shadow of the barn, giggling as she dodged a large bee. This side was generally unused and had grown weeds that Gracie loved. She did not know the true name, but Grampa Ike called the orange-blossomed weeds 'pop-de-didilies' after the way the bean-like pods flew apart to spread their seeds. But she had no time today to stop and touch.

Arc ran behind her, laughing to himself at her excitement, surprised at his own rising anticipation of showing her what he'd planned. She waited at the side door, but he ran on to the ramp and through the larger doors to the main floor.

"It's up here, Gracie. There's nothing down on the bottom floor, all the cows are out to pasture this time of day. We've just used up the last of the hay and we'll soon bring in the first crop of the summer. This is the only time you can find the great barn empty."

The sweet smell of hay lingered yet in the huge empty building. The heavy plank floors were worn and shining from the polish of years covered in hay. The upright beams and cross pieces arched overhead to the window openings far above where sunlight poured in, highlighting the darkness, spotlighting the hay dust that filled the air. Pigeons sang their cooing to each other, flapping and fluttering from one perch to another, and in then out of broken windowpanes. Barn swallows darted and dived.

Gracie sucked in a deep breath, her eyes scanning the dim interior of the huge space. The acrid smells from animal stalls below came to her with a change in air currents, then the smell of the river behind the building, and again the hay, the ever present sweet golden hay that usually filled the interior. She had never thought of the great barn as anything near this large.

"Where's my surprise, Archie?" she whispered.

"Why are you whispering?" he asked softly.

"I don't know. It just seems a place where whispering is enough and talking out loud wouldn't be. It's like a church, isn't it? I could get lost here, like in the woods or in the night." She looked up at her brother and reached for his hand. "I'm glad you're with me."

"Now you're being silly. We're Keltys, and at home anywhere on Kelty Farm."

"You've been a Kelty longer than I have, and you've lived here seven years more."

"But now we're both here and we'll always be Keltys. We own Kelty Farm, and we own the great barn. And now, the surprise!"

Arc dropped her hand and ran to one of the center supporting beams near the middle of the barn. From behind it, he pulled a board and some ropes, letting them fall from his hands and swing toward the waiting girl. The contraption swayed from side to side and then settled into a clear arc moving forward, stopping just short of her outstretched fingers before falling backwards again past her brother.

"Oh, Archie. You've made a swing! Is it for me?" Her voice was full of wonder, she had forgotten to whisper.

"Of course, it's for you. Here, get on." He held the ropes steady as she backed onto the wobbly seat. He smiled as her knuckles whitened on the ropes. He drew her back the limit of his strength to pull and hold her then pushed, running behind till she flew above his reach.

She squealed in a high pitch, then laughed as the swing flew backward into the dark space, paused a breath-taking instant, then rushed again toward her brother near the open front doors.

Arc laughed and shook his head. His cheeks hurt from smiling. He clapped hands and laughed aloud as she streamed toward him and away.

Grace lay back in the air, her toes stretched forward, her arms rigid, her hair and skirts flying behind. She stared upward into the dimness of the roof, glancing up and down the ropes that suspended her from that height. She breathed a deep sigh and felt a tear run from the corner of her eye down her cheek and off into space.

"You want another push, Gracie?""

"No, I want to just come to a stop for a minute." She sat upright and dragged her feet as the swing slowed.

"You want a turn, Archie? It's so much fun." She relinquished the seat and stood aside as her brother took hold on the ropes.

"No. I already tried it. I had to be sure it was safe. I went higher than you did so I knew it would be all right for you. Sit down again and I'll give you another push." He held the seat steady.

"First I want to know how you got way up there to tie the ropes for the swing. It's near the roof. Did Phillip or one of the boys help?"

"I did it all by myself. I just wanted you to have some fun. You don't get to go some of the places we boys go with Dad, and I thought you'd like having something especially for you. It won't last for long. When we bring in the hay the barn will fill up and this space will soon be gone until next summer."

Grace was looking up at the beams and rafters overhead. "Did you see any spiders?" she whispered.

"No. Are you thinking of Grampa Ike's stories about the great barn spiders?"

"Yeah. Did you see any of them? Weren't you afraid to go up there where they are?" She was whispering again.

"That's just Grampa wanting to scare us with his stories. I didn't see any big spiders, nor little ones either. And it's no wonder there aren't any spiders. The birds would get them before they got very big." He could see her fear and he wanted to laugh it away.

Gracie looked unsure.

"Archie, Grampa said when he was a little boy, he was missing his beagle and came down to the great barn to call for it. He heard a muffled sound and he looked up. There was a beagle tail wagging out of the bottom of a spider's cocoon right in the middle of the biggest spider web he ever saw. He said he had to take a board with him when he climbed up to rescue his dog, just to fight off the spiders."

Her eyes were large saucers as she carefully scanned the underside of the roof. She was still whispering.

"Gracie, don't believe it. Grampa was just joshing with you. He's told that story to each of us boys and we laugh when he tries to tell it again.

Think! Do you know how big a spider would have to be to catch a dog, even a beagle? We'd be able to see them from here, and our cows would start to worry if there were spiders that big! Besides, the birds would catch all the spiders when they were small! Now come on, let's give you another push on the swing." His smile reassured her, but before her feet left the ground, she took another cautious look upwards.

Arc pulled back until she was suspended in the air above his head. He held her for a moment and then ran behind her as the swing completed its reach toward the doors. He laughed again as she shrieked with joy.

"Oh, Archie! This is the best surprise I ever got!"

"You're not let down because I said it was a ride and you thought we were going somewhere?"

"This is the best ride! I get to go on it and never leave the Farm! I want to swing forever!" She laughed and lay back, closing her eyes, delight on her face.

11

1915: ELISHABET, POSTSCRIPT TWO

The sun was still high, the far edge of the valley in shadow. The cool shift in the breeze brought a bouquet of river water and late summer grasses and lingered around the front porch swing. There was something soothing in the complaint of the anchor bolt on each forward glide, the squeak of the floorboard on the push backward. Gracie nestled against Grampa Ike's warm belly, her right arm stretched to his left knee, her body rocked on the bed of the swing.

Grampa's breathing had slowed. His right hand held his pipe and rested on his other knee. She could smell the sweet tobacco rising in a slow plume of near-invisible smoke. Chickadees chirped in the lilac tree at the end of the house. She heard the clink of dishes being washed and dried in the kitchen, of chairs being pushed back to table, all being straightened and settled from another meal. Calves in the barn below the house called for their mothers.

She heard Grampa sigh. She waited, just sure a story was coming into his mind.

"I never knew why everyone was so quiet around Gramma Elishabet." He drew on his pipe, poised it in the air inches from his mouth then exhaled slowly, dropping his hand to his knee.

"Of all my aunts—some Keltys, some married to Keltys—no one spoke up to her or did anything but defer to her. 'Will you have some tea, Mother Kelty, will you have some bread. O, pray, take this slice, it is the freshest of the bread, the most tender of the roast.'

"That's how they talked to her. No one sat near to her at table, but approached from behind, leaning over her elbow to speak, to serve. I always wondered at the treatment accorded to the shriveled up, white-haired woman who was mostly blind when I knew her." He paused. He sighed again.

Grace wondered what had made him think of Elishabet, but then she considered. Everyone seemed to think on Elishabet. Sometimes she believed she knew Elishabet and had to remember that old Elishabet had been gone since the time Grampa Ike had been a little boy.

"Among themselves the women laughed and played, they were happy women, hardworking, always at a task, but happy women. And their men—my father and uncles—brothers, four of them, they were all easy to laugh together, quick with a joke in the barns, at the sawmill, in the fields—or even on this front porch of an evening."

A cloud moved and warmed Gracie again. The breeze died away or had gotten to another end of the homestead. She put her hand upon her grandfather's hand on the back of the swing. She liked his large hand under her own.

"But in the house, especially at the table with Elishabet, their own mother, there was a different normal that reigned. A meal was often silently gotten through, save for the clink of flatware, the hollow sound of an empty mug being set to table."

"How old were you then, Grampa?"

"Well, I was ten when old Elishabet died...went home, as they used to say then."

"That's funny. She was already home when she died, and they said she went home. That's funny, Grampa."

She heard him draw on the pipe and then exhale. He gave another push off with his foot and the swing rocked a little further out and forward.

"Well, it's the way they used to talk. They didn't say died so much then, they said, 'called' or sometimes, 'went home.'"

His voice seemed far away. Grace wondered if he would say more or if she should ask.

"People change the things they do and say through the years. Many years have gone between when I was ten, and now you are ten, my little missy." He laughed softly and drew again on the pipe.

"It is funny to think of you being ten years old like me, Grandpa."

"I was ten just two days before she died. It was in the morning. Aunt Jane, one of my grandfather's two sisters that lived with us, found her. Aunt Jane slept in the bed with Elishabet since early the night before and had risen to start the fire in the kitchen stove. When she returned to dress for the day, she was brushing out her hair when she glanced in the mirror and noticed Elishabet's mouth open as she lay abed. Jane went to see if anything might be amiss."

Grace held her breath. The squeak and groan from the rocking had stopped, the swing slowed.

"Now, I was a child, but as I close my eyes this moment, I can hear Auntie's voice from the top of the stairs. I was partly asleep, but she sounded like a bell being rung in my ear. She said, 'The Lord has delivered her up from this vale of tears. The Lord has taken her unto himself. She has gone home. Praise be the name of the Lord.'

"The men were staring, being used to an early start for their day's work, and some of the women of the house were dressing themselves in preparation of morning duties. Children were left to sleep till the breakfast hour.

"But at the sound of Auntie's requiem, everyone crowded into the hall. Aunt stood as if carved in stone, her hands clasped at her heart, her head hanging chin-to-breast-bone, her hair usually in a tight bun was all astray, some over her shoulders, some in front. But her eyes, clamped tight, yet streaming tears which rolled down her cheeks and bounced off her brown dress.

"Everyone stood, waiting, I guess, for her to explain her strange words and behavior. I remember the faces of the family as they glanced about to each other and then stared at Aunt Jane. All the men and the four sisters-in-law—Aunt Orvis was away tending another Kelty brother then—I remember this so clearly because she was ever the one to boss all about and never would have stood for Jane's silence. At the last, Jane began to sway back and forth across the doorway to her room, muttering prayers.

"We had a family funeral that night. The women argued which quilt they would put over her. And that was all I saw of Gramma Elishabet."

He pushed off with his foot and the swing began its ebb and flow, Gracie felt her body leaning into the swing back and then forward. She thought of the pendulum on the big clock at the church.

"No more Elishabet," Gracie said sadly.

"I was never sure of that, Gracie…"

She glanced quickly up at him, studied his face, his green eyes.

"What's that mean, Grampa?"

He looked down into her wide eyes. He smiled, seemed to consider a moment then laughed.

"Oh, Gracie, your maw would have me in the fire for scaring you. I'd better not." He laughed again. "Still, it's better to know a thing than to wonder about it, and it's a grandfather's business to tell the family stories."

"Tell me, Grampa. I want to know."

"And if you don't sleep tonight, missy, don't you tell your maw it's my fault." Again he laughed. He kicked off, letting the swing gently rock them, the bolt above complaining. Looking down into her face, he drew on his pipe and settled back.

"Sometimes of an evening, it was the family's custom to sit out here on the porch together, but when it was cold, we might sit in the parlor. That was the original one room of the first building raised on the homestead. As the family grew, especially during Grampa Arthur's day, side rooms were added, the ell was built on for a kitchen and dining room, a second floor was added above for more bedrooms. By the time I came along, as the family prospered, the main room had become the parlor." He sighed a great sigh.

"So, we sat together, the men smoking and rocking, and sometimes picking on an instrument. My father played the fiddle, just the same one your father plays, Gracie. All the women, my aunts and mother, hired girls, would sew or crochet as they talked.

"Mostly, we talked about ourselves, of the things that interested us, our work, our world on the Farm. Whenever a stranger was among us, the evening was mostly silent. No one could think of anything of interest to a stranger. We always went to bed early, but never earlier than when we had company." He laughed, his eyes closing for a moment, his pipe tucked in between his teeth.

Grace liked leaning on Grampa's belly when he laughed.

"Another thing that drove us from the parlor was Gramma Elishabet in the room above us. She never joined us. If she was quiet, we knew she was content. But the sound of the rocker grinding away above our heads told us a restless night was on Elishabet. Mostly no one spoke of Elishabet, just didn't say much about her. And you wouldn't have thought anything of that except if you saw the four of her sons talking about their pa."

Grampa pushed off with a strong shove and the swing rocked, his feet coming off the floor. Grace smiled with the movement.

"Their faces would near crack with their wide smiles, the four brothers, and each one would interrupt the other to throw in some story or another to tell on him. 'He did this, he said that, this happened or that there.' They would never be tired of the hearing nor the telling. And everyone wanting to be heard, to say more, to lap up each other's words like they was hounds to gravy. They'd laugh and exclaim, 'Yes sir!' in agreement with all that was said."

He finished on a high note, paused, and the glider slowed down.

"But if anyone mentioned gramma Elishabet...," the swing stopped, "it was as if a frosty window was raised, or a door thrown open to the cold. Everyone finished their stories, stopped looking at one another and got what I called, 'hunted eyes.'"

Grace snuggled closer still to Grampa.

"Suddenly it would seem that children would get fussy and need to be put abed. Men would bethink themselves of one last chore to do, or something to be looked after in the barns. Thread would break, needles would stick fingers, eyes would be sleepy. The mention of Elishabet sent people out of the room as surely as did her chair a rocking over our heads."

He took another suck on the pipe but found it had gone out and sighed. He set it in the standing tray beside him. He pushed off with a gentle force and they rocked for quiet minutes.

"Sometimes the adults played music, softly at first, and if we were out on this porch, people sang along. I don't remember many of the songs until I hear them again, I never had an ear for music. My father tried and tried to teach me to play that fiddle, 'the instrument,' everyone called it. It had belonged to my grandfather, Arthur Kelty. They said he played sweet music that made people weep.

"Anyway, I could never get it, and years later, he was glad to teach Jackson, your father, so's to have someone to pass it on to." Grampa laughed softly. "Jackson would never play sad songs, always wanted to play the songs people danced to. He was a popular young man with the ladies, I can tell you, and the sparkle in every eye when he played…well, it was something to see."

"So, Grampa, tell me about Elishabet, about her going home."

"Yes, yes, I was coming to that. Now where was I…?"

"People playing, people singing, here, on the porch…"

"Yes. I guess I was going to tell about after she died, old Elishabet." He pushed off again and went on thinking a moment. "We had these two aunts, the Kelty sisters, sisters to Arthur. They had taken care of Elishabet for years and they kept to themselves, didn't seem friendly to the rest of us. They never went anywhere, usually stayed right here on the Farm. They never went to church, not one time that I remember. Yep, stayed right here all the time…"

"Grampa, the singing, you were going to tell about the singing."

"I'm getting to it, Gracie. So, one night when it was colder, about a year or two after she passed, old Elishabet, that is, we were in the parlor, all of us, and the singing and the playing had started softly, like always. The two sisters came down, sat a while, and then one of them began to play something we called an Ellen pipe, and the other sang along with her.

"And Gracie, you know I never remember songs, but I can see this just as sure as it was happening right here, right now. Aunt Jane was playing, and everyone became very still. We hadn't heard this often, and never this melody. Then the other aunt, Orvis, she begins to sing with the tune, and then Jane stopped playing and sang with her. I can see them now, the lamplight on their old faces, the way their eyes looked off, as if they could see something no one else could see."

The swing had stopped, but Grace knew he hadn't noticed.

Suddenly, Grace heard his voice, cracked, high, alone. He was singing.

"Come home, now, Ned, I need you.

Come back from the wide, wide world.

To this hillside that bore you,

Come home, now Ned.

Kiss me before I die.

What ere the world has promised,

Is nothing you can't leave behind.

Come back before I go away,

Come kiss me Ned

Before I pass over.

I'll f'give it all, Ned,

Come home, come back home.

I'd forgive it all, Ned,

If only you kiss me,

Kiss me, Ned, before I die."

A last strange note hung there. Not music, Gracie thought, but more a sound you remember, different than what it might have been, but the sound you might make as you remember the sound that was. He had become silent. She glanced at him, surprised to see his eyes shut.

"Grampa, are you sleeping?"

"I guess I was in a way, just for a second." He shook his head.

Grace sat up, close to him.

"You look like you might cry, Grampa."

"It's always a surprise to me to remember some moment from the past as clearly as if I were seeing it for the first time. Oh, I was there, but seeing it now, it's colored with everything I didn't know then, couldn't feel then. I realize now what private people the Kelty sisters were, kept to themselves, never really took part in things. For them to come down among us, to share that bit of song, it was like giving a part of themselves. I can see now how special that was."

"Grampa, sometimes it's hard for me to remember about Elishabet, about Arthur and all the rest, that they were really here in this house like I am, and I wonder if the reason all this has happened is so somebody could tell it to me. It's hard to think that so much happened before I was even born. I feel like I missed a lot of the life of our homestead."

Ike laughed and hugged her closer to himself.

"Someday, Gracie, you'll be telling your grandchildren about me, and they will think I'm just a story too. But let's finish what we were talking about."

"Elishabet going home."

"Yes, well this night that the Kelty sisters sang for us, we began to get, oh, I don't know, louder, I guess." He began to swing again. "After the next song, and the next, we sang and played faster music, songs more of us could sing along to." His toe began to tap against the floor. "I think we were happier that night than we had let ourselves be for some time. And it got later than we usually stayed up, but no one offered to stop, to go to bed."

He paused the swing and looked down at Gracie.

"And then it happened."

"What happened, Grampa?" Grace asked in a whisper.

"It didn't happen all to once, but by ones, by twos and threes, people stopped their playing, stopped their singing and looked up at the ceiling, hearing the noise from the empty room above us, Elishabet's room.

It was her rocker. Back and forth, the squeaking of the floorboards above us, the chair rockers going back and forth, back and forth…"

His voice faded; his eyes focused on something far away. Grace squirmed closer, pulled his arm tightly around herself.

"So, what was it, Grampa? What was happening?"

"As we stood there in silence, the sound stopped. I saw my father glancing around the room. Everyone was frozen in place, their mouths open, eyes looking upward or at each other, questions on their faces. Father looked at my mother, and she at me and my sisters then back to him. He says to me, 'You afraid, Ike?' and I said, 'Yes!' right off quick and too loud.

"Everybody laughed, and began to talk together again, but in a hushed sort of way. Dad held out a hand for me to take and he says, 'Come with me, son.' I took his hand and he walked out of the room, leading me to the stairs and up we went, right to the door of old Elishabet's room. He pushed the door open and whatever else was in that room, all I noticed was that rocking chair towards the back, right in front of the heart-shaped window. We hadn't brought a lamp nor a candle with us, but the moon was shining in directly on the rocking chair and there was some light from the hallway behind us.

"He starts into the room, but I pulled back, wanting him to let go of my hand. He says, 'Ike, there's nothing to be afraid of but you'll never know that unless you come in with me.' So, in we went. One step at a time. Some of the furniture was draped in dust covers and stood back in the corners, forms in the shadows. Most of the floor was a braided rug and our steps were muffled. The chair, set there by the window, seemed to be larger each time I looked away and back to it.

"As we came toward it, Dad let go of my hand and I, without realizing it, grabbed onto his sweater. We walked past the chair to the window, but I kept my eye on the chair. Dad leaned on the windowsill and called my attention to a space near the bottom where a draft blew in from outside. A small part of the clay chinking had come loose from the wall. He looked at me, wanting me to know without his saying that this was the reason the rocker had been moving.

"I straightened up, breathed a sigh and let go of his sweater. 'Tomorrow I'll fix this,' he says. And as he walked toward the door, he kicked over the rocker onto its side, looked at me, and said, 'And tomorrow we'll put that old rocker somewhere else.' He left, me not far behind, and that was the last time anybody had a rocker in that room."

"Grampa," Gracie whispered, "you don't think…"

"Gracie, I've thought it over again and again. I know that chair was rocking when we were playing the music, and I couldn't believe the draft caused that big, heavy chair to rock hard enough for us to hear it downstairs." He searched Gracie's face. "But I never liked to think what else could have caused that chair to move, nor why my dad took the chair out of that room. "

"But Grampa…"

"And as crowded as we have ever been in the homestead, no one ever offered to take that room for their own. Your four brothers crush into the smallest bedroom in the house when Elishabet's room is so much bigger. Now there's a story you can tell your grandchildren when you swing them here on the porch. But if you tell your mother I told you this tale, I'll say I was only fooling you, that it never happened at all."

"I'll never tell her, Grampa. I'll never tell Mama."

12

1916: THERE IS A SEASON

JOURNAL ENTRY: March 27, 1896 IKE KELTY

I love this land. I see it in naked season. I plow deep furrows, plant seed, and water with sweat. I place my hand on every swell of it, on all the hard places.

I walk among the bare trunks of trees in fall and know the true shape of the land seen only then. I cry at the bite of frost; I watch and wait while the land sleeps tucked snug in winter snows. I brown my back when the sun shines on it and worry if the rain is enough or will be too much. I moan, moved at the beauty of the land, and wonder at the clean lines of the hills and the shadows of the trees in the moonlight.

JOURNAL ENTRY: AUGUST 28, 1910 IKE KELTY

When I first noticed horses, I most noticed the work teams. My father and his three brothers ran the Farm then, and there were several working teams, but only one Dad used. The oldest of the pair was a white mare he called "Soon." She worked in harness with her son, a grey about six years younger. "Hat" was his name. He stood fifteen

"

hands, somewhat taller than his dam, though she was as broad at chest as he.

I rode in front of Dad in the fields as he plowed, harrowed, and planted circuit after circuit, always moving in smaller turns from the outside towards the middle. Come haying in June, August, and late September, I again rode his rig with him.

He was a silent man, uttering few sounds in a day, expressing his expectations to his team in ways I only slowly learned. As his habit of silence left my childish questions unsatisfied, I sought answers in his hands, in the pull of a rein, a small tug, a loosening or tightening of the leather, all signals to the knowing animals. I felt the sway as they drew us on a bend avoiding a large rock, and their strain as they plodded an incline. Somehow, without Dad saying to, I learned to hitch the team, and one day I left without him.

JOURNAL ENTRY: SEPTEMBER 4, 1912 IKE KELTY

I am a work horse who never asked why. I step into traces of a morning, and move through the work as my eyes see, as my hands know, as my back is willing. I could, on any day these sixty years, have been my father or my grandfather, so near to their path have been my footsteps. Then I look ahead and see my only son following behind me, and his sons after him.

My granddaughter, Gracie, says, "Aren't they lucky."

I wish it could be different for her brothers, that they would be here because of their need to be, not the Farm's need to have them. I wish I could change that, but I can't.

Gracie says, "Gramma always warns to be careful what you wish for 'cause it might come true."

I say, "Everybody wishes for something, Little Parrot, even you. What is it you wish for?"

"Mama says I'll marry a man with a farm of his own and I'll go there to live with him. I wish I could stay here always, with you and Gram, and Mama and Dad, and the boys. I want to marry and have my children and live, all of us, here on Kelty Farm."

I say, "Now it's you who should be careful of wishing or you might get your wish whether it be what you want or not."

JOURNAL ENTRY: SEPTEMBER 26, 1913 IKE KELTY

I lived the seasons of the land—not just the spring, summer, fall, winter that most people know—but the real seasons that begin as soon as the snow and cold of January briefly loosen their grip. There's the rush to bring up more wood from the piles left to dry last summer, to check the sugarbush, to set new trap lines, bring up bundles of ash saplings cut and left in the brooks early winter until then to be pounded into strips and woven into new baskets. As winter again regains its hold, we resign to days of short light, spending more time inside, mending harness, mending and making clothes, checking the tally of preserves put by, the hams hung, the cheeses stored—will we have enough to live out this season when so little is produced and so much is consumed?

The animals—the horses, the oxen—so used to hard work, so restless when not put to it—the cattle—milkers and those about to freshen with newborn—the sheep, our goats and pullets, cats, dogs, and the varmints that haunt our grain and corn stores—all seem the more demanding the first months of a year before the start of a growing season.

This is to say that I spent my life adjusting to the reins and harness, the guideposts that kept me on course through the seasons, kept me absorbed and committed to getting through, to getting by, through the next season and the next, into another year and still another –always my head down, plodding resolutely onward, determined not to be beaten through any shortcoming of my own.

And one day I looked at the apple-laden trees and I knew I had increased the crop by my early pruning, by my diligence with bees—but to what end? Did each tree have fifty more apples, a hundred, or were they bigger apples? And the fields beyond—did they yield an increase of corn or barley? Were those crops more valuable to my farm this year, and by how much?

Did not these increases find more open mouths to feed, or mouths open wider because there was more?

The land—this land that the generations of my family have wrestled the elements for, winning by a slim bounty which encouraged us to spend our lives here—this land does not love us for molding its hillsides nor planting and pruning its trees, redirecting its water, no, nor anything else we do to call it our own.

Soon, when I lie among their number like those before me, this land will cover me over in uncaring embrace, will thanklessly accept those parts of my shell that return to earth, and will little note or care that I walk upon it no longer.

Men grasp toward some idea of greatness but of necessity fill their hands with the next task, and the next, maybe never or only late seeing greatness in the weave and braid of life at the last.

Somehow, I must have always known this, or maybe I didn't want to know so I ignored the truth that seems so evident to me now.

Did my father judge his success against his father's as I am left to judge my own by my father's? Will my son judge himself by me?

Today I sit on my porch in my rocker, heedless of the call of whatever season began this morning.

1916 AN OCTOBER CONVERSATION REMEMBERED

GRACE: "So, Grampa, how come you pick a cold day like this to walk way up here? The wind always seems to be blowing on this side of the hill. Are you going all the way up to the burying ground? Why don't we go down to the big elm instead, where the wind doesn't blow? Let's go back, OK Grampa? Let's go back. Grampa? Do you hear me?"

GRAMP: "Hear you? That's all I've heard since we left the dooryard. Why don't you be quiet and listen on our walk?"

GRACE: "Listen to what? Are you going to tell me a story, Grampa? Tell me a story about your gramma—tell me about great, great, Grampa Art. Do you have a new story? It's OK if you don't. Tell me any story—any one! I'll like it."

GRAMP: "No, child—no story today. Just be quiet now. When you're quiet, you can hear things you'd never notice if you're talking. Now be still."

GRACE: "What do you mean? What's there to hear? There's only birds and squirrels on this side of the hill."

GRAMP: "Don't be sassy, now, Miss. I'll send you back to the house and you'll have to answer to Gramma for leaving me. Now don't you look surprised. I know it was her that sent you to follow me."

GRACE: "She didn't say to follow you..."

GRAMP: "I know what she said—probably said to ask me could you go with me."

GRACE: "That's what she said, all right—and if you'd have said no, I was going to come anyways..."

GRAMPA: "That's why I didn't say no. But now you're here, I want you to hush up a while. You don't have to listen if you don't want to, but I want it quiet so I can listen."

GRACE: "But if you aren't going to tell a story, what am I listening for, Grampa?"

GRAMP: "Well, my girl, we could listen to the wind in the empty branches, the creaking of the trees as they twist and turn. Or maybe we'll hear leaves fall, a butternut drop, dry grass rustle, or our own feet scuffing on the path. And if we're really quiet, we might hear voices in our heads. All that's quite a lot to be listening for, don't you think?"

GRACE: "What voices, Grampa?"

GRAMP: "Well, maybe it would be the voices of your ma and Gramma talking in the kitchen this morning, or your brothers in the barn yesterday, or some others... I've often found it useful to quiet myself down a while and just listen. The words I hear aren't words I pick, they're just words that have hung on, like they'd be worth the hearing again, or maybe because somehow, I heard 'em, but didn't understand 'em the first time. Maybe when they make a second run by me, I hear something in them that I didn't hear before, or something else that was meant by 'em that I didn't get right then. I never know why they come back, I just know they do whether I know the reason or not."

GRACE: "Are you sure you don't want to go back now—we're nearly at the top."

GRAMP: "No, I don't want to go down, I want to go up. We're almost where I meant to come today."

GRACE: "Why did they choose this place for the burying ground?"

GRAMP: "My grampa was the first to be buried up here, the day I was born. My dad said Grampa Art told him this place was where he found it easiest to believe in heaven."

GRACE: "I believe in heaven. Don't you, Grampa?"

GRAMP: "Good gosh, child, can't you be still? I used to believe a lot of things that I'm not so sure of anymore."

GRACE: "I don't know why it's any easier to believe in heaven up here."

GRAMP: "One reason might be that it's usually quiet up here."

GRACE: "You believe in heaven, don't you, Grampa? I do."

GRAMPA: "Gracie, tell me about heaven."

GRACE: "As far as I can make out, it's a place where you are with all the people you love, that nobody is in want of anything, and that people are happy all the time. It must be like Kelty Farm, like going right to our house forever. Is that what you want heaven to be like, Grampa?"

GRAMP: "I've had so much of all those things in my life, Gracie, it's hard to believe there could be more. It seems selfish to expect more."

GRACE: "But you do believe in heaven, Grampa. I know you must."

GRAMP: "Gracie, what do you see when you look down from here?"

GRACE: "Why, everything! You can see all of Kelty Farm from up here—all but the house. The trees are in the way of seeing the house from this side of the hill."

GRAMP: "No, you can't see the house—but you had to walk right by the house to come up here, so you know, even if you can't see it, that the house is there."

GRACE: "Sure, but you can see the great barn, the orchards, the fields, the dam by the saw mill… If you see all that, you'd know there's a house somewhere…"

GRAMP: "Yes…a house somewhere…somewhere. Seeing all this, anybody should know there's a house somewhere…"

GRACE: "You can't see it from here, but you know it's right over the hill, Grampa, right behind the trees."

GRAMP: "Yes, Gracie, I believe you're right…"

13

1918: THE PRICE

It was the day that Stewie died that I knew I couldn't stay at Kelty Farm.

I had been all the morning in the tack room rubbing soft soap into harness, checking every inch for wear or cracks that needed fixing. Dad had come in twice, looking each time at the worn leather I had set aside to show him, and at the harness I had greased and hung on the pegs. I watched his thumb and forefinger take position on either side of a strap, squeeze and slide along a length. Then thumb and finger rubbed against each other, telling him without having to look if there was too much or too little grease applied. The second time, he smiled when he turned to leave and said, "Good work, Arc. You're doing a fine job, son."

I didn't answer him. When he was gone, I stopped and sat thinking. I knew in my heart that my father loved me. I just wondered, over and over again, why he didn't trust me. Looking down at the harness, I knew somebody had to do this job that took time rather than skill, and that any of the twenty men who worked our land could have done it better than me. It pained me to hear his compliments, his praise given so easily on my ordinary performance.

I thought on Stewie, the best, the brightest of my father's four sons. Stewie was the one that so easily did the hard work, so quickly put his shoulder to the task, so handily accomplished a day's work with never a backward glance, never seeking our father's praise. I am the youngest, and yet, all the helping hands and the patience of my brothers is never enough for me to put my heart in my work. My hands are slow, my mind wanders, I never see the connection between what I am set to and the needs of the family. Everything I am given to do turns, for me, into an obstacle that looms larger than my skill to have it done and be on with what I want to do.

And yet, my father will compliment me on any pretext, on every turn. I know I never will work the Farm. I know there is a place in the world and things to do that I will do well and know in my heart that they are well done. His heart tells him that Kelty Farm needs sons, but my heart tells me these sons will not be my sons.

* * *

The wild shrieking and rage of a horse in the fenced area outside calls me on the run. I see others rushing down from the house and up from the Great Barn, and from the far hillside of the opposite wall of the valley.

As I reach the split rail fence and peer over, the horse rears up, screaming, shaking her front hooves at me as if warning me away. I feel a spray from her hooves splatter my face. I am captured by her wild eye which pierces me and holds me in its power. I touch my face absently, and when I look at my hands, they are wet and red. Then the hooves are up again, waving, shaking at me, dripping red, spraying red into the air. My eyes follow them to earth as they stomp on some bloody rags. I struggle to make sense of what is before me, unable to say what my eyes see, unable to hear anything but the howl of wind that fills my head.

I wrench my eyes away, finding the maple at the end of the yard, seeing a few dozen leaves floating gently to earth, too gently for the wail of wind in my head. I spin around, tearing my hands from their grip of the rails. My head says there is wind, my eyes say not. My eyes see people running toward the gate that holds the horse, but the silence in my ears says they cannot be there.

I turn again, seeing men inside with the horse, seeing the horse rear at them shaking her huge head, threatening with kicks of her forelegs. I see men's mouths open, their tongues moving, but my ears hear only the wind.

Suddenly, below the horse, behind the horse who takes her threats closer to the advancing men, behind the horse and closer to me, the rags take a form and make a horrible sense.

There are work boots on two stems of denim. There is a leather belt held by a silver buckle with a black letter S. There is a chest covered with a blue shirt, and arms flung wide and still. And if this form could make any pattern I know, above the row of silver shirt buttons should be a head of brown curls, and a face of the brother I most love. But instead of those laughing eyes and that grinning mouth full of teeth there is a bloody blossom, a tangle of flesh in no shape meant to happen, in no shape that can hold life.

And under the blackness that wants to hide this from me, sounds come back to my ears. There is the rage of the horse who bellows, shrieks and snorts, her hooves pounding again and again on the hard ground. I hear shouts and cries. Above it all there is one clear note, a sound larger than the wind it has driven from my head. It grows louder, closer, levels all other sound until only it lives.

Just before the darkness squeezes the last light from my eyes, when a terrible knowing presses at my heart, just before my mouth fills with bitter puke that will not wait for thought, I know the sound is my own scream.

* * *

I dream I am with Andrew and Phillip, my oldest and second oldest brothers. I know they are at the war in France, but I don't wonder how I can be with them. Andrew pats my shoulder and says, "Don't cry Arc. Don't cry. Dad's gonna need you more than ever." My cheek is hot as he holds me against his woolen uniform.

Somehow, at the same time, Phillip grasps my hand tightly in his own. Phillip says, "You have to be strong, Arc. You've got to be the strong one now." I cry and cry and my brothers hold me, but there is no comfort.

Waking with a start, I am on a cot in the tack room. I can hear the horse outside screaming and snorting. For a moment I can believe I dreamed the whole awful thing and I want to be glad. I run out of the barn into the bright noon sun. At first, I can't see anything, but I rush to the board fence and climb up to lean over the top rail.

The horse screams again, pounding the rock-hard ground. I hear a whistling sound I can't place then jump back as the horse crashes against the wood of the fence. Another shrill screech, another whistle sound. In my mind I see chunk wood splitting, but I can make no sense of this image. The horse struggles, her cries equal part rage and pain.

Another whistle followed by a sickening dull thud close at my feet, then silence. I see the double edges of the splitting ax raise high in the air in front of me, poise a long moment, then blur with a whistle and land with a thud.

I reach again for the top rail and set my foot on the bottom. I see my father, though not my father as I ever knew him to look. His clothes are soiled with bloody splatters and dark stains. He has lost his hat. I see the line between weathered tan and pale white that crosses high on his forehead. His hair hangs askew, falling across his eyebrows, hiding his eyes for the moment. His bulging arms yank at the ax handle that seems stuck beneath his foot. He grunts with the exertion of moving the ash handle backwards then forward, finally heaving it free.

His face is jumbled. I cannot place it on the familiar frame. The mouth is all wrong. It is a tense slash. His jaw grits then quivers. His cheeks contract and expand with the suck of wind needed for this unholy exertion.

I follow the dripping ax head into the air then lose it as it is pulled earthward again with a whistle and thud on impact. A growl escapes from this man as he frees the tool, this extension of his arm, his strength, his will. Again in the air, again a whistle to earth, again the sinking, sickening dull thud. Upon delivery of each blow, my father's chest gulps breath, he growls with the lift of the ax to the full height of the arc, then howls as he slams the ax forward again.

My eyes slide down his body, finding his feet planted in muddy gore that gleams brightly in the sun. It is black, yet red as I know it must be. In the mire of severed flesh, an eye stares with disbelief into my own eyes. I blink, but it is still there. For an instant it is lost in a fresh wave of blood then reappears in large white reality, its black center fixed on me.

I recognize the tawny mane that lies in the blood, the shape of the great head now severed from the powerful body. This is Dream Girl, Stewie's pet, the close friend to his heart and apple of his adoring eye, and today the instrument of Stewie's death.

With each thud of my father's ax the sentence is served. While I stare into that eye slowly setting into a filmy gaze, I know the certainty of what I have seen here in this yard—that Stewie is dead.

At last, the ax is too slippery to grasp and is too deeply embedded in the rib cage of the great chest to pull free. With a wrenching cry, my father begins to kick at the dead horse and when he slips and falls onto the bloody carcass, he beats it with his fists until his strength or his rage gives out. He lies across the open gashes and blood soaks into his clothes.

I climb over the fence, dropping inside. I wonder if I dare to look at his face. What has it cost him to satisfy this blood debt, the ancient demand of an eye for an eye?

He lies weakly sobbing ten feet from where I stand. Some of the hired men are on the opposite side of the yard. I suddenly realize they are not watching my father. Six heads I see, all watching me from across this yard where a man has done battle with his soul, where a horse has lost her life in the carnage. They seem to be waiting, as if expecting to be told what to do, for someone to assume the fallen reins of Kelty Farm.

These are good men, willing to put their hands to any task, but men who need to be told, to have someone direct them. Good willing workers, yet they ask what to do, what job should be next.

My heart is empty, too desolate to direct another to any task. I want only to lay down even here in the yard and just sleep. I hear the words of my brothers in my dream. In my head Andrew says, "Dad's gonna need you more than ever," and Phillip, "You've got to be the strong one now, Arc."

I look at the mangled horse, at the man upon the horse's legless body, and a part of me surrenders. What others call strength I know is weakness. I walk around the inside of the fence, sealing my fate with every step, goaded by Phillip and Andrew's words.

Old Paul is the first of the men inside the fence. I stop in front of him, hesitating one last moment, needing this pause to settle my new authority they so readily—gratefully--confer upon me. The other men lean forward as if the sooner to hear my words. I wonder which of them carried me, in my faint, back to the tack room, away from the grisly scene of Stewie's death and into my dream of Phillip and Andrew.

"Where's Stewie's body?"

"We took him up to the house. The women have him in the kitchen." Old Paul removes his worn hat, holding it in his hands as his fingers work the brim. His eyes beg approval.

"He's dead?" I cannot stop myself asking.

The other men take their hats off. Several answer, "Yes."

My father's sobs break the quiet.

Old Paul's face silently asks me a hundred questions.

"Two of you men get some shovels and bury that horse—bury her deep. Scrape up the blood in the yard and throw that in too." The two youngest walk away toward the tool shed, adjusting their hats, their faces looking relieved to have an assignment.

"Someone go get Doc Craven," I say as an afterthought.

Old Paul looks at me funny. "Stewart don't need the doctor, Arc," he says gently.

"No, but Dad will, and probably Mama will too. She hasn't really been strong since Andrew and Phillip went for the Army last year. This will be hard for her." I hear myself say these things, but I can't credit my ears.

"Yer right, Arc. I didn't think on that." Old Paul turns to another, motioning him to go. "And stop to the preacher and tell him what's happened." He turns back to me, waiting.

"We're going to have to make up a box...a coffin...for Stewie." I choke on the words. "Use the wide pine in the loft above the carriages." I turn away, keeping my tears to myself. I look at my father, silent now, yet shoulders heaving with great sighs he cannot control but I dare not hear. Old Paul sends two more men away.

"What's to be done with yer dad? You can't bring him in to the house like that." Old Paul's hat brim fairly spins in his hands as his fingers turn it round and round. I want to laugh, and if I was myself, I would.

"Go up to the house and get him a change of clothes. Bring them to the spring house—no—to the river, by the big elm. I'll take him there and clean him up."

"You'll need fresh clothes too," Old Paul says.

"I'll be all right. Then you better ask Mama if she needs anything— no, ask Gramma Lucy—she'll know. Tell them Dad and I are OK." He turns away from me, putting his hat on.

"And, Old Paul..." He turns. "Thank you."

"Yer welcome, Arc," he answers very quietly. He hurries away, one hand holding his hat on his head as if needing the reassurance of knowing where it is. The gate swings slowly shut.

The two young men return. One has a long-handled shovel, the other a pick and a short-handled shovel. They stand some distance from me as if reluctant to impose on my solitude. Both are older than I but are always called and referred to as "the young men." I'm not sure I know their names.

I walk toward them and open the gate, giving it a push outward. As it swings wide, I hear a hinge complain and somewhere inside my head I make a note of it. I walk through a black puddle to my father, putting my hand out, hardening my resolve to touch his bloody shirt.

"Dad. Dad, get up now."

"Huh?" he mumbles.

"Dad, get up now. Come with me, Dad, we've got to clean you up. We can't let Mama see you like this." I speak softly, not wanting the men to hear. I want to protect my father from them, from their seeing him so unresponsive, so out of himself. Somehow, I know they need to be protected from this too. As if I have sent them this thought, they lay down their tools and walk into the carriage barn.

The sun has moved, and the shadow of the barn approaches my father. Flies are gathering, their buzz droning in the quiet.

"Dad," I shake his shoulder. "We've got to go to the river to clean up. You can't go into the house until we clean you up. Now get up." I tug at his arm.

He twists slightly, sliding off the carcass, his knees touching to earth. He pushes onto the body, lifting himself away, and then stands. He is a big man, taller than I am by half a head. His tears wash clean furrows on his bloody face. His hair hangs stiffly in several directions, his shirt has lost some buttons and is open across his chest. His eyes are nearly closed. He stands before me, but I believe he does not see me.

I take his hand and he follows my lead out of the gate, across the yard away from the house toward the river. The path to the bottom land is well worn. The big elm, as everyone on Kelty Farm calls it, stands by a wide place in the water. This is a favorite end-of-day wash-up spot used by most of the family men and all the hired hands. In late afternoon the giant tree shades the water, offering protection to pale body parts usually hidden from the sun by work shirts, hats, and trousers.

At the river's edge, I drop my father's hand. Coming down the path he was easily led but as I face him, I am in doubt as to the task before us. I'm shocked to find no recognition in his face, no recognition in his eyes of where he is, who he's with, or what is required of him. We both are at a loss as to what to do next.

"You need to wash, Dad."

He stares blankly over my head, unmindful of the sun in his eyes. I nudge him forward toward the water and he steps into it up to the tops of his work boots. There is no change in his face nor in his lack of focus. I know he is far away, somewhere too distant to hear me, to know what I want of him. I hope that place is peaceful for him, safe.

I unbutton his shirt the rest of the way and unbutton his sleeves. I pull the shirt bottom out and peel it away gently where it is drying to his skin. He makes no movement nor speaks any word.

I loosen his belt and unbutton the front of his pants, then think of his work shoes. These I untie and slide each one off as I steady his legs against my shoulder. The pants are soaked through with blood, slippery, and hard to hold. My hands are wet from the shoes, and now are red from the pants. I hurry the rest of his clothes off to get him into the water. As I drop the last of his things on the pile, I begin to take off my own clothes which are now near bloody as his. He stands, his face vacant, his body slack.

Taking his hand, leading him deeper, I back into the water. There are springs on this side of the river, and it is coldest where we enter, but the cold is a welcome feeling where I had been feeling nothing. His face does not change as I lead him deeper still.

The clear water colors around us, swirling away in brown spirals. I splash at his arms, at his chest, cupping water onto his shoulders. He does not move. I rub at the cakes of blood dried on his chest, his jaw, and one cheek. Though it seems so natural a thing to do for him, I am surprised at his allowing me to do this.

I scrub his body with my hands, bringing fresh handfuls of water to his chest, his shoulders, his back. I draw him to the side, sitting him on the rock that lies just under the surface. I kneel behind him and gently rinse his hair, shielding the runoff away from his face. I bathe his forehead, his neck, and trace my fingers in the folds of his ears, finding bits of flesh and chunks of hide dried onto him.

Wading back to shore I find the canister of soft soap used every summer for the men who swim here after a day's work. The lid lets go with a hollow ring and I fill my hands with the slippery yellow stuff. It smells of clean pine. I put a handful on my father's back where it looks like soft butter on white toast.

I wash myself, scouring my hands and unseen places, feeling the need to know I am free of the gore. I wish I could wash the awful taste from my mouth, from my nostrils. I wish I could scrub this day from my mind.

Returning to Dad, who has remained where I left him on the rock, I wash his hair and protect his eyes from the soap. I glance at his face. There is no recognition on his part. I urge him to stand and I soap him thoroughly, splashing him to rinse. Then he sits again. I hate the blank gaze, the eyes that see past what I can see, his mind that wanders now in some place where there is no pain. I hate him, I envy him, I love him.

He is a large man, not only tall. His face, thick corded neck and arms are near to brown from seasons in the sun. But his hairless chest and belly are baby white. And that's what he is at the moment, a baby to be cared for. He sits on the rock in the river, naked but for the hair men have, yet in every way dependent. I hold him to me, his back to my chest, my arms across his larger body. He sits, unmoving, unmoved, and I weep.

I call to him, "Dad, Dad...," but he does not answer. After a time, I look to shore and see white towels and two piles of clothes, two pairs of shoes. Old Paul has done as I asked.

I guide him back to the gravely riverbank and dry his body as he stands before me. I ask him to help himself to dress, but he does not answer, in words nor in movement. I have never dressed a grown man and I am awkward and fumbling. I have him completely clothed before I realize my own nakedness and think to dress myself.

"We're going back to the house, Dad, back to the homestead. You must be able to speak to Mama when we get there. She'll need you, Dad. You can't let her see you like this." I have no hint from him that he hears. Except that he breathes shallowly, and walks when I lead him, I might believe him dead too.

Too. I think on this day of death. Too.

When we are nearly to the brow of the hill, nearly to the carriage barn in front of us, I remember what is waiting there. I wish I had taken another path, wish I had considered more before coming this way. It is too late. We pass the corner of the barn and approach the rail fence. Dad stiffens, slowing his pace, his steps hesitant. I hold his hand tightly and speak softly.

"It's over now, Dad. There's nothing here. Holly and the other man are cleaning up the yard. They will be done soon. You don't have to look, Dad."

I walk backwards, slowing my pace to his, holding his hand, studying his face. "We'll be at the house soon. You'll need to talk with Mama. You'll have to be strong. She's going to need you strong, Dad." I hear my brothers' voices in my head, about half a word ahead of my own tongue.

There is the sound of shovels full of earth being tossed and landing. The men are digging just inside the fence. I didn't expect that. Dad stiffens again, but I pull him forward. At the far end of the fence, he stops and takes his hand away from me. He covers his face with his hands and lets out a wail that chills me and wants to break my heart.

"Stewart!" he yells, he demands. "Stewart! No! No!" he cries. He sways and would fall except that I step closer and take him in my arms.

The shoveling stops. There is silence again, except in my head. Andrew and Phillip are repeating their litany. I curse them for not being here, for leaving Kelty Farm. I know the Great War sounded a call to adventure for them, but they are oldest, their place is here. I am the younger son—it is for me to go off, to make my way in the world, to have my dreams.

Then Dad puts his arm over my shoulder and he wipes his eyes. He pulls me closer and whispers, "You've got to be the strong one, Arc."

I hold my breath. My heart stops.

"I'm gonna need you more than ever now."

I had said these words to him. I try to hope he is only repeating them back to me, but my heart knows.

He releases his hold of me, straightens up, turns his back on the fence, and walks directly across the yard toward the house. I watch as he hesitates at the side door, then watch him go to the front entry instead.

Old Paul stands beside me. I had not heard his approach.

"The women are doin' for Stew. They got him on the big table. Mrs. Lucy told us to bring the coffin in the front door. It'll be ready soon. I set up some sawhorses..."

I hear his voice catch on the word horses. I turn and step up to the fence. The hole is man-deep and wide. The men have worked fast. I thought this ground was hard, but now I see it is softer below the surface. Like Dad.

In the house everything is hushed. I stand on the door sill waiting to hear anything that will tell me where everyone is. There is a muffled hum of voices from the kitchen. There is no sound from the parlor nor the dining room to my right. If I were stronger, I would go to the kitchen and see if I am needed. Instead, I go through the parlor and up the main stairs.

The door to Dad's room is open and I see his feet up on the bed. He still has his shoes on. I ought to stop to talk with him, to be with him, but I don't think either of us wants that.

In...my...room, a room Stewie and I shared with Andrew and Phillip, I see the quilt is gone from Stewie's bed. I remember now that Gramma Lucy put a quilt on Grampa in his coffin. I asked Mama about it. She said we do it for all our people going way back. They don't have any such custom in town. I'm glad Stewie will have his quilt.

I see his good shoes are gone from under his bed. Stewie's feet were small for a man bigger than me, almost as tall as Dad. The closet door is open. The women must have taken his suit to dress him. Stewie never liked that closet door open, said he couldn't sleep with that darn door open.

I'll close it for you, Stewie.

Gramma Lucy comes to my door. I'm surprised. She doesn't go up and down the stairs much because of her knees.

I wait. She walks into the room and hugs me. She puts her head on my chest and I embrace her. I wait.

"Why did this happen, Gram?"

"Arc, there is an answer, but it is not given for us to know it for now."

"But why do such awful things happen?"

"We may know all the whys someday, or we may come to where we don't care why." She steps out of my arms, gathers the folds of her apron into a knot, clutching it to herself.

"But Stewie was so young…"

"Arc, it helps if you know that everyone lives their full life, be it eight days or eighty years. Stewie lived every day he had, right up to his end." She looks down at the wide board floor, not at me, and she speaks slowly, deliberately. "He died on Kelty land, in sight of the homestead where he was born. When they carried him into the kitchen, he was clutching a piece of leather rein in one hand and in the other, a handful of mane. He had to have been up close to that horse, the one thing he loved most."

"The thing that killed him!"

"Is it so bad to die where you lived doing what you love to do? Most of four generations of Keltys buried on the hillside above died of what they loved—the men of loving their land till they'd given more of themselves than they had left, the women for lifetimes of care for their children, their men. And even then, we put them in coffins made from their own trees and place them under the sod they worked."

She puts her head on my chest again. I fold her into my arms. She sobs quietly and I don't know what to do for her so I just hold her, patting her shoulder. Downstairs pots and pans clang and armfuls of wood drop into the wood box near the back stairs. Gramma loosens her hold of me, wipes her eyes and looks into mine.

"You'll need to be strong. You're the man of the family now, Arc. We're all going to need you."

God damn you, Phillip! God damn you, Andy! Shut up! Shut up!

"We still have Phillip and Andy, Gram. They'll come back when the war is done," I say. Her blue-ice eyes look up into my own. I suddenly know I don't want to hear what she's going to tell me.

"Arc, they're gone. If you don't know it yet, you'll know soon. I prayed for them, Arc, every night since they left the Farm. Every night I knew my prayers went up to heaven and right into God's ear. But last night, well, last night…" She looks away from my gaze. She drops her arms from me and turns toward the door.

"What, Gram?"

She looks at me. There are tears. "Last night my prayers couldn't get out of the room. I even opened my window, but they wouldn't go to heaven. They just swirled around my head. I knew it then." She is standing very still. I touch her blue-veined hand and find it cold.

"Maybe that was because of Stewie. Maybe God wanted you to know."

"No. It was Andrew and Phillip. They're gone."

Her tears are running freely; she doesn't try to stop them. Her lips stretch thinly over her teeth, where she'd always had a smile. "I wanted to tell someone this morning, but I just couldn't…and now I can't tell anyone else. I had to tell someone strong."

I take her into my numb arms. I try not to look over her head at the two empty beds. I know that behind me is another, and my own freshly made up this morning. I always thought this was the smallest room in the house but now it seems the biggest, the emptiest.

Gramma Lucy holds on to me a long time.

"You're all that's left of their sons, Arc. There's just you and Grace left".

"They'll come back, Gram. Andy and Phillip have got to come back," I say, wondering if I believe my own words. I don't have time to think of Andy and Phillip. Now is the time to think of Stewie.

"We'd best not say anything to the others. They'll think we're borrowing trouble when we have plenty to home. Bad news will wait. We'll get word soon enough." She walks out of my room and I follow. The room is too empty for me to stay.

At the foot of the main stairs, we meet Doc Craven coming from the kitchen.

"I sent Emma to bed. All has been done for poor Stewart that earthly hands can do, and she needs her rest. Mrs. Lucy, you'll have to direct the kitchen. You stir up cakes and such, the likes of which can't be found in three counties around. Your neighbor ladies will be descending with food before nightfall, and no one will bring any deserts because you put them to such shame."

He holds Gramma Lucy's hand as he talks, patting it and smiling into her face. His voice is understanding and kind, a voice you would turn to as flowers turn to the sun. I can see that he has dealt with Mama and now is giving Gramma Lucy something to do, something to keep her hands busy, and engage her mind and heart. I know I will be next on his list.

"Nothing will ever be the same here. We think if we don't ask for much, nothing will be required of us. We lull ourselves into believing we're safe in a little world we make. How easy falls our house of cards." She weeps, struggling to get the words out.

"Nothing will be the same, but it will be…some…way. We have to hold the pieces together as best we are able." He puts his arm on her shoulder, making her seem even smaller than her five-foot height. "Now, get every pan and pie plate out, and fill them with sweets that everyone expects at the Kelty table. Don't you disappoint anyone." He smiles broadly. She looks sadly at me then walks away.

"How are you holding up, Arc? This is an awful loss to you." He pauses. I cannot look at him.

"How's Mama?"

"She seems reconciled. I'm going to see your father now. He's in the parlor with Stewart. Come in with me."

"I don't think I can, not yet."

"Whatever we find, you'll have to face soon or late. I don't know what to expect." He looks at me, waiting. I cannot bear to see his face. I stare out the open door into the late afternoon sun.

"What do you mean?"

"I heard about the horse."

I glance at his face and find a certain uneasiness, a reluctance to say more.

"He had cause, for God's sake!" I am angry that my father would be judged. "Stewart..."

"I know—I didn't say I might not have done the same thing." He grasps my shoulders to assure me. "I only mean to say that what your father did as a reaction to and on top of the loss of Stewart took something out of him that can't be put back, at least not for a while. I'm telling you because you're the man of the family, now. You need to know what to expect."

I am an over wound clock, ticking, ticking.

"Your parents are going to need you more than ever. Give me a little time with your father, and then come in." He goes into the parlor.

I dread going into the parlor, seeing Stewie there.

I thought I knew death. On the Farm, death is as common as life. It is there anywhere you look; you just don't think about it. The animals become food, chicken for supper, steaks or roasts, venison, hams and fish from our land. I know that babies die sometimes. I'd heard there was one before me, and one after me, before Gracie. Old people die, like Grampa Ike last year. We go to other families' wakes and funerals, and they go to our peoples'.

On Kelty Farm, we have our own way to take care of our family in death.

In the loft over the carriages, there are wide pine boards left to cure. These were the center cuts—the widest boards from the oldest trees on the land. Every board is rough cut to about one and a half inches in thickness and seven to eight feet in length. When death occurs within the family or among the older workers who are thought of as family, some of the boards are taken down and cut up to make a pine coffin, pegged or nailed together the very day of the death. No coffin is ever made up ahead.

Home wakes are observed. Our dead are washed in the kitchen and dressed by loving hands. Sawhorses are set in the parlor to hold the pine coffin through the night. Someone always sits up in respectful attendance and funerals are held by noon, followed by a potluck meal brought by neighbors who attend.

Burial is in the family cemetery on the hill above the house. There, small groups of white marble tablets are placed in rows, those who have been together in life now together in death. I don't know why, but all our people lie facing the sunsets. In the front row, the first to be put on the hill above the house he built, is my great-great-grandfather, Arthur Kelty, and his wife Elishabet. Beside them are two sisters who never married, and, it is told, who never left the Farm. Then are two of Arthur's sons and their wives, and some small markers for babies and young children.

In the second row are my great-grandfather and his brother, two more of the sons of Arthur and Elishabet, and then their wives and some children. In the third row is Grampa Ike. We buried him there last year. I know Dad and Mama will go in that row after Gramma Lucy. I guess Stewie will go there too. There are two baby markers, and that fills the row.

I can see all this in my mind as I think of it. It too is a part of life on Kelty Farm.

The parlor has nice wall covering, several lamps on brackets, and a big fancy stove at the far end where the fireplace is that we don't use anymore. There are two divans and several large chairs. Our house is home to many and used to large families. When we have company, other chairs are brought from the dining room and other places in the house. I have seen fifty people seated in this room, though some of the other furniture had been carried out to make room for chairs. The windows are draped over with black today, just the way they were for Grampa Ike. All the wood gleams except the plain rough-cut pine of the coffin. As I look around, I see Dad in a chair with Doctor Craven bent over him. They talk in low voices. Bracing myself, I walk up to the coffin, which is set waist high.

The first thing I notice is that they've used my suit on Stewie. I was always glad that he...was...a little taller than I am and couldn't ever borrow that suit. I notice the sleeves of the jacket show more shirt cuff than they did on me, and I know without looking that the pants are too short. His hands look softer than I know they are and seem to have come to rest on his chest that is strangely silent. I watch, sure that his chest will heave, and great breaths of air will fill it, but no, it doesn't.

One more thing we do, here on Kelty Farm. We bury our dead with a quilt around them, sometimes just for them to lie upon, sometimes tucked over them. Stewie has a quilt that Mama made for him. It is mostly red, his favorite color. It seems to be under him, and his head is covered over with it. I know there could not have been anything to show of his beautiful laughing face, but it hits me now how hard a thing it is not to be able to look one last time at a face I love.

I don't know what I believe as far as heaven is concerned. I guess if he had his choice, Stewie would wish to stay on Kelty Farm. I think maybe the dead stick around for a while. They may not get used to being dead all at once and are curious how we're going to do without them. Gramma Lucy said that Grampa Ike talked to her every night for over six months after he passed. I hope Stewie's not mad at Dad about the horse.

I hear a shuffle of feet at the door. I cross back to the hallway to see who it is so that Dad and Doctor Craven will not be disturbed. Old Paul stands at the door waiting to be invited in. His eyes hardly come off his boots, and he stammers as he speaks in a low voice.

"I'm glad it were you to come to the door, Arc. I was wanting to know is there something more to be done." He pauses. "I moved the…well, the other horses down to the great barn so as to have room for them that will come, and we cleaned out all the stalls." He looks up into my face, waiting. I can see his willingness to take anything he can off my shoulders. I know I have only to think of something for him to do to make him happy. I just do not know what to say.

"I got one of the men bringing extra hay up and we'll stick around to help at the barn. Do you want me to dig the… the…? Well, I guess if you wanted me to, you'd tell me, wouldn't you." He turns away. I am failing him. I just stand there. I know he is suffering too.

"But look, Arc. I dug your Grampa's grave, and I wanna dig Stew… I wanna dig Stew…" He turns back to me as I look away. "Arc, I know I'm old, but let me do this. It's easy diggin up there, almost all sand. I can do it, Arc, I wanna do this for Stew… for Stew…" He turns toward the door, his hat chest high, his hands working the brim as if they can't decide to hold the hat or put it on his grey head.

I sense more pain in this man than I have yet allowed myself to feel.

"Old Paul, would you like to come in and see Stewie?" I put my hand on his arm and receive the full attention of his glistening eyes, of his great round face. There is some glimmer of hope for a moment, but then it falters and goes out like a candle.

"I can't come in, Arc. This is a time for yer family. And I'm not cleaned up, I'm all dirty. No, I can't." He looks away again, out through the door, his head high like he is looking across the valley to the road that goes to town. Then his gaze falls to his boot tops again, and his hands spin and work his hat brim. "No, I can't Arc. Not now, anyways."

"Old Paul, we think of you as family. And the dirt on your boots today is from doing the things that had to be done for Stewie. Don't think about it. Stewie wouldn't, would he?" I speak gently as he has always done to me, sliding my hand around his forearm, pulling him to the doorway of the parlor. I feel his muscles rigid under the worn coat, I feel the jolt of his heels as, step by step, I draw him forward. I walk backwards as if towing him, not wanting him to slip away, needing to give him what I know he wants. I hear my own heels, softer on the parlor carpet, as we leave the hardwood of the hallway.

Concentrating on Old Paul, I am startled when my hip brushes against the rough pine coffin. I read in the old man's eyes that he is looking at the quilt that covers Stewie's head, and that he is relieved not to have to face again what he certainly had earlier today. Before I can look away, his face grimaces in a dry-eyed crying, his mouth draws down and he heaves a sigh of great pain, great regret.

"Ah Stewie… ah Stewie." He reaches a great paw over Stewie's hand and holds it a moment, then draws away. He looks at me. We are a fellowship of loss. His eyes embrace me though he does not.

"How are we to bear this, Arc?" He struggles with the words, barely whispering. I take his arm again and turn him away just as my father steps up behind.

"Thank you for all you've done today, Paul."

"No thanks needed. You know I'd always do anything I could. You know that. You know that…" his voice trails away. He takes Dad's hand, Dad that I always thought had big hands, Dad that is a foot taller than Old Paul, he takes Dad's hand, and Dad's hand disappears inside of that great brown and dirty hand. "I'm just so sorry about Stewie. I love him like he was my own, you know I did. I love all yer boys like they was my own. I'm just sorry."

Then tears burst out of his old eyes splashing down on his hand, making watery-clean spots in the dirt that covers it. Though neither move, I see these two men reach out to the other in a way that says they each know more than I can know, now, or perhaps can ever know. I step back, somehow humbled by this silent exchange.

Old Paul walks away in a sort of shuffling that is louder as he reaches the hallway. I hear him on the steps outside where he pauses, then he is gone. Dad takes my arm and steers me to the chair he had been in and where the doctor waits.

"You look washed out, Arc. Are you going to be all right? You've had a rough day. Maybe I should give you something and you lie down a while." Doctor Craven seems far away as he speaks.

"You need a walk outside, Arc. Go ask my mother to pick out a spot for… for Stewart. That'll get you out in the sun. Be good for you." Dad sounds like he wants to sound better than he feels.

"Do you think that's a good idea, Jackson? Your mother's busy in the kitchen and that may be best for her now." Doctor Craven looks worried, his suggestion is a question.

"She's going to do it soon or late. She's the one that has picked out every grave up there these last fifty years. She knows how many places over each should be so everyone fits in like fingers in a glove. And she won't have it any other way, so we might as well let her do it." He laughs mirthlessly. "She's all but the boss on Kelty Farm anyway, and it's only the more so since Dad died."

"I miss old Ike. He was a good man, none like him." Doctor Craven nods his head as if in agreement with his own statement.

"It's like she knows where each person should go… it's just something she's always done." Dad turns away from the Doctor and looks at me. I feel like he is going to kiss me and send me out to play. "You go find your gramma, Arc. Tell her to pick out a spot for our Stewart."

* * *

It is only late afternoon, and the sun is still warm on this high spot. Alone, I could walk here from the house in twenty minutes, but I rarely come, and never come alone. This is a silent place, right at the heart of Kelty land, the silent place that everyone comes to at the end of lives lived in labor on the Farm. The hired hand, kitchen girl, babies that left too soon, the family patriarch and matriarch, and so many others in between them all lie down in long sleep, in line after line, all cares left behind, all questions quiet.

I think they lie in this peace, listening to the beating of hearts still pumping blood not far removed from their own. I imagine that they wait here, knowing who will be next to join them. I believe now that they know Stewie, my beautiful Stewie, the happiest among us, will be here tomorrow to stay with them forever. I told Gramma Lucy all this on the way up here.

She walks across the rows of graves and seems to be reading every name. Finally, she comes to Eikenhous "Ike" Kelty, my grampa. She closes her eyes and embraces the tall, cold marble. I come closer.

"You're partly right, they do know a lot more than most. I know a lot too, but they see it clearer than I can. You could know, Arc, if you would quiet yourself and accept the gift." She opens her eyes full on me. I nearly step back. "It comes to some, the gift, if they want it or no, but most that have it had a choice. It doesn't come without a price; I surely do know that." She looks away.

"Everything has a price, Gramma. The question is: Who is it that has to pay?" I know I am being bold, but Gramma Lucy allows me to talk direct, at least when we are alone.

"We pay, each of us, for what we accept, and sometimes more besides. You mother is paying the higher price, and she's not half paid."

"All I know is it's Stewie dead, and Andy and Phillip not here—whose shoulders will this come down on? Dad's going to expect me to take up where Stewie left off, and it's not in me. You know that. It might as well be my life that's ended today. Old Paul will be digging my grave next."

"No. That's not going to happen." Her voice is cold.

"Gramma, if you know something about that, can you tell? I know you know things other people don't know, and you never tell. But you can tell me." I wait. I only half want an answer.

"All possible futures can be had starting with the next step you take." She points at my feet, looks into my face, then sweeps her hand out and away past the valley below us. "I look at you and I see lines traveling out from where you stand.

"Every line reaches past where I can see, so I know you will outlive me. And anyway, Old Paul will soon lie beside his own son, and won't dig my grave, either." She sounds sad, resigned.

"I didn't know he'd had a son. It must have been a very long time ago. How come nobody ever said?"

"It was his story to tell. If he didn't then you have to respect that. It was a long time ago, maybe thirty years. His son is over there." Her eyes move to the back of the grounds, the far side of the flat, the low rows of markers where workers on the Farm were at rest. "You'd find a small white marker that says, 'Paul, Beloved son, 1878, Age 20,' and an open plot beside for Old Paul. He dug the grave and buried his son, and he didn't come down to the house for three days. He paid for the marker and put it there himself. I watched him do it. I've seen that loss in his eyes all these years, but he's never spoken about it, at least not to me. I'm probably saying too much. We have other work to do here."

For a small woman, she walks fast. She paces to the end of the row and puts a stick into the ground. She measures three feet across and puts in another twig, then seven feet toward the bottom of the row and places another small branch. "Do you want me to show Old Paul the place you've marked?"

"You won't have to; he'll know where to look." She turns, staring into my eyes. "Tell me what's the matter."

"What's the matter? Stewie got his head mashed by his own horse! Dad… Dad chopped the horse to pieces! Wouldn't that be enough the matter? What else has to be wrong?" I am close to shouting. Gramma doesn't flinch.

"That ought to be enough, but you've got more to say. You've hardly begun." She steps closer and looks directly up into my face. She doesn't give an inch. "I've never hidden a thing from you. I tell you things that would be too big a burden on others." Her voice softens. "Now it's time you told me your heart."

"Stewie should have had the Farm. Or Andy or Phillip." She waits patiently. "They were the ones to beat Dad to doing every chore, who made a game of knowing the thing to do next. Not me. Never me." She has resignation in her face, on her shoulders, in her body. "I did what they wanted to do just to be with them, to do what they were doing. It didn't mean anything to me." I can't stand her gaze. I turn away into the setting sun. "It just didn't mean anything to me. I never really cared. How will I care now?"

"It would come to you if you put your hand to it."

"I see what caring does—look at Dad, look at Mama. And if it's true about Andrew and Phillip…"

"It is," she interrupts simply.

"I can't be here to see their faces when they know that too, not after Stewie."

"What is the center of your fear?" She puts her hand on my shoulder.

"I can't say it… I can't." Tears are coming.

"You've got to get it out and have a look at it. Say it. Say it!"

"I'm afraid they'll look at each other and their eyes will tell one another that they have nothing left, that everything worth having is taken from them, and that they are left with only me." I cover my face with my hands and fight the tears that insist.

"They are offered no choice about this. And their way is to take comfort in each other, count their blessings and go on. And you, Arc, are chief among their blessings, you and Grace." She is insistent, urging me to look beyond what I can see.

"But Kelty Farm! It eats up its men, and I'm the next. What's in my life for me? I never wanted the Farm and now what choice will I have. If I stay, my big reward will be to pick a spot up here with the rest. If I leave, I'll be letting everyone down. They won't say it, but I'll know."

"What would you do if you had the chance, Arc, if the whole world were open to you?" Her voice, her words call me back. This is an invitation to dream.

"I don't know. I have always believed that I'd know when to go, where to go. I'd know when the time was right. I have lately thought the time was near..." I turn to look at her. I see the great caring I always find in her face.

"Arc, you'll do your duty, now. Yes, your parents need you, and Kelty Farm needs you. But your turn will come. You father will see that your heart is elsewhere, and another choice will be made known to them."

How I want to believe her.

"Gramma, the name of the place is Kelty Farm. After Dad, who will they have but me?"

"They have Grace. She's a young girl now, but in five years..."

"In five years, what? She's going to marry. Then she won't be Kelty anymore." Why doesn't she see it?

"I'm married over sixty years, and my name's Kelty. It's just a name. It takes more than the name to make a Kelty, to live up to this land and to take everything, good or bad, that it would give. If it's not for you, then go where you've got to go. If you can't be who you need to be here, then Kelty or not, you've got to leave. Your parents will come to see that." She is stern, solid in her stance.

I look away, at the sticks that mark tomorrow's new grave.

"Gramma, is there a place for me up here, with all these Keltys?" I have to ask, to know, if she can tell me.

"Stewie is the only one of you boys that will be up here, Arc."

"Stewie. I should be thinking about Stewie, and I can only think of myself."

"There will be time to think on Stewie. Be patient. You'll get what you want. You've got to be strong. But you'll pay the price for it. It can't be helped."

Five years for freedom. I sigh. "Five years."

14

1919: IDENTITY

"Sorry, Mr. Kelty. I hate being the one bringing bad news. Specially... Well, after all... that's already gone on, for you, this last year I'm meaning."

"I thank you for your thoughts, Ronald, but there can't be much bad news left to come out from town. Why don't you come down off your mount and go out to the kitchen? Mrs. Kelty will give you something to eat before you go back."

Jackson held the envelope away from himself, resisting the urge to put it in his pocket. He watched the youngster walking away from him as he watched all the young men who came into his sight. He wondered if he was trying to see his own sons in these left behind, maybe Andy or Phillip, or, God knows why he'd be expecting Stewart. At least Stewart he got to see put in the ground, for whatever blessing that was.

The screen door slammed shut behind the boy, and Jackson went to the rocker on the porch. There probably wasn't any bad news left, but whatever it was, he'd face it sitting down this time.

The envelope was not a telegraph envelope, but it was from the depot. Carl had sent young Ronald up here, the youngster knowing its contents and saying it was bad news. Ronald was probably telling his information to the women in the kitchen right now.

Jackson stretched his legs before him, leaning back into the chair. He looked again at the envelope, fighting off the dread he felt in his flesh, deep in his bones.

The last message coming from town was that Andy and Phillip were missing and presumed dead. "Regrets, etc." filled the rest of the paper. His mother had warned him to expect some rough news about his boys off in France, and though she had spared him for the moment because of so recently having lost Stewart…Stewart…that telegram hadn't been a complete surprise. While the message left room for a slim hope, she warned him to have no hope. And he knew she wouldn't say that if she hadn't known for sure. He'd always been aware Lucy Kelty knew things—some things—before there was any way for anyone to know.

So now this envelope. Jackson opened it carefully, noting his name written on the front. The plain paper was folded in four but only said, "Jackson, you better come soon, and bring someone with you. Carl"

Jackson thought where everyone was at the moment. Some part of his mind had a constantly updated inventory of the whereabouts of his dwindling family members. At this point none of the hired hands were in town either. His dread lightened a bit. Whatever this message was about did not feel the threat it might have been before recent events at Kelty Farm.

Soon his mother and wife would be out here wanting the news, so he savored these few moments of solitude in which to decide his next steps.

Archie came out of the carriage barn across the yard just as Jackson was thinking to call his son. He watched Archie's eyes sweep the yard, the kitchen door, and come to rest on his father's usual perch of the porch rocker. Archie smiled across the yard as he caught his father's eye.

Jackson brightened at the sight of the one son he had left. He waved his son to the porch and felt a sense of gratitude as Archie moved in his direction.

Archie brushed himself off as he approached, glancing at his father, at the paper in Jackson's hand. He noted the horse at the hitch and wondered whose it was, and what it might mean that there was no stranger in sight to go with the horse. The question was on his face, but he waited for his father to speak. Archie had recently developed a sense of waiting, a hesitancy heretofore unnoticed, unneeded. Of late, he seemed to consider every possibility in what he saw before him when deciding his path through any situation.

"Archie, I have a message from Carl at the depot to come see him. How's about you get a wagon ready and we go find out what he wants of us."

Archie wiped his forehead and neck with his bandana, replacing it in his back pocket. He put a foot on the bottom step.

"Are we picking up supplies? Is that what we need a wagon for? Otherwise, horses would make a better ride on that road."

"Until I know what Carl has in mind, I think we'll take a wagon. There might be something needs hauling." Jackson appreciated the caution in Archie's face, in his thinking. He understood Archie's need for caution.

"You want to take any of the men with us?"

"No. Let's us go for now. If we need anybody, later we'll send them in. Let's go as soon as we can."

"OK, Dad. Did Carl say to come right away?"

Jackson could see the concern in the query but shook his head. "No."

"Maybe we should go after lunch. It must be almost ready."

Jackson smiled. Archie was stalling for time, wanting a better handle on this before he moved forward.

"If they have something ready to go, we'll take it for sure, otherwise, we'll get something in town." The porch door opened behind him.

"Mr. Kelty, your mother says for you to come see her. Hey, Archie. How ya doin'? Haven't seen you around much. They keeping you close to home?"

"Hi, Ron. Guess there'd be enough reason to stay to home. It's a big place, lots to do." Archie's tone was light toward his young friend, but there was pain in his eyes. "You headed back to town? Tell your dad we're on the way in."

"Ronald, do you know what's caused your father to want me to come see him?" Jackson watched as the boy hesitated, his eyes looking at his horse as if the answer was over there.

"Well, it might have to do with a big box that came off the train this morning. Dad had some men put it over in the shade, but I don't know anything more than that to tell you, Sir."

"You go on back then, and we'll be along shortly. Thank you for your trouble, Ronald."

"Oh, no trouble, Sir. Glad to be of any service. See ya later, there, Archie." He stepped into the stirrup and mounted, turning the horse in the same motion. Jackson thought of Stewart again.

"Should we change clothes to go to town?"

"No, Archie. This isn't going to be that kind of trip. And I don't think there will be time to visit Anna May. Not today, anyway." Jackson smiled at the carefully hidden surprise on Archie's face. Archie liked to keep his thought to himself lately. The father regretted that Archie had had to take on such a load since his three brothers were gone. "Wait, Archie. You be quick and clean up, I'll see about the wagon and some food to take with us." He smiled at the relief on Archie's face. He saw in this unguarded moment Archie's need to see his young girl in town. Jackson also realized Archie's depth of interest in young Miss Brist. He more than hoped it was a passing thing.

He walked to the carriage barn to see who else might be available to hitch up a team and have the wagon set when Archie was ready to go.

"Ah, Holly, glad it's you up here. Get a team hitched up to the long wagon and bring it around in the yard. Archie and I are going to town." Jackson admired the young hand, a steady boy just older than Stewart had been. He showed promise and seemed willing to stay on after all the bad turns for the Kelty family this last fall. Some of the hands, especially the younger men, had left, probably out of their feelings about Stewart's death. Jackson himself knew he had blocked some of that day out of his own mind.

"Will you need any help in town, Mr. Kelty?"

"No, but thanks for thinking ahead. You've got a good head on your shoulders, Holly. I notice your good work." Jackson stopped himself from calling the man 'son' as he had called all the young workers in previous times. He turned for the kitchen door, expecting a fresh batch of questions about the note and his going to town, at least from his mother. Emma didn't ask much about anything anymore. She just accepted what came her way and steeled herself to bear up as she was called upon to do. As he reached the first step, he saw his mother waiting inside the screen door she held open for him.

"I don't know what this is about, Ma. It was a note from Carl at the depot to come see him and to bring someone with me. Archie and I are getting ready to go. Is there some food we can take with us?" He knew she wouldn't be satisfied with this.

"What could Carl want with you and why would he say to bring someone with you? I don't like it, Jackson. I should go along too." She put her arms inside her apron top, keeping her ice blue eyes on her only son.

"Where's Emma? I want to tell her I'm going."

"She's upstairs. She looked poorly after breakfast, so I told her to lie down. I think she might be sleeping. But you go see. I wouldn't want you to leave and her wake to find you gone." Emma needed lots of assurance since Stewart's funeral and then news about the other boys.

Jackson turned down the hallway and up the back stairs to the room he shared with Emma. He opened the door carefully, but found her looking at him as he poked his head in.

"Is something wrong? Do you need me for something? I heard a rider come to the house and leave. Who was it?" Her face seemed calm but that was a thin coating over her feelings these days.

"Nothing for you to worry about. Archie and I are going into town. Is there anything you need at Dudley's Store? Some thread for your quilting maybe?" He kept his voice light, knowing how little it would take for her to worry.

"Thanks, no. I have plenty. I'll come down and have lunch with you." She swung her legs over the side of the bed, but Jackson stopped her before she could rise.

"You stay there, Em, get some rest. Archie and I are going to eat on the road. Ma's fixing us a basket now. Probably enough for the next week." He laughed, hoping to deflect her interest, hoping to get away with as few questions as possible.

"I'd better come down and see to the basket myself. And what's the hurry? You should have your noon meal before you go. Eating on the run is not good for you." She stood up, but he came into the room and kissed her forehead.

"I really just stopped to kiss you goodbye before I left. I'm glad I found you awake, but you lie back down and get your rest. Ma said you didn't look well a bit ago. Are you feeling better? Should I send the Doctor out to you?"

"No, but I will rest. I'm sure your mother won't let her boy starve. And she baked some of Archie's cookies this morning. He'll get a share of those if I know Lucy Kelty." She sat back on the bed, adjusting the pillows behind her. Jackson leaned down and kissed her again.

"I don't think it will take long. So, I'll see you at supper tonight unless I see you sooner. You be well when I get back." He reached for the door.

"Jackson. Thank you for your thoughtfulness, your kindness toward me. I am getting stronger. I'll be better soon."

"My dearest Emma. You are all that matters to me, you, Archie and Gracie."

"And your mother."

"Yes, and my mother, it goes without saying. Sometimes I think of her as part of the Farm and forget to include her in those I care for, because I love the Farm so much." He enjoyed her small laugh. Jackson admired the relationship the two women shared. He knew it had been a safety net for Emma after the loss of her three sons. Since last fall his mother had been a good balance against Emma clinging to the last of her children.

* * *

The wagon wasn't as comfortable as other carriages they had, but its long bed made them ready for any need they might face. Jackson wondered about the big box Ronald had mentioned. He and Archie munched on the sandwiches and drank the root beers in the basket and were well on their way before having something to say.

"I see you dressed up pretty well. You have your new shoes on. I'm surprised you didn't wear a suit and tie." He smiled at Archie, knowing his gibe was expected.

"You always say you never know who you'll run into in town. I was surprised when you wanted me to wear dusty work clothes instead of putting clean ones on. And it's not just because I could see Anna May, she's likely to be in school at this hour. Although we might see her father. I always want to look my best for him. I get the feeling he expects it of me."

"Humm. I guess he's about the last person I ever want to see when I go to town. He does seem to cross my path more than I need. But Archie, you remember who you are, and that you have no reason to feel second best to anyone in this town or anywheres else. And you sure don't have to feel second best to Brist. His family were all…"

"I know, Dad. They were pig farmers. And before that… But that's not who they are now. And Anna May thinks a lot of me. I can tell. Her father's always polite, glad to see me…"

"And he's lucky to have a fine young man such as you showing an interest in his daughter. Even at her young age."

"There's only a few years difference between us, Dad, and you know nobody's rushing into anything. We're just, well, mutually interested, that's all. Mr. Brist always asks after you and Mama. He seems concerned how we're doing since…"

"I can guess his concern. Remember to keep family business in the family, and that means Farm business too. He doesn't need any information from us. He soaks it up everywhere he goes. And frankly, I never liked his interest in Kelty Farm."

"Let's not get into this now. What do you think is waiting for us at the depot? What could they want us for? Have we ordered something that's been delivered?"

"I don't know, and glad to change the subject."

"None too soon, I'd say. Are we going to pick up any supplies while we're in town? I'd like to look around and see if there might be some men to hire. We're short a few men and could use some help."

"Good thinking, Archie. Check at the grain store, the livery, and at Dudley's. If there's no one around, ask who is looking. Anyone in need of work would check in one of those places." As he said this, he knew Arc would have already thought this far ahead.

"So, you don't want me to check the ice cream parlor, the café, or the jail first?" Archie had a quiet smile on his face that made Jackson laugh out loud.

"Son, you got me there. I guess you'd know where I would look. But first, let's get to the depot and see what Carl has in mind. The strangest part of his message was that I should bring someone with me. I feel some concern about that. Do you have any ideas?"

"No. But we're almost there. We'll find out soon enough. And if it is bad news, like Ron seemed to think, it will wait for us."

* * *

"Young Mr. Kelty! Good to see you about. How are you doing, son?"

"Just fine, Mr. Tibet. Thank you for asking. We are all well at the Farm." Arc shook hands with the station master, a portly man younger than his father. "Dad's just getting the horses some water, and he'll be right along."

"I don't envy you that road in that wagon. It's not built for comfort, nor is the road." He laughed at his own joke, his merry eyes sparkling as they squinted. "Come. Wait inside out of the sun."

"I'd better stay in sight so Dad will know where I am." Arc looked around. "Ronald said something about a box. Is it for us?"

"I ought to wait for your father, Archie, but maybe it's best to tell you first. We got a crate from the military this morning. There's a letter attached addressed to Mr. Kelty of Kelty Farm. My guess is that there's a body inside. What do you think?" Mr. Tibit took his hat off at the mention of a body and turned to face Jackson at his approach.

"We'll have a look at the letter and decide," Jackson said. "And let's get right to it. Let's not spend any time dreading the task."

Mr. Tibit put his hat on and led the way around the corner. Under the lilac trees was a sturdy wooden container, stenciled across the two visible sides with the words, "Military Priority." On the top of the case was a letter addressed as Mr. Tibit had said. The letter was held by a wooden cleat across the heavy envelope, a nail in each end.

"There it is Jackson. I didn't know what to make of it is why I sent the note out with my son." He spoke reverently, lowering his voice to near a whisper. "I got a crowbar out for you; it's laying against the side there."

"Thank you, Carl. Let's see that envelope." Jackson pulled at the cleat, and it came off with no trouble. He reached for the envelope, glancing behind to see Arc nearby.

"Want me to open it, Dad?"

"No, Archie, just stay nearby. Whatever it is, it's not good." Each of the three men had noticed the sweet odor around the box, drifting in and out of the fragrance of the lilacs in full bloom. He opened the envelope, tearing off one end, pulling several papers out. First was a letter. Jackson stared at it a minute, then looked at Archie.

"What is it, Dad?" He reached for the letter in his father's hand just as Jackson released his hold on the papers. Arc grabbed at the falling papers, making a jumble of them. He glanced at Jackson, then read the letter.

"What's it say, Archie?" Mr. Tibit asked as he leaned forward to get a view.

"It's from a Lieutenant Hodges. Says he was newly assigned and didn't know many of the men from the battlefield. Says this man was badly wounded and taken to a field hospital, and later was shipped back to the states hoping for recovery. The Lieutenant only knew he was one of two sets of brothers from the same place, and one of his men remembered the name of this town and Kelty Farm. He says it is unfortunate this man died unidentified but hopes family members would identify him. Says there's a flag inside." Arc studied his father's face, fearing to see the far away and vacant state Jackson had fallen into the day of Stewie's death.

"Get that bar, Arc. Let's not labor this thing." Taking the crowbar from his son, Jackson studied the crate, deciding on the weakest point to open first. Sliding the thin teeth of the bar between the planks, he pried and released the top with a wrenching sound. Repeating this action at the far end freed the cover and they set it aside.

The men looked at each other. Jackson removed a paper-wrapped parcel on top of what appeared to be a metal casket. He handed the parcel to Mr. Tibit.

"That'll be the flag, I'd guess." Jackson's voice was steady, but Arc watched his father carefully.

"Do you have in mind opening that casket, Jackson? Maybe we should get Rinker the undertaker over here." Mr. Tibit had taken a step back as he spoke.

"Is it going to be necessary to break the rest of the crate to get the casket open, Dad?"

"No. But let's take a minute. There is a man in here. The remains of one of the sons of our families, mine, or someone else's. This was a brave man who died answering the call of his country. I've already accepted that my sons are gone, and if this is one returned, it won't matter which one. If he's not my son, he still is someone's son, likely Mr. Robbins, as both his boys went in right after mine and were reported lost." He paused a long moment. "Are you ready, Arc? Let's take a quick look to see what we can tell. It's not going to be good; we know that from here, and who knows what condition we'll find the body in."

Jackson reached for the release bar on the side nearest him. As he pushed on it the top sprung open, lifting only inches. The men stepped back again. Jackson steeled himself and flung open the cover.

Inside, the body lay at ease, at first glance only the bandaging around the head spoke of wounds too terrible to survive. On closer inspection, the hands were missing at the ends of the jacket's sleeves. There were medals pinned to the breast front. Though Jackson had only meant to take a quick look then close the casket again, he was fascinated by the peace and composure of the uniformed body. The lilac trees added to the moment, their freshness sweeping away all but faint odor from the casket.

"He's not ours, Dad. Our boys were taller than that. This man is about my height. I'd say it was Truman Robbins if it's one of those two."

Jackson closed the casket with reverence.

"Good call, Archie. I might have come to that." He turned away for a moment, then reached for the parcel in Mr. Tibit's hands. "Let's we make use of this, Carl. It's all we can do for the man now is respect him, and those he represents." Jackson unfolded the flag. He tossed one end toward the bottom of the casket, and a breeze caught it, spreading it across the lower end. He carefully stretched the corners over the top, then stepped back to survey his work.

"Should I send Ronald out to the Robbins Farm?" the station master whispered.

The three men walked away from the casket, heading back to the depot.

"No, Carl. Now that we're pretty sure this is one of his boys, I think I'll go myself. I would like to borrow a horse so's I don't have to ride that bucking wagon out there. His road is worse than mine."

"I'll go, Dad."

"No, Archie. He'll take it better from me. And you have to check the jail and some other places, don't you?" Jackson's half-smile was a relief to Arc.

"You got a friend in jail, Archie?" Mr. Tibit seemed confused. "Oh, Jackson, I'll get Ronald to saddle a horse for you. He's right here somewhere. He's usually under my feet. Can't seem to find him enough to do."

"Maybe you'd send him my way. He's a likely lad and I could put him to good use."

"Might just do that. Got to check with his mother first, though. You know she takes a keen interest in her pup. Can't blame her, so many of the youngsters from around here never made it back from the war." He stopped abruptly. "Oh, Jackson, I'm so sorry! If anyone knows that it would be you, and after losing Stewart. Oh! I've stepped in it again!"

"That's all right Carl. I'm working on getting used to it. I'm careful myself not to bring it to mind too often. Mostly, as Emma says, we count our blessings. We've got our Archie and Gracie."

Jackson's voice was even, but Arc wondered how much that cost his father.

***

As Jackson approached the Robbins land, he noticed fields un-plowed and unplanted. He thought it was late to be this far behind. He'd heard Mr. Robbins had sold off his cows, and anything else he'd gotten an offer on. The older man was seated in a cane rocker on the porch watching as the horse came to a stop in front of him.

"Mr. Robbins."

"Jackson Kelty. Don't guess I've seen you in a while. You don't come out in this direction much, and I stopped going to church. Come on down. Sit a spell." He indicated the chair next to him with his pipe stem.

"How's the Mrs.? She doing any better?" Jackson sat in the old chair but did not rock.

"Some. She has to think hard what she's to do next. Some days doesn't get up at all. Doesn't eat much. I was never what you'd call a cook. Been livin' off the canning jars lined up in the cellar. They'll last till winter, I guess. If she's not better by then I might bring her to her sister in the next county. Don't know what else to do.

"But what brings you out here. Is there something left of my farm you'd want to buy? Everything's going cheap, you know. Land and all."

"No. Got my hands full with what I got. Not in any real position to buy much anyway. How are you doing, Mr. Robbins? What are you doing to keep busy?"

"Well, I'll tell you, Jackson. I'm pretty busy these days sitting right here on my porch just watching for what God's going to send my way next. Yes sir, I hardly sleep at night, want to be awake for what He's going to send along."

"I guess it's me He's sent along to you today. I got some news. Glad to find you at home and sitting down."

"I imagine it's bad news." He chewed on his pipe stem. "It's the only kind that comes down this road of late." The older man shifted in his chair, settling down in the same position.

"But don't let that hold you back, Jackson. You and me, we've had about the worst news there was and we're still standing—well, sitting anyways."

"Mr. Robbins, I know you were friends with my father. And you married late and got your two fine boys. Our boys are gone, and for myself, I think I'm getting used to the idea that's the way it is and isn't going to change. How's it for you?"

"Can't say I'm planning to get used to it anytime soon. Seems like I got a little grudge with the man upstairs I'd have to work out first." He leaned forward, looking full into Jackson's face.

"Well, this morning I got a message to go into the depot to see Carl. I got in there to find a box from the military with my name on it." He paused. "There was a letter explaining that somebody thought the boy in the box was one of two sets of brothers from this town. They thought it might be one of mine."

Mr. Robbins sat back in his chair and began to rock slowly, sucking on his pipe.

"I opened the box, found a casket with the body of a young man pretty bad off, but in a clean uniform." Jackson waited. Mr. Robbins brought his gaze up to meet Jackson's eyes.

"He's not one of my boys. My boys were taller, well, all but Archie, but he was standing there beside me at the time." The old man put his pipe down and stared away across the field.

"Archie thought it might be your Truman. "

"Truman? He's over in France, they said." His voice cracked and Jackson looked away.

"They sent me a letter saying he was buried beside his brother. It was the only comfort we could have from it all."

"I guess they had a battle, a lot of bodies, and a list, Mister Robbins. And first priority was likely to get them into the ground. In the end, the name might have been guessed at in some cases."

"Who's to say you're not right, Jackson. And it wouldn't make a difference."

There was a long moment of silence between them. A bird called from a nearby tree.

"The letter with the coffin said this man had been badly wounded, had lived to be sent home, but died since. They had no way to know who he was but for someone who remembered something about Kelty Farm and him being one of two sets of brothers."

"And you say he ain't one of yours? Must be in bad shape if you had to speculate."

"His head is all bandaged. I wouldn't think anyone would want to look under that. There are no hands out of the sleeves of his jacket. Is there some other way you might know your son?"

"Did he have shoes on?" he asked quietly.

"Yes, and a nice shine on them, too. Why do you ask?"

"Well, if I was to look, I'd want to look at his right foot. If it's Truman, he's missing a couple of toes, and has no nail on his big toe." He thought a moment. "I guess I could come on in, but I'm not sure I could look."

"Maybe I could do that for you."

"It can't be pleasant. I wouldn't put that on you. I ought to be man enough to look at my son myself."

"It's not so bad. Except for the bandaged head, and the hands. They embalmed the body, but I don't know how long that's supposed to stand up. Did you want to come in?"

"Can't see any way around it. I can't ride a horse anymore, but I've got a buggy and a gentle mare to pull it."

"You might want a wagon to bring him back here."

"No. I made my mind up this minute. If it's Truman, if we're lucky enough to have one of my boys back from that cursed war, he'll be buried in town, and I'll take Brist up on his offer on my farm. It's near a fair offer, but I've been waiting to see if someone else might come along. Brist will only sell off the land in lots. I was holding out that someone might want to farm it. Now, this minute, I decided I just don't care what happens to it. And I know Marion won't care, maybe it'd perk her up to live in town."

"That Brist. He's like a buzzard wanting to pick the bones. He has his eye on every farm in the county."

"It's different for you, Jackson. You've got one son left. The war took all I had, even my identity. I have no reason to keep the farm. No one to give it on to. I feel like I don't know who I am anymore, giving up the farm. Like there's no reason to be, when I give it up. I think that's how Marion feels without the boys."

His words lay there, his shoulders slumped, his chair at rest.

"Jackson, I'd sell the farm to you for even less than Brist is willing to pay."

"I know that's a kind offer, Mr. Robbins, but I can't think of buying anything at all. I'm glad to hold on to our Farm as it is. And you'll need every dollar you can get from the place, especially being you'll be selling to Brist. He never buys anything for a respectable price. It's a bargain or nothing for him." Jackson had a sour taste in his mouth. "Do you want me to hitch up the buggy? We can tie my horse to your buggy, and I'll ride in with you."

"Kind of you. If it's Truman, I'll call in the undertaker and we'll have a funeral in town. You'll help, Jackson?"

"We've all missed out on some funerals lately, my family and others, a chance to pay respects and honor what all these young boys died for. This one may be for a son of yours, but he was the son of this town, and represents so many others lost to us.

"My family and I will be there, all of us. We'd be honored to attend, Mr. Robbins."

15

―――

1919: LILLIAN, POSTSCRIPT ONE

Lucy shaded her blue eyes with her hand and squinted at the figure on the road across the valley. It was a woman wearing a cape out of season and carrying a satchel that was either too heavy or too heavy for her to carry. The dust rose around the figure as she passed the point on the road of being seen from the front porch. Lucy determined to go to the carriage barn across the yard and send a hired man to help the walking woman.

Lucy questioned herself why she felt concern about the stranger. So many came here hoping for a job to guarantee some income or at least the dignity of being housed and fed for the worth of their work. Lucy knew this was different.

No men in sight at the barn. "Must be out in the fields or at the great barn. But she didn't stop there. I guess it's the house she wants." From the back of the barn, she could look down onto the road that rose to the land shelf where Lucy stood and to the house across the yard.

The woman on the road below lingered as she came to the bridge crossing the river in the valley. Lucy watched her gaze downstream to the big elm before continuing up the steep grade to the homestead.

"Something familiar in the walk, in the gait, but don't just know…"

162

She decided to wait outside the barn, at the edge of the dirt track that passed from the far hillside through the valley and upward to the house. Again, she shaded her eyes, but even as the stranger neared, Lucy could not tell why she should know her.

"Good day..." Lucy offered, waiting for the distance between them to narrow before having more to say.

"Hot one, good or no..." the woman returned without altering her pace, making as if to pass Lucy by.

"I'm Lucy Kelty. Should I know you?" Lucy put her fists on her hips, turning her back to the sun as the woman walked past. She felt satisfaction as the stranger paused and looked over her shoulder.

"You've changed since I saw you last but haven't we all." She set her satchel down in the dust and sighed.

Her voice was tired, old. Lucy noticed the lines in the woman's face. A worn bonnet covered her hair, and the cape hid her dress. Dark colors, Lucy thought. Wrong for the season. She guessed the woman was older than herself.

"When did we meet? I'm sorry, I don't remember you."

"No reason you should. You were Lucy Jackson, and I thought you'd marry one of the Brist boys who were all around you. I was always surprised you settled on Ike. I thought he'd be too quiet for you."

"Well, now you've surprised me. You speak so casually of days I've forgotten, they are so long gone. But I'm glad to say things turned out all right for Lucy Jackson. She did just fine without any of the Brist men for a husband."

"I heard." The stranger turned back toward the house, as if she remembered something and looked to find it again.

"Well, come along to the house and you can sit and tell me what you can say for yourself. I'm sure you're too tired to carry that carpet bag any farther, and it's too hot to keep that cape and hat on." She reached for the worn handles, but the woman was quicker, picking the bag up and holding it against herself.

"I guess I got this far on my own steam, and I can make it from here across the yard to the kitchen. I hope you're not baking, that kitchen is hot enough a room without the stove being full of limb wood." She turned back to the house and continued at the relentless gait Lucy had noted before.

"Walks like Ike," Lucy said softly, remembering her husband, dead two years. She found herself following along behind the stranger when she was most used to leading.

At the path to the house, the woman chose the branch leading to the back door. Lucy was surprised at this display of knowledge of her home. She made to step past the woman to reach the door first, but the woman had gone up the two stone steps and pulled open the screen door. Stepping inside, she let go of the door without thought of Lucy behind her.

"Sit yourself down," Lucy commanded, firmly grasping a hold on the situation, asserting possession of her home.

The woman dropped the bag to the floor and untied her bonnet as she slowly stared at every item in the room in its turn. Lucy thought the woman was checking against a mental list of the room's contents, and she felt uneasy in her own domain in a way she seldom had before. Suddenly the stranger dropped her bonnet and began to cough, doubling over in obvious pain.

Lucy crossed the room to the stranger's side, reaching for her shoulders, backing her into a chair. The woman's hair came uncoiled, falling white against a lined face and closed eyes. She had a look of great age.

"Tell me how I can help you. Do you want some water?"

The woman shook her head yes, resting her chin against her chest, her hair hiding her face. Lucy filled a tumbler from the pitcher on the shelf. She took the woman's hand to give her the water, but then held the hand and tumbler and brought it to the woman's lips.

"I'm sorry. I didn't mean to be any trouble. I didn't come here to cause anyone work. I wasn't sure I would come at all, changed my mind near every step of the way," she said weakly.

"Why don't we start with your name?"

"No reason to think that would help you. I used to live here, but I was gone before you came. And I was older, too old to have been your friend in those days." She put her head back, her hair falling away from her face. She closed her eyes and smiled.

"Too old? What days do you speak of?" Lucy had the uneasy feeling again.

"Can't tell now, but I was out of school when you graduated. I often saw you looking at Ike." She smiled, her green eyes shocking Lucy.

Ike's eyes, Jackson's eyes, young Arc's eyes, and Grace's.

"Lillian Kelty…"

"The prodigal daughter…" Her mouth opened in a grim silent laugh.

"Lillian, I…, we…, I'm sorry, but we thought you were…"

"Dead?" The grim mouth again, the pain behind the eyes.

"We never heard from you. Ike…, Ike asked about you whenever someone came here from away. There was no way to know…"

"That's the way it had to be." She looked away from Lucy, at the things in the room, the door behind the stairs. "Momma kept that door open in the summer, said it cooled the kitchen."

"Yes, it does, but we're not baking today, no need to overheat the bedrooms. Arc don't like… You don't know Arc, my Jackson's youngest son. I didn't marry a Brist, but he's likely to."

"A Brist finally gets Kelty Farm. Circles, all life is circles." She coughed again, but kept her head erect, closing her eyes with the effort.

"Circles, Lillian?"

"My father used to say the Brists wanted our Farm. Said he hired the old man of the pack to mind our pigs and was sorry he gave them a foothold here."

"I've heard that. But it was so long ago. Your father's been gone…"

"I knew when he died. Knew when Mother died and knew he wouldn't last long without her. Did he ever say anything about me?" She searched Lucy's face.

"No, not your father. Sorry, Lillian. Your mother sometimes. Ike and Hatti often spoke of you. Always wondered where you were, why you didn't come home… You know they're gone too, Ike and Hatti?"

"I knew about Ike, and Jackson's three boys, read it in the papers. Sometimes I got a newspaper from here. Found out about Hatti today.

Went there first, thought she might... But I didn't know any of her children, at least they didn't know me, said they didn't know their mother had a sister... So, I came here."

Lucy saw false courage in the other's face.

"Can you stay long? We have room... You'd be welcomed, Lillian. Jackson and his wife, they'd know you, who you are. We have room..." Lucy suffered for her, for the long moment of indecision. There could be only one answer.

"Well, I could stay, but I won't be staying anywhere for long, not for long..." She looked for understanding and seemed comforted by Lucy's eyes.

"The cough... I know that cough. I know..."

"Yes, well, I couldn't stay and be charity, especially not here. I can work. If there's a loom around, I can weave, I can stitch fancy work, quilts, shirts, most anything." She seemed poised to go if the wrong words were said.

"That's a skill to have. I could never do anything but plain stitching, plain quilts, never worried much about patterns, colors. I remember now, your mother showed me some of your handiwork, said she was always proud of your work, of you..."

"Mother. A kinder soul never was born."

"I still miss her, and your father..."

"My father. I'm only glad I didn't have to come hat-in-hand back to him. I'm sure he expected me, I'm sure he looked for me to come..." Her voice fell away, she began to get up from the chair.

"I hope you'll stay, Lillian. I was always sorry I didn't know you. Ike and Hatti... Well, when they spoke of you, I felt left out, like there was something they knew that made them sad, and I was left out, couldn't help."

"I'm sorry I missed Hatti. I knew Ike was gone, but I'm sorry I missed my sister..." She fell back into the chair.

"You and I, Lillian, we're sisters. I always felt it, just never had the chance to show it. Say you'll stay, if only a little while..."

"That's all I've got to get through, a little while. Don't think it'll be long..."

"Maybe the air here will help. I think it's clean air and rest for what ails you, if I'm right."

"I'm pretty near the last of it, nothing much to hope for now except..."

"Except?"

"...not to be alone, not to leave things undone..."

"What is left undone, Lillian?

"Circles. Circles are closing. Need to close them up, to finish... to finish."

"You must be tired, hungry... All this can wait. Let's get you settled first..."

"I have bad days, days when I'm too tired to do much. But this is a good day. I want to do one other thing before I decide to stay."

"Do you have other people to go to?"

"No, no one I know. Have some children somewhere, but they never amounted to much, sorry to say."

A grim false smile. Lucy again felt her pain.

"Decide now, Lillian. I want you to stay."

"I don't want people saying..."

"There's no one left that matters, no one to say anything. Please stay."

"I'd need to work. I can't stay and be charity. Just couldn't do that. Just couldn't." She finished the water.

"I know we have a loom, and wool as you need. And a needle is always busy here, especially a good one. Jackson's Emma is good, but has other duties, and we have young Grace that would benefit from a great Aunt's skill, from the company."

"As long as I work. Just don't want to burden..."

"Family is never a burden, sister."

"Thank you, Lucy Jackson."

"Kelty. Lucy Kelty. No one left that would know me as Lucy Jackson anymore. It's been a long time, a lifetime."

"Sister… Still, there is a thing I want to do yet today. I want to walk up the side hill, to the cemetery. I want to visit Ike, Momma."

"There's time for that. Eat first, get settled."

"No, I want to close circles. I can't tell when I'd feel like it again."

"We could pick some flowers from the side yard and I'll go up with you…"

"This is something I need to do alone. I'd thank you for the flowers."

* * *

"Always hated the wind up here. With the trees gone, it can't help but be windy." She looked at the valley below, straight down to the river, up the opposite hill. The open land, the tall standing trees along the stone piled fence lines. "Used to be father's favorite spot…" she said to no one. "It's never going to be mine." She caught her breath from the climb then turned her back on the valley.

Nothing had prepared her for the lines of standing white tablets. She got her bearings from the first two at the far end of the front row. "Arthur and Elishabet…" She remembered faces of the uncles, the aunts, some of the children, "Had forgotten they might be here…waiting." Others were here she had not known.

"All waiting," she said. "Circles… Circles…"

She shivered, feeling a weakness in her legs, knew she had to move onward while she could. In the middle of the second row, she began to recognize names and came to the largest tablet there.

"Beloved Husband, Eikenhous 'Ike' Kelty, 1840—1917"

"Sorry I worried you, Brother. Sorry to have missed you. Won't be long till I'm up here too." She put the flowers down, retrieving one stem of yellow mums. "I won't come back, Ike, until I come back for good. We'll have a good talk." She pressed her lips together.

No tears. A circle closed.

At the last of the front row, she found her mother. The white marble was inscribed with flowing letters, "Till the Morning," and words too numerous to read now. She looked at the fountain, the weeping willows. She saw the cherubs, the urn, the hand pointing upward.

"Till the morning," she read again. "Father did well by you, Momma. Father always took good care of everything, saw to everything. Always knew what to do. No doubts."

She put the stem of mums down. Her hand read the figures in the marble, found the shapes, caressed the letters.

"Madeline Eikenhouse, Beloved Wife."

A circle closed. No tears.

The companion tablet. Thicker by an inch. Only slightly taller. Similar etching, lettering. A heavier touch on the letters, she thought.

"And Ike did well by you, dear Father. But then Ike was always one to try to please you, a task I never accomplished. You'll be glad to know I'm back, that I'm likely to be buried up on this hill at the end of it all. I'm sure you're pleased by that, at least. Take what pleasure in it you can. I'm back to making shirts for the Kelty men, the farm hands. I can see your face. Smug. So knowing.

"I didn't bring you flowers." She unfastened her cape, pulled it from her shoulders, laying it over the marble.

"I can only hope you know my regard for you, for your caring, for the thought you always took for me. I've thought of this a long time. I've walked miles when I wanted to sleep. I didn't wait after I got here. There is only another moment to wait."

Standing in the center of the grave, she gathered up the worn and dirty dark blue skirts, pulling them from behind into her lap, exposing naked legs and buttocks. She squatted, bringing the material higher around her, spreading her feet, leaning backward but balanced. She released her stream, strong, flowing onto the ground, steaming even in the heat of the day. It stopped. She waited a moment. Stood.

She retrieved her cloak. She walked away. A circle closed.

16

1920: THE LETTER

"Lillian, I've found the letter! Ike told me about this letter he had for you but never told me where it was. Just now, I found it in his journal from 1916, of all places." Lucy had spoken in her excitement without realizing her sister-in-law was still sleeping. She made a mental check of Lillian's breathing and general coloring. There was no sign of fever this morning, though of late, fever came and went without giving notice.

Lucy put the old letter on the bedside table, standing it against the unopened Bible, making sure the name faced the sleeping woman, then left the room.

"Now, what did Ike tell me about that letter? I don't even remember who it is from, but surely it will say inside." Lucy wondered if she should wait to give Lillian the letter when she was awake and having a time of clarity. Yet, how many days did Lillian have left, she thought.

"What's the matter, Gram? You look worried," Grace said. "Are we still canning mixed vegetables today? I'd like to get them picked before the sun gets too hot. Dad said one of the boys would bring up a sack of corn. When he comes, I'll ask him to get the jars from the cellar."

"I'm sorry dear. My mind was elsewhere. Oh! Yes, we'll do the vegetables today. Mixed vegetables are the most work, each kind having to be blanched separately, different times, different pans. But the rainbow of color when we mix them in the jar is so beautiful, you forget the work on a cold winter day when they steam in a bowl on the table ready to eat." Lucy put away her concerns for Lillian in favor of the project before her and another opportunity of working with Grace.

Among her duties, as she saw them, making sure Grace knew how and when to do things was very important. Lucy thought again of Lillian, and then of the dwindling number of her own days. How many more late summers would she have to do this ritual of claiming the wealth of the garden for the winter table. And could she still do these tasks with joy, imparting the need of their doing without feeling the endlessness of the lists of things to be done, season by season, all in preparation of a future need?

"We should heat some water to wash the jars first. That will give them time to dry in the sun before we need them."

"Why do they need to dry in the sun, Gram? Couldn't they just air dry on the shelf?"

"I only know that's how Ike's mother did it and my own mother did the same. I think the sun sterilizes the jars. Anyway, that's how we do it. And here is that boy you like coming up the path with his sack of corn. Good thing he's stronger than he looks, they've loaded that sack more than just full. Probably playing a trick on him, or he's showing off for you!"

"Oh, Earle. I don't know as I like him a bit better than any of the others. He is very strong, though he doesn't look it. He's still smaller than Archie, but he's stronger, and he'll grow some more, I'd think. Do we have any more molasses cookies? I'd like to offer him one or two while he's here."

"After he gets the jars up from the cellar, you can fatten him up as much as you want to. If he doesn't have to get right back, maybe he'd shuck the corn. That would be a good job done." She heard a cough from the side bedroom and listened as it came again. "I've got to tend Lillian. You know what to do. Get about half a bushel of carrots, beans —green, yellow and pole beans--, and anything else that's ready. I can't think now what's out there, but you know what to do. I'll be back as soon as I can, but I'm going to stay with Lillian if she's up to it. I don't think we have much time left with her."

"Maybe I should come with you. Is there anything I can do to help?"

"No, Gracie. Enjoy your time with your Earle."

"He's not my Earle, Gramma! You better stop that. If Dad hears you, he'll find Earle work fixing fences along the road to town and won't let him back here."

"Gracie. Your father has eyes in his head. My Jackson always sees more than anybody thinks. He just doesn't talk about everything he knows. Don't let him fool you."

* * *

"Lillian, your eyes are closed but you are breathing heavier. I wonder if you're just resting or still asleep," Lucy said softly.

The older woman didn't move but cleared her throat. "I'm not sleeping. I thought I was, but I heard you come into the room, and I understood you speaking to me. It seems a great effort to open my eyes. I hope you don't mind." She cleared her throat again.

"I see you opened the letter."

"I saw it there and thought I had enough strength to get it open, but I can't make out anything on the pages. Is this the letter you said my brother had for me? Is it from Ike? Words from the grave..." She coughed again then was silent.

"It's not from Ike. He had it for years, and I had forgotten about it till lately. I've looked everywhere and only found it this morning. Do you want me to read it to you?"

Lillian sighed. A moment later she reached for the papers on the table and slowly handed them to Lucy.

"Who is it from? I didn't leave many friends when I went off. I never thought I'd live to end up back here. Life is a circle, they say. You wouldn't say that, I guess. You've been standing still all this time." She coughed then breathed with great effort till she was quiet again.

Lucy watched her closely. "This may not be a good time to get into this. Maybe I should bring you some broth. It might be good for your throat."

"Just tell me who the letter is from." Lillian's eyes remained closed.

Lucy arranged the sheets of paper. They were yellowed and stiff. As she looked the letter over, a memory stirred, and she recognized the handwriting. Skipping to the last of the three pages, she saw no name, but knew who had authored the letter. Words from the grave, she echoed Lillian's thought.

"Lillian, it's from your father."

Lillian locked her fingers across her chest. She pursued her lips, frowning. There was a silence in the room that Lucy noticed. In fact, thought Lucy, the whole house is silent, not the usual bubble and gurgle of things going on and people conversing. Only silence.

"Lillian…" she began softly, wondering at the reaction this information had cause.

"You take it away, Lucy. He didn't listen to me when he was alive, and I'm not going to hear him now he's dead. My only fear in dying is that I'll be buried too close to him and lay all eternity aware he might speak to me, even in death. I'm sure you think I'm foolish, but still, that's the truth of it." She turned her head toward the wall, her eyes clamped shut, her fingers white from the pressure of their grasp on each other. She stifled another cough.

"I'll leave you, Lillian. In a while, I'll bring you some broth."

"Take the letter with you."

* * *

Lucy sat at the kitchen table. On the stove two canisters of water were beginning to steam. Corn shucks were on the floor and a pile of husked ears on the shelf. Out the screen door she could hear Grace talking in the garden, laughing, and someone answering her. The folded letter remained in her hands. She turned it over and over, slowly unfolding it, spreading it on the table. She hesitated but could not stop herself from reading the words written so long ago by her father-in-law.

She pictured old Mr. Kelty, "Dad," as he finally asked her to call him. She had been willing to love him, his son's bride, new in this house. He had never paid much attention to the young woman till his wife died then had only slowly realized how dependent he was on her. The last few years of his life, Lucy saw him mellow toward her, and even become affectionate and was delighted with her young son, Jackson. He had loved his own son, Ike, was loving toward Hatti, his married daughter living only a few farms away. How had it happened that Lillian missed that part of her father? How could she have left so long ago, and what grudge did she still bear in this last part of her life?

"Maybe the letter explains," she said to herself. She set the envelope aside and smoothed out the three pages. She hesitated a moment but knew she had decided to read the letter.

24 April, 1876

My dearest daughter, Lillian,

You have been gone so many years I have little hope you will yet return, at least while I may see your face again, hold you in my arms, assure you of my love, and ask your forgiveness. I write this letter against the day we will know where to send it to you, or, Dear God Please, you come back to the bosom of your loving family and reclaim the life you left behind. I write this letter because I no longer believe I will be able to say these things to you myself, things that must be said, things that weigh on my soul. I cannot trust my life will go on much after these poor lines are written, but I will leave them in care of your brother Ike who, as best he is able, will honor my wish that they come to your hands.

When you and I spoke of your desire to leave the farm, that long ago day, I believed you had heard my caution, my fear of the life you would find away from our home. This was my error. I did not sufficiently color my deep fear of the world outside our own. I did not weight my caution with the things I had learned of the world you would rush into. That was my failing, a failing that I fear has cost you a terrible high price and may have cost you all. If I could have prepared you better, if I had given you my support, and made a plan for your well-being, or at the least, given you money to do as you must, I would have some peace now and your life would have been as safe as I could make it for you. This failure has cost me a daughter I so loved, and these years of not being in each other's lives.

While I have hoped against hope you would find a different world than my fear allows me to believe you have, I have, all these years since, wished you only well, and have daily begged our kind creator to watch over you as the loving Father I believe in. I pray your life will allow you the quiet to hear when He whispers into your soul to remember a life you left behind, a life here waiting your happy return, a return that will bring joy to many.

Though you left believing Kelty Farm a curse one had to endure under the misfortune of having been born to it, I must have faith that you soon would have realized there is nothing for free but misery, and even that sometimes comes at great expense. Please, please find the right day to come home to us. Whatever day that may be will be the right day for your family.

Come back, your head held high. Deceived by your youth, you were yet brave enough to seek a destiny you could only have guessed at. Whatever you have found cannot replace what awaits you here. Bring with you any you call your own but come home and we will call them our own as well. Do not fear scorn nor reprimand, there will be none. Open arms, welcoming hearts, glad faces, and tears of joy will meet you. Come back and share your life with us who love you.

If not for our sakes, come back for your own.

In closing, may I again assure you that from the day of your birth you were most precious, most dear to me. To my dying day, this will remain true, and if after death, there's any will, then my love for you will live.

We remain here, at your home, Kelty Farm. Your loving family and a father awaiting your forgiveness.

Lucy leaned back in the chair, drained by the sentiments in the letter. She wondered if Lillian would be able to hear its contents. Lucy again glanced through the pages then folded them to replace in the envelope. These certainly were words from the grave, as Lillian had suggested this morning, but were also healing and balm for wounds Lucy could only guess were inflicted in the passing years since Lillian had left the Farm. She considered the burdens of life she had lived through, and yet believed they were outweighed by the blessings of security of life on Kelty Farm.

She determined she would pass this letter and its contents to Lillian one way or another. These were words that would compel Lillian to understand, perhaps make her willing to forgive her father for the wrongs she had held against him her whole life. It might occasion Lillian accepting her own part of their loss.

Lucy prepared a tray with a mug of broth, some buttered bread, a cup of tea and a cookie to tempt Lillian if she were awake. She carefully placed the folded pages between the cup and the dish of bread. Carrying the tray down the hall, she gathered the courage to face the problem with Lillian, and to bring it to some resolve. Lillian had little time left and should come to peace and comfort at her end.

Opening the door quietly, she set the tray on the stand then gave her attention to the elder woman who seemed to be sleeping. Lucy was about to speak when she noticed Lillian's chest was not rising and falling.

"Oh, God."

This is a cruel trick, she thought. But then, Lillian had been in decline for weeks. A conflict arose, regret at the loss, relief of the suffering for this late-found sister. She sat in the chair at the bedside and calmed herself. Acceptance was a part of life, a part with which she was well acquainted. She was surprised to find tears falling freely. She did not deter them. The tears were a sign of this loss, a necessary part she allowed herself. This moment of privacy had seldom been available in previous events of loss in her life.

"I'm also closer to my own end," she admitted softly.

Returning to the kitchen, she regained her command, knowing what to do. She opened the screen door to find Grace and her young man on their knees in the garden. "Grace, come in and wake your mother. See if she's able to come downstairs. You, young man. Go find Jackson and send him up here as soon as he can come." She clapped her hands, waking them from the stupor her orders seemed to cast over them. "Now! Go now!"

The spell broken; the young pair moved as directed without a backward glance at each other.

"What's wrong, Gram?"

"Wake your mother if she's sleeping. Ask her to come down if she's able. We'll discuss everything when your father gets up here." Lucy was too distracted to notice Grace's confusion. There were things to do, decisions to be made.

In the meantime, the family had to eat, so she would fix a lunch. If they ate it or not, it would be ready for them. And everyone could use a fresh pie, and bread. Grace would help.

* * *

"What is it, Mother?" Jackson hadn't shut the screen door behind him before asking. "You scared young Earle to death. He was out of breath when he found me and couldn't talk till he calmed down. He said you yelled at him?"

"Never mind that. Sit down. Emma and Grace will be down here in a minute. Oh, don't worry, it's not Emma. She isn't much better, but she's on the mend."

"Lucy, what did you want? I was going to come down for noon anyway."

Jackson searched Emma's face. "How are you, Em?"

"I'm all right, Jackson. Do you know what this is about? Is Archie OK?"

"He's on his way here. I sent one of the men for him."

"I called you here because Lillian has passed, just half an hour ago." Lucy surveyed the faces surrounding her, some of shock, most of surprise. "She was talking to me this morning, and I may have upset her with a letter left for her by her father."

"Her father? You mean my grandfather?" Jackson was incredulous. "My grandfather Kelty left her a letter? And you've had it all this time?"

"I didn't remember it till recently. He left it with Ike, and when I remembered, I started looking for it. I found it just this morning."

"The letter upset her? What did it say?" Emma asked.

"Let's sit down. I have some dinner cooking. I started bread and a pie. I don't know when I thought there'd be time to finish them. I'm a little shaken. I've been expecting this for some time but didn't think it would be today."

"Rest a minute, Mother. Catch your breath. There's no reason to rush now."

"Do you want some tea, Gram? Mama? Or you, Dad?"

"No, Gracie. Give me just a minute. In fact, I have the letter here, I just read it."

"I'll look in on Lillian, Gram."

"No! Gracie, you stay out of that room till I get it cleaned. You know what the doctor told us. The less traffic with that room, the safer it is for all of us." Lucy paced the room while the others sat quietly, chastened by the reminder.

"It upset her that there was a letter from her father, but she didn't read it. I took it to the kitchen to read, and she was gone when I went back again."

"What did Grampa have to say, Mother? Is it something we can hear?"

"Jackson, I think you should hear it, we should all hear it. The words hold meaning for us, at the very least, telling us to count our blessings."

Archie came in through the screen door, letting it slam behind him.

"Sorry. What did you need, Dad? Why are we gathered here at this hour?"

"Sit down, Arc. Aunt Lillian's died," said Jackson, pulling another chair away from the table for him.

"Is that a letter? Who's it from, Gram?"

"Archie, it's from your great grandfather. Your gramma is going to read it to us." Emma put her hand on Archie's hand as he sat beside her.

"This letter was written about forty years ago. Lillian left Kelty Farm years before, and her father never knew where to send it, so he left it with Ike. Ike didn't open it and didn't mention where he had put it. I only found it just this morning. When I gave it to Lillian, she refused to read it, and asked me to take it out of the room. She was upset. So, I brought it to the kitchen, and I read it."

"What did he say to her, Mother?"

"He said what any of us would have said in his place. She was very young when she left her home, and his heart ached for the suffering he was sure would meet her in the world. She never spoke of those years, but we can see what thanks the world gave her for the little she got out of it. I will read the letter, and we can, perhaps, each find a meaning for ourselves in it." Lucy looked at Archie, who held her gaze for a moment then looked away.

"Before that, I want to remind you of the Doctor's instructions. Lillian must be buried right away. I know you have a coffin ready, and that should be brought up and put beside the bed. I'm going to wrap her in a quilt I made long ago, and we will close the coffin. Unless you say otherwise, Jackson, I think we'll put her father's letter in with her. I've marked out a grave so if you'll have some of the men dig it out, we will bury her this afternoon."

"This haste is unseemly. And aren't there reports of death to go to the town clerk? People may think we're hiding something." Emma hesitated to add her opinion but felt the need to be heard.

"Em, we're not concerned about that. The Doc said we could keep her here and care for her ourselves if we followed his instructions. I'll send someone to town to notify him and he'll take care of anything official. Is there anything else now? I'd like to hear the letter."

"In fact, Jackson, you read it. As I remember his voice, yours is like to it. Do you remember him?"

"I remember a lot about him. He taught me to play the instrument. Pa said he could never learn, so Grampa taught me. Give the letter here."

Lucy passed the letter on, and then went to stand behind Arc's chair, her hand on his shoulder. He glanced up at her, then away. He knew she was warning him to listen closely.

* * *

In the morning light, the family, the doctor, and a few of the hired men gathered at the side of the grave freshly dug the previous afternoon and filled in upon receipt of the coffin. Flowers were brought from the gardens near the house and fresh flowers adorned several other graves as well. The minister read his service and spoke of death as a homecoming. The family sang a hymn and then Jackson took up the instrument.

The music wordlessly spoke of hills and streams, of air and trees, of grass and home. The bow washed over strings lovingly, releasing sounds rarely heard in this open place, yet at one with all. Jackson's eyes were closed, as if he searched for the music he needed, though every note was the right one, everyone there gathered into the moment.

When the music stopped, people let a sigh mark its end, and slowly walked away, down the side hill to the homestead, leaving the white marble tablets and the unmarked grave in the silence.

Jackson put his arm on his son's shoulders. "This was a homecoming indeed. A homecoming to Kelty Farm."

Jackson was surprised when Archie stopped and gave him a fierce hug. He held his son a moment. "Are you all right, Archie?" he asked softly.

"Yes, Dad. And thank you for letting me keep Lillian's letter"

17

1922: THE SPRINGTIME OF GRACE

"Ike's mother came here as a hired girl. Oh, there were women enough and more to do all that needed doing, but it seems there was some trouble among them, some who looked down on others, gaps, you might say, that grew between them and what wanted to be done."

Grace watched as Gramma Lucy's hands worked the dough more slowly. Then Gramma sat back in her chair, her eyes shining. She seemed to Grace to be seeing life in this kitchen as it had been years before she came here. Grace waited for Gramma to find the thread to pull that would bring a story out. Then, as Lucy began to smile, Grace relaxed: Gramma had found the string.

"Elishabet was distant from the family in those days, apart, staying in her room and waited on by Arthur's two younger sisters. She sat up there, old Elishabet, in the room over the parlor, the room where the heart window is. She was going blind, but her ears were better than eyes for knowing who was where, what was said."

Lucy reached across her bread board and took the sifter by the handle, turning the red knob back and forth, seeing no flour drop from the screen bottom. She rose from her chair, walked into the pantry, pulled out the flour bin and scooped another sifter full, returning to her chair at the table. Grace waited, an apple in one hand, a paring knife in the other. Lucy set the sifter on the edge of the board then looked down at her hands.

"Everyone lived quietly, if you can believe all those people could live quietly under one roof."

"How many people lived here then?" Grace asked.

"Well, there was Elishabet. Arthur ran the Farm and didn't say anything about the house unless it meant building on to it. There were two married sons and their wives, and some children. Two brothers were unmarried, but one was sweet on a neighbor girl. The two Kelty sisters, Arthur's sisters—set in their ways like—and any hired girls on the farm lived in the house. The hired men stayed in the barns or went home nights. Summertime, some camped by the river. They didn't keep many hired people in winters."

Lucy shook flour out of the sifter, set it down and kneaded the waiting dough.

"The Kelty sisters felt the running of the homestead was theirs to order, more than it was their nephews' wives. The sisters kept the wives working like hired help. The sisters had their own hands in everything, allowing the wives only drudge work, the humble work—work that everybody does some of and thinks nothing of, but if it's all you get to do, you soon come to know you're not an important part of the family, of the household, that you don't count for much in a house where those born Kelty have say over those who married Kelty."

She folded the dough into itself, lifting it, slapping it down again on the floured board.

"Women working under women have tough taskmasters where there's no love to smooth feathers," Lucy said absently. She stopped to look at Grace, though Grace felt her gaze slip right through herself and out onto some point beyond seeing. Grace shivered.

"So, came a time," Lucy continued, "when the younger boys thought to move on, not wanting—not able—to bring more women into the household. But the older brothers didn't want the younger to leave and pressed their aunts to leave off their harsh ways, to lighten the burdens of the wives." Lucy tore the dough into smaller pieces, forming each portion, flouring it, setting it aside.

"The sisters ruled the house. They made as if to move men and wives out of the homestead. It was like to be war—and the first to surrender were the brothers, leaving their wives to the untender mercies of the aunts." Lucy shook flour off her hands and walked to the lower cupboard, pulling open a door. She reached inside and lifted out a stack of bread tins, returning to the table.

Grace wondered how her grandmother could know all this. Grampa Ike hadn't been born when this story took place, and Lucy was younger than her husband.

"Soon the wives stopped doing the work left them to do, not doing anything the sisters directed be done, and the house was in sixes and sevens. The sisters began to cook, to wash, to clean only for themselves, retreating to their rooms, in service to themselves and Elishabet only."

Lucy floured her hands again, reaching for a handful of lard from the can on the shelf. She picked up a bread tin and coaxed the lard into each corner, along the bottom and sides, then set the tin aside and picked up the next. Grace put the apple and paring knife down.

"Well, the wives were unused to ordering the household, who should do what, when, and so on. Soon they were both baking bread and no one making meals, or both cooking meat and no one tending gardens. There was a winter week where only ham was had to eat, no one taking thought to preparing anything else." Lucy laughed to herself then became silent, intent on the row of bread tins she had assembled.

"Then what happened, Gram?" Grace prodded.

"So, help was needed, and Ike's mother, Madeline, came to live and work as cook. She could do it all and smile too. Anyone who watched knew where a hand was needed. She listened more than she talked and laughed or cried with the wives as no one had before. And it's not that she told anyone, 'do this,' or 'do that,' but that the wives—so unused to kindness and gentleness—wanted to help the person who was help to them, to their home, their lives."

Lucy dropped flour into the first waiting tin, swishing the pan, making the flour slide from side to side, into the corners, around the inner walls and top edges. She reached for another. "It's not always necessary to flour the pans but I do it anyway." She went on.

"If someone needed a dress made, it was Madeline who started them off, guided them through it. If someone needed hair curled for church, who but she did they turn to? Then when it seemed that this good soul had caught the eye of a younger brother, the wives turned their thoughts to smoothing the way for this ally." Lucy sat in the chair nearest her, dropped her hands onto her apron and stared at the floor.

"I suppose she loved him and that's why she stayed. It can't have been money nor the kindness of the Kelty sisters. And when they married, there was talk of them building another house, somewhere on the Farm. But it came to nothing because no one would tell old Elishabet about it, you see, to ask her permission. So, in the end, another Kelty brother and his wife settled into the homestead, and they did what the Keltys had always done, they built on. First it was just a bedroom for their privacy and then another and another for children that came along.

"Ike was born about a year later, the day they buried Arthur."

She smiled, more to herself than at Grace.

"By the time Ike came along, there were other children but no babies here. Madeline's second boy lived only two years, then came Hatti and Lillian.

"After Elishabet died, and finally lay to rest beside Arthur, the sisters moved into her room and gave up two rooms. That made some space. Then two of the brothers were carried off with influenza, and the wives went back to their families. The other brother lost his first wife, married again, but never had any children.

"Grace, look outside and see if any of the boys are around. I want some limb wood carried in to bake my bread by. I get a hotter oven with limb wood. Your folks will be back soon, and I want the house to smell of baked bread when they come." She got up from her chair, looking at the waiting row of bread tins.

Grace knew there would be no one about, that she would bring in the firewood herself. A couple of trips to the woodshed would fill the wood bin and she hurried, hoping Gramma Lucy would go on with the tale. No one else seemed to have time to listen to Gramma Lucy, at least not a whole morning. Though Grace had heard many parts before, this telling seemed more complete than she remembered.

"That will be enough, dear," Lucy said when Grace returned with the second armful. "Put it down gently so's not to raise dust on my dough." She was stirring the deep stewpot on the back of the stove, banging the wooden spoon on the edge of the pot before replacing the cover. Returning to the table, she spied the unpeeled apples and glanced at her granddaughter. "You'll have to peel faster if we're going to make pies, won't you?"

Grace laughed. "I'll peel and you talk."

"By now, you've heard every story I can tell. But I've always said it's a grandparent's job to tell the family stories. Still, I think you got a full load from your grampa and shouldn't need to hear much more from me." As she talked, she put a waiting loaf into a tin, set them on the warming shelf above the stovetop and covered each group of four with a damp cloth.

"Sometimes I feel like I'm still in school. It's like history, all the stories. They're just not written down. And every time someone tells more, I find another detail I hadn't heard before, or maybe had never caught. How do you remember so much of it, Gram?"

"Now I mean it, Gracie, you peel those apples. We're going to need them soon enough. As for all these tales, well I think they hang around in corners of the old house and finally just fall onto the heads of everyone here. But just you listen to whoever is telling because you will have to tell others."

"I want you to tell my children all you've told me."

"It may not happen the way you want, Gracie." Her voice was soft, regretful.

"Then I won't get married and have any children!" Grace reached for another apple and thrust the paring knife into it, cutting deeper than she meant to. She concentrated on the red of the apple, trying not to spill the sudden tears she felt.

"Gracie, there's no use worrying over things that will be whatever way they're going to be anyway."

"Archie says you know things, that you don't tell everything, but you know things. What does he mean?"

"Peel those apples, my dear, or we'll have only pie crust for dessert, and you can explain that to your father."

"Archie says you knew when Old Paul was going to die."

"He was an old man. It didn't take much knowing that when he got so sick, he probably wasn't going to get better." Lucy's brow furrowed.

"Archie said…"

"Your brother talks too much. His head is in the clouds, and he doesn't mean all that he says." Lucy threw a sideways glance at Grace.

"So why did you say you might not tell my children the stories? Won't I have any children?"

Lucy stopped avoiding the subject and faced Grace across the table. The dough and apples waited.

"Grace dear, I see sparks in you that will likely be your children, but I don't see your children. I think this means something to me more than is meant for you to know. And, yes, sometimes I know things, but I can't pick and choose to know, to not know. And sometimes knowing is more painful than not knowing. Now, peel those apples, my girl."

Grace watched her walk away, feeling very alone even with her grandmother in the room. Lucy opened a cupboard door, reached up onto an upper shelf to bring down a large glass bowl.

"This bowl has been here a long time. I like to use it when I make apple pies. If you fill it to the top with sliced apples you have enough for six pie fillings. We're only making four pies today, so you put your finger down the inside edge till you hit your knuckle, then fill it to there for four pies."

"Gram, how am I going to learn all these things? How will I remember it all?"

"Gracie, you've been learning since you were a little girl. It's only difficult when you worry about knowing it all to once. You already know most of what you'll need. Ike's mother told me about that bowl, and I just now thought to tell you." She set the bowl on the table in front of Grace and sat beside her, taking up a peeling knife and an apple.

"Tell me about Grampa's mother." Grace began to peel, dropping the peeling into the pail on the floor.

"These apples are going soft, it's a good thing to use them up."

"Gram, tell me about Grampa's mother."

"You sound like a little girl when you ask like that. It's hard to remember, even when I look at you, that you're all grown up, that you'll soon be off getting married."

"Tell me about Grampa's mother."

"All right, Missy, just see you keep peeling." She laughed, looked at Grace, then at the apple whirling at her knife. A long spiral of peel dropped off the end of her blade into the pail. She reached for another apple.

"Madeline was a do-er in the house from the day she came here. As the other women got older, left the homestead or died, she absorbed the work and carried on as if she were still the hired girl. And as the brothers gave up their responsibilities, Ike's father stepped in to take up the reins.

"When I came, all I ever got to cook was baked goods, sweet desserts and the like. No one ever asked me what I wanted for supper tonight nor thought I might have wanted anything different than what was set before me. Madeline ran the kitchen, and yes, the whole house, like she was set upon this earth to do just that and would till God told her different."

"But she had help, she had her children?"

"Ike followed his father around from the time he could walk, Hatti married before I came, and Lillian…she went away." Lucy stared into the bowl at the few white crescents of apple. She stopped peeling, her knife still under the apple skin.

"Then one night Madeline went off to bed and never woke the next morning. Come breakfast we had yesterday's bread, scrambled eggs and my double egg coffee cake." She sat back in the chair, sighed, and looked at Grace.

"I had no idea what we'd do from that day on. The good woman was dead and all I could think of was what I'd serve for dinner. Those were hard days, Gracie. I still miss her. I think of her often."

"You loved her, didn't you?"

"Yes. Everybody did. She was kind, easy to love."

"How did you know you'd love Grampa?"

Lucy laughed again; her eyes lit up as she considered the question.

"I know your tricks, Gracie. You peel those apples or I'll stop talking right now!" She beamed at Grace. "You know, I don't think anyone's ever asked about that. It's so long ago. Well, Gracie, this will be a new story for you." She picked up an apple that Grace had peeled and sliced it up, emptying the slices into the bowl, the core into the pail. She reached for another.

"Some things I knew from the start. Ike was an honest and upright man. He was well known to be temperate, and a man of some humor." Her hands again fell to her lap. She studied them.

Grace settled her elbows on the pine table, cradling her face in her hands.

"I could have had any of a dozen young men, landed, and bound to their land. I was Lucy Jackson, and my father had means." She thumped the table on the last word, paused then smiled.

"What are you smiling about, Gram?"

"Oh, I don'no. Sometimes I just laugh and smile at everything. The years fly by so fast I can't remember where we've got to when I awake of a morning. I set out breakfast for nine yesterday, when there are only five of us left in the house. And last week, I made a peach pie and asked one of the young men to take it down to Old Paul, never remembering the poor man's been dead these three years." She sighed.

"Anyway, you asked me to think back, and it stirs up days I had put away, and hardly have thought of since they happened." She laughed softly and smiled again to herself.

Grace waited.

"When I think of him, I see him on horseback, riding up to my father's house. He had a suit of clothes on that took my eye, and beautiful brown leather boots with shinny buckles on the sides." Her voice was edged in wonder, her face softened, and a smile flickered on her lips.

Grace sighed.

"Lord, that was near sixty years ago. It was in May." She sighed, remembering, then studied her hands in her lap again. "He had on a white shirt that dazzled my eyes in the sunshine. I was picking flowers from my mother's garden in the front of the house, snipping the stems against my thumb with a small knife and watching him approach. When I realized he was looking right at me and getting close enough to speak, I snipped a hollyhock off at mid-stem. And he laughed right out loud.

"Well, in fact that wasn't the first time I'd seen him—I guess I'd been watching him for years at church socials, at weddings and funerals—anywhere the Keltys came, I looked for him. I just, until that moment, had never seen him look at me—nor had any other man before that—looked at me the way he did as he sat high on that horse. Funny, I can never remember the color of that horse…"

Silence lay on the table for a moment. Lucy hummed a few unrelated notes. Grace waited till Gram's memories would bubble up and spill out again.

"When did I know I'd love him? I think I always knew." She laughed again. "The wonder was I didn't make more of a fool of myself before he declared his intentions toward me." She laughed another soft laugh. "Oh, we broke a lot of hearts, Ike Kelty and I, but never each other's."

"But how did you know he was right for you?" Grace insisted.

"Gracie, why don't you tell me what's really on your mind? I know you can't be wondering about your grampa and me at this late date. Aren't you really asking about yourself…? And young Earle?"

"Archie told me there would be no fooling you, Gram."

"What is it you want to ask?"

"I asked about you and Grampa because I know how that turned out and I wondered if it started like this…" Grace stood up, crossed her arms and walked to the window. The sunlight was bright outside but did not reach this window till afternoon.

"Grace…"

"It's only that I'm so confused whenever I see him. It's all I know how to tell you." Grace folded and unfolded her arms, finally squeezing her fingers into a two-handed fist before her.

"Perhaps you'd better tell me more, Gracie," Lucy said gently. "What is it that confuses you? Is it little things or big things?"

"Little things and big things both!"

Grace faced her grandmother. She came back to the table, sitting on the edge of her chair, her fisted hands on the table.

"My, my. That sounds bad…" There was a trace of a smile on Lucy's face.

"No! It's not bad, at least it's not all bad. It's just… confusing! I know it's April, but don't you find the flowers up early, their colors so bright this year, so beautiful? And the birds—the red-winged black birds are back, picking out their territories! The grass is showing green! And the willows are golden…" She searched her grandmother's lined face, her blue eyes. "They're so golden for April!"

Lucy took Grace's hands in her own.

"Gracie, the spring always turns this time of year. What do you find confusing in that?"

"That's not all. It's other things, a lot of other things."

"Tell me, Grace…, tell me, my dear girl."

"I love my home, Gram. How could I ever leave here?"

"Why would you have to, Gracie? Tell me about Earle."

"Earle isn't the only thing on my mind."

"Tell me what's worrying you."

"Well, Archie is getting serious with Annie Brist, and if they marry, she'll be the new Mrs. Kelty. But if I marry, I won't be Kelty anymore. I won't belong here."

"Grace, you'll always belong here. Don't worry about that. And I can tell you Mr. Brist didn't raise Anna May to be a farmer's wife."

Grace heard the disapproval in Lucy's voice.

"So, you don't think Annie will marry our Archie?"

"She very well may marry your brother, but she isn't going to be a farmer's wife, and she won't marry Arc till she's sure of that." Lucy pursed her lips. "Now let's talk about you and Earle."

"I want to stay here with you and Mother and Dad. I don't want to leave my home. I always want to be Grace Kelty and live on our Farm." Grace looked into her grandmother's blue eyes. "But I like Earle."

"And why shouldn't you, child. Earle's a fine young man. Your father tells how hard a worker Earle is. Not quick but determined. Always figures things out at his own pace." Lucy considers then continued softly. "He doesn't come from farmers. His folks don't have their own place. Seems to me he might be glad to stay right here if you gave him a little encouragement."

"Well, I like Earle…"

"You've said that, Gracie. Is there some question you want to ask?"

"It seems I ought to more than like him before I encourage him. Am I wrong?"

"Yes and no, my dear. I see you sit with Earle on the front steps and sometimes you're talking and laughing and sometimes you're both very quiet. I notice a lot of young fellows trying to get your attention but it's Earle that you feel confused about. You may be waiting to feel something you've never experienced before, but Gracie, maybe you feel about him the way you feel about everything you care for."

Lucy slid out of her chair and walked to the window.

"Grace, where would you go, where would you live if you had the whole world to choose from?"

"I wouldn't go anywhere. I'd want to be right here," Grace answered quickly.

"And how would you feel if Earle were going away?"

Grace stood up, hesitated then joined her grandmother at the window.

"I wouldn't like it. I wouldn't like it at all, but does that mean I love him?"

"Love? Is it love you're wanting, Gracie? Yes, and why shouldn't you have love? It's a good thing to have. I've seen people who loved one another but couldn't sit quietly together or talk for hours as you and Earle do."

"You and Grampa had love."

"Yes, and your ma and pa do too, though it's a quiet kind that many people miss. They lean on each other. They look for one another in a room, they smile at each other. They can sit for hours and never say a word. They seem to listen to everyone else talk, but they're really listening to each other listening. You and Earle do that. I've seen you."

"I thought love would be more…, I don't know, more something!"

Lucy laughed.

"Love will be whatever it is, Gracie, and usually more than anything you could wish."

"How would I know…"

"Gracie, just sit quietly, let love come to you. Be patient. You know that good things take time. You know that. And when it comes, it'll last."

She went back to the table, patted Grace's chair.

"Now come back here and peel those apples."

18

1922: A TIME FOR EVERY PURPOSE

"Earle, my boy."

"Yes, Mr. Kelty?"

Willing to please, I can see that. A good boy, will make a fine man for Gracie, thought Jackson.

"Maybe it's time you called me something besides Mr. Kelty. Seeing as how you're going to be family."

"Well, we're still a ways off from that but that'd be fine, sir. What do you suggest?"

"Grace calls me Dad, but as you recently lost your father, maybe you'd call me Jackson." Jackson knew the other hired men were watching for a sign from him that Earle was family. He saw the thought taking root in the young man's mind, the pleased look in the eye, the slow smile on his face.

"Mr. Kelty, I don't mind things the way they are, but if we come to it, I'll try to call you Jackson. It just may take me some time before that feels natural to me. I hope you understand."

"Earle, I hope you understand that it would be strange to have my Gracie marry a man who'd call me Mr. Kelty. That's what the hired men call me, not family."

Earle walked to the edge of the porch and put his hands in his back pockets. He was a slight figure seen there against the valley before them. He was very strong for his size. Jackson often was surprised by that quiet strength.

"The day you call me something besides Mr. Kelty, you and I will plant some trees in a place I've always wanted to see an apple orchard. But the season is short when planting is done. And there are other things to speak of that can only be spoken of as family."

Earle turned to face Jackson. The sun at his back threw a shadow across his face. He wasn't tall, not like Jackson's sons, slow to think, but sure of himself when he figured a way things had to go. Jackson thought there's a lot to like about this boy.

"I'll call you Jackson when I can, but sometimes I may call you Mr. Kelty. Don't take nothing by that, it would just be a slip on my part and wouldn't have any meaning."

"My wife calls me Mr. Kelty on occasion," he said with a smile.

"And your mother does now and then, too." They both laughed at this.

"Yes, well, Mother does about as she pleases, I guess. Nothing will change that." Jackson smiled again. "So when will you start?"

"Start, sir?"

"Calling me something besides Mr. Kelty. You and I have things to speak of and I'd like to get on with it. I also have some seedlings that need a new home." Jackson laughed.

"Well, today, I guess…Jackson, sir."

"You can skip the sir part, Earle. Jackson will do it." This was going better than he'd hoped.

"OK, Jackson. OK, I guess it's today then." Earle seemed pleased with himself.

"Well, my boy, you take a wagon in to Dudley's Store and pick up the saplings he has saved for me. They came special but you see that they all have new growth on them, and the roots are damp or have old C.P. take those off my bill. Sign your name on the receipt. He'll know that's all right."

"And the other things we need to speak of?"

"This afternoon when you return from town, I'll meet you on the hill closest to the road, opposite the house. I'll have some men working on digging the holes and we'll be ready to start. You and I will plant those trees over the next few days, and we'll talk then."

* * *

"Everything go well in town, Earle?"

"Yes, Mr. Kelty..., I mean Jackson. Mr. Dudley was ready for me and let me sign, just like you said." Earle handed the first bundle of seedlings down from the wagon to Jackson who set them upright on the ground.

"You looked them over? We're not going to pay for any dead trees." Jackson examined every bundle, handling each delicate twig and new leaf before taking the next bundle.

"Mr. Dudley said he looked them over close when the shipment came in, that you are to tell him about anything you're not satisfied with, and he won't charge for those. He said to tell you, 'Usual terms apply,' that you'd know what he meant."

Jackson laughed.

"That's the good thing about knowing someone for years and years. You can depend on them. You know what to expect, and they know you."

"Mr. Brist sends you his regards."

"Brist? How'd you come to talk to him, Earle?" Jackson turned his attention to Earle, the trees forgotten.

"He must have recognized the wagon, came over to me while I was loading and asked a lot of questions. Said he was an acquaintance of yours, Mr. Kelty. Is there anything wrong?" He wondered if he had made a mistake. Earle waited while Jackson thought.

Jackson went back to the trees he was examining. "No, son, you couldn't know. That's a man to exercise extreme caution with. If you tell him ten cents worth, he'll make a dollar out of it. Never tell him your business, nor anything about the Farm. For years he's had a weather eye out for our Farm, for our land, for anything else he can get from us. Don't give him the time of day."

"He wanted to know my name, asked about my mother, and Grace, like he knew us. Seemed real polite, Mr. Kelty."

"Jackson, remember? Let's forget about Brist for now. Let's get some of these trees upright with their feet in Kelty land." He pointed off to the left where the shelf of land was wider. "Someday I mean to build a barn over on this side of the valley. Up here, nearer the road, away from the house. We don't really have the right kind of barn anymore. We've made do with what buildings we had but soon we're going to need to modernize ourselves. I'm glad Pa isn't around to hear me say that." Jackson reached for a bundle of trees and carried it to the edge of the hillside where the land dropped gently to the river below.

"I can see the end of the valley from here, all the way to the big elm, Mr. Kelty."

"You're going to have to call me something besides Mr. Kelty for us to have this talk, my boy. Let's start down at the lower end where the holes are ready and get some of these trees in the ground before supper." Jackson walked away carrying two bundles. He smiled as he heard Earle scrambling to catch up.

"What talk are we having…Jackson?"

"These holes are paced twenty feet apart, ten to a row. We'll have fifteen rows between the bottom and the top by the fence on the road. I think we've got a little more than a gross of seedlings. I count twenty-five bundles of six, so that should work out. Let's carry some of the trees down first then we'll do the planting."

Earle was unusually quiet as they carried and placed the bundles in the middle of each waiting row. Finally, they broke open the first packages, separating the young trees carefully, protecting the tender roots. On hands and knees the two men put each tree in a prepared hole, pulling the rich soil onto the roots by the handful.

"Feel the texture of the dirt on your hand, the grainy clumps that stick together. Stones would grow in this soil!" Jackson laughed, silently remembering his father and grandfather before him making up that old saw. He glanced across the river, up past the house to the land above. He couldn't see them from here but was aware of the rows of white tablets marking the lives of the people who had wrung a living out of this dirt on his fingers, under his nails.

"How long have you worked at Kelty Farm, Earle?"

"I worked some summers, then on and off for two years, and now almost a year steady, Mr. … Jackson."

They both laughed at the hesitation.

"So, you've been here through every season. You've seen how we get from spring through the winter to spring again. Pretty much we do the same things year by year. Always something to be doing." Jackson noticed his handprint in the soft soil around the newly planted tree, larger than Earle's.

"This was my first winter on the Farm. I never realized there would be work to be done in the winter too. I mean I knew the stock had to be cared for, milked and all, but the everyday work, I just never thought of the Farm as an all-season workplace, I guess."

"Have you found any job here you wouldn't be willing to do every day?"

"No, I don't think so. And anyway, there's always people around to help, people who have done any one job so many times they hardly notice when they're doing it again. I like the variety of things to be done. There isn't anything I mind doing, and I hope to get better at doing what needs to be done as time goes on."

"So, you like working on the Farm?"

"I've never really thought about anything else. My dad and I used to help out on my grandpa's farm when a time came they needed us, and when Grampa sold out, I came here to work summers and sometimes in the fall. Now Dad's gone, my ma's living with my sister and her husband, so I was glad to find work and a place to live here."

"And now there's Gracie…" Jackson carefully spread the net of roots around the bottom of the hole, scattering handfuls of soil to cover the moist, delicate tendrils.

"Gracie… Yes, she and I have known each other a long time. And I get to see her every day since I've been here. There's surely no one else like Gracie. I'm going to take good care of her, Mr. Kelty, you can depend on me for that."

"Jackson, remember?"

"I mean Jackson. You can depend that I'm going to take good care of Gracie."

Jackson smiled to himself. He could hear the earnestness, the determination in Earle's voice. He recognized the tone of a man making a promise to himself. Jackson didn't worry about Gracie, she would always be sure she was being taken care of, at least as little as she ever needed someone else to care for her.

"I will depend on you for that Earle. I just wonder what you have planned for yourself, for the future. What kind of work you see yourself doing to provide for your family, for children?"

"I know I'm always going to work hard, I know that, sir. I haven't any real plans, if that's what you mean."

"Do you think you'd mind living here, being a part of Kelty Farm? This has always been Gracie's home. I think she'd be glad to stay here."

"Would you want me to do that, Mr. Kelty?"

"I wouldn't want you to stay unless you thought it was the best thing for you. Kelty Farm is good to those who want to be here, but hard on those who'd rather be somewhere else. This is already Gracie's home. It could be yours too. That's one thing you need to think out and be real clear about with yourself, and with Gracie."

"Is this one of the things we need to talk about, Jackson?"

"Yes, it is."

"And there are others?"

"Just a few, and we don't need to look at them all today. While we have this time together, just you and I, maybe we'll take up another of those things we need to talk about. Are you willing?"

"I think so, Jackson."

"Earle, if you're going to live on Kelty Farm, I'll be sure you get a good view of everything that needs doing season by season, year by year. You'd want to know these things to be better able to look ahead and plan your work. You wouldn't always have someone to tell you what needs doing next, what to have the men working on."

"You'd always be here, and Archie."

"I mean for you to look into the future, to see the long years ahead. I won't always be here, and maybe Archie wouldn't be either."

"I'd be here by myself?"

"You'd have Gracie. But leave all that. I just want to say that if you think you'd stay here, then I'd want you to take on some responsibilities, to be alert to what needs doing, and to learn to do things well enough to show someone what to do, how to do it. Just like today. You've seen me plant these seedlings, and if you watch carefully enough, you could do it yourself. This isn't a job needs doing every year, but when you come to do it, you need to know how or get someone to show you."

"I can see that. And everything needs doing sometimes, so if I was to watch, I'd eventually see everything done now and again."

"That's what I'm telling you. I would want to be sure you know what's expected of you and give you the chance to ask questions and know what you need to know. Are you all right with my telling you these things this way?"

"Sure, Jackson. I appreciate your trouble. "

"This will be no trouble to me, son, it will be a joy."

"I'll really try hard to pay attention and get things right the first time."

"That would be a lot to expect of yourself, but it's a good thing to aim for, Earle. Now we're going to talk about one of those things, and you stop me if this is too difficult for you to talk about."

"Too difficult? Like if I don't understand or want to ask questions, you mean?"

"Like everything else you have to learn, this is something I've taken time to tell each of my sons just as my father told me. So now I'm going to talk to you like I would if you were my son. I don't know if your father had anything to say on the subject of women…"

"Well, sir, knowing my ma, he didn't have much to say."

"I didn't know your folks more than to speak to at church, but I always thought your dad was respectful of his wife, and that's a good thing. Now, I'm not going to speak to you like you was some blear-eyed pup, but there are things a man ought to know, things it behooves a man to know, things, well, things that are on a man's shoulders as to how they turn out. And if they don't turn out well, so much else is closed, lost, and maybe lost forever."

"I guess I don't know what things you might be referring to, Mr. Kelty."

"I mean to be talking about the congress between a man and his wife."

"Oh, that! Well, my pa said that happens as it happens, and there's no telling aforehand how it will be between any man and his wife, nor any telling afterwards either."

"I'd disagree with your father, no disrespect intended. My own pa had words with me on this subject. I kept them in mind all my married years and they still hold weight with me. Some things we'll talk about closer to your wedding, but some I'd like to share with you now."

"I've some idea what's required, sir,"

"Maybe you'll already know all these things, but it would ease my mind to tell you anyway. The first thing a man must know about a woman and to keep in mind is that women are always stronger than they look, sometimes and some ways stronger than men are. That never excuses you from doing everything you can do for them. I just tell you because it comes as a surprise to a man that his woman can be depended upon to bear his burdens with him, can be expected to know as much as he knows about how to get through a problem that concerns them both. Just store this away and keep it ready, the time will come when you understand this better."

"Yes, sir."

"And remember, this woman is your friend for life. She's always going to be beside you; she'll bear your children and probably be there to hold your hand when you die. Respect her. Honor her. The better you are to her the more you can respect yourself, the more right you will feel inside."

"This is not what I thought this talk would be about."

"I expect you know what you need to know about the other, and we may talk another time about that. Today, I'd only add one thing. Never do anything she says no to. You'll pay the long dollar when you go against her, believe me."

"I'd never do anything Gracie said no to."

"That's a good resolution. But anytime you have thought a thing through, and you don't think she has seen your point, talk it out. Don't give up easy on something important to you.

"We've done enough for the day, Earle." Jackson could feel his back complaining about the bending and reaching he had accomplished today. He surveyed the stand of new trees in the first rows planted.

"It's not every day you do a day's work and can see the results of that day. Most days you have to work along believing that this day and all the days together will add up to something worthwhile. One day's work is often forgotten in the middle of the next day's. But in a few years, we will sit on our porch with babies all around our feet and we'll look over here to see the white blossoms in the spring, the red of ripe apples in the fall. In between, we won't have to see the traffic on the road beyond our fence line."

"I'd say this is a day we'll remember, Jackson."

"Why don't you come to the house and have supper with the family tonight, Earle?"

"Thank you, Jackson. I'd like that."

19

1923: GOD'S GOOD TIME

"I don't know as this road ever will be good enough for a car to run over. It's never as smooth as the sleigh in winter." Jackson's hands gripped the steering wheel, his eyes intent on the road ahead. "The creamery complains our milk is almost gone to butter when they get it into town. Course, when there's a better road, it'll be better both ways, and Lord knows we have enough traffic to the Farm."

"Everything changes, Pa. All in God's good time, Gramma used to say." Arc watched his father's face and saw the wince at the reference to Gramma Lucy.

"You're only remembering half of her saying, son. The way she'd say it, you knew she meant that God's good time went a lot slower on Kelty Farm than other places. We Keltys aren't big on change, in God's good time or not."

"Getting on towards town, Pa. If you've got something that needs saying before we get to the station, you might want to bring it up now." Arc studied his father, a big man, larger than Arc, taller, broader in the shoulders though still farmer-lean, strong even now in his late fifties, stronger, Arc thought, than he himself would ever be. Jackson gritted his teeth, pursing his lips, a sign Arc had been watching for, revealing the muddied waters the older man tried to hide under light comments on the condition of the road, and the shabby appearance of the several farms they passed on this ride into town. Arc watched his father tug at the collar and tie worn for the occasion of his son's train departure. Jackson hunched his shoulders a hundredth time, trying to find the freedom for his large body that his usual farm overalls allowed.

"I only bought this car so's my father could have a ride in one. He didn't like cars, thought nobody but a fool would give up a horse and carriage. I wanted him to try a car. Couldn't see any way for that to happen so I bought one." His eyes stayed on the road; his jaw relaxed.

"I remember when you got it. Could it be ten years?"

"Eleven. In the summer. You boys were so excited." Jackson laughed. "Everybody was crazy to be the first to ride, everybody but Stewie. Couldn't get him off a horse. He was just like Dad for having a horse under him." His voice fell away.

"You took Grampa on the first ride, Andy, Phillip and me in the back seat. We were doing fine until we came down the long hill and you couldn't remember where the brakes were."

"Your grampa didn't know anything was wrong and near the bottom we passed Mrs. Wilder in her surrey. Pa tipped his hat and said, 'Good day.' You boys were laughing, and I couldn't find the brake. I couldn't guess what all your noise was for… Finally had to aim for the swamp. We sunk to the bottom of the doors. Pa just looked at me and said, 'What'd you do that for?'" Jackson laughed again, sharing the moment with his son.

"One of you boys had to run back to the Farm for a team of horses to pull us out. Pa never let me live that down."

"Stewie was sure mad he missed that…"

Jackson's jaw was tight again.

"Let's talk about us, Pa, you and me." Arc faced forward, not wanting to meet his father's eyes.

"Arc, seems we've said it all, I guess. What's left?" He paused. "I mean, we've talked this all out. You're set on going and we're in agreement, your mother and I, you need to go. You've got cash money in your pocket. You've got a suitcase full of new clothes. You've got our blessing. What's left to say, son?"

"Pa, I feel like you're letting me off the hook too easy, that I'm running out on you, on Mother, on the Farm." Now he found himself pulling at his own collar and tie, wondering if he could wear one the rest of his life.

"Well, like we said, Archie, we've talked this out. You're doing what you want to do. I can't begrudge you that, it's what I did myself." He glanced at his son. "And you're more important than the Farm."

Arc looked away.

"Archie, I've said it over and over, and if one time more would help it go down easier on you, I'll say it again. You weren't cut out for the Farm. You never had your mind to it on good days when you were trying. Where's the sense of giving it more time than you have? The family knows you gave it all you had. No one thinks of you as running out. You'll have to come to some peace with that. You'll have to find peace with yourself." His voice was even. "Maybe it'll come in this opportunity you're looking into." He was not saying more than his words said.

"Pa, I don't know how this is going to be. A day without seeing you? Week in and week out in this school? I wanted to go to school, would have done it sooner except..."

"Except for Andrew and Phillip going off to war? Off to die? And Stewie and that damned horse? I know all that, son, and I appreciated that you stayed when we needed you." Jackson looked away; his eyes strained toward something he could not see but knew surely was there.

"A man doesn't raise his sons and love them to cast them out into the world. But what can he do when the world comes for them, and they are willing to go? But God's voice is to be heard everywhere. It is in the silence. We hear it, but do not know the given words. His voice tells of miracles, of prayers answered." He turned back to his son.

"Now you need something for yourself. It would be wrong to stay, wrong for anybody to want you to stay."

Arc heard the words, had heard them before as often as he'd asked. The words were right, but something still wasn't settled inside of him.

"If this doesn't work out, I'm coming back."

"We're all expecting you to make a big success. You've got it in you to do well in this. It's something you want, there's no reason it won't work out."

Arc knew his father would give anything to have a pipe in his mouth, in his hand, the sweet smoke rising from it, sucked in and exhaled. It relaxed his father, the holding of the pipe bowl, the spaces the smoking allowed in his speaking. His father had never mastered driving to a degree that would give him a free hand to hold a pipe.

"Mr. Brist says a year of this school and a year working for his insurance company will put me right out in front, in a position of having my own branch office, maybe in Boston or Albany. Then I'd have the where-with-all to marry and have a family of my own."

"If it's married and family you want, Archie, no Kelty ever depended on a Brist to give him that. It's being away from the Farm, that's what you want. You don't need Brist and his company. You go to your school. When you're done, you look around and see if there's not something else that you'd like better than Brist is offering. A young man with your character could do well in many endeavors."

"Pa, you're forgetting Anna May."

"Anna May Brist. Well, Archie, if she's the one, you don't need her father nor his business to have her. If it's right, it won't matter if you take her father's offer or not."

"It matters, Pa." He had purposely kept his voice low but the words seemed to take on heaviness he had not meant.

"Matters? To you? To her? Or to Brist? Archie, don't do anything depending on that man's future good will. He's not to be trusted. I know the man, knew his father, his family. His people have been around..."

"I know all that, Pa. Almost as long as the Keltys. They used to be pig farmers, worked on Kelty Farm, used to spell their name differently. You've said all that. It doesn't change anything."

"It does. If you don't know who a family has been then you can't know who they're going to be."

"People can change. Look at me. I'm changing who and what I'm going to be."

"Leaving Kelty Farm doesn't change you into something else. You'll carry all of us with you. You'll still be the fine person you would be here. It may be harder on you, but you will be. You won't have any choice."

"No choice?"

"Archie, you come from strong stock, good, honest, upstanding people. An apple doesn't fall far from a tree like that. Whatever you do, you have the inner qualities to prosper. And that's something you can depend on."

"Some would say Mr. Brist has prospered. Some would say his family's done well."

"Brist has prospered, but by means you'd never employ. And he hasn't done near so well as he'd like. Time and again he or his father has tried to interfere with the Keltys. At every setback I've had, he's been right there, offering to buy the Farm, wanting to buy land. He's a crow, sitting high up in a tree, watching, waiting."

"That's nothing to do with Anna May."

"It's good that you'll be away now. You have a look around while you're gone. You take a good look around."

"Anna May and I have spoken of a future together. I know her father is agreeable, as long as there's no hurry."

"Well, enough said about that. A lot can happen. Let's not get too set in our thinking. There may be choices to make that you can't see from here. You may find you don't want what seems so ripe for picking now."

Arc heard the reserve in his father's voice. He thought of all that had passed between them this morning, more words than his father often said in weeks.

"Gracie seems happy."

"Are we done talking about you and me, Archie?" Jackson snorted. "You better not play cards for money, son, you're pretty easy to see through."

"I just mean that Gracie seems to be taking to married life pretty well. She's always whistling, walking around singing to herself. Like she and Earle have some secret life they've discovered that no one else knows about. It's kind of funny, and special at the same time. I'm happy for her."

"It's the second flowering of love."

"The second…?"

"Well, son, there's the bloom of love, when two people set eyes on each other and don't see anyone else in the world even standing beside them. It's like that other person was some new continent they've discovered. Then the first flowering, when the two can talk it out, can agree on what it is they want from each other, what it is they have to offer the other. That's when they decide that everything is possible. That's commitment, marriage, the straightening of the paths between one and another. The looking down the road and knowing you've made the right choice." Jackson smiled as he expounded.

"You sound like the wise old man, Pa, like you've been there!" Arc laughed.

"Then comes the second flowering, the love you fall into that you couldn't have guessed at before. This can happen soon after the first flowering, it could happen over and over again. But only to those lucky few!" Another broad grin for his son. "And Archie, my boy, there's nothing like it, nothing like it in this whole world."

"Pa! I'm so surprised at hearing all this from you."

"Nothing like it in the whole world, Archie." He looked sideways at his son and then back to the road ahead. "And where do you think you and Miss Anna May stand in these matters?"

"I don't think I can say, Pa. I guess I don't know."

"That's something to think about while you're away. And I recommend you not settle for anything but the bloom that leads to the flowering. Don't settle, Archie. Don't you do it."

Arc thought about his father's words, watching the distance between themselves and the station shorten.

"I'm going to miss you, Pa."

"We'll all miss you too, son, but we're happy for you." Jackson slowed the car and glanced at his son, eyes meeting eyes. "And you can believe that, Archie." He brought the car to a stop near the loading ramp. He turned the key and sighed when the engine sputtered and stopped.

Jackson glanced the length of the station platform. Finally, he stepped from the car, stretched his back and arms, and reached for the two smaller valises.

"Looks like the train is already here, son. We must have taken longer to drive in than usual. Better hurry."

Arc carried the larger bag, striding a length behind his father. He couldn't seem to focus on leaving, kept thinking ahead to coming back, maybe for Thanksgiving or Christmas. He saw a porter reach to take the cases from Jackson, but Jackson strode past the man as if he hadn't been there. Then Arc saw Mr. Brist waiting at the station doorway, smiling past Jackson to Arc.

"Good day to you, Jackson. You're not a moment too soon. Train's runnin' early. And you, Arc. You look ready for your journey. I envy you, a young man at the beginning of his quest." Brist smiled broadly at Arc as if he had already forgotten Jackson.

"Sir, I didn't know you'd be here. It's kind of you to see me off." Arc was suddenly aware of the cheap cloth suit he was wearing, the meanness of its cut compared to Mr. Brist's fine suit.

"Yes, Brist. Kind of you," Jackson offered gruffly.

"Nonsense, and I have a gift for you. I've purchased your ticket. Here it is. You can put away your money." He stuffed the ticket in Arc's hand and patted the fist that closed around it.

Arc stepped between the men and thanked him, ignoring his father's glower.

"Yes, sir. To be young and reaching for the future. It stirs me, I tell you. It stirs me." Brist tapped his walking stick on the board walkway.

"This stirs me pretty well, myself," Jackson threw in.

Suddenly the conductor called an, "All aboard!" The locomotive blew a huff of steam and a bell clanged.

"I'd better go. Thank you again, sir." He shook hands and turned to his father, his hand still outstretched.

Jackson easily gathered Arc into his arms, hugging his son, speaking into his ear.

"I love you, Archie. I want the best for you." He let go and stepped back.

Arc forgot the noise and the world. He saw his father in this moment, older, alone as Arc never thought of anyone on Kelty Farm.

"I'll miss you Pa. Say good-bye to everyone for me." He saw the sunshine glisten on his father's eyes, and he wished himself already aboard and away. He looked for the steps and the conductor's waving arm.

"Anna May says for you to write her as soon as you have an address. Good luck to you, my boy." Arc heard the words but kept his eyes on his father.

He stepped aboard just as the train began to labor into life. He looked back but the sight of his father was lost as the town receded from view. He sighed and wondered just what he was really feeling.

"God keep you, son," Jackson said to no one.

* * *

"That's a son a man could be proud of. Yes, proud of." Brist smiled after the departing train.

"I'm used to being proud of sons, Brist. There would be no need to remind me." Jackson watched the train grow smaller, picking up speed, belching smoke in its wake.

"Yes, of course. But he is the only son you have left, and you must feel a certain disappointment… I mean about the Farm and all. He was your last hope."

Jackson looked toward his waiting car.

"My hope as regards my children is my own business, Brist, my own and my family's."

"Jackson, I meant no offense."

"Didn't you?" Jackson faced him with no false smile. "I ignore your baiting so often that I may be wrong about this. It seems to me your son led the way when my two sons went to France and to their deaths. Your son sold that wild horse to my Stewart, and it killed him. And now your daughter expresses some small interest in my Archie, and he leaves us to go off to school, and looks to a future in your insurance company. Is there anything I've forgotten?" He raised his finger accusingly in Brist's face.

"Ah, yes. You want to buy my land, my family's Farm. Do you want to buy my name too?"

"No," Brist answered in his most polite voice. "Some of my grandchildren will have that name without my having to buy it. But Jackson, you can't think that the tragic deaths of your sons are my responsibility?"

"Stewart made the decision to buy that horse against my opinion. I respected him for his strength, and I take no joy that I was right and he was wrong. Andrew and Phillip? I couldn't advise them against going to war. I never took thought of the world outside of our valley. I didn't see the growing evil in the world that could reach into our quiet lives and wrench my sons away from me.

"I take responsibility for that. But how often I've wondered if they would have thought to go if your son hadn't beat the war drum and sounded a trumpet charge to justify his own going. And again, I say that my sons were fine young men and able to decide for themselves." He kept his voice even, his emotions private.

"And Archie? Do you respect his decision, a future that takes him away from you, from Kelty Farm?"

"I do."

"You can't think my daughter will ever be a farm wife?"

"I never had that thought." Jackson let go of a slow smile.

"I see your barns in disrepair. I notice your fences left down after a hard winter. You have land that's not grazed yet not under cultivation. We're looking at the end of Kelty Farm, aren't we?"

"You'll never see the day, Brist. Don't count us out."

"Change comes to all, even Kelty Farm," Brist said.

"Only in God's good time." Jackson smiled again at Brist, then walked to his car for the drive home.

20

1934: TRACES OF FIRE

"Don't ask me again. It's in your hands, Earle. You're leaning on me and I'm not going to be around to live with the results. You decide. You will live with your consequences." Jackson sat back in the rocker. He shifted his gaze to the far rim of the valley, at the blossoming apple trees. There was no sun this overcast morning.

Earle stepped off the porch but turned back. He studied the hard lines on the older man's face. Jackson had been saying the words for years. Maybe he meant them this time.

"I'll live with whatever I decide. I hope you can."

"If you're going to tell me again that we don't need the extra buildings which are putting our taxes out of our reach, I'll agree."

"I wasn't going to bring that up now." Earle looked across the valley, his back turned.

"If you're going to tell me that the new barn by the road is the only one we need anymore, I'll agree with you again." Jackson gazed into the distance, past the worn floorboards of the front porch.

"Jackson, ten years ago we both knew building that new barn nearer the road was the right move to make. Neither of us could have known these hard times were ahead, that things would go this way."

"And if you're going to ask me what to do about the buildings we have that have outlived their usefulness, I'm going to tell you again: I don't know." Jackson did not look at the younger man.

"What would be the use...?" Earle scanned the threatening sky.

"Don't ask me about the great barn my grandfather built with his father, that we don't need nowadays and can't afford to fix..."

"No one has put any work into that barn in twenty years and now it's beyond fixing. The roof leaks, the sills are rotting, it's leaning into the wind. Snow's going to take it down some winter. Would your grandfathers want that? Maybe we could save some of the beams if we had the manpower to take it down ourselves, but what do we need them for? Where would we store them?"

"I tell you I'm not going to decide about that barn or anything else."

"So, we're back to that." Earle stepped up one stair. He squared his shoulders and glared at the granite profile.

"You're not going to decide? Isn't that a decision? Leaving it in my hands alone is a decision, Jackson."

"I know that. I made that decision a long time ago." Jackson turned toward his son-in-law. "Were you listening then any better than you're listening now?" His voice had risen to a tone neither man was used to hearing from him. Somehow it felt good to him, raising his voice. He guarded his impulse to soften any word he had meant to say to this young man who had become more than a son-in-law, but his son as no other had before.

"Catch fire, Earle! If you don't do it now, son, you never will." He turned his gaze back to the tender blossoms of the orchard and, locking his fingers around his belly, he settled into another level of comfort in the old chair.

Earle walked away in a silence that lingered behind him, his steps slow, never rushing to a new thought, to any new solution.

"You want some tea, Dad? I'm making a fresh pot. Is Earle gone? I thought I heard him out here with you." Grace started to open the screen door but sensed she hadn't been invited. When he didn't answer she decided for him and returned to the kitchen.

Both hands on the tray, she elbowed the door aside. The cups rattled in their saucers and the pot spouted steam. She stepped past her father and down one stair, setting the tray by his feet, glancing at him, seeing him take no notice of her. Though she had been in the kitchen and the words between the men had not been clear, she wondered at the volume and intensity of voice she had heard.

"Where's Earle working the men this morning?"

"That's not up to me to know, Daughter. Your husband is master of Kelty Farm. It's time you both knew it."

She looked across the valley trying to guess what had his attention. Nothing seemed out of place. It had been warm for a month and the new orchard had budded and blossomed early. The river was still high with spring runoff and if it rained today, it would be higher tomorrow.

"Have some tea, Dad." She poured a cup and handed it to him. He stopped rocking and set the saucer on his knee, lifting the cup to his lips. There was hardness around his eyes she noticed. She thought again about the raised voices she'd heard from the kitchen.

"Is it going to rain, do you think?"

"That's not up to me either, Daughter. Never was."

"What's wrong, Dad? Did you and Earle have words?"

"No new ones, just some that don't seem to get heard unless you say them a little louder each time till they've been noted. I think Earle has noted some words today I've been telling him for years. I expect to have more rocking time in the seasons I have left." He glanced at her, then away. The hardness around his eyes spread to the set of his mouth.

"The baby's crying. I'll come back when I see what ails her." She went into the house letting the screen door slap shut behind her. She paused and bit her lip. She had forgotten how tight the spring was on the door. She looked back at her father, but he hadn't seemed to notice. He often told the boys not to let the door bang behind them. He said it was like the crack of a rifle when left to slam.

Grace wound her hands into her apron and went to see after the crying Marjory. She seemed to be sick often these days.

Jackson let the rocker start its mile less journey, its quest to work through the floorboards before wearing off its old rockers. He thought about the Farm, about how times had been when he was younger and his own father sat in a rocker on this porch wanting only peace, not command. He remembered his own mixed feelings of guilt and exultation when making decisions without asking Ike's approval. He remembered making mistakes, some big ones, and how Ike had never mentioned them.

His father had a way of saying, "It's a good morning to butcher hogs. Cold weather ahead." Or "Do you think there's dry maple enough to smoke hams this fall?" Ike had had a very light touch. Maybe Ike should have said, "Fix the great barn's roof," or, "Tear down the old carriage barn."

Ten years ago, when he and Earle had built the new barn on the other side of the valley, Jackson had thought of taking down the great barn, but couldn't bring himself to remove a board or beam. It'd seemed to him that if he wanted a new barn, he should be able to build it without tearing down another for the wood. And the great barn was a beautiful thing, well built, tall, graceful in a way all barns were but more so. Those beams still had strength then, but that strength had waned each year since with the leaking of the roof and the weight of the snow.

He pondered if it had been the use of the barn that had kept it alive. Perhaps filling it with hay every year had anchored it, had insisted on it being upright and in repair. Maybe moving to the new barn with its more updated and convenient design, its distance from the living area of the homestead, had been the reason he had let all the old buildings go. The new barn made it easier for the milk pick up, for the health of the wintered cows. Its roof didn't hold the snows yet allowed plenty of room to store the hay needed to get through a winter.

Jackson hated to think that it was pride in his vision to build a new barn that had cost the usefulness of the older building that his fathers before him had found to be enough. He knew he had loved seeing the beautiful lines of his design come to life under the labor of his new son-in-law as the building had risen from vision to reality. He suspected he had been very prideful in the achievement.

Yet there was truth in the need of the newer building. They didn't keep horses anymore for work teams, and a lot of the space seemed wasted in the great barn. Just a stall for a tractor took less space in the new building and was the only place they had to work on the machine when needed. The herd had been cut in size, getting more milk from a smaller number with improved graining and feeding methods. The newer building was easier to keep cleaned out, especially in the heavy months of winter when there was no way to distribute the end product the cows so cheerfully produced by eating. In fall and spring, it could be spread on the fields, whereas storing it sometimes caused discomfort to the cows within the closed spaces of winter.

Jackson searched the lines of the great barn from his porch rocker. He well knew without having to see the patches of missing shingles, the lean towards the rear that became more pronounced each season. Still, as he surveyed the building, he could see the pride built into it, the reality of someone else's vision, his grandfather, and great-grandfather, Arthur Kelty. In some way, deep in his heart, Jackson felt the history of Kelty Farm rested in that great sagging edifice. And he wondered where his eye would rest if it were ever not in his line of sight.

It did seem inevitable that a morning would come when the snows or wind would have taken it victim, that it would be a fallen giant, more rubble than worth the sorting. They would perhaps have to burn it where it fell. How far off was that day and how will he feel about it when it did come? As it surely must.

"Everything wants to come earthward," he reflected softly to himself.

The new barn had been the right move. The stock had changed. The tractor had made a big difference in how they did their work. It gave relief to the house from the noise and animal smells. The milking business was better served and more efficiently. Yes, the new barn had been the right move.

Who could have known crops would bring in so little these last years? It hardly paid to feed a cow for the price milk brought. Lately they had cut the herd again, selling off any animal they could do without. They had given away the last team of work horses to another farmer just to be rid of them. The scrap metal had sold, gutting the old sawmill that hadn't been used in Jackson's lifetime.

The town wanted to tax unused open land, so Kelty Farm had planted extra pastures in pine. They wanted to tax farm equipment, so he'd sold off or scrapped rigs and machinery that had been left behind in the change of times. Now it was the farm buildings. The number of buildings on Kelty Farm qualified them as a larger farm than any other around and therefore liable for the highest tax assessment.

"That's what comes from abundance of land and the years on it to build new and leaving the old standing. It's a wasteful way but I'm sorry to see the day we aren't allowed the luxury to walk away leaving unused buildings. We can't build up the Farm and use those old buildings anymore. It's the times. They're against us.

"Maybe it's true, what people are saying. Maybe we're at an end for Kelty Farm. Maybe when a man runs out of sons, he ought not expect things can go as he'd planned all his life. But I hope the day never comes when someone like Brist owns the land I'm buried on."

The rain began in gentle waves that marked the porch steps in dark splashes at first, then filling the spaces between. There was no wind. The rain fell downward, soaking the earth, ladening the blades of grass, weighing down the leaves of the flowers and bushes planted around the porch. Jackson wished for his pipe but it was inside the parlor by the chair where he'd left it last night. The porch door opened behind him. If it was one of the boys he would send them in for the pipe.

"Are you cold, Dad?" Grace asked.

'No, Gracie. I'm fine. Thank you for worrying."

"I brought your pipe and tobacco. I'll set it here on the..."

"Give it here, Gracie. Thank you again. I wish every father had a daughter as thoughtful and kind." He stopped the rocker, sorting the folds of the tobacco pouch, filling the pipe bowl, packing it tightly.

"I'm sorry if I was sharp with you earlier."

"It wasn't like you, Dad. I know you have a lot on your mind. Let Earle handle things. Sit back a while and rest yourself." She stood behind him, her hands on his shoulders. She noticed his shirt seemed too big on him, or rather that he seemed smaller inside the same shirts he had worn for years. For some time now, she had watched his belt being drawn up one extra notch at a time. She wondered if he was eating well, if he had made the change over to her cooking from her mother's since her mother died.

The smoke of his pipe rose in the still air. She smelled the cherry blend he always favored, that Grampa Ike had smoked here on this same porch. The rain made a dull roaring sound as it hit the ground. The soil had been well watered this spring and had stayed moist. This rain was more likely to run off than soak in.

Then his shoulders tightened beneath her hands. His gaze was fixed intently toward the top of the big elm that stood at the foot of the mill pond beyond their sight. Black smoke rose toward the sky. It grew in strength then changed to angry grey billows. Licking tongues of fire rose with the smoke.

"What is it? Should I go find Earle?" she asked.

"It's the icehouse. It's all but fallen down anyway. And Earle will see the fire… if he doesn't already know."

His voice was calm, his words spoken slowly. She felt the tension in his shoulders again that gave lie to his calm.

"I haven't been to the icehouse in years, not since Joseph was born. I guess I don't get out around the Farm anymore." She gripped his shoulders, caressed his neck, felt of his hair, a great shaggy mane wreathing his large head in grey.

"You'd have no reason to go there. We haven't used the place in a long time. No need to." He sighed.

Another column of black rose not far from the first. Jackson leaned forward in the chair.

"The mill," he said quietly. "Arthur's mill."

"The mill is afire? I've got to find Earle. Where was he working this morning, do you know?"

"I think we're looking at his work, Daughter. There's no wind. That's too big a blaze and too soon from the first to have caught by sparks." There was a deliberate pace to his words, a resignation.

"Dad, you can't mean that the mill has been set afire on purpose?"

He didn't answer. She felt his shoulder slacken beneath her hands. He sighed again. The rain hissed as it fell, splashing in water already on the ground. The smell of wet earth came to Grace but went unnoticed as she kept her eyes on the rising smoke at the end of the valley, below the rim of the hillside, beyond her view.

"Gracie, get me the instrument."

"Your violin, Dad?" She understood his words but didn't understand his need. "Shouldn't I send for Earle? Should I get him? Don't you want him to explain what he's doing?"

"I know what he's doing, and he doesn't have to tell me anything. It's his place to do as he decides. His and yours. Have him tell you if you need to know."

"Did you tell him to do this, Dad? Did the two of you decide to do this?" She was suddenly aware of holding her breath waiting for his answer.

"No."

She waited but he said nothing more.

"You want the instrument? Is it in your room?" She didn't recognize her own voice.

"It's in the parlor, behind my chair. Joseph and I were playing it a few days ago."

"Sunday. Yes. I remember. He seems to be catching on. I'm glad he has you to teach him." She patted his shoulders but couldn't let go.

"Joseph is going to play as good as Archie or Stewart. Maybe better. I offered Archie to take the instrument with him when he got married but he said no that it belonged to the Farm. I guess he was right. It was Arthur's from his father. I wanted to pass it to a son of mine but I'm going to give it to Joseph when he can play it better."

"You keep it, Dad. Joseph can learn it from you better than he would on his own."

"Gracie, I think you show someone what you know and then you stand back and let them go. It works out how it works out."

She dropped her hands from his shoulders and went to the door. She paused, sending her thoughts through the rain to her husband.

"What are you doing, Earle?" she said more to herself than not. She entered the house.

The soft thump of the screen door as it came to rest behind her seemed a signal to Jackson to continue rocking. He relit his pipe and coaxed it to burn, sucking hot smoke into his throat. He exhaled slowly, the pipe in his hand, hand in his lap.

Grace brought the instrument to him. She set the case across his knees and sat on the top step by his feet. She drew her knees up and cradled her arms inside the high front of her apron.

Jackson thought she looked more sixteen than thirty.

He watched the tractor come out of the orchard, down the far hillside and onto the road across the bridge in the valley. It turned off before the bridge and went out of sight again. He could hear the motor chugging and popping through the rain.

His hand rested on the smooth wood of the polished case. He felt the bulge of its center over the bridge of the instrument nestled inside. He half remembered his grandfather opening this case to show him the treasure. He certainly remembered the first time it had been put in his hands, the first time he had drawn the bow across the strings, the sound created where none had been. Jackson remembered the look of pride on his father's face as Ike's father had shown Jackson some elemental but necessary fingering exercises, the correct way to hold the bow, the setting of each string to perfect tone.

Jackson remembered the longing on Ike's face, the wanting of the ability to do what his son so easily learned from his grandfather. Ike never had had an ear for the instrument and so it had never come into his hand. Of Jackson's own sons, only the last two had any aptitude, and neither had the interest. Now there was Joseph, and maybe his brother Stephen.

The pipe set aside, he opened the case, took up the polished curly maple instrument and set the case down. He took out the bow, set the instrument beneath his chin and drew forth the first sounds. Its voice was clear in the heavy air. He set bow and instrument in his lap and peered through the watery curtain as a new column of smoke rose black on the other side of the river.

"What's over there, Dad? I don't remember anything being on that side of the river that far down."

"It's the sheep sheds. Haven't needed them for years. We should have torn them down and burned them at the sugar house. I think they're all rotted. He musta used gasoline to make them burn in this rain."

"What's he doing, Dad. Do you know?" She leaned forward, her chin on her knees.

"He's doing as he's decided it best to do. There's no one to tell him different. He'll have to live with what he's doing, and he knows it."

"Couldn't you tell him to stop?"

"I couldn't and I wouldn't." Jackson's fingers played with the strings, raising a sound akin to the rain.

The tractor came into view and four men sluggishly followed. Jackson held his breath a moment as they passed behind the great barn near the bridge, but they continued through the orchard along the riverbank. Near what Jackson had always called the back side of the valley, were the old chicken houses. Snows had flattened the best part of the unused buildings several winters back.

The tell-tale plume of smoke rose.

"I should have done that myself. There was never a reason before. They weren't in the way, we just didn't use them, just left them lay where they fell. Well, I'm glad to see them go." His palm and fingers caressed a circle on the violin's face, and though it was uniformly smooth, he traced the swirls and burls of the patterns in the wood.

A whiff of burning wood finally reached his nose. He drew it in as if it were as sweet as cherry blend. He had expected the odor of this fire to come to him as he had not found the smell of the burning buildings in the lower valley. He'd always believed the air in the valley flowed with the river, had often thought of his life as laying in that river, waters rushing constantly over and away from him.

"Maybe it's not life but time I'm feeling," he murmured.

"What did you say, Dad?"

"Nothing, Gracie. Nothing that makes any sense."

"When's he going to stop? Do you know?"

"Maybe he'll take a notion that the house has been here long enough and burn it down around our ears. He'll stop when he stops."

"There's nothing funny about this!" she snapped.

"Do you see me laughing, Daughter?"

"I'm sorry, Dad. This must be painful for you. I don't understand Earle doing this without talking it over with you. What's come over him?" She stared across the valley to the base of the rising smoke, willing herself to see, to comprehend.

"There is no need to talk it over with me. I'm not the master of the Farm now, Gracie."

"But Dad…"

"Only one person can be in charge on a farm. My day is past, Gracie. Your mother and I hoped for this day. Today Earle stepped into the traces. The Farm is finally his own."

"Why do I feel so sad about it?" She was close to tears.

"It is only sad if you look back, on what's ending. Look ahead, Gracie, to what is beginning. If not for this day, what would the past be worth? If the Farm doesn't continue, what would we have worked for?" He needed to tell her and tell himself. "When I lie beside your mother on the hill, I want to have known that things are going to continue, to go on, to support life for you, your children, and someday for their children. Otherwise, my life would have been only for me and not for, well, for you and those to come after. No man wants to think his life was only about feeding himself."

Another source of smoke showed itself. Jackson and Grace observed but did not confirm this with one another.

"It's the carriage barn. Been empty since last fall. We don't need it for sleighs in the summer nor carriages in the winter. We have the car now, and the truck and tractor. All the old-time hay-polished-wood in the horse stalls has been ripped out and the horse barn remade to house the gas guzzling machines. Not a horse on the place. My father wouldn't know his Farm anymore."

"Not after today."

"You're right, Gracie, Pa wouldn't know the place after today. But his day is gone and now my day is gone. And to say the truth, I'm glad I lived to see this day."

On the floor of the valley below, the tractor chugged back into view. The men followed behind carrying red cans. In their bib overalls, their jackets hanging rain sodden and heavy on their shoulders, they marched in a solemn line. They disappeared behind the great barn by the bridge for long moments before reappearing and circling the old structure.

The building had a decided lean toward the south of the valley as if wanting to follow the river as the air did. Above it all the proud roof line was straight as the day Arthur Kelty had nailed the copper weathervane onto it.

The view of the great barn from the porch was not hampered by the softly falling rain. A mist would have been a mercy. Jackson laid the bow beside the instrument across his knees and his large, gnarled hands gripped the smooth arms of the rocker. Grace moved to sit at his feet, her attention riveted on the ant-like men in the valley. She couldn't make out which of those was Earle. She felt torn between wanting to be with her father and running to Earle's side, to see, to understand as both men seemed to understand.

Some men entered the building. The others waited. One crawled out the top window, pigeons flying out ahead and fluttering to the roof line. The man carefully worked his way along the ridge to the weathervane and loosened it with a hammer and bar. He lowered it from its perch on rope and worked his way back to the window.

There was an air of waiting, of expectation.

Jackson tucked the instrument under his chin and closed his eyes. As the bow took its place on the strings, a small trail of smoke came from that top-most window, another from the central air vent, and another from the peak closest to the bridge. The strings strained for a pitch and melody Grace had never heard but one with which the ancient wood of the instrument seemed familiar. The lick of flame followed the first black billow, and she hid her face in her father's lap. The music flowed, slow drops of blood leaking directly from a heart wound, beautiful, fatal.

Grace's tears fell onto his knees, but she could not look at her father. His melody floated into the rain though his eyes saw nothing of the engulfing flames covering the roof, the waves of heat returning steam for raindrops, smudge for redeeming baptism.

The instrument seemed to know pain and played chords and crescendos in deep and somber sentences. From the porch the "whoosh" of the falling roof was heard, and the heat felt, but neither player nor mourner was moved to look its way. The sound of the rain underscored all.

The voice of the fire joined the harmony in base and tenor, the shouts of the attendants added staccato beat. The sound of the tractor motor moving from the scene faded from the choir. The newly homeless pigeon flock circled the rising smoke. One end of the great barn buckled and fell into itself, crashing to the fiery floor, sending another towering wave of heat to beat a path up the hill and be caught under the jutting porch roof. Each sidewall sagged and leaned toward one another unnaturally, two strangers never meant to meet.

Through the maelstrom the notes of the swelling strings rose and fell without need to explain nor excuse the tears of all, though only each one knew his own. Player, mourner, fire bearers in the valley were witness to the death of the building that had stood proud and served well a hundred years. None had known this break of day that by evening smoking embers would mark where the great structure had hidden the earth below it for the century past.

A man built it with his son, the son had passed it to his own son, and that son on to Jackson. From this day Arthur Kelty's great barn was not a part of the heritage to pass on at Kelty Farm, except in memory.

21

1939: PASSAGE

"Joseph, get my pack basket from the shed, the smaller one with the harness on it."

"Where you going, Grampa? Mom and Dad'll be gone all day. Aren't you going to stay with us kids?"

"Joseph, you are old enough to stay with your sister and brothers. I want to go out for a walk. I'll likely be back before they get home. Now, please get me that basket." Jackson didn't like asking twice but he reminded himself all the time that he was no longer the ruling hand on the Farm anymore. These children had seen him surpassed by their own father and mother and didn't accord him the authority he had felt all his life before they came to be.

"Maybe you could go tomorrow so I could go with you. If you go tomorrow, Mom will make us some sandwiches and things to take along for the day. And we could do some fishing."

"Joseph, for now, will you get the basket or not?"

"I'll get the basket, Grampa, of course. I don't know why you want to go today instead of when I could go with you. You've taken me before. Remember we stayed out one night in that cave? Wasn't that fun? We could do that again sometime."

"Sometime, but not this time."

Joseph went away, and Jackson didn't have to see his face to know there was disappointment around the lines of his mouth and forehead. That was one way Joseph was like his father: you knew what he was thinking. Jackson laughed to himself. That was the reason he was so easy to teach. Anything they talked about, anything they did together, Grandfather and grandson, you could always tell when Joseph was done learning and you might as well stop teaching, the same as with his son-in-law, Earle. For all these years of working Kelty Farm together, Jackson knew when Earle was paying attention and when his mind was off somewhere else.

Knowing this, recognizing when teaching and learning time was over had saved a lot of heartache between them. Jackson had the opinion that there would always be another day. Nowadays, his instructions to Earle often fell on deaf ears, and he would soon realize Earle already knew about this thing or that as came to Jackson's mind to tell. Maybe there wasn't anything left to show the younger man, anything new to teach him.

Lately, Jackson didn't sleep so well, and he lay awake in the wee hours trying to remember if there was anything left that he hadn't told Earle, worried that a day would come when Earle would scratch his head and say, "Jackson never mentioned anything about this..."

"Maybe that's just my fear," he would answer himself. After all these years, if anything new came along, how could he have warned Earle, how could he have guessed about something that had never come up in his own time.

"I got the basket you asked for. It still has the Indian blanket in it we used last summer. I shook it out to be sure there were no mice nests in it, but Mom will want to wash it."

Jackson smiled to himself. Joseph had not given up on going with him and hoped the blanket might cause his delay.

"Just put it there on the chair. Now get me two bottles of root beer and a jar of blackberry preserves from the cellar. Go on, now. Is everything going to be an argument today?" Jackson watched Joseph's feet dragging to do this errand. He smiled again. He folded the old blanket so that it would protect the glass bottles from one another, then went to the shelf for bread and the ice box for meat. A nice hunk of roast would do. "Sandwiches indeed!" he exclaimed to himself.

Earlier this morning he had put his shotgun out at the end of the yard leaning against the fencepost. No one would see him taking it along, so no one would worry that he had it. He added the ammunition he had readied, the food stuffs, and when Joseph came up with the items from the cellar, he snuggled those in place as well. Since early this warm November morning, he had dressed for the day with extra layers of clothes and his warm hat with the earmuffs. His gloves were in his jacket pockets, his hunting knife on his belt, and loading the basket was the last touch. He was ready.

"I still don't see why you couldn't go tomorrow so I could go with you."

Joseph had a pout on his face, not a good look for a boy that age, his grandfather thought. "Next time, son."

"So where will I say you were going when they ask me. You know they'll expect I'd know."

"You could just tell them I didn't say." Jackson put his hat on making a mental list of things he might have forgotten. "Oh, I need a spoon, a soup spoon. And some matches."

"But they'll think I should have asked you. And none of us goes off alone without saying where we're going. So just tell me. And if they come home early maybe I could hike up to meet you."

"No, don't do that. You make me feel I'm too old to go off by myself. Did your folks give you that idea?"

"I don't have that idea at all. I just want to go with you, Grampa. You know how I like to be with you, to learn things from you. You see how well I'm playing the instrument these days. Mom says she's not heard such happy tunes from that old fiddle since she was a girl."

"Joseph, you're a good boy, a smart boy. And you learn very fast. But today, what you have to learn is that sometimes a man has to go off by himself, to kind of get reacquainted, if you know what I mean.

So, I'm going to follow the river up a ways and then turn off where the stream comes down from the mountain. I don't know how far I'll feel like going, but nobody has to worry for me. I can take care of myself, and I guess you'd know that by now."

"Grampa, you're not mad at me, are you?"

"No, boy. I'm never mad at you. Never. I just want to go off by myself, and being young, you don't understand that." He headed for the door, expecting some final word. But here again, Joseph was like his father. He would think it over and get to an answer that gave him peace. In many ways Joseph reminded Jackson of his own father. "Apples don't fall far from the tree, even if it's from a different branch," he said to himself as he left the yard.

Looking back to see if anyone watched, he grabbed his shotgun on the way down the path to the river. He was on the lookout for any of the hired men who might see him and report to Earle. When he thought about who would worry or not, he was thinking of Gracie.

He crossed by the stepping stones just short of the bridge and headed off to find the path going out of the valley. This was a cross of game trail and farm trail. It went across land they didn't oversee often, mostly planted in pine for the future.

Finally hitting the trail, he began to feel the weight of the basket on his back, but he shrugged it off, knowing it actually was light and he might not go very far. As the trail wore out, going from worn path to grassy divide of wild stalks, as the land passed from open to branches swishing in his face, he walked more slowly, reminding himself he was in no hurry. Jackson only had half an idea what he might do with this day. Walking along he realized that the day was warmer than he was dressed for, so he stopped by the river to remove some outer clothes which he put in his pack. "Maybe I should have taken the larger basket," he wondered.

As the land began to rise, the river branched several ways to smaller streams. He crossed the water again in a convenient place, watching for the stream that came down from the mountain. Finding it, he prepared for the upturn of the land, the lesser traveled way, and the rougher terrain. He adjusted his pace to match the path, determined not to wear himself out before finding a spot to rest.

He thought of his words to his grandson, about wanting to get away, to get reacquainted with himself. He had originally thought he wanted to get reacquainted with the land, perhaps to check on a far border, though he had no reason to believe it had to be looked over. Generally, it was the idea that he hadn't been there in a long time, and in this part of his life, a part where giving away and letting go of things was the norm, getting to a far point of used-to-be seemed a good idea.

These years, especially since Emma was gone, giving over to Grace and Earle, teaching Joseph and Stephen the instrument, letting go of doing things his way in favor of Earle finding a way that was right for him, had become Jackson's life. Deep down he knew he was getting too familiar with his rocking chair, too ready to be an observer on Kelty Farm instead of his years as the director of others toward some goal they could not see, did not know. Earle often made Jackson feel the job was done. Earle had been a slow learner, but stored everything said, shown to him, done in his presence. After a round of seasons, he put it together and had added lesson after lesson to his experience, making it easy for Jackson to believe that everything was well in hand.

For a time, Earle's success had been Jackson's success. With any goal met, any season's work completed, Jackson had taken secret pride in the younger man's progress. At some point, Earle hadn't noticed the compliments, the atta-boy pats on the back which were Jackson's way of saying that Earle was meeting and exceeding expectations. And the relief Jackson felt when he could step back and know everything was going well, if not his personal way, but going well enough to let go, was appreciated both by Jackson and Grace, the watchful eye on this process of change.

Today, something that had been stirring in him for a time had finally grappled with Jackson's excuses, and the time had ripened for this last challenge a man places upon himself. Was he still up for today's jaunt? Could he do this at all, or maybe he had passed the point where it was possible for him to strike out on his own, go where he pleased, take care of himself? Jackson knew he was well on his way to finding what limits were on him, what lengths he could allow himself to a point this side of being foolish.

He came into a clearing he had been expecting. It was a small meadow that soaked up the sun and acted as a run-off for the stream at its height. Perhaps the ground was too often saturated to allow tree growth, but the many times he had lingered here, he had enjoyed the sunshine. Long ago, he and Emma had shared a summer picnic in this spot. He savored the memory of a charming afternoon over which the two of them had shared secret smiles through the years. Jackson knew he could easily get back to the homestead from here in daylight if he were to turn back now.

There was a large web some absent spider had woven between stalks of dried weeds. He considered the design for a moment, wondering as he often did over spider webs, how the spider knew the design he would create. Did the insect know the full pattern or only know the next step to take that eventually led to the whole of the creation? He again thought about Earle and Kelty Farm. Earle sometimes did not show any evidence that he was aware of the big picture, but somehow all the little steps he took came out to a complete season, a complete year. Time after time Jackson had marked with satisfaction the progress Earle made.

Jackson sat on the grass and drank one of the root beers from his pack. Grace made good root beer, but not as good as his Emma had made. He considered the path of return, but it held no interest for him. He knew he had made preparations for a bigger adventure should he arrive at this spot and feel he could go on. He looked back at the trail but turned and walked forward.

"Sorry, Gracie," he muttered to himself with a smile.

His path was seldom out of sight of the stream flowing merrily away from him. The trees closed in again, but the birds didn't hush at his presence. They seemed as happy as the stream. The deep smell of the woods encouraged him onward. There were many tracks of small animals living in these woods. He had a sense that everything was where it was meant to be, including himself.

He came upon ground covered with beech nuts newly fallen since the last frost. There was no sign any animal had recently claimed this prize, so he helped himself by filling each pocket with the three sectioned nuts, remembering how many made a mouthful. Except in great quantities and with the addition of much patient labor, beech nuts were only a passing enticement. Having to depend on them was too much work, but the freshness of his breath and mouth that followed was worth a little effort.

When next he crossed the stream, he bent to drink from the fast-flowing water. It was cold and good, satisfying more than thirst to a man with a life-long claim on this land. He filled the empty root beer bottle and replaced the cap. He spotted the tracks of several white tail deer in the stream bank. Jackson was pleased with himself that his senses remained keen and that his breathing was steady. Perhaps he would reach the far outside of his half-realized plan for the day: the cave where the spring rose that fed this stream.

A few years ago, he and Joseph had come upon it from another direction, and he had shown the boy the old cave. Ike, Jackson's father, had said it was an Indian shelter, but Jackson had never seen any evidence of that statement. Ike often had a story to go with something, some place, but whether it was tradition or made up on the spot, Jackson could never be sure. Jackson himself had never been very good at storytelling and shied away from the opportunities that came his way.

But Gracie, now there was a storyteller. Her head was full of things Jackson only half remembered or didn't know at all. Sometimes when she told her children a story, Jackson was as entertained as were the children, though he had known some of the people the stories were about. Sometimes memories stirred of his own grandfather telling him tales of the family founder, Arthur Kelty, and many times he wondered if he knew anything but parts of the stories, too vivid to forget the small details of their make-up but too incomplete to tell anyone.

Maybe stories were more about the kind of people who the Keltys were--had been now that he was the last on the land to have the name. What stories would they tell about him?

Nothing much about what he had done, but maybe about how he had lived through all that had happened in the years of his life. He didn't think of himself as having accomplished much, mainly doing the same thing year by year, trying to keep up his inheritance, wanting to pass it on in some better condition than he perhaps had been given it.

Sometimes, looking back, he was astonished that he could still be standing. He and Emma had taken a lot of hits through the years, some bad ones. The loss of three sons had cost them mightily, but watching his Emma bear it had been the source of his own strength. Seeing the heartfelt effort his son Arc had made on the Farm, though his own dreams were shunted aside, had forced Jackson to take up the reigns again, to lighten his youngest son's load. And when Gracie had found a sweet communion with young Earle, Jackson discovered the way to let Arc go into the world as was his wish, and to marry though Jackson had held misgivings about the choice of bride.

And now were these last years. Actually, he laughed to himself, how many more could one man ask. His aim had been to see Kelty Farm to the hands of a new generation, and this he had done against all odds. The new generation was not named Kelty, but Jackson had found peace with that last vestige of thinking the name made the person. It was heritage that mattered, not the name. He had even offered Grace and Earle an opportunity to change the Farm's name, but they had declined. Jackson and Emma had been pleased with their decision.

He stopped again, taking his basket from his back, rubbing the places the straps had worn on his shoulders. He drank from the stream again, appreciating the clear water, the cold in his mouth. He looked around, unable to judge distance in this closed spot of woods, unable to find a point to pin a memory on. He and Joseph had traveled home by this route, and he hadn't been back since. The second growth of forest from his father's time was near maturity and could be claimed again if needed in the years to come. He'd have to mention this to Earle, or had he already?

Soon he would reach a place where the trees were stunted from the wind, where the growth thinned out and allowed more light. He should be thinking of the availability of firewood for an overnight stay. Though following the stream would lead him right to his objective, he felt confident he would make it to the cave with time to prepare for the night before full dark. But he must not rest a moment longer. The day was moving on, and the air had a chill in it to warn him not to be caught without shelter.

There it was, just through the remaining trees, only a shelf of land above his position. He was cheered by finding this place as he had expected he would. Things being where they ought to be, where they can be depended upon to be, always cheered him he realized, and only more so these late years. He hurried the last steps to the shelter, picturing the twenty-foot depth, the ten-foot width it opened to behind the narrow entry. He stepped inside, seeing again the trough the spring's water had worn down the side of the even floor and out to the sun.

Jackson set his burdens down, deciding to gather a wood supply as his first task though he would have enjoyed a moment to savor just being here again. Inside of him, a small voice added to his thought, "For the last time." He shook this off and began to look for the broken limbs and branches of trees that might have fallen from the mountain above the cave. As he remembered, there was many a blow down just below this site. The wind and rain had all but swept any soil from this area leaving what trees that had developed roots powerless to stand. He remembered a resolution from his last visit that he should leave a hatchet up here for this purpose. "Next time...," he said, though he wasn't really listening to himself.

He brought the wood inside as he gathered it knowing how suddenly a rainstorm could appear. Finding an abundance of dried dead wood, he was encouraged to bring in more than he initially had thought he'd need. Always a good idea to have more than less, he knew. Starting the fire was a matter of a few matches, grass, dried twigs, and patience. He used the same shallow pit from previous years, a place where the wall was well covered with soot.

Away from the entrance, behind the fire, he set up his stores, deciding to cut narrow strips of the meat for a meal with the bread, to be followed by some of the berries. When the fire offered him some security that it would not easily burn out, he decided to start his evening with a nap. This was so out of his experience, he laughed and said to himself, "Why not?" He spread his blanket with two layers under and one over him, drew down the flaps of his hat, and fell into a peaceful sleep.

* * *

It was late afternoon when Earle and Grace motored into the yard to hear the news Grandpa had left that morning. Grace immediately began to worry but Earle suggested they wait a while to see if he'd come home. Further investigation revealed the pack basket and blanket, as well as the food he had taken. With Joseph's report of the direction and possible goal Grampa had been forced to tell, Gracie escalated her worry, prompting Earle to say he'd go looking for the older man. Joseph claimed to have been on that trail with Grampa in the past and went along with Earle and got the large pack basket out with the blankets they might need. Grace packed some food while Earle went to get a gun. He discovered Grampa's shotgun was gone. This gave Earle some comfort, but worried Grace the more.

On the trail, Earle and Joseph settled into a steady trot, discussing what they would do if they hadn't come across Jackson by dark, and decided they would continue their trek as long as they felt sure they were on the right path. As the river broke off into several streams, they watched for the stream coming from the mountain. Earle had never been in these woods before and depended on Joseph's memory. At intervals, they found reason to believe they were on the right track.

They reached a place Jackson's boots had scuffed as he sat on a log, another place where rocks were freshly disturbed near the winding stream flowing from the mountain. He had crossed and re-crossed the stream with no apparent reason, but Joseph remembered having done this with his grandfather the time they returned home this way. As the light failed, they took council with one another, but determined to continue. The going was slower with the day's end and the temperature dropped fast. Their main defense against the cold was to keep moving.

Joseph had told his father to keep a look out for the open space they would come to that should be just ahead. In a short time, they reached the place he had described, assuring Earle that Joseph had a good grasp of the lay of the land. As they walked along, the noise of the leaves would have warned off any surprise sleeper, and they were undisturbed by the wildlife. When they found a log by the stream they rested and took stock of the situation. Joseph was pretty sure the cave was still some distance higher on the mountain, but certain that following the stream would lead them to the exact place they believed they might find Jackson.

About the time the pair was stumbling from fatigue, they came to the scrub Joseph had been expecting, and looking ahead, they saw the fire-lit entrance of the cave. Joseph regained his energy and sprang ahead with a shout while Earle stopped a moment in relief that the fire told of good news ahead. At the entrance of the cave, Joseph was calling to his grandfather with no response. He turned to Earle with a worried look. Earle entered the cave, his son at his heels.

The fire was burning low but revealed the sleeping figure of the man wrapped in the old travel blanket. Earle stood over Jackson, watching him breathe, then gently shook his shoulder. Jackson opened his eyes and smiled up at Earle, then closed his eyes again.

"Jackson."

Jackson opened his eyes again then sat upright.

"I thought I was dreaming that you and Joseph were here. I was glad then, and even more so now. How did you find this place in the dark? Is Gracie teed off at me for leaving?"

"Yes, but all she really wanted to know is that you're all right. Our coming after you was the only comfort we could give her. She promised not to worry, but you know our Gracie." The three laughed together.

Jackson stood up, meaning to build up the fire.

"I'll do that, Grampa. You must have gotten here early to gather this store of firewood."

"In the last of the light, Joseph. But then I was pretty tired and decided I'd have a nap. If you hadn't come along, I might have slept through the night."

"Might have been good for you, Jackson."

"But then I would have missed my supper! I had a snack when I got here, but if I hadn't been so tired, I would have eaten more. Let's get the food out and have ourselves a feast, mountain cave style!"

"We brought some food too, Grampa."

"Gracie packed it for us herself. We'll eat some but then we've got to lie down. The trip up here was about all I can do in one day."

"Not me, Grampa. I can stay awake with you all night."

"I guess if you stay awake, you'll be by yourself. I remember when I could stay awake all night, but I don't remember accomplishing anything worthwhile the next day. Let's eat, maybe talk a while, but then we need a good night's sleep."

Jackson got out the bread and cut up some slices, putting them on a cloth he had spread. He took out the hunk of beef, but Earle showed him sandwiches and cake Grace had packed, so they all set to the food.

"Earle, you've never been here, to this cave before. There's something I want to show you." He stood, taking a burning branch from the fire, and motioned the younger man to follow. Joseph jumped up, tagging right behind his father.

At the back of the cave, on a dry wall above the source of the spring there were letters carved into the rock. At first, they were not clear, the light flickering on their indentations, but as Earle stepped closer, he saw they were sets of initials in a row, one under the other.

"What am I looking at, Jackson? I see they are initials, and all end in K, must be for Kelty. And here, the last one is J.K., so maybe that's you. Does this list go back to Arthur Kelty? And then his son, and then E.K.—is that your father, Ike? And then you?"

"I thought you'd get stuck on the E.K."

"I remember the gravestone with Eikenhouse 'Ike' Kelty, and I hear his name often enough or I might have forgotten. Glad I got it right. I guess I've been listening all these years pretty well." The three laughed and Jackson clapped Earle on the back. "But why are they here? You've never said anything about this, and you've been here, Joseph, you never said anything either." Earle looked at his son, his eager face shining in the torchlight.

"He didn't know, Earle, I didn't show him. These are here because Arthur said this was a far corner of his land and he marked it anyway he could. I guess his son marked it when the Farm came to him, and I know my father and I carved our initials at the same time. I was about Joseph's age when we did that, it was right after my grandfather died, Arthur's son. So, while we're here, you should put your initials on the list."

"And mine too, Grampa."

"I guess that remains to be seen, there, young man. This is a list of the masters of the Farm. If you are master one day, you come back and put your name right here." Jackson pointed to a place below space for Earle's initials.

"But the Farm will be mine one day, won't it? I always thought so. Who would you want to have it? Stephen? He doesn't even like horses or cows; I don't know what kind of a farmer he'd make. He doesn't even like dirt! How are you going to farm if you don't like dirt?" Joseph's voice sounded shrill in the end of the cave. Earle smiled at the boy's passion.

"Joseph, I'm not even sure I feel right adding my name here, these being all Keltys."

"You've taken your place at master, so why not? Of course, your initials go on the list. And probably Joseph's too, but that's not for me to say. You and he will decide that. I know what Joseph has said is true, he is the boy whose ears are open when we talk, and he's followed you around since he could walk. That's how you learned, Earle. That's how I learned too. It was a proud day when my father took me up here to add my name, proud for him, and proud for me. I'd want that for you in your time too. You consider it tonight, and in the morning, you put your mark on the wall."

Jackson turned, and the three walked back to the fire-lit area, each wrapped inside his own thoughts.

As they lay down on the rock floor, Jackson could sense questions wanting to be asked. He waited, but the moments slid by in silence.

"My father said this cave was called 'Heart of the Mountain.' I don't know how far back the name goes. He told me his father called it that. There was something special about the water here, something about... I guess I don't remember now, but it was something good. Did everybody have a drink of it tonight?"

"I did, Grampa."

"I did as well. What could it have been? Is it healing water? I've heard of that. Could that have been what it was, Jackson?"

"I don't remember right now. Maybe it will come back to me. Well, happy dreams, boys." The older man soon breathed deeply then softly snored.

"What do you think it is, Dad?"

"I can't guess, Joseph. But he said it was something good, so I think we're OK. Good night, son."

* * *

Jackson. Jackson.

What? I'm sleeping.

I know, son. This is a dream. I'm sure you haven't forgotten my voice.

No, Ma, I knew it was you right away. Is it time to get up?

No, Jackson. You only have to hear me. You don't have to get up.

I haven't heard your voice in a long while. I've heard your words, and remember things you said, but I haven't heard your voice. Where have you been?

I'm never far. We are all here, so close to you.

Who? Who do you mean, Ma?

You know our names. We shared blood with you, and our names are writ on the stones.

The Keltys?

Yes.

I miss you, Ma. And Emma, my boys. And Dad. And Grampa.

I Know, Jackson. It's the way of things, to miss what changes. But you were well prepared for our passing, each in turn. We gave you what you needed, and you've done well in your time.

Have I, Ma? You know that? I have often wondered what Dad would think, what you would think, about some of the things I've had to handle. I wonder how you think Earle and Gracie will do. I think about Joseph, if he's the boy to teach.

You have good judgment, Jackson. You always did.

Thanks, Ma. I used to be sure of myself, more than I feel lately.

We all felt that way near our end. I think it's a sign that we recognize it's not all dependent on us anymore. But you've had good judgment, son.

I think what you or Dad would do, it's the way I learned and has stood me in good stead.

Sometimes, we look out of your eyes. We don't always know what we are looking at, but we see you happy, more than that, content.

You know I didn't have a son to pass the Farm to?

But you had Grace, and her Earle.

Grace isn't Kelty anymore.

She is now all she ever was. You know that.

True.

We look out of her eyes. She is our blood.

And after Grace?

It's the blood, Jackson. It's in the blood. You have no reason to fear. There will be Keltys with or without the name. It's the blood, Jackson.

...the blood. It's in the blood.

We love you, Jackson.

* * *

How will I know?

You'll know, Earle.

But how will I know?

The same way you know anything, Earle. You keep your eye out, see the signs, and act on them. It may take you some time to come to it, but the signs are there.

If I had to guess, I could, but what signs am I missing?

Who listens to every word you say? Who watches? Who is by your side even if you don't notice? Who is hungry and thirsty to know what needs to be done and how to do it?

I'm not really sure I know what needs to be done and when, how can I be teaching?

Even when the things you do don't turn out, who watches you figure it out? Who sees you do it different next time? You learned by doing. He's learning by watching, by listening.

Joseph?

Who plays the instrument as well as his grandfather, as well as any of his grandfathers, except me? You can't know this, but we do. Believe us.

Joseph? My Joseph?

When you put your initials in the line on the cave wall tomorrow, under mine, under Jackson's, remember all this.

I'm dreaming. I might not remember.

Then just know. You don't have to remember.

Isn't this a lot to put on him? He's just a boy.

It's in the blood.

…in the blood. It's in the blood.

* * *

"Earle, wake up Earle. Did you sleep well?"

"Jackson. Morning. You don't catch me sleeping many mornings. Where's Joseph?"

"He's just stepped outside. Lucky we have some food left, that's one hungry boy."

"He's growing. Got big shoes to fill, if he's ever going to run the Farm."

"You feel ready to say that?"

"You didn't see him find his way up here! You didn't see the sureness in his every step. For someone who only came this way once, and that was from the other direction, I was amazed at him. I guess it confirmed a lot I have been noticing, a lot I've hoped for. How do you see it?"

"I'm not blind, Earle. But I'm glad to hear this from you. For my part, it's good to see the future, but for you, you're picking up a new partner, as I see it."

"Good way to look at it. But is he ready to hear it?"

"Maybe it's not something that has to be said, but just is. Let him know you take him seriously. Ask his opinion sometimes. Don't just let him listen and watch, tell him and show him. Let him put his hand to it once in a while. Joseph is your son, Earle."

"This has a familiar ring to it."

"You lived through years of exactly that. You didn't just wake up one day and know what to do next, did you?"

"Actually, Jackson, I wondered if you remembered those painful years?"

"There was no pain in it for me, Earle. You gave it your best, and most days that was really fine, and those days got closer together as we went on. You got there, and he's an apt student. You won't have any trouble with that boy."

"Thanks, Jackson. Your opinion counts a lot with me."

"Earle, you should ask Joseph to tell you about his dream from last night."

"I had a strange but comforting dream myself."

"Here he comes."

"Morning, son. Your grandfather says you had a dream last night. Want to tell?"

"Sure but look what I've found! They look like arrow heads!"

"That's what they are, all right. My father used to talk about this being an Indian place, I guess he was right. You have a good eye, Joseph." Jackson turned the arrow heads over in his hand, smiling.

"Now, what about that dream, Joseph?"

"I can tell you what I remember, but it doesn't make much sense to me. It seemed that things were happening over and over. Like the grain in the field would come up, get cut down, come up again. The apple blossoms appeared, then the fruit, then the trees would go bare and blossom again. Cattle would drink at the river then go to the barn. When they went to the river again, it seemed they were different cattle, and more of them. There was snow, then sunshine like spring, new leaves, summer breezes, fall then winter again. It was day then night, then day again. Maybe there was more but it was all the same, over and over, and in no hurry. It seemed to flow, peacefully, slowly, but over and over."

"How did you feel during the dream? Were you worried?"

"No. No, I felt calm, even satisfied. In the dream it wasn't a mystery to me, what I was seeing, what was happening in front of me. I guess, now, it's all a jumble. I can't see any meaning to it. Don't dreams always have a meaning?"

"I remember now. The water. My father said it was so pure it gave you dreams you could trust."

"So, what do you make of it, does it make any sense to you, Grampa?"

"It probably makes more sense to me than to anyone of us. I think you were seeing seasons pass. You were seeing the land produce, respond to the work we do, the years going by. You didn't see anything come to an end, but going on and on, season after season, year by year. I'd say it was a good dream."

"I'd say so too, son. Let's get back to that wall. We've got some initials to carve."

"We, Dad?"

"You understand the initials are those of the masters of Kelty Farm? Do you think you're ready to make a commitment?"

"I'd be ashamed to ask for this privilege before either of you."

"That's the answer of a man, Joseph. I'm proud of you, son."

"And we have the dreams to go by. I think it was a good time to look the future in the face. I'd be glad if you would put your initials on that wall, Grandson, right below your father's."

22

1940: THE SKELETON

Jackson swung his foot in an absent-minded arc. Grace wondered if he knew he was standing on his father's grave. There weren't many leaf bearing trees up here, mostly pine around the edges, but what leaves fell seemed to always pile up against the monuments and had to be swept away about twice each year.

Broom in her hand, she watched her father as he struggled with something he had asked her up here to tell.

"I only heard this once, and it was long ago. I didn't know what I was being told, and I was surprised to hear these words from my father. I think I only heard the first part clearly, then I was too shocked to really listen. At the time I had bad dreams for a while. When I told my father, he said they would pass, that they had with him. All these years I've only remembered it a few times, but once was last year when your Joseph and Earle slept in the cave with me, and I've been thinking about it a lot since." Jackson seemed to study the toe of his work shoe.

"I have, at times, thought it was all a dream. These things, they don't sound like my father. And even now I remember he didn't look at me while he told me.

"It was as if he didn't want to tell it, to tell me. It seemed he had to, like he had to lift it off himself. But that can't be it, because he wouldn't have given me a burden to take it off of himself. He wouldn't have done that.

"I'm thinking he felt it was his duty to tell and mine to know." He paused, cleared his throat and glanced at Grace for assurance.

"So now, I'm worried that I may be relieving myself by telling you, yet I think someone should know, and I'm the only one now who knows.

"But if, I mean when, I tell you, you should decide if it needs passing on or not. It will be yours, and you do as you think right to do, Gracie."

"Well, Dad, you sure have my attention now. I'm curious about what you're going to tell me, but I'm more curious about your hesitancy. Whatever it is, just tell me. It will be easier on you than this build up."

"I hesitate, Gracie, because even now, I'm not sure it is the right thing, telling you. I always felt this a burden and I don't want to give you anything I think of as a burden."

"Yet you asked me up here to the cemetery with no one else about. We're as alone as anyone gets on Kelty Farm. And, Dad, I'm not worried about any burden. I can handle it, especially if it helps you. So, are you going to tell me or not?"

"Gracie, it's like un ringing a bell. After I've told you, I can't un tell you. I can't say if you will feel the weight of knowing it has been for me. I don't want that for you."

"Dad just tell me. I'm here for you." Jackson sighed. He sighed again.

As she seldom saw him, Grace thought he looked very old now. He closed his eyes a long moment, let another sigh escape.

"It was a long time ago. I don't know if Arthur Kelty or Elishabet ever knew, but I guess they must have. Their sons, some if not all four of them, did something, something bad, with consequences, that seem to always come back to haunt us at Kelty Farm. I don't know. It was a long time ago as I say. Maybe it really doesn't matter anymore."

"Dad, maybe you should think about it some more, if you want to tell or not. I hate to see you in such a state. And if it's something about the Farm, I'm surprised you haven't told Earle. You often remind my husband that he's Master of Kelty Farm."

"No! I couldn't tell Earle. What would he think of the family he married into if he knew! No, no, I couldn't tell Earle. You may decide to tell him. Just when I'm not here. Today is the last day I want to speak of it or hear anything more of it. I don't even want to think of it again. Promise me, Gracie." Now he faced her, his eyes pleading.

"Well Dad, you have me almost as worked up as you are. You had better just tell me. If it's something that goes back as far as Arthur and Elishabet, or their sons, I don't see how it could be as important as you are making it to be." Then, more softly, "Tell or don't tell me, Dad, do whatever is easiest on you..."

"Again, I can't take it back after you know. That's all I'm saying." He turned from her, putting both hands on the marble tablet as if needing it to steady himself. Again, she wondered if he realized it was his father's tablet that he leaned on.

She walked a few steps and swiped at the buildup of leaves against a tablet. Scattering them was the trick, the wind would take them from here.

"My great grandfather, Arthur, had two younger sisters, about the age of his sons, born about the time he built the homestead we live in, and he and Elishabet left the old Kelty home of his parents. The sister's names were Jane and Orvis, I'm not sure which one was older. Their mother was very hard on everyone, and especially hard on the women around her." He paused more than a minute.

"They were young, probably foolish or at least silly, and somehow got mixed up with some wrong-headed boys, not much older than they were. I'm pretty sure I never knew the details, but their mother threw them out of the house, called them harlots and I don't know what all. Arthur and Elishabet took the girls in, though I'm sure it was mostly Arthur's doing—they were his sisters. After the way old Mrs. Kelty had treated Elishabet, I doubt she'd want to do any more than she had to for that whole family." Jackson turned around, but his gaze was on his shoes.

"At first it was a matter of keeping the girls safe from those boys, who, I guess were persistent in the search for them. Then it took some warnings from the Kelty men to scare them off. Later, it became evident that one of the girls was with child. I don't know which one it was, but I guess it could have been either one." He sighed again. The burden hadn't shifted yet.

"Someone thought that marriage was the answer but neither girl would tell which boy had been the one to father the child, and both were actually too young to want to be married, so that solution seemed blocked. Whether he knew about it or not, Arthur's sons, some of them if not all four, took it upon themselves to bring comeuppance to both the offenders. They tracked them down and got them out to the woods. They tried to beat the truth out of the boys, but if they knew who had been with which girl, they wouldn't tell. So, the brothers beat them some more.

"They were left in the woods with a firm impression that they should leave town or get some more of the same."

Jackson paused again. He turned, stepped between the monuments and stared up at the mountain behind.

"Is that the story, Dad?" Grace felt some relief, though only hoping that was all of it.

"No. That's the easy part." Another sigh. "I guess in those days the word 'rape' wasn't some word you spoke aloud. The family's name couldn't be splashed with such a word. It wasn't only the girls' reputation, though of course that would be done for. It surely must have seemed to be the right thing, to beat those boys, to run them out of town." He turned to face Grace, catching her eye.

"Those boys, their family, didn't have to worry about that. They were pretty low folks, and probably they had acted as you might have expected. That family hadn't amounted to much, were beneath the notice of most folks around then, except there was a lot of them, they were a big family of boys, all unruly. And the two boys that got beat were not the oldest nor the youngest of them."

Jackson turned from his daughter again. In the silence, a breeze cleared the leaves Grace had swept from the base of a tablet. She knew without looking whose grave she had cleaned. She itched to sweep away more leaves from the bases of the tablets but was afraid to break the spell her father had woven. She leaned the broom against the marble and stepped closer to her father, reaching for his arm, grasping his sleeve.

"It was long ago, Dad. It's really nothing to do with us. Why does it trouble you so?"

He turned away again. The breeze died down.

"It's been the most of thirty years I've known. Dad never mentioned it again after the day he told me. I couldn't stop thinking about it then and had bad dreams, but when the dreams passed, I kind of forgot it. Still, ever once in a while, it would come to me, or a part of it. Mostly, I put it away where I didn't have to look at it." He seemed to notice the lettering on the tablet in front of him. He traced the letters, "I K E" and went on with his tale, but with a lowered voice. Grace stepped closer still.

"Those boys were left where they lay, but the next day all the town was searching for them. Word was out that they might have run off from their folks. Most people thought the better of the boys for having left. But at the Kelty Farm, there were sharp glances passed from one to another though no one spoke about it." He glanced up at Grace. "This is one of the hard parts. Should I stop?"

"Get it out, Dad. Get it over with."

"The Kelty brothers, one at least, went back to the place they had left the pair. One was gone..."

"And the other?"

"...was dead."

Both father and daughter were stunned, one from the telling, one from the hearing.

"What happened next, Dad?"

"The Kelty brothers discussed it among themselves. There were few choices, but they made one. It seems they drew lots, or somehow decided between them, and one only was chosen to bury the body, away someplace, where it wouldn't be likely to ever be found. And he wasn't to tell the others where the grave was, nor of course, would they ever speak of it again."

"So that's the story you have carried and now you've told me. You can let it go now, Dad."

"That not only a part of the whole."

"What more could there be. One of those boys ran off and the other died and got buried. Did anyone ever find out?"

"The Kelty brothers gathered some things they had found through the years, arrows, broken bows, arrow heads, a stone ax, you know, Indian things from around the land. They had all these things put in with the body. They planned to take the dead boy's clothes off of him and bury him like he was an old time native. They thought if he was ever found, someday in the future, it would look like an ancient grave.

"That's why I've been thinking about this so much after Joseph, Earle and I slept in the Indian cave last year. Joseph found some more arrow heads, and I was afraid he might have found the grave. I didn't want him to dig around there in case that was the place."

"Is that the place?"

"I don't know. Nobody knows now. Only one of the Kelty brothers knew and he took it with him to his grave."

Grace stepped back, looking at the names on the tablets.

"Which one was it?"

"I never knew. I know it wasn't my grandfather, it was one of the other three of Arthur's sons. They were all gone by the time I was little. But my dad said the one who buried the boy had a hard time over it. He couldn't get past it, was mostly sad and eventually hung himself, though they told everyone he had died of influenza. Nobody questioned that, it was so common in those days. His wife never told, again, to splash shame on her or the family wouldn't have been done. She moved away. I don't know how they kept this all secret, but I guess my granddad told this to my father, and dad told me, and some details were probably lost in the telling, or in my case, in the hearing."

"Now, that's all of it?"

"I wish it was, Gracie."

"What more could there be?"

"I know they always worried the other boy would return to tell about the Kelty brothers and their involvement. That never happened. It was thought he may have died elsewhere, and it never got back to the town folk. They also wondered why only one of them died when they were beat the same and neither should have died from it. Could the one boy have killed his brother for having gotten them into the mess to start with? There got to be speculation between the four brothers who again swore they never would speak of it again."

"So, that must be all."

"No. There's more to know. You didn't hear what happened to the baby, or who the family of the father was." He turned and pointed across the family graves to a line of markers around the outside where were buried people other than family.

Grace looked where her father was pointing. A small round-topped white marker peeked out from a pile of leaves. She walked over to it, sweeping away the leaves.

"J. O."

"That's the name of the baby? How old was it when it died?"

"It died right away. I didn't ask how. The initials are the initials of the two sisters. I don't think anyone ever asked who the mother actually was."

"And the father's family name? It's not on the marker."

"Please God, that name will never be on any stone up here. Their name was Bristholtz."

"I've never heard that name around here. Did they all die out or move away?"

"No, Gracie, they changed their name."

"Changed their name?"

"They changed it to Brist."

"Brist?" Grace took a step backward, bringing her hand to her mouth. She stared at her father. "You don't mean my brother's wife's family? Anna May? And all the bad feeling you have toward her father—I never knew what that was about. I thought it was about him always trying to buy our Farm from you, trying to squeeze us with taxes from the town, trying to find out our business. I can't say I ever liked the man, but that's not who Archie married. He married Anna May, not Mr. Brist. I'm so ..."

"I know, I know. It never was clear to me how important it is to keep our land out of his hands than when I knew the story. I don't know how much those people know. I suspect they don't know what we know. I think they always wanted to blame us for their boys coming up missing, running away as they must have thought. I don't think they know all I've told you. I don't think the one who did run off ever contacted them, ever wrote them, let them know..."

"But Dad, Anna May has no interest in the Farm. And you've signed it over to Earle and me. You've settled all that with Archie. He has no expectation to inherit..."

"No, Gracie, there's nothing to worry about there. You and Earle and I are in partnership, and when any one of us dies, the Farm goes to the remaining partners. You'll take a partner when I'm gone, probably Joseph, I'd expect. But that's up to you.

"No one can ever claim Kelty Farm but a partner. We always make provision for anyone from the family, but the Farm stays in the hands of the partners. Archie has received his provision and expects nothing further from the Farm. It won't go to Anna May no matter what. And her father's kind of cooled down, I don't think he has his eye on us anymore. Maybe he grew out of it. Maybe he knows he may outlive me, but he won't outlive you and Earle. And I'm content he'll never own the land the Keltys are buried on."

"There's still his son..."

"He's not amounting to much as I can tell. There's no threat from that quarter."

"And things are going well, aren't they Dad? The Farm is doing well?"

"I have no complaints, Gracie. You know that. Earle and you, well, I couldn't have hoped for more. I know your mother and I worried a lot when the boys..." He hesitated, turning away towards Stewart's grave.

"You mean when Stewie, and then Andy and Phillip died. But you still had Archie."

"Archie wasn't going to stay. We knew that from before all that happened. We kept him past time for him to go, and, being honest about it, past when he was doing any good here. But your gramma Lucy told us you would be the one. And she was right."

"I don't know how you dared to pin you hopes for the Farm on me. I was just a little girl."

"But my mother knew things, she always knew things, and she was definite about you being the one. And besides that, we needed something to hang our hope on. It didn't matter for us anymore. We could have given up. But we had the time to wait. My mother, your gramma Lucy, told us we had the time. And she lived to see it come to fruit. She pointed out Earle when he was no thicker than a fence post. She said, one day, 'That's your boy. That's the next Master of the Farm.'"

"I knew she had feelings for things waiting to happen, but she didn't share much with me." Grace paused a moment. "Mostly she shared her hopes, her intuition with me. She never answered the questions I asked. Or maybe she did and the answers she gave weren't the answers I was listening for. I knew she liked Earle. I knew she was happy when we married. I wish she had lived to see my Joseph, my other children. I wish I knew that she knew about them."

"She knew what she had to know, and never asked for more. She had faith in things, Gracie. She didn't have to see them happen. I always wondered if she knew about the Brist thing. She never said."

"I can't picture Grampa Ike knowing that whole tale and keeping it from Gramma Lucy. Do you think he told her, Dad?"

"Gracie, I never knew any two as close as those two were, but even then, there would be room for something to be left unsaid. I never told your mother. She died not hearing a word of that from me."

"She didn't need to know. I wonder if I needed to know either." Grace swung her broom at another nest of leaves, and then another. She looked at her father. A wisp of her hair blew away from her face as the breeze picked up. "I don't think we feel any worry that the skeleton would be found after all these years, nor is there anyone left that would put all the facts together. I'm glad you got it off your chest, Dad, but I think it will lie silent after this."

"Whatever you say, Gracie. I knew you'd know the right of it."

23

1981: THE HOUR OF REMEMBERING

Grace is sitting in her kitchen, her hands idle on the table. She glances around the orderly room, seeing everything in its place. She straightens the tablecloth, though she knows it is already smooth. She glances at the kitchen door, expecting it to open any second.

Like a gust of wind Sarah rushes in. "Gram, I'm sorry to be late. I meant to be here sooner, I'm sorry."

Grace rises to hug her granddaughter. "Sarah, Sarah, you're here now. Don't cry over spilt milk, honey. Take off your coat."

"It's my last day of Thanksgiving Break, and I feel guilty I haven't spent more time with you this trip home," she says apologetically, taking off her coat, hanging it on a wall peg. "I love you, Gram. I probably won't be back again till Spring Break or maybe not till summer. I hope you're not upset with me."

Grace takes the girl's hands in her own. "Well, I hope you'll come home sooner, but don't worry so much, dear. I know you love me, even when you're not here. Let's not spend any more of our precious time worrying about not being together, when, here we are, together now." Grace lets go of one hand, reluctant to let go at all. "I know you have to leave tomorrow. My word! Back to college. You're the first of the family to go. I'm so proud of you. We all are."

Sarah pulls her grandmother into an embrace, hugging past where Grace would let go.

"What's the matter, child?" Grace asks softly.

"Gram, I hate to see you alone in this old house. I just can't bear to think of you all alone."

"Here, here, child!" She lets go with a laugh. "Your father and the family live right where I can see them, just across the valley. Everyone calls me during the day, and I see your father often—and your two brothers. Don't think of me as alone, honey. I don't."

"But you are alone, Gram," Sarah insists.

"Sarah, I know what you mean, but I don't need others here to trip on not to be alone. Now stop worrying. I want us to have a good time together, and we can't do that if you're worrying." Her tone says they are finished with the subject.

"Now, are you hungry? Can I get you anything? Do you want to sit here and talk, or would you like to sit in the front parlor?"

"Oh, I love to hear you say, 'The front parlor.' Nobody has a front parlor anymore except you, Gram!" She laughs and gives Grace a hug. "And I don't want a thing, just to be with you. I love you, Gram," she adds with a serious note.

"I love you too, dear." Grace stops to really look at Sarah. "I just can't get over it. You're so grown, so very beautiful. Seems like only yesterday..." Grace looks away, carried back by memories.

"What, Gram? What is it?" she asks in concern.

"Well, I see you there, but I hardly can believe it's you, Sarah, can hardly believe so many years have passed. It was only yesterday that you were a baby. Now, tomorrow, you get back on a plane—heavens! an airplane!—and fly half across the country to school." She shakes her head but shrugs off the serious turn.

"But now I am the worrier. Let me finish up here, and we'll go into the parlor." She takes off her apron, shakes it out and hangs it on a peg.

She looks around and turns out the light, following the girl into the hallway, and on to the parlor. Their steps are muffled on the runner.

The parlor furniture, heavy and dark, is from a previous era and a tall wood stove stands in front of the fireplace. Sarah walks directly to a favorite chair. Grace stops at the stove, swings open the door and puts a large maple chunk inside.

"I've saved that maple chunk all day. By morning, it will be a beautiful bed of coals to start off my day. By God and the maple chunk we'll be warm this night!" She laughs. "Your grandfather used to say that every night, and now I say it for him. Sometimes..." she pauses as if considering, "sometimes, I say it in the summer, too. It starts my nighttime, like a signal. It triggers the kinds of thoughts I put myself to bed with. It probably sounds foolish to you, Sarah." She sits on the couch and motions Sarah to join her.

"No, Gram, I know what you mean. A lot of things change, but Kelty Farm isn't one of them." She speaks reassuringly, then more seriously, "That's good for you, I guess, and for Dad, and maybe my brother, Kelty, too. I used to want to be just like you. I wanted to make cookies and bread, to make quilts. I thought I'd be a farmer's wife when I grew up, just like you."

Grace hesitates, but asks, "You don't want that anymore?"

"I don't mean this disrespectfully, Gram. I just want more than you or even Mom got. This place is the way you made it, or maybe, you are the way this place made you. I've got to find my own place, my own life. I don't know what I want, or where it will take me, but Mother says not to worry now, that I'll figure it out. I guess that's what she did. She never wanted much that she didn't get. Maybe it will be the way she says."

"Sometimes we overlook what is within our own fences."

"Gram, Mom has her career, her family, her house, and Dad is always there for her. But there's something else... I feel it. She's never at rest, she's always watching... I'm not sure what, but she's still looking for something."

Grace hesitates then lowers her voice, "I expect your mother would say if there was more she wanted."

"I've only been gone three months, but I've thought a lot about things while I was away. There's something I'd like to say."

"What is it, Sarah?"

Sarah hesitates and begins slowly. "You and Mother, you… never got along. I know we don't talk about it, but I wouldn't want you to think no one noticed." She stops a moment then her voice is stronger. "I don't know what is between you, I just know that I'm a part of it, even though I don't want to be." Her statement hangs in the air.

"Sarah, I…" Sarah cuts her off.

"I often felt like there was a tug-of-war going on over me, and I didn't know why. Anyway, I'm out of it now. Maybe that means Mother wins, I don't know." Her face reddens, as if the effort to say so bluntly what she really meant took a lot out of her.

Grace looks away, her fingers fussing with a lace doily on the arm of the chair. There is a short silence. "Adults are so foolish to try to hide things from children. But you are no longer a child," she says softly.

"I know Mother is furious because my brother didn't go on to school. He says he's going to spend a couple of years on the Farm, and then think about college. I don't believe he'll ever go. I think farming is in his blood. She says it was a mistake to name him "Kelty," after the old people, that now he thinks it's his fate to be the next generation of the Farm."

"It's not such a bad thing, here on the Farm," Grace continues softly.

"This has always been your home—your place. And Mother, she made it hers. But Kelty Farm is where I'm going from, not going to. I'll find a place for me. I only hope I'll be happier than Mother has been."

"Your mother has been happy enough."

"I wouldn't want to look back, like Mother, and wish I had made different choices. I want to look ahead and feel sure of myself. If I stayed here, I would only be trying to live your life over again." Sarah looks for understanding in Grace's eyes.

Grace gives a forced laugh. "Well, in defense of my life, there are worse to choose." She gets up, walks slowly around the room, looking at the photographs displayed on various surfaces.

Sarah speaks softly, "I'm probably not saying this very well, Gram. I think some people are cut out for this. You and Dad, for instance, have been perfectly happy here. You don't look for anything else than what you have. I think that's great, but I know, I really know, it's not for me."

"You have a lot of your mother in you, but I hear a different voice, a strong voice: I suspect you've grown up since leaving here only months ago. I think I'm hearing Sarah the woman, and not the girl I knew."

"I haven't changed so much. I hope I'll always be the girl you knew. I liked her, and don't want to give up much of her." She stands and hugs her grandmother.

"Oh! I love you, Sarah. And Kelty Farm will be a home for you, wherever you go, as long as any of us are here."

"That's how I think of it. But we've talked too long. You look tired. And no one will have to sing to get me to sleep tonight!" She laughs, enjoying the lightness of the moment.

"Sing?" Grace asks.

"Dad used to tell how he'd put us youngsters to bed, talking softly all the way up the stairs, stopping to look at the nursery rhyme illustrations hung up over the cribs and beds, telling each one. Then lastly, singing a song as a lullaby. He said his babies were often sleeping before he finished, though some evenings he'd have to sing his three old songs over and over. It put the children in the mood to sleep, he said, or at least set the pattern so they knew sleep was next on the agenda. I don't remember Dad singing me to sleep as a baby, but anytime I had a bad dream, he'd be there, and sing to me till I'd fall asleep." Sarah smiles at this memory.

"Well, I have a good-night routine too." Grace touches some of the photos.

Sarah smiles at her, "Do you mean the 'Hour of Remembering'?"

"I'm surprised you haven't forgotten that."

"Gram, I've thought of it often whenever I looked out the window from our house at night. I watch your lights. I remember the times I stayed over with you, when you told me about the Hour of Remembering."

"Then you should understand why I never feel alone."

"Whenever I heard all those old stories, I wondered if anybody ever learned anything from them. They sound alike after a while. I don't know how anybody could remember them all." Sarah yawns and stretches.

"You worry too much—you were always old beyond your years. Just like your father." Grace scolds but she smiles.

"Will you do the remembering tonight? I'd like to hear it again, word for word, don't leave anything out. It'll help me to keep it in my mind while I'm away."

Grace smiles, thinking she has glimpsed the little girl again.

"Well, child, I don't remember everything, not every time. Some of it comes and goes. But we'll do it tonight. You're a rememberer. I know you'll carry this a long time."

"Let's do it, Gram. Just like you've done before."

"Well, my girl, I do it differently each time. But I always do it some way. I guess I really live it every night. I don't just remember at night, you know. I divide up my remembering, keeping the day for the people who are still living, still in my life, for my waking and walking hours. I keep all their pictures downstairs in these frames." She touches more of the pictures. "All day I write them letters, phone them, or see them as they stop in at times. I try to only think of them during the day."

Grace moves to another group of photographs, picking one up and smiling over it. "I haven't really been conscious about it, but I've been saying good night to all these dear faces smiling at me out of their frames. They're with me all day. Now I'm going to leave them downstairs for the night as I go up to bed. From the bottom of the stairs, I think of the other people in my life, the ones who are gone now, but who remain in my heart. I do this to keep them present a while longer. They are with me more and more, but I keep it to this time and make it special." Grace looks at Sarah to see if she's understood, if she should go on.

"I know most of these faces, Gram, but I want to know the ones on the stairs too. Tell it all to me, every bit, don't leave anything out. I want to remember the way you do this." Her eyes brighten in anticipation.

"Sarah, Sarah!" Grace laughs. "You make it sound like a show. It's just my way of calming down after the day, getting ready for bed. It puts me in the mood for a good sleep." She checks the stove again, adjusting the damper. "Now come along."

Grace stops at a small table at the bottom of the stairs, picking up a candlestick.

"I do the rest of the evening by candlelight." She strikes a match, lighting the candle and shaking out the match, unaware of the elegance of her movements. "I like electricity fine when I'm baking cakes and cooking, but when I'm going to remember, it's candlelight for me."

Sarah turns off the light and steps to her grandmother's side. She looks into the picture of a frowning woman on the wall. "Who is this, Gram?"

"This was my mother-in-law. That makes her your great-grandmother." Grace raises the candle and sighs, speaking to the portrait, "Ah, Eudora, another day is done. Again, I forgive you your dislike of me."

"She didn't like you, Gram?"

"I often think of her in these quiet years. What a comfort my family is to me, my sons and their families. I'm never the lonely, bitter old bird she was. Still, I know her better each day I live on." She moves up a step, shining the light into the face of a smiling man, a frame matching the first. "Mr. Charles. I never knew you, but every day I thank you for the fine son you raised. He had your smile." She glances back to Eudora's portrait, "I'm sure you have a special place in heaven, Mr. Charles."

Sarah notices a painful grimace on Grace's face as she takes the next step. "It hurts you to go up the stairs?"

"My knees complain about the steps. When I come down of a morning, I don't go up again till night because of them."

"Maybe you should move to a bedroom downstairs."

"Someday, but, oh, not yet! Not yet." The candlelight reveals two small portraits at this step. "My littlest darlings!"

"Who are they, Gram? I've forgotten."

Grace points to one, "This is Lori, your Uncle Alden's third daughter. She was two when she died of pneumonia." Then she looks at the other, a warm smile on her face and in her voice, "And this is Baby Willis, your Uncle Stephen's first born. I only saw him once." She sighs, "I'll know you better in heaven." She moves up another step, "Oh, my boy. This is my son Phillip, your father's younger brother."

"I know this one. Dad still talks about Uncle Phillip. He got hit by a car," Sarah steps into the story.

"Almost fifty years ago." She shakes her head in disbelief. "How fragile the thread of life is." She sighs.

Sarah puts her hand on Grace's shoulder. "It still makes you sad, Gram?"

"It amazes me that I might have tears for something that happened so long ago. But I mourn the lost years we would have had together, and for his life that was unlived. Ah, well…" She takes the next step and brightens at the oval portrait. "This is Rose."

"I remember her."

"You do, dear?"

"I remember her at a picnic we had here. I think it must have been the Fourth of July, or Labor Day. She was laughing, and she had a big sun bonnet on. I remember when she died you cried. You kissed her as she lay in her coffin, and Grampa put his arm around you."

"Sarah, you remember a lot. But there was so much more." She looks at the picture with a faraway stare. "We were girlhood friends. I guess we laughed about everything, from our own silliness on through the tricks time plays on all women, young and old. My dear Rose. She made me laugh through some hard times and was my friend in the storms."

"That's a great compliment, Gram."

Grace smiles at Sarah. "Every woman deserves a friend like Rose. I've had very little 'girl talk' since I lost her. And it's hard to keep everything to yourself." She grimaces as she takes the next step.

"I hate to see you in pain, Gram. Do you take anything for it?"

"Well, Dear, I'm heading toward eighty and pain is the only physical reminder I have of that fact—and then only going up the stairs. It's not as bad when I go down, in the morning. Most of my day I don't notice my knees, so," she laughs, "they get my attention this way." She looks up to the next frame, as if to see where she is.

"And Marjory! Sometimes it surprises me that this picture is here, and not downstairs with my other children. It's as if she slipped away unnoticed. She died suddenly, 'her heart' they said. Well, maybe…" She looks thoughtfully at the picture and is still a moment, as if she has a private thought. "It seemed to me she more gave in, than gave out. That's a difference you might see if you had known her well all her forty-six years or if you were her mother, I guess."

Grace looks up the stairs into the darkness, a slight bitterness in her voice, "A parent never gets used to a child dying before themselves. It isn't the order of things. I always wonder, as with Phillip, if there was something—anything—I could have done."

"You can't think like that, Gram. No one can change anything."

"Well, maybe…" She moves to the next stair, and leans back against the rail, closing her eyes a moment.

Sarah looks at the five frames, the center one of four boys, with four frames of individuals surrounding the middle. She points to the group portrait in the center. "These are your brothers! I know their names but not which one is which. These other pictures are of them as individuals when they were older."

Grace gazes calmly at the arrangement, focusing on the center picture. "I never knew them as children because they were all pretty well grown when I came along. This picture of the four of them was in the parlor when I was a child, and I used to pretend that we played together. Sometimes I think they were there—were my playmates. And then I remember…" She looks closely at the group picture.

"This is my favorite photograph of them. Look at the short pants and ringlets on Stewie and Archie. I never saw any of them this young. They were seven to twelve years older than I, and would have been out working the Farm when I played by myself in the parlor. But the impression of them as my playmates is so strong..."

"These other photographs seem somehow alike."

Grace surveys the other photos. "I think they were each taken when the boys came of a certain age, probably eighteen. This is Stewart. He was killed by his horse. Andrew and Phillip were gone off to the Great War then, and never came home. They are not buried up on the hillside with the rest of the family."

"I've been up there at times. When the sun shines and the wildflowers are in bloom, it's so pretty. And those neat rows of white marble tablets...all with names and dates. I used to think they looked like teeth when I was little."

Grace is still absorbed in the photographs. She says, softly, "I was the little girlchild they tossed high in the air. They used to chase me out of the barn by threatening to pull my hair. How I used to scream, and how they would laugh..."

"What wonderful memories, Gram, of so very long ago," Sarah adds.

"Long ago to you, Sarah, but only yesterday to me."

Sarah points at the fourth individual in his frame. "Is this your brother Archie?"

"Yes, Archelaus. Our family names its boys after the old family, and he is the only one who was ever named after Almost Grampa Arc, who died out west.

"But that's another story." She pauses, sorting out her memories. "All my brothers were fun loving rascals. But after the others were gone, Archie found it a burden to be the last living son. He had the best education and expected to go into business. But my father kept him on the Farm. And he tried, but his heart wasn't in it. He left us after a while. He married and had a business started when he died. He had two children. He's not on the hillside, either."

"That's a sad story..."

"Well, he got the chance he asked for, and got to do what he wanted." She looks at the five-picture arrangement a moment. "They were all such lovely boys. I still hear their shouts, their taunts, and the rough-housing that left the house with them, not heard for another generation." She and Sarah move up a step.

Sarah speaks up quickly, "This is Great-Great-Grampa, Ike Kelty!"

"Yes, dear. You wouldn't remember him."

"But Gram, I do! It's true I never met him, but you've told so many stories, I feel like I know him."

"Sarah," Grace says with a laugh, "pretty soon you can do the hour of remembering yourself, and you won't need any help from me." She looks back at the photograph.

"Don't say that, Gram! I'll always need you. Even when I'm far away, it's nice to know you are home, on Kelty Farm."

Grace turns to Sarah, looking directly at the girl. "If you think of the Farm as home, you'll always come back. It's your home, your heritage…, for as long as you claim it for your own."

Sarah sidesteps the seriousness of the moment. "Tell me again, about Grampa Ike."

"My Grampa Ike's real name was Eikenhous, after his mother's family. But he never reminded people of that, he liked to be called Ike." She pauses. "I've lived a safe and secure life, but I never felt safer than when I was leaning against him, rocking on the porch, feeling the rhythm of the rocker, the ebb and flow of his breathing. Sometimes I sit in that same rocker, on my same porch, my grandchildren around me, and I tell the same stories he told me and more besides that I lived through."

"And that's where I know Great-Great-Grandfather Ike from."

Grace smiles as she moves to another stair. "And this is my Gramma Lucy, the most wonderful woman!"

Sarah examines the small, old-fashioned picture. "Her hair is pulled back so tightly, and her eyes are so piercing. How come she isn't smiling?"

"I've never found a picture of her smiling, though I never remember her not smiling. She had real joy in her. She taught me the 'cook's secret'. She'd say, 'Think of how much you love your family when you're cooking. It will show! And put an extra egg in everything!'" Grace's voice gains strength. She no longer seems tired. "Gramma talked as she worked, explaining what she was doing, who used to do the same job, but maybe some other way, who lived here, what they died of, who was named for who, how far back a name went in the family and so on."

"What did she cook?" Sarah asked, caught up in the enthusiasm.

"Breads, cakes, party preserves that were the envy of all. She used to say her everyday fare was 'nourishing,' but she was the first to admit that my mother set a better meal on the table. She didn't believe any kitchen big enough for more than one cook, and she always complimented my mother on the meal. Gramma loved my father, her son, Jackson, named after her own family. She loved my mother and was a good friend to her." Grace leans back on the railing, living a moment from the past...

Sarah sees the pause, and adds, "Lucy lived a long time, didn't she, Gram."

"Lived to be over seventy, past her husband. She died just before my first child, your father, Joseph, was born. I so wanted her to see my baby. I was disappointed and heartsick when she died." She sighs. "But here, we've lingered too long on the stairs tonight. Joseph will be watching for my light." She looks again at the picture then takes the last step.

This picture is in an oblong frame. "These are my parents, the twin oaks of Kelty Farm, the last to live here and bear that name." She looks at Sarah, as though passing on a hidden meaning. "They lost all their sons and offered the Farm to Earle and me. We were newly married, and Earle didn't know farming. They worked their retirement as farm hands to help us get on. My father was so patient with Earle, showing, explaining, seeing him through the seasons, giving him the lessons of long experience. One of the first jobs they did together was to plant the orchard where your father built the house you live in."

"How was your mother through all this?"

"She took each loss and found some strength to give thanks for, to endure. Then, one day, my parents came to us and asked Earle if he would want to change the name of the Farm, there not being any Kelty owners after them. We were stunned at their generosity, their consideration of Earle's feelings. Without a moment's hesitation, he assured them the name would stay, 'In honor of the generations who had lived and died here and to guide those to come.' I was so proud of my young husband!

"Your father knows you are with me tonight, but he'll be watching the window. We've got to go along." She glances down the long hallway then turns away.

"Don't hurry, Gram. He knows if anything was wrong, I'd call him." She notices Grace pause beside a doorway. "That was your room with Grampa, wasn't it?"

"Yes. I usually stop and look in. I could do a tour of the room with the door shut. My mother's Wedding Ring quilt hangs over the foot of the bed, another quilt on the bed. Our wedding picture is on the dresser. It's a comfort to know it's all there, unchanged."

"You don't use the room anymore?"

"It had always been 'our' room. We talked everything out as we lay in each other's arms every night through a generation and a half. Earle died so peacefully there, so quickly. And I didn't feel the room could be mine alone. I felt like a different person without Earle and needed a place that was mine. I tried every room in the house till I settled on Elishabet's."

Sarah laughs. "All us kids used to say Elishabet's room was haunted."

"Well, children have a way of seeing things."

"You mean it is?"

"Now Sarah! You ought to know better than to think I'd say anything like that. Maybe after a good night's sleep, you'll know if the room is haunted or not." She turns to another doorway and enters, leaving Sarah in the dark hallway peering into the room lit by Grace's candle.

"Yeah…after a good night's sleep. Maybe I'll know."

As Sarah peers through the doorway, she sees Grace walk to the heart-shaped window at the far end of the room to light a lantern. Grace then returns to her dressing table, seating herself and looking into a gold framed photograph. Sarah walks slowly into the room.

"Will you be warm enough, dear?"

Sarah drifts past her grandmother, stopping at the dresser with the lantern in front of the window. "It's nice and warm, Gram, right over the parlor stove. I'm just looking out the window, realizing what it looks like from the inside. So often I've been across the valley at Dad's house, seeing this window from there. Your lights signal him where you are in the house. Did you know that?"

Grace brushes her hair, still looking into the picture frame. "Your father and I have this all worked out and we've never really discussed it. He worries about me, so I do things in a way to help him not worry."

"When your lights go out downstairs, he gives you time to get up here, then he watches for the light in this window—it looks like a heart even from over there. If he can't watch, he sets one of us by the window to tell him when this lamp is lit. First we see a spark that must be your match then the light in the shape of a heart spills out of this room into the night."

"But then he worries if I leave it on too long and don't go right to bed. He's a worrier. I used to be a worrier. I guess it's his turn now."

Sarah traces a zigzag crack in the window with her finger. "When I was first away at college, I dreamed about the heart-shaped light shining on me. I felt so secure. I think about this window often."

Grace stops brushing and turns toward Sarah. "I wouldn't have guessed that. I'm glad to hear it."

Sarah traces the line in the window. "I never noticed this was broken before. How long has it been like this?"

"It has been broken since it's been in this house. It's part of the story. I thought you knew."

Sarah comes to stand behind Grace, watching her. "I don't remember. Tell me."

"It's not a bedtime story. I'll tell you another time. I've been thinking about your grandfather tonight."

"Tell me about the years with Grampa."

"My dear, that would be telling my whole life's story!"

"I remember Grampa. He was tall and walked slowly."

"There's no accounting for the things people remember. He's gone now, near ten years. That's half your life ago. You remember him as tall because you were so small. He wasn't a tall man, but he was determined, and that made him seem tall to me...and to his children. He just put his head down, and worked through whatever he was at, and finished everything he started. He said he had to be that way because he didn't have any natural talent and had to work hard at everything. But I don't think there was anything he couldn't have done if he had a mind to. He only walked slowly when he was thinking things out. He always got where he was going." She takes the picture off the table, looking into it.

"You still miss him a lot."

"Sometimes I forget he's gone. I have so many memories of him. All those seasons, days that seemed endless at the time. In spring, how he loved every little thing that poked a green leaf out of the ground. And summer, the orange drink I used to carry out to him wherever he was working. I remember how he'd pause to watch my approach, the brightness of his eyes when I'd hand him the cool drink. Once I saw wet furrows tears had made on his dusty cheeks. Oh! I loved that tender hearted man. I never forgot that he fulfilled my father's dream for the Farm to go on, that my husband may have had a plan for his own life, but his first consideration was that I would want my life in my home."

"So, he took up farming with your father..."

"Fall...well...fall completes things, ending some, resting others." Grace closes her eyes. "I remember the last bale of hay, the wood pile stacked, the rows of canned vegetables lined up on the cellar shelves. And Thanksgiving... Most of our children were born in the fall. And

Earle died in the fall." She pauses. "Winter nights, safe in his arms." She puts the photo back and takes up her brush again. In the candlelight, her hair is a silver wreath around her head.

"This is the hour of remembering and I must remember it all, so it will live, so I won't lose it. Sometimes he would watch me brush my hair as he lay in bed. Sometimes, he offered to brush it for me, though his hands were rough, and somehow clumsy, as if he might be nervous. It thrilled me, that those hands that worked so hard all day would want one more task before bed. Sometimes he put his face into my hair as we lay in bed. It told me what he was thinking." She turns to look at Sarah. "I had the chance to be everything I wanted to be in life. I know I'm the rare exception to be able to say that. I owe thanks to my wonderful parents and to my darling Earle." She puts down the brush, turns the picture to face the bed, and stands.

"In this house, I sat on my grandfather's knee and heard him tell of his grandparents. And now my grandchildren come, and I talk about my life and the others I have witnessed. My whole life has been a re-membering. I've never thought of it quite this way but remembering is appreciation of those who have been here, who added in some way, to what life is like for me and for others who will come. It isn't a burden, but I worry that I am the last one who carries all I remember. After me, a few will carry some of it, but no one will carry it all."

Sarah takes her hand. "I'll remember it, Gram. Just as you told me. It seems a lot, but you tell it so lovingly. Someday I'll tell my children too. It probably won't be as real to them. They won't have the quilts, or the old house to see, or the marble tablets on the hillside."

"These things will still be here…"

"But there's not much chance I'll be here. My life will be different than yours, Gram. The things I want to do, to achieve, can't be done here. And this will be my brother's home, not mine."

"I'll leave this house to you if you want it, Sarah. When I'm gone, it'll be your home to come back to, wherever you go, whatever you do."

Sarah laughs. "I take Kelty Farm with me, Gram. If you're not here, what would this place mean to any of us? You are Kelty Farm. I'll just try to remember all the faces, all the stories."

"Well, child, you'll remember as you remember. You'll have your own life to mix in it, your own feelings to change how you see it all. And, I guess, that's as it should be." She pauses a moment, feeling the weight of her words. She goes to the window and turns down the wick in the lamp. As the light goes out, the end of the room is in moonlight.

Sarah opens the closet door and begins to hang up her clothes, slipping a nightgown over her head, letting it fall to the floor. As Grace changes, Sarah puts her hands onto a quilt at the bottom of the bed. "Did you make these quilts, Gram?"

"No. I give away the quilts I make. My Gramma Lucy made this top one. I like it the best of all my quilts because it has pieces of everything from her daily life. It's a time capsule. I recognize pieces of work shirts, probably from my brothers, Grampa Ike, and my father. There are pieces of Gramma Lucy's dresses, my mother's, and even some from dresses I wore when I was a little girl. When I look at it for a while, at any one piece, its pattern blossoms in my mind into the whole garment it was cut from, and soon I see the person who wore it.

"This little square is faded from its original dark brown, but I can still pick out a tiny, embroidered flower that wasn't yellow like this, but was orange. I saw Gramma Lucy's sister Lillian wearing it. She was a silent woman who liked to weave and sew in her last years on the Farm. There's a square from one of those shirts in my mother's quilt underneath." She lifts up the top quilt to show the one below it.

"Your mother made this one?"

"Yes. In the summer it's the only one I use on my bed. It has a pretty design. She didn't just sew pieces together haphazardly. Her quilts had to have a pattern. I think it's because of all the sorrow she lived through, the things she had no control over. When it came to making a quilt, she was so exact, so conscious of colors, of patterns."

"But you like Gramma Lucy's quilt better?"

"Yes. It's very special to me... Sometime, I'll tell you more about that..."

"Tell me now."

"No, dear. There's an obligation that goes with it, and you're not ready for it, yet. I'll tell you another time."

"Why can't you tell me now? Why is this quilt so different from the other?"

"Please, Sarah. I'm just not ready to tell you. And it's not that the quilt is so different, it's just that I feel differently about it. It gives me comfort that my gramma's and my mother's hands made these, and that their quilts are keeping me warm, even so many years later. They made these quilts with love, and when I sleep wrapped in them, I feel the love." She laughs.

"One time I had a dream that my mother and Gramma Lucy were cross with me about something, and that when I woke up, I found all the knots on their quilts untied. The morning after that dream, I was afraid to open my eyes. I felt with my fingers to find knots still tied, to see if it had happened." She laughs again. "But it was just a dream. It shows how important it is to me to live right and know they would approve."

"I have a quilt you made. It's true that it makes me think of you. I'll appreciate it more, now that I see what your quilts mean to you."

"I can make you another quilt—in fact I have. I've made you a Double Wedding Ring quilt, like my mother made for me as a wedding present. I know your mother doesn't make quilts, so I made it...to give you...someday."

Sarah hugs her grandmother. "Oh, Gram, thank you. If you're saving it for a wedding present, you're going to save it for a long time. I have a lot of living to do before I ever marry."

"I've made one for each of your brothers, too. But don't tell them. They wouldn't understand. Now, let's go to bed. Do you want to sleep with me or I can make up the trundle bed for you? We can just pull it out, like when you were a little girl."

"No, Gram, I'd rather sleep with you."

Sarah gets in first and Grace gets in beside her, pulling the quilts over them. She reaches for the candle on the bedside table, but Sarah stops her.

"Don't put out the candle yet, Gram. Let's talk some more."

"Joseph will be waiting. But a while more won't hurt. What did you want to talk about? College is going well, isn't it?"

"It was a leap of faith to leave here. It's what my mother thought was right, and my brothers are watching to see how I do. I'm a little scared. It's frightening to face what has just been a dream till now."

"Just you know you have all of us at Kelty Farm behind you, believing in you, loving you."

"But I'm the one on the line, living in a strange place, among people I don't know."

"You're the pioneer of the family, Sarah, blazing new trails, doing new things. You're very brave. Whenever you doubt yourself, remember the people you come from, the people who hung onto what they wanted, who always found a way to get through."

"But that's different. The Farm is a very little world. Everybody knows you and all about you. And, because of that, you act in a certain way. I don't mean 'act' exactly, I mean everyone who knows everyone else doesn't try to be anything they really aren't. So, people are real in places like this. Out there, where I'm going to be, I'm the only one who knows who and what I am. It'll be up to me to keep me honest, to keep me straight. I'm the only one who will know when I'm off course, or over my head, and I'll be alone doing what I'm doing."

"All struggles are the same. We really are, every one of us, alone in our struggle, but there are many who would aid us if we ask. You asked for the opportunity to go to college and you're getting it. It's like that, in life. No one needs to help a person who is not doing anything. But if someone is working, trying to accomplish a goal, everyone wants to lend a hand. You only have to ask."

"I'll remember that, Gram."

"It's a good lesson to learn because you'll use it all your life. As life goes on, the things you struggle over change, but that principle stays the same."

"It must be nice to be past this kind of struggle."

"My dear girl! Life has fresh tests and trials in store for each of us, every day. It never stops…until it all stops. The things I work at and worry over are my issues, and I make a little progress every day."

Sarah takes a moment to think this over. "What did you mean before, about the room being haunted?"

"Most children that have lived here have been uncomfortable in this room. I understand that. Remember, I was a child in this house, too."

"When you were little, you thought this room was haunted?"

"I just know that my brothers all crowded into a smaller room at the end of the hall when this larger room was empty. We used it as a sort of attic, storing odds and ends of things that were seldom used. I never came in here as a child. There were no lights until much later and so it was dark. I emptied it out to use as a playroom for my children, but they wouldn't play in it. I fixed it up as a guest room, but anyone who slept here complained of a very restless night."

Sarah clutches the covers, looking toward Grace. "Did anyone ever see…anything?"

Grace laughs, "You mean like a ghost? No, not anything like that."

"Tell me about the crack in the heart-shaped window."

"That's a long story. Aren't you tired?"

"No, Gram, tell me."

"That window is the whole story of Kelty Farm. My great-great-grandmother, Elishabet, was the most beautiful girl in the county, and had many a beau. When she was younger than you are now, she chose a young man who came from a landed family. On her wedding day, her husband, Archelaus Kelty, gave her this window, its frame carved from a single piece of oak. He then announced his intention of going away with his bride, 'To the west, where a man can come into his own.' Elishabet begged him not to go, not to take her, for her father not to allow this. But everyone applauded the young man's courage to strike out on his own and warned her that none of them would help her if she disobeyed her husband."

"I can't imagine being forced to leave like that."

"Seven years later, Elishabet returned. She was haggard and worn, beaten down by sorrow. Her husband had died, and a child had been born dead. She had slowly worked her way back home. Her parents were dead, and her brother wouldn't take her in. He said he had inherited all, that there was no portion for her. He sent her to her in-laws, the Keltys.

"The Keltys were reluctant, but they felt bound to take her in. They had four younger sons living with them. Elishabet had brought a crate with her from the west. When it was unpacked, it contained some linen towels she had made for her wedding, and the heart-shaped window, which had been chopped free from a wall. The Keltys called her bad luck and tried to find ways to justify making her leave."

"That's terrible. What did they do?"

"They worked her very hard and found fault with everything. Finally, they told her their Bible dictated she marry another brother. She wanted none of them. They said it was unseemly that she, a single woman, live in the house with so many unmarried men. The youngest, nineteen-year-old Arthur declared his wish to marry Elishabet. She was taken aback, but demanded he build her a house of her own, high on a hill, so she would never have to be beholden to live with anyone again. He agreed.

"There was family land from a Revolutionary War grant, though it was burdened with a tax debt. Arthur petitioned the town for his portion and paid the tax off by cutting and milling trees into lumber for the town hall being built then. He showed Elishabet the place he had chosen to build. She complained that it was under the brow of the hill, when she wanted her house on the top of the hill. But he convinced her they were more likely to have water here and not have to lug it, and the house would be protected from storms."

"And this is the very house he built, right Gram?"

"It was added to several times, but the parlor was the original one room, and this room was the loft. Arthur put the window into the wall of this room for her, in memory of his brother and the child who were buried in the west."

"How did it get cracked?"

"Arthur noticed a small crack in the glass when he put the window in. Elishabet told him to leave it that way, that it suited her to have the heart broken. Then, years later, when it had broken in a jagged line all the way across, someone had it leaded as you see it now."

"What a story! And was she happy after she got her own house?"

"Elishabet was never a happy woman. Art was the second man to make her Mrs. Kelty. He worked tirelessly in an effort to prosper and gain his bride's admiration and love. He had a sawmill, the farm with both sheep and dairy, and raised four sons, but he went to an early grave before he was fifty, never hearing a kind word from Elishabet. He was the first Kelty to lie on the hillside above this house." Grace pauses, reluctant to continue. She gets out of bed and walks toward the window, then stops. Sarah sits up, waiting.

"She wrapped him in one of her hand-made quilts, and they laid him in a coffin made of pine boards he had sawed himself. She stood silently by through the funeral until they were mounding the earth above his grave. Suddenly, a sob ripped from her heart. She covered her face with her hands. Her body quaked in grief. Her snow-white hair, tied in a bun, shook loose and covered her face, falling toward the earth. As her sons reached for her, she threw herself onto the fresh sandy earth, pushing her face into the dirt, moaning, tears flowing. In front of her shocked family, the dam in her heart spilled out her sorrows, stored from childhood. She declared she had not known a man was capable of loving her as this man had."

Grace sits on the bench at the dressing table. "After that day, Elishabet lived quietly, never complaining, weaving and stitching till her eyes gave out, sitting with grandchildren while their parents worked the Farm. When she died, they laid her to rest beside the man who had loved her." Grace pauses, as if she is stunned by the story.

"Are you all right, Gram?"

"Some of these family stories get started and have to run their course."

"So, how did you decide to move into the haunted room?"

"Haunted? Child, you don't believe in ghosts, do you? If there was such a thing, it would be the presence of Elishabet in this room. But I am the first mistress of Kelty Farm who was born here. I have lived in this house longer than anyone. I couldn't concede one inch of space to any unfriendly presence. I never found a picture of Elishabet, but I found two of the linen towels she made before her first wedding. They were embroidered with the initials A K E, for Almost-Grampa-Arc, Elishabet, and Kelty. My Grampa Ike, Elishabet's grandson, said that Arthur's initial being the same as Arc's was another reason she consented to marry him."

"What did you do with the linen towels?"

"I decided to use them as side curtains for the heart window, reuniting the efforts of Elishabet and Arc in the house Arthur built for her. I moved into this room myself. I filled the room with things I loved, and that was the beginning of my 'Hour of Remembering'. I found peace here that eluded me elsewhere. That peace spread out of this room, across the hall, and down the stairway. It brought together all those I have loved and remember, who would otherwise be a part of a void their passing left for me. Most of my life is in the past now, but I live in the midst of strong memories that cannot, will not be denied."

Sarah settles down, yawns. "It's so much to remember. I don't know how you can."

"It's not remembering so much as it is knowing. All of my life, these things have been here for me to know. Sometimes I forget one thing or another, or something starts to fade. But telling it makes it live again. "

"I want to remember it all too, the way you did tonight." As her eyes are closing, "Will I remember, Gram?"

Grace pulls the covers over Sarah's shoulder and kisses her forehead. "Well, child, that's for you to choose." She reaches toward the candle, hesitates, and walks to the window. Looking out, she speaks into the moonlight, "Joseph, we're making it through another generation who know Kelty Farm as home. As far flung as all our family is, like the seeds of milkweed on the wind, you and I, Joseph, give them a place to come back to. Let's promise that it'll be here, for them that were, for us that are, for those who will come."

Grace gets back into bed, kisses Sarah again and blows out the candle. "Good night, Joseph. Tomorrow, I guess tomorrow will take care of itself."

24

1989: DAYS OF DECISION

Day 1, Grace's Kitchen

"I'm glad you could come home, Kelty." Grace brings a cup of coffee from the shelf to the table and sits with her grandson. "It's been a strain on the Farm since your father had the stroke. I hardly know any of the hired hands anymore."

"I knew when I heard about Dad you would need me, Gram. I hope I didn't scare you, coming in so late last night." He sips his coffee, toying with the food on the plate. She notices he has dressed for work today.

"Scare me?" She smiles. "Who else would open the refrigerator before closing the outside door?"

"I was trying to be quiet and not wake you."

"Living alone so many years, I know every sound this old house can make. I hear the wood snapping as it dries near the stove. I hear the breeze against the windows. Sometimes I think I can hear the nails popping loose in the shingles. The sound of your feet on the stairs was music to my ears. I didn't get up because I knew you'd be tired, and we'd talk all night." She takes her plate from the table and puts it on the shelf near the sink.

"I stopped at Mother's house first. There was no one there. And I knew you'd have a room made up for me, that it would be warm at the homestead." He hands her his plate as she reaches for it.

Grace laughs, "'By God and the maple chunk, we'll be warm tonight,' your grandfather used to say. I wish you remembered him better. He was a fine man."

"When I worked with Dad, he talked about his father. Every hillside and tree seems to remind Dad of another story about someone, usually his father. Sometimes I'm not sure whether I'm remembering things that happened or something Dad told me so many times it seems like I was there to see it myself. In any case, I know you and Dad, and what kind of people I come from." He sits back in the chair, his big frame comfortable at the table in the kitchen of the old house.

Grace looks fondly at the young man. "It's good to have you here. Things are not going well since your mother took Joseph, your father, to the medical center."

"I was so caught up in things at college this spring, and Mother said things were being handled. But I know it took everything Dad had in him to run things."

"It would have been easier on him all these years if your mother had been here helping him instead of having her 'career.' A career for a farmer's wife is the farm."

Kelty sighed. This was old territory. "That was between them, Gram, and nothing you or I could settle now." He had sidestepped this argument before.

"Anyway, I have a better feeling about things now you're home. Your mother will be upset you left school." He lifts his cup and saucer as she wipes down the table.

"Dad would expect this of me. I left her a message I'd be here. I'm sure she'll call today. I told them at school I had a family emergency—they already knew about Dad being in the hospital, so it was no surprise to them I had to leave. I tried to call Michael but couldn't find him. I don't even know where to call Sarah. I'm not much of a big brother to those two since I left for college."

"Oh, I hear from Michael every other Monday. He's always fine, never has any news. And Sarah calls every few weeks. She talks about her two kids, about her job and the few courses she's taking. I always ask her to come for a visit. She says, 'Sometime, Gram.'" Grace sits at the table, folding her hands in her lap.

"I ought to do something for Sarah, I just don't know what."

"Kelty, your brother and sister know you're busy. You're older. You stayed on the land after they left. It must be harder for you in college than for them. I never thought you would go after so long."

"I finally gave in to Mother. She thinks farm life is a sentence to work off."

"Your mother has never understood the hero it takes to do the same job day after day, committed to something bigger than your own lifetime. That's the person it takes to run Kelty Farm."

"It was heaven to me. She said if I was going to take over from Dad that I at least had to have a good education. Mother never valued the real education I got right here working with Dad, season by season."

"You and your father are...were...a pair!" Grace begins to cry and pulls her apron from her lap to her face. Kelty puts his hand on her shoulder. "I'm sorry. I promised myself I wouldn't do this, that Joseph needs us to be strong. I'm not sure how things will be without your father. It's so hard to believe he isn't just across the valley in his house, or even right upstairs covered in quilts, not up yet this morning. The years slip in and out on me. Sometimes I catch myself fixing lunch and waiting for your grandfather to come in from the fields, and here, he's been gone all these years."

"It's all right, Gram, I'm here now. And Dad will come out of this."

"I only know what she tells me, so I don't know much."

"Mother has taken an apartment near the medical center. She said Dad was worried about me missing school. I thought that was transparent of her."

"I wish she had kept him in the town hospital. The medical center is so far away. She said the stroke was brought on by overwork and worry. I think it's from her pressuring him to leave here."

"None of that matters, now. Mother loves him in her own way."

"It's just hard to hear her self-serving accusations without having my say. Your father never did a thing he didn't want to do."

"But Father never slowed down, either. And now we know he should have, that we should have made him. Being in the hospital and the rehab they have there is going to be hard on him. He's used to the outdoors, to coming and going, not staying put."

Grace looks into Kelty's eyes. "He'll come to see that getting well is his job now, what he has to do. If I know Joseph, he wants to get back here."

He takes Grace's hand across the table, lowering his voice. "We may have to face the fact that Dad isn't likely to come back the way he was before the stroke, that some things are already changed."

"Well, we are not making any decisions now, unless we let everything slip away and there's nothing for him to come back to." She stands, unsure for a moment, then puts her back to the broad shelf, and wraps her arms in her apron front. "I'm not going to stand by and let it happen. I'd never be able to face your father. I wouldn't want to be the last Kelty, and the one that let the Farm go. My parents gave it to my husband and me sixty years ago. It was unheard of then, to let a daughter inherit the land. But they did exactly that. They even offered to change the name of the Farm. You were given the old family name."

"I know all the stories, Gram, but they're not going to help now."

"Joseph will never get well if we let anything happen to the Farm. We might just as well take a gun and shoot him, and I bet he'd rather we did."

"Gram, you're not in this alone. We're going to be here with everything running smoothly when he gets well. If any decision has to be made, it'll wait till then. For now, you better stop feeding me these muffins and doughnuts or I won't be able to get away from the table!" Kelty stands and embraces Grace, her arms still inside her apron front. She leans against him.

"It's been a while since I had anyone to feed. I'd forgotten how good it feels to take care of someone."

"New curtains, too, I see. They're pretty bright, aren't they? They don't seem like you."

"I guess I've got a few surprises left for you, haven't I. I needed something to pick me up last week and I ordered them from a catalog. I can't remember ever having store bought curtains in those windows. And you're right, they are bright. I'm not sure that's the color I meant to order, but I like them. I guess change isn't all bad, and there are still some things I have say over. I felt better as soon as I put them up. Right after, you called to say you were coming home. I decided things had taken a turn for the better."

He smiles at her but reaches for his jacket. "I'm going out for a quick look around and talk to the hired hands. I'll be back about lunchtime, and we'll figure out what needs doing first."

"I'll think of something special for your lunch."

"I know you will, Gram." He reaches for the doorknob.

"Wait, Kelty. When I knew you were going to sleep under this old roof, that you'd have breakfast at the head of this table, I decided it was time. When you're walking around Kelty land, you should know how closely you're connected to it. I want to give you something my father gave to my husband. My dad said it came from his father." Grace takes something from her pocket and places it carefully in Kelty's waiting hands.

"It's beautiful. Is it a compass?"

"Yes. It's supposedly from almost-grampa Arc, the brother of Arthur Kelty, my great, great grandfather." Grace laughs. "I know you don't need it to find your way around," then, more seriously, "but when you feel it in your pocket, it will remind you who you are, and where you belong."

"Oh, Gram! I couldn't take it—I'd be afraid to lose it."

"I offered it to your father once, a long time ago, but he said to save it to give to you someday. See how the leather case has darkened in the smooth places. All the old timers here held that compass and added their sweat to it. Now it's yours."

Kelty puts it in his pocket, kisses his grandmother, and closes the door behind him. She watches after him then hears a knock at the front door. She looks puzzled and goes down the hallway to open the formal door.

"Rachel!" She steps back in surprise. "Come in. When does family knock at the front door? Why didn't you call?" Suddenly she is alarmed. "It's not Joseph? Nothing's happened to Joseph?"

Rachel breezes past Grace, removing her coat. "Joseph was fine when I left him last night. And I called this morning—there's no change. He had a restful night. I didn't know how early to call you, so I just came up. There are a few things we've got to settle."

"Settle?"

Rachel sits on the sofa, putting her coat across her lap. She looks up at Grace. "I got a message from Kel yesterday. When I called him back, the school said he had left on a family emergency. I only know of one family emergency and I'm managing that." Rachel changes her tone. "So, I suspect that you are manufacturing an emergency of your own. I'm sure you're trying to lure him away from school."

Grace, still standing, puts her arms inside her apron front again. "He's here. He came last night."

"I thought as much. I thought I could catch him at home this morning, but there was no sign of his having slept there. Then I looked across the valley and saw his car here. Is he still sleeping?"

"No. He's gone out to have a look around. He'll be back for lunch."

"He and I will be leaving then. We won't stay for lunch."

Grace unwraps her arms, folding her hands before her. "Kelty will decide that for himself."

"After I talk with him, he will decide to do things my way. I know you must have called him to come back. I want you to stop interfering with my family."

"Your family, Rachel? This is my family too. You are my family. I'm not interfering. I just want everything to be here when Joseph gets well."

Rachel gazes at Grace. She speaks firmly, "Joseph may get well, and be back on his feet again, after a while. That remains to be seen. He's still in guarded condition, and I don't want him worried about his son leaving college to be here. That's what hired help is for. If they're not enough, if you can't get by on what help you can get, then it's time we take a look at the future. One thing I know: Joseph will never come back to work here. I'll see to that. And if you have your heart set on Kel taking his father's place, then take a good look at where his father is right now. Is that where you want to see Kel, too? What's it going to take to see the day of one man running a farm this size is over..."

Grace interrupts: "Joseph will decide that."

"Joseph is past deciding anything. He's not going to be influenced by you and your ancestors buried on the hill. It's not just the work that is the heavy load to carry here. It's the history, the weight of all those generations—it may come down to letting them go to save his life. Joseph is worth more than all the headstones--and so is my son. Kelty Farm put your grandfathers in their graves, your father, your husband, and all the Kelty women except you. But you're not going to get my men."

"Rachel, Rachel. You give me too much credit. I let all that go long since. Joseph is his own man. He decided to cut firewood for sale, to increase the cattle herd and enlarge the barns. He decided what crops to plant, what land to put to trees, how to market the apple crop. Whenever he asked me, I gave my advice, but he decided."

"I know you won't accept the blame..."

"If you're blaming me because he's a man who makes his own decisions, then I guess you're willing to give me the credit for some of his decisions that were made directly against my wishes, like building a house for you in the middle of my father's orchard when we all could have lived in this house."

"Well, that damage is done. You've never liked my house, but he built it for me, to have us both, and have peace. If we'd had to live here, in this old place—with you, he'd have lost me, lost his children, and hated you for that. My house has stood in that orchard thirty years—you can have it back now. And if anything happens to Joseph, I have his power of attorney—Kelty Farm will be for sale!"

Kelty comes into the hallway toward the parlor in time to hear this last remark. He has the compass in his hand but slips it into his pocket. He stands in the doorway unnoticed.

"I guess you've forgotten. You spent your years chasing other rainbows, your businesses. I'm glad all that paid off well for you. You never needed Kelty Farm or anything we could give you. But I am still partner with Joseph on the Farm—which ever of us outlives the other becomes sole owner. God forbid anything happens to Joseph, but if it does, the Farm belongs to me." Grace's voice is soft, but somehow full of steel.

"Stop it! Father's not dying—he'll get through this—he's got to! And you two won't pull his world apart while he's getting well. I'm here to see to that. Everything will be as he left it."

Rachel turns to her son. "Kel, darling, your place is in school."

"I would have finished this year anyway. I say I'm done now. I'm moving in with Gram."

Rachel eyes her son. "I'm your mother, I'm in charge. It'll be the way I say…"

"Gram has the say here, and I'll stick with her on Father's behalf. Do what you want to do, but Kelty Farm goes on as before, the way Gram and Dad want."

Grace leaves the room, walking slowly toward the kitchen.

"Kel, you don't know what you're saying. The last thing your father would want is for you to give up on your future, your own education. Your sister Sarah doesn't feel any obligation here, nor your brother Michael. This is your life, Kel, not your father's all over again. That was the way it was for your father, trying to please his parents, wanting to do what his mother would think was the right thing. Now he's in the hospital—and can't speak for himself—is that his reward for making Kelty Farm live another thirty-five years? Is that what you want for your next thirty-five years?"

"We're not talking years, here, but only till Dad is on his feet. Then he and Gram can say what they want to do."

Rachel reconsiders her approach. "Kel, if your father could tell you today that he was all done here, what would you do? Would you try to go on anyway, just because your grandmother can't let go of the past? That's what this is about, you know. This problem exists because your grandmother thinks she owes something to her parents, to her dead brothers, her husband, and I don't know who else! She would sacrifice the present and the future—your future—to her past. You could change all that, Kel, right now. You could do what you want to do with your life. What they wanted was to be here married to the Farm. You haven't made that choice yet—it's not too late for you."

Kelty's hands clench, but he speaks evenly, "I would have decided years ago to live here, working with my father. That's the thing I wanted, to make the Farm my own in my turn. You insisted I go to college. I put it off years past when I should have gone. Right now, I'm the oldest in every class. I even have one professor younger than I am."

"Kel, I only wanted what was in your best interest..."

"I know—and Dad knew too—that it was your hope I'd get my education and move on, that I'd find the need for more than I could have here—just like Sarah and Michael."

"I only want what is best for you..."

"The best as you see it. But I've come to see that no one is all wrong or right. I think it's asking a lot from someone to want this life—I think it was asking a lot of you to want the life Dad had here. I'm worried about who I'd find to share my life. On the most casual date I start wondering if she'd like this life, like me—love me, as I would be on Kelty Farm. So, you see, the years of niggling thoughts you planted in my head are bearing harvest. I see why Dad married late. I don't want that. I want to be young with my children. I want a wife who wants me as I am, who will appreciate the life we can have here, together."

"Really, Kel, we're off the main issue..."

"Mother, you accuse Gram of pushing Dad into what she chose for him, and maybe it's true. But can you really say that you're any different —to me or to Dad?"

"Kel, you're upset now because of the responsibility you're taking on your shoulders. This is not your burden."

"But it's Dad's." He sits beside his mother. "It's all I can do for him. I'm just glad he gave me some experience and now I'm not lost here without him."

Rachel sits back against the sofa, her hands kneading her coat. "Be realistic, Kel. We aren't talking about a weekend, or even a month. The best we can hope for your father, with rehab, is to return in some limited capacity in six or eight months. That's a big chunk of your life to commit when we don't know if the opportunity is worth it."

"We'll be able to talk to Dad sooner than that."

Rachel's eyes flash. Her face sets in a frown. "We will not bring up the Farm to your father until he's well enough to be on his own. If he's got any chance to recover, it has to be to get rest from these cares. What we should do is to get a professional in here to run the Farm like a business then sell to the first buyer who comes along."

Kelty stands, turning to face his mother. "That's not going to happen, not as long as Gram's alive, and probably not ever. Let's not waste any more time. I'm home now, I'm staying. It's settled! What my brother and sister do is up to them. Michael's never been interested, and Sarah, well, she's got her own problems."

"You've got to finish school. You promised me!"

"You made me promise! All bets are off now. Besides, I could go back when the time is right…"

"That's what Sarah said…"

"It's the same thing…"

"It's not the same thing. She was pregnant. The situation couldn't be ignored." Rachel spit out the words.

"This can't be ignored either. There's no use in any more discussion without Dad's input. If we have to wait for that, at least someone with experience will be running things. If I couldn't do this, six months from now we would find our decision already made." They stand their ground, a test of wills. Rachel steps back and slowly puts on her coat.

"You know where to reach me."

Kelty kisses his mother but does not walk her to the door. "Take care of Dad." She lets herself out, and he returns to the kitchen.

Grace looks up from her pots on the stove. "Is she gone? I didn't hear her car drive away."

"Her car is quieter than that four-wheel-drive she had before."

"She's not quieter…"

"I don't want to be put in the position of having to defend my mother, any more than I want to defend you to her."

"You're right, Kelty. I'm sorry. When I think of your father, so far away, so alone… But at least she can be with him. And Michael's in the same city, so he can see his father."

"Dad's job is to get well, and our job is to keep going, at least for now. You and I make a good team. I've got a great feeling about this. So, let's get to work."

"First, we'll have lunch."

Day 2, Two weeks later, local hospital room

Sarah comes to the doorway, finds her grandmother sleeping, Kelty sleeping in a chair beside her. She looks around the room then touches her brother's shoulder.

"Kel. Kel. Wake up, big brother."

He wakes, stands, and embraces her fiercely. "Sarah! I wasn't sure you could come! I really needed you here."

"I got that from your message. It's one of the few times you've really tried to reach me. Of course I'd come! Mother told me you were here, and I'd been thinking of coming up. I'm glad you let me know about Gram. How is she?"

"She needs some rest. She's been doing too much, worrying too much. She took over the worrying from Dad."

"Does Dad know Gram is in the hospital?" She studies her grandmother's face.

"I don't think so. I haven't been to see Dad this week. Mother won't even let me discuss the Farm with him, so I'm sure she hasn't told him about Gram. He's doing better, Mother says."

Sarah takes off her coat and hat and puts them on the chair next to Kelty.

"It's great Mother is so devoted to Dad's care. It's been a godsend for him. And he is getting better all the time. She seemed glad to hear from me yesterday. She's been distant to me for some time. I sensed her disapproval still, but she was friendly enough. She didn't ask how I was, or about the children. I think she feels that's my bed and I've got to lie in it."

"That's not an issue for me, Sarah. I want to know how you are, what's going on for you, for the kids. Where are they? Who's keeping them? Did you bring them with you?"

"Lucy and Mike are at Gram's house. I think they'll be all right."

"Sure, they'll find something to do. They've been there before. I get such a kick out of Lucy calling her brother Ike instead of Mike. What about Steve. You and he are not together?"

"I don't want to talk about that. Anyway, won't this chatter disturb Gram?"

"She's been given something to sleep. Let's sit over here." He takes her hand, and they walk to chairs further from the bed. "I should have gone back to the Farm, but everything seems so empty without Gram. Here, at least, I open my eyes and see her breathing quietly, resting. I've found a lot of comfort in that. I'm glad she's here, in town, and not far off like Dad. I've been feeling alone, and no one to talk to about it. Mom surely doesn't want to hear it."

"That's her disapproval, Brother. Anything about Kelty Farm brings it out—you know that. We've heard it since we were old enough to talk. She resents having to live there all those years, resents Dad wanting to work after she sold her business in town and was ready to retire. I thought she'd blow a gasket when you refused to go to college. I wasn't surprised you finally gave in. And now you're the oldest living junior in the state college system."

"Be careful, sister. You're aiming for the funny bone but hitting tender spots that don't take ribbing well. Besides, I'm more than a junior. I'm working on senior credits and headed for early graduation. But that's all off for now. I don't think I'll ever go back."

"It's Kelty Farm, isn't it? I see it hanging over you like a sword. I often thought Mother's determination to keep you away from it only drove you toward it." Sarah studies her brother.

"Let's not talk about Mother. Let's be glad we're together. God! It's so good to be with you, to talk to you. I've forgotten how much I've missed you, how much I love you, Sarah!"

"My dear sir—you could turn a girl's head with that kind of talk—if you weren't my brother!" They laugh together. Kelty takes her hand.

"Seriously, Sis, it means a lot that you came when I called. How does it work out with your job?"

"Job. That's the real problem. I hate to say it, but it worked out just the way Mother said it would—no sheepskin, no career. All I could ever get was a job, almost enough to keep body and soul together. And, as the kids came along, well, the choices were slim. Anyway, it was no problem to say I needed a week off. The reality? The job won't be there when I get back."

"Hasn't Steve been helping?"

"Steve can hardly help himself. In fact, he's one of my major charities. I love the guy, but he's not growing up fast enough to be my husband, or father to the kids. There's no solution to that problem."

"How's that with the kids? I feel so out of touch. They must be in school by now..."

"They're in preschool and first grade. They have a break coming up next week, so they're only missing a few days. As for their father, they think of him as a giant teddy bear, a live, adult-sized playmate. They don't really have a father figure."

Kelty turns more serious. He grips her hand. "Tell me what's going on with Steve."

Sarah pulls her hand away and stands looking out the window. "I told you I don't want to talk about it."

"Damn it, Sarah!' He stands behind her at the window clenching and unclenching his fists. "That works on the phone, in conversations a month apart. It's not going to work here."

Sarah faces Kelty. "Be quiet, you'll disturb Gram. And don't you have enough problems? I know you're being out of school is not going over well with Mother. You're not fooling me. You were always a push-over for Gram and the Farm. But look where it got Dad."

"That's different. Dad couldn't discuss any problem with Mother because her solution to everything was to sell out and move away. I don't have anything big to decide. I'm only maintaining. And you're right. I love it. There are new ideas to try, new ways to market. I'd do it for free, even if I wasn't doing it for Dad and Gram."

"Or for the cemetery full of Keltys that are looking over your shoulder. I always wondered if you felt trapped by being named after the ghosts who ran the place so long."

"Dad must have really wanted me to have that name. I can imagine how hard it was to convince Mother. I admire him when I think of it. As for the Farm, I can't remember ever wanting to do anything else. It seems my rightful place."

"That reminds me. Tell me about all the old journals on the table at Gram's." She rummages around in her purse and brings out an old book. "Some of them go way back."

"Gram got them out. She thought I should go through them to see if there were things done in past seasons that we might be forgetting now. They're pretty interesting. It's so weird reading words and handwriting of people I've only thought of when I saw their names on tombstones. I've often been startled to find conversations—almost word for word, faithfully written down fifty or a hundred years ago—that dad and I had again only last year. It certainly gives you the idea that there aren't too many new things under the sun, at least not on Kelty Farm."

"I'm amazed at the journals themselves. I never knew about them. It's like one of Gram's patch-work quilts, every time you look at it, you see something you'd swear wasn't there before. In different light, you see colors or combinations you never noticed, and sometimes a certain patch seems to stand out, making you wonder about where it was cut from, why it was put in that exact spot. You just can't know; you just can't know everything."

"Are we still talking about the Farm or Gram's quilts? Tell me about Steve."

She pauses, looks past her brother. "Well, to continue the metaphor, Steve is a patch you're really glad to have, thrilled about in fact. But then you find out it doesn't fit in anywhere, doesn't go with anything else you've planned, or want. When you're determined to use this beautiful square that you so tenderly cut to size and shape, and even if you're willing to rearrange the whole pattern to accommodate it, it just won't go with anything else." She pauses. "Then finally, when you've thrown everything else away just to keep this one special square, this one special patch you want so badly to fit, well, then when you have nothing else left, you find that you really don't want only this."

Kelty reaches to embrace his sister as she continues.

"That's when you begin to find wisdom hidden in things like quilts. When you have nothing else—except what you wanted bad enough to throw away everything else to get—well, you find out why you thought quilts were so beautiful your whole life. It's the idea of everything fitting together, one square sitting beside the others, everything coming together to form the pattern." She buries her head in her brother's shoulder, gripping his shirt. "But it's all the pieces together that keep you warm and gives the quilt its value."

"This is hurting you. I want to know how I can help."

"The worst part is that all the things they try to tell you all your life...well, it turns out they were right. Your father, even your mother..." she walks toward the sleeping woman on the bed, "your grandmother. Every old story they ever told you, well there was a lesson here, about the people...not who they were—that's what you try to remember—you think the stories are about who they were—it's not about that at all. The stories are about what kind of people we come from, what happened to them, how it turns out over a lifetime. We can't know for ourselves how it will be; it hasn't fully unraveled yet, we are too close to see any meaning in it. But we can hear the stories, read the journals, look at the tombstones—we can know all about what it was like for them."

"Look, Sarah, I didn't mean to get you so upset. Drop all the metaphors; I never was good at following them."

She laughs. "Kel, my dear. All those lit classes must be hell for you."

"The Elizabethan poets went down pretty hard. As soon as one said, 'My love is like,' they lost me. But I got by."

"You are such a sweet man, Kel. I love you. The reason metaphors are lost on you is that you're so direct. And you don't see the need for any other way. The short story between Steve and me is this: Boy meets girl. Boy gets girl. Girl has children, becomes a woman. Boy becomes a father, remains a boy."

"Well, that's direct. I think I got it that time." He looks at his hands, Sarah gazes out the window. At the same time, they say: "Look, I didn't mean..." They laugh.

"Sarah, I didn't mean to pry..." Sarah interrupts him, putting her hand up.

"Kelty, I'm sorry to be so blunt. I could have been more kind. I know you and Steve are friends. I just haven't had time to deal with my feelings about this. I hate to keep offering excuses, but I've been working very hard to keep life close to normal for the kids. I'm putting everything I've got into their needs, and I haven't got time to consider Steve, or even myself."

"Sounds like you could use some help."

"Dad was helping. He sent a check every week, always something, some weeks more than others. I don't know what Mother thought of it, but it stopped when Dad went into the Medical center."

"She hasn't said anything?" Kelty felt some resentment toward his mother.

"No, and I haven't asked. I just didn't realize how much I'd come to depend on that check. It was like a shot in the arm, like coming home from work and finding the table set or the meal cooking. It made me feel I wasn't alone, that someone cared..." Sarah sighed.

"You should have asked Mother to keep it up."

"Well, to be fair, the checks were written on the Farm account, maybe she didn't know. It was from Dad, something to let me know he was thinking of me. Probably sold a cord of wood, or a few bags of potatoes. Knowing him, it was a little game he played, making that extra, giving it to me. Do you mind, now that you know?"

"What I mind is that you needed it and I didn't know. I always had whatever I needed and didn't carry a job to get through like most of my classmates. That's why I took extra courses. And I know Michael never wanted for anything. If he did, you can bet he asked Mother and got it!"

"That's the way it was for me when I was in school, but when I dropped out, the support stopped."

"Sounds like a message from Mother: 'Do it my way or do without my help.'"

"Brother of mine, I'm surprised to hear you talk that way."

"Sarah let's be real, here. Just between you and me, it's not news that when Mother disapproves, she stands aside to see if it's going to be sink or swim, and she's not above tipping the scale to get things to come her way."

"Kel! You've been listening to Gram too long!" Sarah laughed.

"What's that mean!" he snaps. "Don't you think I've got eyes, or opinions of my own? Gram's not putting words in my mouth. I'm nobody's puppet, not Grams, not Dad's, and not Mother's. It's a big job to keep things going for Dad and Gram, but at the same time, if I consider my own future, then I'm fighting for Kelty Farm, and Mother is not on my side." He sits in a chair and looks directly at his sister.

Sarah sits beside him, takes his hand. "I'm surprised to hear you say that. I know it's true, but I didn't think you realized it." She pats his hand and smiles. "Brother, I want to be in your corner. I'll roll up my sleeves and pitch in. I want you to win, for Gram, for Dad, and for yourself."

He squeezes her hand. "Sis, you're all right. I try not to think of this struggle as sides to choose, but just to keep everything in place. Dad getting well and Gram and he coming to terms with the future is my goal."

"But there's got to be something in it for you, Kel. What do you want out of this?"

"If things go well while Dad's away, and he and Gram are pleased, then I want them to consider my taking on the Farm. I've thought a lot about this, and that's what I want. I'd like to live in the homestead with Gram and look forward to the long run."

"I hope it turns out the way you want. I'd like some of us to be happy. Look at Gram. I've never seen anyone as content with life."

"I keep getting this picture of a lost little girl, all alone in the world…"

"It's even worse than that. The lost girl has two children who don't know she's lost, and that delusion seems to her worth the struggle."

"That's it! You're coming to live at the Farm, you and Lucy and Mike."

"Oh, right. The simple solution to everything: rescue and retreat. Not this time, Kel. That's why I call Gram so seldom. That's her solution, too. Coming home would be a step backwards for me. I've moved past the off ramp to Kelty Farm. Sometimes at night, especially if I've had a bad day, I close my eyes to sleep and I seem to see a light around the Farm. I could imagine a voice saying, 'Come back, come back.' It makes me laugh just telling you, it's like a bad cartoon."

"I've seen that cartoon, too. But I never laugh, I just see all the obstacles in my path, and worry if the Farm will be there when I come back. This is an insecurity Mother has planted. I don't know what I'll do with my life if I don't have the Farm." His voice falls away.

"You'll probably marry somebody rich and live happily ever after."

"Happily ever after for me is the Farm. And as for marrying, well, school's not the only thing on the back burner."

"Tell, tell! Is there someone special, someone you met at school?"

"Now it's my turn to say I don't want to talk about it." He laughs but looks away. "Really, it's nothing. Whenever I meet a woman I like,

I think of her in relation to the Farm, and…well, they all start to look like Mother. I guess I'm looking for someone more the 'Gram' type."

"Maybe you should just let each person be their own type, and not try to fit them in some 'either-or' category. It's like prejudging people before you find out who they really are. Try to think of them in relation to you, not anything else. If there's one you like, find out how she feels about you before you look deeper. You're not auditioning a wife for the Farm, Kel, but someone for you." She laughs, then: "And now that I've straightened out your life, tell me you've met someone special."

"Well, the answer is still that I don't have anything to report. But you've made me look at myself and given me something to think about. I guess I've been trying to line up someone who would be on my side, someone who would…"

"Sounds like you're looking for a 'Yes Woman.' Your girlfriends sure have a lot of qualifying rounds to get through. OK, you're off the hook for now, because I know we'll cover this again. Since Gram's sleeping, I'm going to go check on the kids and make them some lunch. If Gram wakes, tell her I'm here, and I'm going to stay in her room." They stand and walk toward the door.

"That reminds me, she said to tell you she left something for you under the dresser scarf, in her room."

"She knew I was coming?"

"She doesn't sleep like this all day. Sometimes she's awake and we talk. I told her I called you and she said she left you something…"

"What is it? Did you look?"

"No, I didn't look. It's for you, why would I look? If she had wanted anyone else to see what it was, she wouldn't have put it under the scarf. She would have left it on top."

"Only on Kelty Farm would anyone respect that kind of thinking. Anywhere else, knowing something was under the scarf would be an open invitation, like, 'The money is in the cookie jar,' or, 'The key is under the mat.' Everyone would look."

"I didn't look, so what's the big deal? Just look at it when you get home."

"'Home,' you said. Home to Kelty Farm? I only wish it were that simple. By the way, what is Gram doing with red curtains in the kitchen? Wow! Those are really bright!"

"I think she bought them on impulse. She said they cheered her up and made her believe that change could be a good thing. This sterile place could use something to brighten it up. If she's going to be here, maybe we should bring some of her things here. She was muttering something about a quilt last night. I thought she was cold, but she said she was just thinking about her special quilt on a shelf in her bedroom closet."

"I'll take a look and see what I can bring after lunch. If it helps her get well, I'll haul the whole place over here. It's only ten miles!" They both laugh at a family joke. "At least she's not as far away as Dad. Will I see you at home, or will you still be here when I get back?"

"I'm staying a while then I'll be along. See you later." He watches her go then sits beside the bed again. He leans his head against the wall for a minute. "Gram, most times I feel like our family's flying in all directions, but then we come together again and it's usually because of you and Kelty Farm. What will the world be without either of you? I don't want to find out."

A young man enters the room, looking around to see if he's in the right place. Kelty brightens and rushes toward the door to shake his hand.

"Steve! Steve! Wow, you just missed Sarah. She didn't say you were coming."

"She didn't know. I went to see her this morning and they told me she had gone home because of a family emergency. I came to the Farm and found Lucy and Mike alone. They told me Sarah was here with your grandmother. How is Gram?"

"She's going to be fine, just needs more rest. They don't make 'em like that anymore. She's really made of iron. The doctor had to give her something to make her sleep, or she wouldn't get any rest here either. Put your plant down on the nightstand so she'll see it when she wakes." Kelty motions toward a bedside table.

"You guys are so lucky to have her and the Farm. My family moved from place to place when I was a kid. I never knew where to say I was from. Your mother told me it was like that for her before she married your father. It's one thing she and I have in common. I saw her last week when I visited your dad. He seemed glad to see me. I asked her how she liked being away from home. She said the Farm never really felt like home to her, and she didn't miss it at all. Then she went on and on about the benefits of the medical center rehab for your father. He does seem to be making progress."

"So, what's going on with you, Steve, and more particularly, you and Sarah? She seems to be having a rough time. Can't you help her more?"

"Sarah doesn't ask anything from me, except a few dollars now and then. I never have much to give her, to be honest. I don't know how she gets by on the little jobs she gets. But she's a great mother to the kids."

"I hope you're not waiting to be asked to help. Because she can do well by herself doesn't mean she couldn't do better with you. Do you still love her? Why don't you make yourself more of a fact in her life? And your kids, don't you know how much they need you?"

"You can't say anything to me that I haven't said to myself. Of course, I love Sarah. I love her enough not to tie myself around her neck like a stone. And sure, I wish things were different than they are. I pick up a little money tutoring, and subbing for teachers, but I'm not anxious to be tied down by a teaching contract. I know I went to school to get those credentials, but it's not for me. If I could make a living growing things like you do on the Farm, maybe I could be the man Sarah needs in her life. Until I figure out what I want, I'm no good to anyone. Anyway, how long is she staying, did she say?"

"I think she'd stay for good if she could find a way to let herself do it. It would be good for her and for the kids too. For right now, she says she staying the week, and if you're not otherwise obligated, why don't you stay too? Maybe you could work off your keep doing some fence mending," Kelty smiles, "or something else useful. What do you say?"

"Sometimes I don't know if you're Sarah's big brother or the big brother I never had! You're a pal, Kelty. I don't ever want to disappoint you and lose your friendship. Why do you have such faith in me?"

"I have faith in Sarah, and she chose you."

Steve laughs. "I thought I chose her!"

"Men are supposed to think they do the choosing." They share a laugh again. "Now, can you stay the week?"

"I'll stay if Sarah doesn't mind. Would you have room for me? Sarah and I, well, we don't share the same quarters anymore."

"We never run out of room at the Farm. We've got rooms no one has used in ages. There were always several generations living in the homestead, but since Dad built the new house across the valley, I'm the first to come back to live there. And I may be back for good if I have my way. It will be nice to have you, Sarah, Lucy and Mike all together."

"Sounds great. You're sure it's not a problem?"

"We'll make the old place jump again! Gram will want to come home sooner. Why don't you go back and talk things out with Sarah and the kids? I'll be along in a while, and we'll make plans for the week."

Steve shakes Kelty's hand again, holding it a second longer. "OK. And Kel...thanks."

Kelty sits beside the bed again, putting his hands behind his head and leaning back. He smiles. "Well, Gram, somehow I don't feel so alone anymore. All the pieces are coming together. We just have to tie them up and we'll make a fine quilt."

He stands, looking at his grandmother, leans down to kiss her forehead, and leaves the room.

From the bed, Grace mummers, "My quilt...my quilt."

Day 3, One Week Later

Grace is sitting up in the hospital bed wearing a colorful gown, a homey quilt over her legs. The room has many personal things in it, including the kitchen curtains installed on the hospital room's windows. Kelty stops in the doorway with a big smile on his face.

"Just the one I'm looking for! How are you feeling today? Was the doctor in? What did he say?"

"He said I wasn't going to live forever. I think he's underestimating me. He did say that I can go home tomorrow morning. I'll have the weekend with all you young folks before Sarah and the children leave. I bet that old house has been shaking this week."

"There does seem to be a lot going on. Sometimes I find someone in every room I walk through. It's more like it ought to be."

"That's how it was when I was a girl." Grace laughs. "I had four brothers, my parents, my grampa Ike, and Gramma Lucy, along with old aunts and others in that house too. The room you're in belonged to my brothers—now that was a noisy bunch. I used to be jealous that they had each other, and I was all alone in my room. And then there was my own family after I got married. Your father and mother lived there when they were newlyweds."

"It's strange to hear about so many people I never knew. I guess there was a lot of life lived before I was born. That's what you've been telling me, but I'm just getting it."

"There's no timetable, dear. It's your heritage, you'll get it all at some point. Many people have lived on our land, and every one contributed in some way to making our lives what they are. Not everyone has the courage to live up to the past, to accept what has gone before as a gift."

"When I look at the lifetimes of effort, I feel I owe a great debt I can never repay."

"There is no debt. It was a gift. Every Kelty who lived and worked on the Farm got their reward during their own time. The reward for doing the right thing is just the knowing you did the right thing. If anything else comes of it, well, that's extra."

"All the same, I know something is changing in me. Always before, Kelty Farm meant my father's work, or even my grandfather's, and behind all that are the Keltys, your own parents, and theirs." He walks to the window, moving aside the curtain.

"So, what has changed now, Dear?"

"It's something I've felt for the first time, while you've been gone."

"Can you tell me what it is?"

"I'm not sure I can explain it. It may be something I'm not quite aware of, something that's not fully realized yet."

"What is it about? Is it about your working on the Farm?"

"I think it's about me, or maybe it's me and the Farm." He turns back to her and looks at her directly. "Somehow this week, I've felt at home there, and Kelty Farm has been mine in a way it never has before."

"In what way?"

"Right now, everything is on my shoulders, with Dad out of touch and you here. Maybe it's because Sarah and the children are home, and the homestead is full of life. Maybe it has been working with Steve and the hired hands this week, people asking me what to do next, trusting my experience, expecting me to know what I'm doing. At the same time, I'm discovering how many answers I have for the questions." He takes out the compass and looks at it, then at Grace. "I don't think I can explain more than that."

Grace looks past him, toward the windows. "Whenever I arrive at the doorstep of a mystery in my life, I comfort myself by remembering that there isn't anything so new that it hasn't happened to someone before. I think a moment on what I know. I think of the old family stories, about the people I knew or heard about. I just have to find the right pattern that this mystery fits and look at how it turned out for someone before me."

Kelty comes to the bedside. "Do you know what I'm trying to say? If anyone can understand this, or help me to understand it, it'll be you, Gram."

"The first thing that comes to mind is the story of Archelaus Kelty, who married my great, great grandmother, Elishabet. You can figure how long ago that was from the date on her stone. She's the second one in the front row on the hill."

"And she was the wife of Arthur, who built the homestead."

"First she married his older brother, Archelaus, and on the wedding day, Arc made a boast that he would go out to the west, 'Where a man can come into his own.' And those are his words, passed down through the family from people who were at the wedding."

"And Elishabet was forced to go with him."

"That's right. Arc took her away and then he died out west. She returned and married his brother Arthur. They began their family on Kelty Farm, our family."

"Arthur is the first one buried on the hill."

"Yes. But anyway, I was always struck by those words, the first story of all our family stories. For many years I didn't know what that could mean, 'Where a man could come into his own.' By the time all my brothers were gone, and my parents offered the Farm to Earle and me, Earle had been working with my father several years, learning what my father could teach him, season after season, learning what my father had learned from his father."

"Just like I learned from my dad."

"Well, I saw my dear Earle work along with my father, like a new work horse is put into harness beside an old horse. At first the new horse struggles against the harness, straining the leather, out of step with the other horse. The younger wants to go faster, doesn't want to corner the same, move the same, not work as steady. After a while, his strength is spent but there remains work to be done and only the older horse willing to do it. Then one day, the younger horse falls into step beside the older. He watches for direction, turning when it's time, slowing, speeding up in step with his teammate, and at the end of the day, he still feels fresh enough to enjoy his supper and a run in the pasture."

"Do you mean he came into his own?"

Grace laughs. She settles back against the pillows. "No, but something like that. A time comes when he's the older horse, and a younger is put with him. My Earle was like that. He was always running ahead of my father, trying to beat him to the next thing to be done. But by the end of the day, it was Earle who was beat, and my father still going. After a time, Earle learned to stay in step with my father, and come out at the end of the day with life still to live."

"I think I see where you're going, Gram." He leans forward in his chair.

"And it was the same for your father. After many years working beside Earle, Joseph found his pace and made his own mark on the Farm. You have trained with your father, and you know what you need to do in most circumstances. You've been reading the journals. You see, time after time, situations arise that have been dealt with before." Grace pauses and looks long and hard at Kelty. "I can't be the one to say. I will only know when you show me. But you will know before that. When you decide what you want to do in a situation, then I think…"

"Maybe that is what I'm feeling. It's clearer to me now than before, that Kelty Farm is what I want. I feel sure it's right for me. I have to make peace with a few other things first. I'm glad you're coming home tomorrow, Gram. I'll miss Sarah and the kids when they go back after the weekend. I wish she would stay."

"What about Steve? Is he leaving when they do?"

"He hasn't said. I don't think he has any firm plans. He's been a lot of help to me, and he just loves all the barns, especially the older one that we've got to fix soon or tear down. He's been great with the kids this week too. He really loves them."

"How has Sarah been with him around so much?"

Sarah comes through the door just at Grace's question. She laughs. "Why not ask Sarah? I thought my ears were burning as I came up the hallway."

Grace smiles broadly at her granddaughter. "Well, you caught us red handed, so you might as well just answer the question yourself."

Sarah leans over to kiss Grace. "I hardly know where to start. This week has been more family life than I've known since the kids were born. Mike and Lucy have been better behaved—oh, not that they haven't been into everything, and out of that and into something else. I just mean that they've been more like kids and less like little grown-ups. I've loved having the house to take care of, and the guys to talk and be with. It's been a real week off, out of my usual life."

"Gram's question was about Steve."

Sarah grimaces. "The question always seems to be about Steve. It's been nice not to have any pressure about him this week. I know that's not an answer. I guess I don't have an answer. If there is one, I don't know it yet."

"Sis, I'm glad you haven't closed any doors. Having a day-to-day life with you and the kids is a great motivation for him. This week, I've learned how hard Steve's willing to work when he's interested in what he's doing. And I've seen again what a good person he is."

"I haven't given him any serious thought in a while. I know he's a fine man."

Grace hesitates, "He is still the man you chose."

"That was a long time ago." Sarah looks at Grace.

Grace's voice is gentle. "You saw something in him. Perhaps you're seeing it again."

"You could be right, Gram. But this is nothing I could decide in one isolated week."

"Sis, I wish you'd stay. This has been a real home since you came, and I don't mean just the cleaning and cooking. I could do that. I mean you're being there, at the Farm—it seems very right. Don't you feel it?"

"I do feel something different. It's hard to say what. At first, I felt like I had swum to some island of safety. I was a little thrown when Steve showed up, and you asking him to stay. But I got past that."

"I didn't ask him to stay to upset you. He came here because his heart's in the right place, and I thought it would be good for him and for…all of us if he stayed."

"I know your heart is in the right place, Kel. But I also know you're intent on rescuing me."

"So, sue me. I want everyone to be happy."

"Then start with yourself, brother dear. I think that's a big enough job. I was angry with you at first and I had a plan to get even, but it doesn't seem to have worked out."

"A plan to get even? What do you mean?"

"I called some of your friends from school to come down to visit, and I asked around to find out who you've been dating. I guess I didn't make very good connections because no one came."

"You two have some growing up to go if you're talking about getting even."

"I'd like to know who you thought was going to come all this way to see me. I think final exams were this week. I didn't talk with many of my classmates when I left."

"Then you must talk in your sleep, and not know it. I spoke with three of your school friends, and all asked about Dad, and said to say hello to you."

"I have to get back to the Farm now, but we'll talk about this later."

"Don't forget to come get me in the morning. I can't wait to be home again." Grace smiles.

"Gram, I want you home as fast as I can get you there. And Sarah will have to return all these pictures, curtains, and quilts. The house isn't the same without you or your things." He kisses her. "I love you. I may get back to spend the evening with you."

"Stay and enjoy your company. I'll see you in the morning."

"Bye, Kel."

"I've been meaning to tell you how grateful I am to have my things around me. The curtains made me laugh every time I thought of you talking the hospital into putting them up. My pictures, all those dear faces I love, and the quilts…especially the old quilt. Thank you, Sarah."

"I'm glad it helped, Gram. This has been a good week for me, too. I've learned a lot about my brother, about my children, and about myself. Kelty Farm is a very healing place."

"It is for those whose roots are there. I'm glad you're finding you belong, too."

"I'm more surprised every day how at home I feel. These years of raising my children, I've tried hard to make up to them that they're not on the Farm, that they don't have what I had as a child. Oh, we have everything we really need. It's the support of knowing where you are, where you belong. Now I know what I would have missed growing up anywhere else. I can't make that loss up to my children. I think that's why I didn't want to come back here, I didn't want to realize."

"The truth always comes out."

"Something interesting came out the other day. I still don't know what to make of it."

"Tell me, dear."

"Lucy and Mike are pretty good at recognizing letters and spelling their names. Their father and I were walking with them up in the cemetery and they were spelling out the names on the marble tablets. Lucy found her own name on one, and then found the tablet beside it that says, 'Ike.' You know that's what she calls her brother."

"That's my gramma Lucy and grampa Ike."

"They lay down on top of the graves, right in front of their names, and they spent the afternoon looking at the sky and talking."

"Sarah, you're like to give me chills. What did they say?"

"They asked how come they weren't Keltys like the names on the tablets. Steve told them they were his children, and children have their father's last name. He told them that no matter what anybody's name was, if Kelty Farm was their home, then they were Keltys." She laughs. "He was wonderful."

Grace claps her hands. "I always liked that young man."

"Now the children want to live on the Farm. I'm afraid Steve and my brother have encouraged them. Mike and Lucy are walking around telling anyone who will listen that their names are Ike and Lucy Kelty, and that they live on Kelty Farm. Like saying it makes it so."

"I'll be glad to meet these new Keltys tomorrow! They are welcome to call the Farm their home. They would be the eighth generation to be home there."

"It's too soon to decide that. There are other issues I have to resolve first."

"Like what, Sarah? If there's anything standing in the way of coming back, I'd like to hear about it."

Sarah looks away from Grace. "All the times I worked hard jobs, or felt alone, or worried for my children, for myself, I've always remembered what it was like, at the Farm. I would tell myself over and over, 'go back, you fool!'" She walks to the window then back toward Grace. "But I didn't come back because I was waiting for someone to tell me it was the right thing to do."

"Your father or I..."

Sarah holds up her hand to stop Grace. "And at the same time, I avoided contact with the very people who might have told me the thing I was waiting to hear. I don't know how to explain this. It doesn't make sense as I tell it now. I told myself it would be taking a step backwards. I felt there was no going back, no chance for a fresh start. Coming back to stay would be admitting I had made a mistake in ever leaving. It would mean Lucy and Mike were a mistake. How could I do that?"

Grace pauses waiting to see if Sarah had got it all out. "Sarah, did you look under the bureau scarf to see what I left for you? I hesitate to ask, since you haven't mentioned it."

"Yes, the very first day. I thought it might be a letter, or even a check, but I found a picture. I think it's you, Gram, as a very young woman. I've wanted to ask you what you meant by the note. It only said, 'I was young once, too.' I've been thinking about it all week. I guess you'll have to tell me what it's about."

"I only meant what it said. I thought you might think I wouldn't understand you, being older than you are, or having stayed on the Farm all my life, not going away like you did. I thought you might have the idea that I never made any mistakes, or that I couldn't know how you felt. I thought it would remind you that when I was young as you are now, I didn't know much the first time out, either."

"But Gram, you've always been so sure of yourself, of your life..."

Grace chuckles to herself. "Oh, my dear! From the time I was a growing girl, I worried that I would have to leave home when I married. I worried I might not love my husband, or he wouldn't want to stay working on the Farm. I worried that I wouldn't have children or wouldn't be a good mother when I did have them. I worried that none of my children would want to work like we had, that I would be letting someone down if the Farm went out of the family. I worried that Joseph wouldn't marry, or wouldn't have children, or that none of them would find value in the life of the Farm."

"That's quite a list, Gram."

"It's not the complete list. It goes to show you that I worried all my life, and when I look at it, I find I worried for nothing."

"Are you telling me I'm worrying about nothing, to forget everything else, and just come back?"

"I'm not telling you any such thing. You don't need anyone to tell you. No one told your father what the right thing was for him, and no one is telling your brother, either. You are your own person, Sarah. When you decide, you'll come back because it's right."

"What do you worry about now, Gram? Is there anything else?"

"When I don't have anything else to worry about, I worry about being cold in my grave." She tucks the quilt around herself.

"What do you mean?"

"It's nothing for you to be concerned with now, dear."

"Over the years I recall you starting to tell me something special about your quilt, but felt I was too young to hear it. I think you had better tell me now."

"It's a part of a tradition I don't want to talk about with you yet. The time isn't right."

"It isn't the right time for you to tell me, or for me to know?"

Grace laughs at Sarah. "You shouldn't play word games with an old lady. It's not very nice and doesn't show good manners."

"I see you're changing the subject, and good manners demands that I let you. I want to assure you that I'm not going to forget this secret tradition you haven't told me about. I'll wait, but I may ask about it sooner than you choose to tell."

"Ask me again if you ever decide to stay for good." There is a knock at the door. "Who could that be? Come in."

A woman younger than Sarah comes in. "Sarah? I'm Ruth, Kel's friend from school. You called me?"

"Oh, come in, I'm so glad to meet you. Thanks for coming. This is my—and Kelty's—grandmother."

"Kel speaks about you both all the time. I'm…I'm a little intimidated meeting you. You should hear him go on about the two of you. I bet you can walk on water!"

Everyone laughs and there is a shared moment of connection.

"It would be hard to live up to that expectation, child. It's nice to meet you, Ruth. Isn't that a pretty outfit? It matches my curtains." They all laugh again. "But you have the advantage here. I don't know anything about you. Call me Gram, like everybody else does. You go to school with our Kelty?"

"I should explain, Ruth. I called Kel's roommate and asked to speak to some of my brother's friends. Everyone I talked to mentioned your name, so I called and left a message for you. I invited everyone down for the weekend, but you're the only one to take me up on the offer."

"Your brother works so hard and is so serious all the time he doesn't have many good friends. He and I had several classes in common our first two years, and we spent a lot of time studying and researching together. I haven't seen much of him this year. He's really ahead of me in classes. I didn't know he was off campus till I got your message." She turns to Grace. "Have you been in the hospital very long…Gram?"

"Actually, Kelty came home some weeks ago. He and I were running the Farm. These last weeks, my fuss-budget doctor decided I needed a rest and put me here. My grandson has done well with me out of the way. He has attracted a crowd of friends and family this week, such as I haven't had around for some time."

"How does it make you feel, to have him doing well without your help?"

Grace examines the young woman's face. "That's an interesting question. I couldn't be happier. This way any success, any pride in ownership, comes to Kelty with no doubt that he is achieving by his own efforts, by his own strengths."

"And you don't feel threatened by that?"

"Ruth! That's very blunt!"

Grace laughs easily, a broad smile on her face. "Calm down, Sarah. I think we're getting to know Ruth better. Ruth dear, your questions are bravely asked and deserve direct answers. If you've been out of touch with Kelty I think you're going to find a change in him, and I hope you like that change."

Everyone looks up as Rachel breezes into the room, "A change in Kel? What are you talking about?" She seems to examine Ruth with cool interest.

"Mother, it's good to see you." Sarah kisses her mother. "How's Dad today? Oh, this is Ruth, a school friend of Kelty. She's come down to visit him."

Rachel remains focused on Ruth. "It's nice to meet you. Kel rarely mentions any school friends to me. And you've come so far for just a day's visit."

"Kel is a good..." she pauses meaningfully, "friend. I don't choose my friends by how convenient it is to visit them. Besides, while I did come for just the day, I'm prepared to stay over if I'm asked. I hear there's quite a crowd of friends and family gathering, and I want to get a look at them."

Grace and Sarah share a smile. Rachel turns to Sarah.

"What crowd does she mean, Sarah?"

Sarah laughs. "Well, Mike and Lucy are family, Steve qualifies as friend and family, and now Ruth. And tomorrow, Gram comes home. Are you staying, Mother?"

Rachel is caught off guard. "What's Steve doing here? I'm surprised he'd show his face. And of course, I'm not staying. I have your father to tend. I just came up to make sure things are going well, so I can give a good report to him. He's starting to worry about things."

Grace perks up at this. "I should think that's a good sign he's getting better."

Rachel turns sharply to Grace. "And I think that's a sign that he hasn't learned where worrying got him up till now. But if things are running smoothly, then he won't have to give it any more thought." She looks back to Sarah. "The Homestead will be too crowded for Grace with all of you there. If you and the children are staying through the weekend, why don't you move across the valley to my house? No one is using it now—and invite Ruth to stay."

"That's a good idea, Mother. Ruth and I will discuss it on the way to see Kelty."

"Sarah! Don't go while your mother is here. Stay and visit with her." Grace seems casual, but some note in her voice warns Sarah.

Sarah pats her grandmother's hand. "Gram, if Mother wanted a report on the Farm, she would be talking with Kelty. And if she wanted to visit with me, she would have said that. So, I guess it's you she wants to see." She turns to Rachel. "Good-bye, Mother. Thanks for the offer on the house. I may take you up on it."

"Well, the house is there, someone may as well get some use of it. Ruth, will I see you again?"

"I hope we'll get to know each other better. Kel has told me so much about you. It is really a pleasure to finally meet you. Good-bye for now." She and Sarah leave the room, and as the door closes, they are heard laughing in the hallway.

There is a pause, the women glancing at each other and away.

Grace says, softly, "Tell me about my son."

Rachel answers sharply, "Tell me about mine."

"Sons…is that what we've argued about for thirty years?

"I think so." She pauses, then in a softer voice, "But something's changed. I've lost. You've won."

Grace is taken aback. "Lost?" She pauses. "Won? What do you mean?"

"I have Joseph, or what there is of him. He's finally mine, though the best of his life's gone to serving you and Kelty Farm. What's left for me is his care, his therapy, the hard work to get back some of what made him the man I loved."

"My dear, no one planned this happening to Joseph. If you want to blame me, well, it's what you've always done, and you'll do it now."

"And the children. You got the children too. I could see Kelty Farm in my son's eyes his whole life, and I never gave up trying to change it. But now…well, I have my hands full with Joseph, and Kel is back on the Farm. I can see there's no changing him without breaking his heart—which will probably happen sooner or later anyway."

"You're being very hard, Rachel."

"And I see Sarah and her children, slipping on the rose-colored glasses, looking like they're going to stay. I didn't expect that."

"Rachel, if Sarah decides to stay, it's probably in her best interest. She has so little else."

"I know. I should have been more active about getting her settled somewhere. I just didn't know what to do. She never listened to me, never…" Her voice trails off. She sits in a chair half-way to the bed.

"I never had to fight for Michael. He was always mine. He's such a dear boy. Kelty was a losing battle from the day I allowed Joseph to name our son. And Sarah was a toss-up between us, Grace, until I got her into college. I thought I had won that fight, but then, nothing has ever gone right for me when it came to Kelty Farm. I fought for nothing. I was bound to lose. From what I saw in this room this afternoon, I'd say it's all going your way. You win." She stands, turns her back to Grace, but does not move toward the door.

"Rachel, there is no winning or losing between us. You and I always wanted things to work out for the best as we saw them. I've never thought you insincere or mean about having your way. It wasn't selfish of you to want what you wanted. If we lost anything, you and I, it was what could have been different between us."

Rachel turns toward Grace. "Actually, we had more attention from one another than any other way we might have lived. There are people who share the same house who don't know each other as well as I know you."

"While what you say may be true, I never believed you knew me at all. And most times, I didn't feel I knew you either. I was only afraid that your discontent would lose my family their heritage. Kelty Farm is for them to decide to keep or not."

"Your family heritage! You always say, 'your family.' Your family is gone off the land now, even if you count Joseph. What's left is my family."

"Why are you so blind? For as smart a woman as you are you do have this one blind spot. Rachel, you are my family too. You never chose to hear advice from me. You went on and did well in your business. I admired you for it, though I'm sorry to say I never told you. Your life is a success, Rachel."

"It doesn't seem that way to me. I don't feel I got one thing that I ever worked for."

"You must not be looking at the right column of figures. You've raised three wonderful, fine and healthy children who all respect you. Your husband worked to keep peace in the family, even building you a new house because he honored your wishes. You worked your way up into a partnership in a business you enjoyed and sold out when you were ready. You chose education for your children and set them on paths you thought were right."

"Little good that has done."

"When my father planted those trees so long ago, he couldn't think of a better use for that land, but you had a different idea, and put a house in the middle of his orchard. That land wasn't my father's anymore by the time you came along. And your idea was a better use than he could have thought of. Now you are unhappy that you have shown your children a path and they don't seem to choose to travel it."

"And except for Michael, isn't that the way it is?"

"A parent's triumph is to see what kind of people our children become, not to choose for them. They did not grow up to be little Josephs nor little Rachel. They come into their own lives to be themselves, and we must be glad for whatever hand we have in that."

"You make it sound as if nothing we do makes any difference."

"We both know that's not so. An apple tree can't help but bear apples. But our children have choices. We can smooth their way, and they can use our help if they've a mind to. We are bound to do our best for our children. Not only must we, but we could not rest if we didn't."

"You always did your best with Kelty Farm in mind."

"Kelty Farm is my home. The years have washed gently over me, swirled around those I've loved, and left me thankful for yesterdays, today, and any precious tomorrow I'll be given. Soon, I will go to sleep some night, and not see a morning to follow. It's a comfort to me knowing that when that time comes, someone else will be taking care of things, someone who has found value in what has been protected and given to them."

"Which brings us back to my children…"

"Our family, Rachel, yours and mine."

"You sound like you're forgiving me."

"There's nothing to forgive. As surely as I have pushed, you have pulled, and that balance has brought Kelty Farm to where it is today. You have helped me to deliver the Farm into the hands of those who will have it tomorrow."

"Next you'll be asking me to wrap a quilt on you when they bury you on the hill. You asked me long ago and I wouldn't listen. Sometimes I've been sorry not to have allowed you the comfort of believing things would go on and on as they have always been."

"I'll never ask you to do that for me, Rachel. Putting a quilt on me when I'm in my coffin is a tradition that's come down through five generations of Keltys. It's a loving thing that women of our family have always done. But you told me how you felt, that it was old fashioned, an out-of-date practice. Soon a new generation will have Kelty Farm. Old traditions will have to prove their worth or they'll be put aside. That's the way people find out what matters."

"A new generation at the Farm—I never thought I'd say this, but my son—and my daughter and her children—all seem happy there, like they belong. And you know what? I'm glad for them. I don't know what makes me say that, but it feels right, them being there. If Sarah decides to stay, I'm going to offer her my house. Maybe she'll settle down and make a home for her brother."

"You aren't counting on Steven in your picture. Don't sell him short, or his love for Sarah and the children. And wasn't it nice to meet Ruth. I wouldn't have picked her for our Kelty, but I didn't have to. He did."

"We'll see how interested she is in our Kelty when she sees that any woman in his life will always play second fiddle to the Farm."

Grace settles back on the bed. "We will see. I think she came down here knowing that and thinking how it might suit her fine. A woman could do worse than share her man with Kelty Farm."

"All of that is for the future to decide, and you and I may not have influence on the future. I have to take care of Joseph now. That's my future. And, the funny thing is, since Joseph needs me more, we're growing closer. We seem to have something now we never had before. Something wonderful."

"I'm glad for the both of you, Rachel. But you're wrong about neither of us having influence on the future. You and I, between us, have made and bent the future. True, we're not the ones to decide who Kelty marries or if Sarah stays at the Farm or gets back together with Steve. We have put the tools in their hands and set these young people in motion. They have choices now that they wouldn't have had without us. You and I, Rachel, we helped to make them and their world what they are, and what they will be."

"I wonder if they'll thank us?"

"Does it matter?" Grace smiles.

"You're probably right. Well, I'm going to leave. I'll tell Joseph you're looking better and are going home tomorrow, and that the kids have the Farm in hand. I...I still think you won, Grace, and maybe that's the way it should be, I don't know.

"Oh, I almost forgot. I have a note for Kel from his father." She hands an envelope to Grace. "I tried to read it, but the writing is so shaky. Best I could make out it says to remind Kel he made his mark on the heart of the mountain. Do you know what that means?"

"No. But maybe Kelty knows. He'll just be glad to see anything from his father."

Rachel leaves the room, and Grace closes her eyes, a smile on her face.

"Gram, are you sleeping?"

"Sarah, you're back so soon?"

"I didn't go with Ruth. I've been in the coffee shop thinking. You can tell me your tradition about the quilt, now."

"Do you mean..."

"I'm going to stay. I want to help my brother to keep the Farm."

"That's not what I'm waiting to hear."

"And I want to offer my children the kind of home I had, with you and the Farm. I even think Steve will stay on if we're settled down. He's a good person. It's what I first saw in him. It's still there. And he and my brother are a great team. I still love him, Gram."

"That's not what I'm waiting to hear." Grace holds her hands out to Sarah.

"All right, all right. I want to stay because I want to stay. I want to wake up every morning and be the me I'd be on Kelty Farm. I know now that it's my own permission I've been waiting for. It's the right thing for me." She pauses, as if to catch her breath. "Since I'm going to stay, I'll need to know the rest of the traditions."

Grace clutches at her quilt. "Oh, Sarah! And I need to tell you all of them."

END